THE PAST WON'T END

THE PAST WON'T END

by

Lauran Paine

The Golden West Large Print Books
Long Preston, North Yorkshire,
BD23 4ND, England.

British Library Cataloguing in Publication Data.

The past won't end
Paine, Lauran.

A catalogue record of this book is available from the British Library

ISBN 978-1-84262-907-9 pbk

First published 1957

Published in Large Print 2012 by arrangement with Golden West Literary Agency

The Golden West Large Print is an imprint of Library Magna Books Ltd.

Printed and bound in Great Britain by
T.J. (International) Ltd., Cornwall, PL28 8RW

CHAPTER ONE

In the clear, razor-sharp air Fred Nolan stood on the observation platform of the train watching the land level out from rolling hills of sage to flat desert. He had his fists dug deeply into coat pockets, his mouth set in a pensive line with little of its customary carelessness showing; greenish eyes soft and brooding, a little stormy looking. Another day, a brassier sun, the edge of the desert and overnight from home.

Up ahead the bell-funnel of the train with a new-fangled steam whistle spewed white vapor and keening sound simultaneously. They were approaching another whistle-stop; another well-and-peach-tree at the side of the tracks, lost and forlorn in an expanse of nothingness.

He looked at the lowering sun. An hour, a little more, then dusk. A tiny gust of wind rustled low through the greasewood, chamise, chaparral, of the desert. For all its smallness there was a biting sting to it. Cold, Nolan thought absently. Early spring and cold, and when the sun dropped over the edge of the world the desert would glow for another hour; twilight. Then darkness.

The train slowed protestingly, gruntingly, kicking up spews of buckskin dust. Nolan stiffened against the expected bucking lurch of the couplings, his nostrils pinched down in expectancy. The smells would come soon now: dust, metal, heat. It was all automatic, the train's reflexes and his own, but Fred, outwardly knowing this world he was in and what was happening in it, was like a stone. A part of it yet apart from it. The clipping in his wallet was in mind again, like it had been since the day he'd unexpectedly read it in the newspaper far back up East.

'...Which makes the third killing done in exactly the same manner which was so characteristic of outlaw Fred Nolan's murder of Jack Beltry, the Texas cowman, in Tucomcori over five years ago. Very obviously Nolan is becoming one of the most baffling, elusive – and deadly – of Southwestern renegade-killers. Nolan's eminently respectable cousin, wealthy Benton Nolan the Tucomcori rancher, told this paper he hadn't seen his cousin, the outlaw, in six or seven years, or before the Beltry killing.'

Three killings in New Mexico Territory by Fred Nolan – who had been working like a slave to put himself through medical college in Massachusetts, as far from Tucomcori as he'd been able to get after the Jack Beltry fight. Years and miles and memories away. So far, he'd thought that the past would never find him. But it had. The past wouldn't die, wouldn't end. It lived and hounded him and very deliberately, very ironically, was creating a legend of outlawry, murder, gun-manship, that was pure myth. A myth that was growing; becoming solid and threatening to Fred Nolan.

So now he stood in the failing light feeling the train's diminishing momentum, thinking that his cousin Benton would know what to do toward killing this snow-balling legend that was attaching itself to his name.

Yes, he had killed Jack Beltry, the Texan, but it hadn't been murder. It had been self-defense. But he certainly had not killed those others. Hadn't even been within thousands of miles of them when he was said to have killed them. The circumstances may have been the same; night-time, knives, two straining bodies, grunted curses, blows, stink of whiskey-breath then a man down on all fours looking up suddenly sober, disbelieving, gushing blood and dying, wagging his head from side to side refusing to accept death; unwilling to put it into words, into thoughts. Dying…

And he could somehow surmise how the legend had grown, too. Unknown fighters, darkness, no tracks, no clearly understood reason for the fight maybe; just the methods of the fight being the same. It wasn't uncommon to kill a man like that; it was swift, certain, customary. The public had waited for lawful retribution. The law was stumped, probably, but there was the precedent and the memory of Fred Nolan. That was palpably the easiest way out.

And this might have been all right too, his mind said, but not now. Not when it was becoming a habit to lay every unsolved knife fight in the Southwest at his feet, because someday it'd grow so big they'd make it a point to hunt him down, then they'd hang him so quick, so high, he'd never have a chance to prove he wasn't the killer lies had made him. Reputations were often built from less substantial things than a real killing, he knew.

When the train finally stopped, he reeled. The cars hesitated then hunched up in a clanking, grinding upheaval before they all settled to rest in sulky bulkiness at the siding where weathered buildings with bleak-looking sides huddled close to the tracks. The red-splashed stain of dying daylight over everything. The whistle-stop.

He turned, unhurried, and watched the passengers disgorge from the cars. There was the customary rush for the hash-house. Tall riders returning south from trail drives, drummers, lawyers, the Lord knew what not, and women. He saw the girl with the supple body, the uncommon red-gold hair, melt into the throng and right behind her was the leather-visaged man who'd been so obviously gallant and solicitous for two days now and still hadn't penetrated her clear-eyed unapproachableness.

It made his eyes crinkle a bit, the way the girl hurried as much to escape her tall, hard-faced pursuer, as to reach the hash-house before the last of the food was gone.

Not hungry, he turned with a rush of loneliness rising inside him, noted the quick-rising white-gray empire of desert smeared with a long, uneven red streak that was the sun's last burst of color.

For all Massachusetts had the green-tumbling forests, the high rolling hills, the misty, blue-tinted distances, the water, the beauty – but especially the water – he knew the peculiar loneliness within himself to be a depth of feeling for this dead, hushed world. The desert.

Born hereabouts somewhere in the bed of a wagon, his parents' schedule and natures not concurring, there was a corner of his soul where the scent of sage and sand, hot sun and crystal nights, lived. And he never felt this way except on the desert or its fringe, like in Tucomcori.

The loneliness was a mood in itself because as a kid he'd had no parents to turn to, after a while; to tell exactly how he felt about the desert. How this dry-hot land was in him forever. No parents – Comanches...

It wasn't an unusual story out there even now, with the iron tracks like dull swords cutting the umbilical of Indiandom forever, but it was a story – a memory – nonetheless.

The little wind rustled the withering buffalo grass with scrabbling fingers. It was sharp and stiffening, the way it cut through heavy cloth. Massachusetts woolen. He turned finally and descended the little steps, walked through the useless shade of the train's west side as far as the hash-house. There he drank a cup of coffee and it recalled another nostalgic thing. As a stripling the wild riders had often said that coffee wasn't fit to drink unless you could float a horseshoe in it.

Wiping his mouth, faintly upward-curving in recollection, he went back outside, found a dim, shadowy position next to the overhang-upright and leaned against it. Smoked a cigar with old memories running like wind whipped sand across the sterile nearness of recent times, and watched the reluctant sunset fade, turn mauve gray, soft-billowing dark, and finally the cold and swift running black of desert nightfall.

The wind rose a little, made soughing sounds under the overhang above his head. Rustled his dark hair a little, worried at the back of his neck. In the near distance men called to one another. The hash-house doors banged. Someone laughed in a musical way, like bells tinkling in a snow-hushed night. He turned. Thinking of the beautiful girl with red-gold hair. But no, it was another.

He took a long pull at the cigar. The smoke was scented, sweet: New Mexico had many things but no tobacco like that. Especially when the aroma was diluted, mixed with tangy desert night air.

The waves of memory were engulfing him now. The tall lazy spirals of dung dust behind the cattle drives when he'd been a boy. The church socials where a massive man with a russet beard and a vast store of gentleness in his powerful hands stood thick-thewed, smiling. And his mother too, a memory somehow not shapely but solid, strong, level-eyed with deep violet forthrightness, forever calm in understanding and a trifle stiff-backed. Cousin Benton and the other Nolan tribe, a different breed altogether. In those days he'd no more than felt it, vaguely, disinterestedly. Different in a hurrying, acquisitive way. A brassy, glittering, rock-hard way. Money and power and sound alliances had meant a lot to the other Nolans, so, of course, as those things happen, the two families grew farther apart with the years.

So many recollections out here in the still desert night with the chill and sounds around him. Many, many recollections. Old Pachise the Apache vaquero who used to sit of summer eves and tell the family of the Old

Ways of his people. How they would all listen, especially young Fred, in deep silence. All, that is, except his mother, who sniffed with her eyes without actually making a sound, at the old heathen. And his father, russet beard glowing like blood under the full moon, listening, enjoying every bit of it, saying finally to the old Apache, that men – all men – are the same underneath. Some curb instincts, some never try to, but they're all the same, and Pachise wouldn't answer for a long time. Just the stingy spiral of smoke from his cornhusk Mex *cigarillo* rising up for a while, then one time he'd said, 'Yes, that is so and there are great troubles for all men. I only wish that all my troubles had come to me when I was very young. Only then did I know everything.'

Then his father, catching the obliqueness of it, had laughed and old Pachise had smiled with a glitter in his muddy looking eyes, and had winked at young Fred.

So many, many memories.

Comanches ... solid ghosts in the night. But he remembered very little of that. Only the billowing fire from tinder-dry buildings, the screams of horses trapped deep in the barn. Gunshots. Something falling on his head where his mother had pushed him under the commode settee, then later, an Indian face all grimed and blood-streaked dragging him, dragging him... Then the burst of sunlight over the far-away hills and clotted blood in his hair where the thick crockery commode bowl had broken over his head and nearby the stiffening form of riddled old Pachise.

He flung the cigar away and took a stabbing deep inhalation of the cold night air. It should have cleared out the rest of those bitter recollections.

The buggies that came for his parents' funeral. The little grave apart for Pachise. The stink that huddled low around the plains where the buildings had been. The long, stoical trip to the other Nolan's place. The months of terrible, gnawing loneliness. The different world of his relatives' making. Starched shirts, dances he'd snuck from the loft room they'd give him to watch, where the lamp chimneys had swayed and the big men with beards and clear blue eyes curvetted with the beautiful women. Corn starch face rouge. No Sunday prayers, no supper graces. A different world. No Pachise; in fact no Indians of any kind allowed within rifleshot of the ranch day or night.

And Benton … fights, jealousies.

He shrugged, disliking the train of his thoughts. But it'd been no more natural. Ben hadn't wanted to share his parents. Well; they'd been just kids and kids're animals. They don't understand. They hurt and enjoy hurting.

Another deep breath with the tingling sharpness of the night air to vaporize things that were unpleasant to recall, only it didn't. It just hurried the tableau-years of his youth to early manhood when a tall, gangling vaquero had been standing in the Territorial bar at Animas drinking alone. Cutting the phlegm and desert-scorch out of his throat after a long drive from the ranch to trail-head. The man-smells of the saloon abetting the not-quite-certain feelings of manhood in a boy who swaggered but was still a boy. The teasing laughter of the big Texan beside him at the bar. Drunk, he'd been. Drunk and bullying in a hazing, half-joking way.

But the boy was struggling with the nebulousness of new-found manhood. He was more deadly than a sidewinder and no one knew it, least of all the boy, Fred Nolan. It was all as clear as white light to him. The boar-scent of the saloon. The big Texan's increasing familiarity, his own white-lipped silence while the Texan reached over and carelessly tilted his hat over his eyes with a coughing laugh.

'Y'got to wear 'em low, sonny, or folks'll think y'still sucking milk.'

The shuddering gorge of fury that swept over him in blinding waves. The way he'd lashed out, caught the Texan in the mouth, broke his lips and knocked him down, swore at him worse than he'd ever sworn at a dog or a breachy critter.

The Texan's broken mouth gushing blood that jetted over his shirtfront. The wild rush of dark blood into his cheeks, the savage flash of his widened eyes. The slow said oaths that dropped like stones into the abrupt silence of the Territorial Bar, then the bartender was between them, a squat, dark faced man with a drooping moustache that swung swoopingly upwards at the outer ends like a Longhorn's hooks. He had a big fist wrapped around a wheel-spoke when he spoke.

'Fightin'–' he jerked the spoke toward the door. 'Out there.'

The Texan's broken mouth was drawn inward and down, his eyes were like coals in a mud bank. He turned toward the door without a word. Fred had followed but then his man-fury was ashes, his heart was nigh to failing him. Fear so terrible, so consuming it made him actually sick inside, had replaced the anger.

Out under the late summer moon they'd fought. It had been the Texan who had bent with an oath, drawn the boot knife and straightened up. 'Use *this* on whelps,' he'd said. 'Jist carve their guts out an' braid me a riata out'n 'em.'

Later, Fred didn't remember getting his own knife. All he remembered was that an instinct – or maybe it was one of the crowd behind him – had whispered, *Don't stand up to him, boy, he out-hefts ye by sixty pounds. Worry him an' hope he tires – or something' – but for Crissake don't get too close or stand flat-footed to him, for he'd split ye like a tree-squirrel.*

The rest of it was just as vague, too, in the usually vivid pages of memory. He remembered very clearly the straining of his lungs, the final grip when they'd closed. The sweat under his steel fingers when he had clung to the Texan's knife wrist with all the sick fear of desperation. The two, low, deep, swift, sliding plunges he'd made with his own knife. The way he was sobbing silently inside and drawing back for another lunge when the Texan just sort of slipped down into the dust before his eyes. Got up on all fours like a gut-shot bear, wagging his head back and forth and staring up at the stripling with the blood splashed pants and stupefied, sick look on his face.

And the flight. The beating of a way so far from the Territory they'd never find him. The dedication to medicine because of the young doctor who'd taken him in, freezing, crying-hungry, in far-off, strange-talking Boston.

'Booard!'

The trainman's shout wrenched him back to the present. He accepted the interruption almost eagerly, a man lost in the mazes of sorrow that go to make every life on earth;

struggling back to the present.

He watched people hurrying toward the little cars. Up ahead a gust of white smoke vomited from the bell funnel. The other trainmen were fighting with the carbide lamp on the front of the train and cursing, but softly.

A fat, short drummer paused in the deep gloom of Fred's vantage post and peered squintingly up at him, a quick mask of fright mantling his features. With a soft oath he said: 'Thought you were an Indian, for a second there. Give me a start. Damned dark.' Then he hurried on. Fred's green eyes followed him amused. An Indian? Not here; not this close to Tucomcori any more. Still out on the desert and skulking along the Mex border and maybe in waylaying places on the immigrant trails, the stage roads, but not here, overnight from Tucomcori.

The conductor's impatient cry whipped through the keen air with frost-taste trailing its wake like steam. 'Booard! Allabooard!'

In the charcoal dusk Fred was hard to see even by those like the drummer, who'd swung close by the overhang-post, but to the tall, graceful figure hurrying past he was altogether invisible. He had only a bare glimpse of a face, clear cut, medallion-like, oval, startled, as he moved away turning toward the train, then they collided.

At that precise moment the trainman's

voice rang out with a definite finality in it. 'Boooard!' The yell drowned out her hastily flung back apology, breathless and blurred. He turned a little, recognizing her as she swung away. He started to move, but slower, in the same direction. A very faintly perfumed swath of red-gold hair brushed his cheek then a bizarre, ridiculous thing happened. Some way, the hair got caught on his coat button. She made a pained exclamation, came to an abrupt halt and Fred reached instinctively for the hair and the offending button.

'Booard! Last call, allabooard!'

'Oh, please hurry!'

She was tugging a little. He pressed his lips together working hard but the pressure, the fumbling of chilled fingers, only made more of a red-gold snarl. In desperation he looked quickly at the trainman who was striding rapidly toward an open car door after making an exaggerated flagging motion forward with a candle lantern in his fist.

'*Do* something!'

There was no mistaking the impatience, the exasperation. On the spur of the moment he grabbed her hand and pulled her along in a spurting run for the train, which was beginning to move in jerky, stiff little spasms. She made a frightened bleat at his side then they were beside the door.

A blob of white face in the tiny vestibule

showed an anxiously aggravated face. He pulled her up ahead of him by brute force, grasped her waist, lifted and grunted, throwing her ahead into the vestibule. He followed but the trainman, rooted, barred their way. With annoyance amounting almost to anger Fred reached around in front of the girl roughly and spun the man sideways. The extra footage allowed him to gain solid footing.

'Look here – what do you think you're doing?'

Fred didn't answer, just pushed the girl ahead of him steering her by the waist until they were into the little car and down the aisle where his bench was. Then he pushed downwards. She sat, Fred very close beside her. He didn't look at her face because he knew his own was brick red.

Working with deliberate and thin-lipped thoroughness, he finally managed to work most of the hair off the button. What he couldn't unsnarl he cut with a knife from inside his long coat. A belt knife with a wicked Bowie tip to it. Freed, she watched the big knife twinkle for a second and then disappear into the belt sheath under his coat; raised her flushed face and angry eyes to his face.

'Did you have to *cut* it?'

He gazed almost stolidly at her for a moment, then leaned back and chuckled mirthlessly with an abrupt head shake. 'Vanity and long hair go with women, don't they? Maybe we should've stood out in the cold and missed the train so you wouldn't lose a lock of hair.'

Her eyes, wide spaced, large and blue with the singing clarity of a desert night in spring, were absolutely flawless. He'd thought frequently that if he ever got up close to her there'd be tiny lines, off-colors, to mar the beauty that struck you like a blow, from a distance. He saw now, however, that there were none; that her beauty was flowing, continuous, like sweet-water creeks after a long cattle drive, the gauge of a desert man's measure of natural beauty.

She took the hair in one hand pulled it over her shoulder and twisted her head sideways to examine the damage. Profile, she was exquisite with a swift, upswept lilt to mouth and chin that reminded him somehow of music, and the line of her jaw, her cheek, the delicate but strong line of brow, were symmetrical, all flowing with a grace, a continuity of line that seemed in motion even while she was still. This, he told himself, solemnly, is real beauty. Real beauty.

'Well – you ought to take it off the button.'

He blinked, jarred from thoughts that were a symphony of linement, of perfection; unsung, unheard music. There was something red-gold snaring the swaying orange light from the overhead lantern, on his coat.

Her hair. Concentrating with quick, sure fingers, absorbed in what he was doing, he went to work. When he spoke it was almost without thought.

'It's a very peculiar shade isn't it? Not red, not yellow. Certainly not auburn; but the red seems darker than most red hair, the blonde more subdued. I don't believe I've ever seen a color quite like it before.'

When he finished he held the hair in his palm, a little tangled puff of it, looking up at her. She was almost laughing at him with her eyes and faintly, down around her mouth. Soundless, pixeyish laughter. With a nod toward the hair ball she said: 'You don't make wigs, do you? It's not a common shade but it's only hair.'

'And yet you're very proud of it.'

'Am I?' Some of the amusement died out in her eyes.

'I think so.' He closed his fist around the hair. 'Otherwise why worry about having a little of it cut off?'

'That's different,' she said waspishly. 'That's personal,' she looked surprised as though what she'd said sounded very rude, discourteous. In a milder tone she continued, 'Well – I'm going to be married very soon and I can imagine what I'll look like now. Hair cut off with a – a – *Bowie knife* of all things. A big snip out of the back of it.'

'Not so big,' he said, settling back, looking at the tuft in his hand. Then, brightly: 'All you'll have to do is have the rest of it cut off to match.' He closed his fist and put it into his pocket, dropped the hair and put his hand back in his lap. 'As for the Bowie knife, I had no scissors or scalpel.' With an upward curl of his mouth he added, 'I don't reckon many people go around prepared for cutting women's hair off their coat buttons, anyway.'

'But they go around prepared to *lift* hair.'

He caught the innuendo easily enough and shrugged. 'Not necessarily. A Bowie knife's not particularly a scalping knife. It's protection, tool, utensil – a lot of things – but not necessarily a scalping knife.'

She was looking at him objectively for the first time.

There was a wisp of doubt and wonder in her expression. 'I suppose New Mexicans carry them out of habit, don't they? Those cowboys up front – they have knives in their boots. I could see the outlines as plain as day when they were sitting down.'

Something inside him knotted up, twisted like gristle, like a muscle. 'Boot knives go with the stockman's trade, ma'am,' he said quietly. 'Mine is not a boot knife, it's a belt knife.' Seeking for an avenue to steer the conversation into, away from boot knives, he happened to see the hard-faced man's boring eyes, unblinkingly hostile, focused on his face from behind her, over her shoulder. He ignored the man.

'If you haven't seen many men wearing belt knives you're new to the Territory, ma'm.'

'It isn't that,' she said, choosing words with care. 'It's that you aren't a Southwesterner, yet you carry one – or are you? I mean, your clothes are definitely Eastern. That goes for the clean fingernails and the way you talk. Oh, the accent's right but the English isn't. And the knife – I don't know…'

The swaying of the car lulled him. Her beauty coupled with the glow from the little wood-burning iron stove up front were tranquilly pleasant. 'It's not hard to explain, ma'm,' he said placidly. 'I was born down here. Lived here until I was twenty years old. Since then I've been away studying medicine.'

'Oh,' the blue eyes cleared. 'A doctor.'

'Not exactly; not yet. I've got another six months to go before my hospital apprenticeship is finished.'

'But you're coming back out here to practice.' A new warmth stole into her voice. 'That's brave of you – unselfish. There were so few doctors out here and so much need for them. There would be much more money in the States but you'll serve a greater need out here.'

His green eyes puckered with a droll sparkle in them.

'Whoa. I didn't say I was going to practice down here, ma'm.'

She brushed it aside. 'I'm on my way to Tucomcori now and if ever there was a place that needed a doctor, that's it. Why, the place is fever ridden all summer and grippe and croup are as common there this time of the year as – as – well, as Nolan cattle are.'

'Are Nolan cattle so numerous?' He watched her enthusiasm dwindle a little.

For a long moment she didn't speak, then she nodded. 'Yes. Benton Nolan is the largest cattleman in the Tucomcori country.'

Looking at her, something inside him suggested the answer before he asked the question. 'You're going to be married in Tucomcori? To Benton Nolan?'

'You're psychic, Doctor.'

Not psychic, he thought, but he knew Ben Nolan. The fastest horses, the breediest cows, the purest blooded bulls, so naturally the most beautiful woman in the Southwest too. It was as natural as falling off a log.

'Tell me about him.'

'Have you heard of Ben?'

He nodded without speaking. Suddenly his ancient childhood animosity for his cousin came up with a rush. It confused him for a moment then he forced it out of his mind with guilty knowledge. This girl whom he'd never seen the equal of, was the cause of that. Nothing more than jealousy. Childish jealousy.

'Well; Benton's parents came down here when the Mexicans still owned the Territory. They went into land and cattle right from the start. They bought huge stretches of land and had the first big overland drive from Tucomcori to the States. They're an old family in the Southwest.'

'I'm sure of it,' he said quietly, smiling crookedly inside. It had been his own people who'd come out first, written back and encouraged the others to come a decade later.

'Benton's parents were killed when a runaway went over a cliff with them two years ago...'

It was like a mule kick in the belly, low, gaspingly low. He hadn't heard of their passing before and coming like it did, so easily and casually, it caught him unprepared. He held his face perfectly blank and the shadow pattern helped. She was going on in the same pleasant tone of voice.

'...ran it like his father had and he's very successful. Really, Ben is very brilliant. But it hasn't all been as smooth as it sounds either. There's been a little unpleasantness, especially over some of their land titles with the fringe ranchers, the little people who get their herds started from the strays and mavericks they – well – they *get* from the big ranchers like Ben.'

'Does he care? I mean – with all the cattle you say he has, what difference does a stray make, now and then?'

'You don't understand,' she said quickly, and Fred could hear his cousin talking in her words, her tones almost. 'If they're allowed to keep it up they'll steal more and more. In time they'll break us. There's just one way to stop it, really.'

'How's that?'

'It's brutal; hang them.'

He nodded in silence. Nothing new; they'd done it when he'd been a boy. They warned a man twice then the third time they rode up to his cabin in the night, took him out of bed with masks over their faces and without speaking a word, hung the rustler. Left him high in the lead-grey dawn for others to see. It had been very effective.

'I know,' he said. 'Two warnings then a lynching.'

'Oh no,' she said. 'They do it differently down here. They ride up in the night, take the criminal out of bed and hang him.'

'That's what I said.'

'But he isn't warned about rustling. Ben said that would scare them away. It wouldn't cure them at all.'

'Times have changed,' he said, wondering how you told when a man had stolen a couple of doggied calves when every squatter he'd ever seen had always had at least twenty-odd scrub old mammycows with calves by their sides.

Her expression changed, became slightly troubled. In a slow and doubting way she said, 'I don't know very much about the cattle business but it seems to me they're awfully quick, sometimes.' She raised her eyes to his face, found him gazing steadily at her. 'Hasn't it ever seemed that way to you?'

'For one or two calves, yes, but you're probably mistaken there.'

'I'm sure that's what Benton told me.' With more firmness she said: 'Of course he must protect himself,' then she paused again. It was very easy for him to see that she was worried, confused, on this topic. 'But it makes the fringe ranchers dislike him and that's too bad, really, because Benton's so dashing, so colorful.'

Watching her, listening to her words, he wasn't surprised that she found his cousin dashing and colorful. Benton had always been that way, had always been domineering and quick-angered too, and *that* was what was too bad, because, unless Benton had changed a lot in six or seven years, he'd break this girl's spirit like he'd broken horses' spirits when they'd been boys. But Ben would've changed. Fred had, surely Ben had too.

'Didn't Nolan range used to run down to

the Line and west of Tucomcori toward the Pinals, some eighty miles or so?'

The blue eyes looked square at him. 'You *are* a New Mexican, aren't you? Yes. Ben took me around the ranch one time, last year. It just seemed to go on forever.'

Jealousy gouged him; dark Ben and this beautiful girl riding together over Nolan range with the summer sun on them.

'And Ben has another problem too. It's this cousin of his. This outlaw Fred Nolan.' She was looking at him frankly, a little worried.

'I've heard,' Fred murmured, returning her look without blinking, conscious again of the hard-faced man's sullen glare over her shoulder. 'What do people think of his outlaw cousin down here?'

'Well – a lot of them seem to think it's another reason for spiting Ben. It's awfully unfair. This cousin – this Fred Nolan – stabbed a Texas drover named Beltry in a little place called Animas one night and fled. Since then he's killed two other men the same way. With a Bowie knife.' She made a slight motion with one hand toward his coat. 'That's another reason why I've never cared for those weapons. They make me think of the way this renegade's reputation is reflected against Ben.'

'Why should it be? Ben's not an outlaw; what his cousin does isn't Ben's fault, is it?'

'Of course not, but people ... like I told you, there's a clique who don't like Ben.' In a tone meant to be reassuring she said: 'Not that they *are* anyone, but just the same it's dislike.'

Fred's drowsiness disappeared. He sat up a little straighter, feeling there was something off-key here. Something that jangled in his head. 'Well; but no one is ever liked by everyone. A little dislike is a healthy sign, at times. Do people think Ben collaborates with this cousin of his?'

'People,' she said philosophically, 'will attach anything to your name if they don't like you. It doesn't have to be rational or true.'

'I suppose so,' Fred said, mildly surprised that she had depth as well as beauty. 'Names have a way of gathering black marks with little or no real basis, I know.'

'But you don't, I'm sure. Not in this case. You see, Ben does everything he can to dissociate himself from this killer-cousin – this Fred Nolan. He hates the man. He'd hand him over to the law quicker than anyone else because of the stigma he's attached to the Nolan name.'

Hollowly the man across from her said, 'You're exaggerating. He may feel indignant but blood's thicker than water.'

'You don't know Ben. If it weren't for this outlaw he wouldn't have half the trouble he does have. Not half of it.'

'Has he ever told you in so many words that he'd turn his cousin over to the law?'

She nodded vigorously. 'He's told me he'd hang him if he ever caught him.'

A long moment of silence settled between them. Fred leaned against the hard back of the seat and lowered his lids. She watched him for a moment then very abruptly stood up.

'I'm sorry. I was carried away.'

Without raising his eyes he said, 'Don't go. This is interesting. Tell me about the cousin. How many men has he killed?'

She remained standing when she answered, swaying a little with the coach and the lantern overhead. 'First, there was the Texas drover, then two years ago there was another man, then a few months ago, a third one.'

The green eyes, hooded, went up to her face. 'Three? Who were they?'

'I believe Ben said the last two were ranchers. This last one was a cowman I'm quite sure. His name was Hull; Mr Hull and my father used to freight together over by Santa Fe in the fifties. It was the first my father knew of Mr Hull's whereabouts, when we heard he'd been knifed to death by Ben's cousin.'

'Only three; that doesn't make him much of an outlaw,' Fred said in a dry voice, looking tired. 'I thought a man had to kill at least a half dozen men to be a real killer.'

She looked closely at him. 'It isn't very amusing to me, if it is to you.'

The sharpness brought his gaze up again. 'Excuse me.' He got to his feet ponderously. 'I wasn't intentionally making light of your trouble.'

She looked up into his face. Her eyes flickered over the broad forehead, careless, rather tolerant mouth that was belied by the out-thrust of firm chin and strong jaw. The strange, disturbing color of his eyes intrigued her more than the regularity, the strength and masculine attractiveness of his features.

'Good night,' she said.

He looked thoughtful. 'May I ask to whom I'm bidding good night?'

'Lillian Malone.'

'Good night Miss Malone,' Fred said, ignoring the obvious curiosity in her face. 'I'll save the revelation of my own name until morning. Curiosity is the best thing to start a new day with.'

He sank back down onto the bench and watched her make her way up the aisle toward her own seat. Out of the corner of his eyes he saw the hard-faced man, his back to Fred now, also watching the girl. He smiled a little. No man enjoys having a potential conquest snatched out from under his nose by a stranger; especially one for whom Fate labors, in the form of a snagged coat button.

He felt inside his coat for a cigar, lit it and blew outward. He felt used up. Not from exertion, it was a different kind of sensation altogether. Weariness from fending off what he must have known all along couldn't be overcome. Ben Nolan hadn't changed, never would change and was the last man on earth he should go to see now, after traveling days and days of endless miles to see him.

An impersonal weariness of the spirit. He smoked moodily. If she'd exaggerated, and he knew she hadn't because she wasn't the type, Ben would hand him over to the law. Why? Because, as she'd said, he was a thorn in the Nolan flesh. He shook his head ever so slightly. No; because Ben had grown to manhood with no more restraint than he'd had in childhood. Had become a man with a man's strength, power, wealth, all the things that confirmed, made all the more fearful and cruel, the brutality he'd had as a boy. Ben would turn Fred over to the law because he was something Ben had always hated. Because he'd evidently become the symbol of hatred people had for Ben himself.

He gazed at the swaying lantern. Involved? Yes; so involved Ben wouldn't understand it himself and for that reason Fred was riding a train to far worse peril than he'd ever imagined, instead of riding through the New Mexican night toward hope and eventual vindication for crimes he'd felt certain Ben would help him clear up.

And a tuft of red-gold hair in his pocket had warned him…

CHAPTER TWO

By morning the sun was warming the night-frosted desert and he was surprised to find out how important that seemed to him. Like a suffocating miasma had been torn away to show a sparkling clearness all around.

Well – in a sense the light was revelatory, for now he knew he'd leave the train before it got to Tucomcori. He'd have to. Seven years would make changes but not complete ones. There would be plenty of people around who would remember Fred Nolan's green eyes, curling dark hair, size, appearance. And the girl; he had to consider her too. Ben would meet her at the station. She'd talk about a hundred things on the ride to the ranch and among them would be the doctor she'd met on the train. The tall doctor who was interested in the Nolans. The green-eyed doctor. Ben would know him right away.

He yawned and gazed at his rumpled clothing, raised his eyes and saw that the hard-faced man was up beside Lillian Malone on her bench. It made his brows lower a little. The girl looked annoyed, harassed. Persistent devil, Fred thought, then he turned to look out the dirty little window.

The desert ran south and cast father than he could see. A flat parched domain of greasewood, rip-gut, chaparral, hidden seepage springs, a world unto itself full of nourishment for those who knew it, understood it. He saw it all but his mind deliberately busied itself with thoughts of Lillian Malone even though he had purposefully looked away from her.

As though pulled to him by his thoughts she came down the aisle with a flash in her eyes like battle flags. Edged in toward the opposite bench and stood there looking down at him uncertainly. He felt rather than knew, she was there.

'Good morning Miss Malone.'

He made no move toward getting up. She nodded without speaking and sat down. Casually he let his glance wash over the car behind her and caught the scarcely controlled hot fury directed at him from the eyes of the hard-faced man. For a second their eyes held and Fred felt an electrifying shock from the impact. It was almost tangible.

'Do you mind?'

He shook his head with a little smile. 'Not at all. I think I know the reason why.'

She let it go by. 'Will we stop before Tucomcori? There used to be a place – maybe we passed it in the night.'

'I don't know,' he said. 'It's been years since I've been down this way.'

'I wish we would. I need to tidy up.'

Gazing at her he thought it very unlikely that any other woman could sleep crouched on a wooden bench all night long crossing the desert on a train and look as presentable as she did now. He yawned behind his hand.

'Have you eaten? I've got some fruit in this sack here. Would you care for some?'

'Thank you, no.' She seemed preoccupied for a while. He left her to her thoughts and went back to his own. The train would slow on the outskirts of Tucomcori. He'd leave it there. After that – he wasn't quite sure what he'd do, but he'd find a place to be alone with his thoughts. He needed that more than anything else.

Gazing out the window again he had a feeling the land was hostile to him, something he'd never felt before. He sighed and turned his head toward the girl. No; it wasn't the land. In fact the land might be the best friend he had. It was Ben who was hostile to him. Ben and those Ben could influence. That and the false, lurid reputation. Probably the best thing to do would be stay out of sight until another train came along then put as many miles behind him going East as he'd put behind him coming down here in the first place.

'It's the prettiest sunup isn't it?'

She was looking out the window at the dazzling desert washed from the spillway of sunshine where the light rebounded with an almost fierce intensity off stones, mica, dewdrops.

He studied her eyes, grave and thoughtful below the line of brows. The fullness of her mouth. He thought she had it in her to fire a man beyond himself, to chill him into despair. He thought of dark-eyed, dark-haired Ben Nolan with his coldness. His churning inwardness that showed out of his eyes like black, wet lightning. The way Ben had always been, like new steel, shiny, colorful, ruthlessly cold. Then he thought with self loathing: *She's going to find out – she'll know,* and he turned toward the window answering her absently.

'Yes, the desert's finest at sunup.'

In the far distance lay a blue blur of mountains. He watched them knowing he'd leave soon now. It troubled him. With an effort he swung back and looked beyond her where the hard-faced man was sitting.

'Will he meet you at Tucomcori?' The name just wouldn't come out.

'Ben? Oh yes; we have it all planned.' She was watching him closely.

'Well – you'll be all right after you get in.' It wasn't what he meant, was thinking, and it sounded clumsy. He tried again. 'If that fellow bothers you, those cowboys up front by the stove…' Her eyes grew steadily wider. 'You see I'm going to leave the train before we get into town. That's what I mean.'

'Oh.' The wildness remained, the close look. 'But there's nothing this side of Tucomcori, or didn't you know that?'

He squirmed. 'Yes, I know.' Dammit; this was getting awkward. She looked more puzzled than ever. 'I just don't want to get into town you see; not just yet.'

She said 'Oh' again, but the inflection was stronger, more bewildered than ever.

He shot a long look out the window again, the mountains looked closer, he arose, towered above her with an emerald brightness to his glance. 'Ben'll be interested in your trip, won't he?'

'Yes,' she said, trying to make sense out of his altered attitude.

'And you'll tell him you met a doctor, won't you?'

That time she just nodded.

He stood there swaying, big, sardonic looking, thoughtful. 'Ben will know me when you describe me to him.'

'Will he?'

He smiled without mirth. 'Yes, he will. I'm his cousin. I'm Fred Nolan.'

The expression on her face hardly altered. It froze, became fixed and stunned, a little tainted with dread or fear but otherwise remained the same. She looked rooted to the bench.

He hated what he saw in her eyes; hated himself for causing it. 'If Ben didn't know I was here I could go away again. That's why I'm saying this. Because if you don't tell him he won't know, but if you describe me he'll know immediately and I won't be able to get away. That's asking too much though, isn't it?'

She slumped at the shoulders, looked terribly upset when she leaned back. She didn't answer his question at all. 'That man up there – the one who has been so friendly; do you know who he is?'

Fred lifted his glance, stared at the back of the hardfaced man's head. 'No. I'm sure I've never seen him before – why?'

'That's Joshua Morgan. United States Marshal at Tucomcori.'

'Oh?' He dropped his glance. 'Why do you tell me?'

Her hands fluttered. 'I don't know – except that he's an enemy of yours isn't he?'

'He is now,' Fred said. 'And what about Ben?'

'I won't tell him.'

He moved into the aisle shot a last look at Morgan's head then moved slowly toward the tiny vestibule where a worn drape of sackcloth supposedly kept the night air from the doorless opening, out of the coach. The conductor slept out there, bundled, hunched up, swaying rhythmically with the train's momentum. Fred dropped the drape behind him, looked at the trainman then out at the desert. It was spinning past too fast so he lit a cigar, with his shoulders against the swaying wall, right hand beneath his coat somewhere and his vision commanding both the drape beyond which sat the U.S. Marshal, and closer, where the slack-jawed trainman slept.

The wait wasn't long but it was telling. Sweat ran under his shirt like dank oil before the train began to lose headway. As though in rapport with the iron monster the conductor's last bubbly snore broke off in mid-sound, resumed, hung up again and stopped altogether. Now, Fred told himself. Now!

He leapt with knees bent and both arms crooked but even so the fall was a hard one and the world spun around until an obdurate growth of greasewood fetched him up short. For a moment he lay there breathing shallowly, then he raised his head and shook it, ran fingers through the tumbled shock of hair and looked after the train. It kept right on going, decelerating, wheezing, clanking.

Beyond it lay the sun-warped village of Tucomcori adobe-colored, old, patient and drowsy looking. He noticed that the scraggly old trees seemed more unkempt but aside from that seven years might just as well have not passed.

When he got up and brushed himself off he heard riders and turned with fear gushing up into his throat from deep down inside somewhere. Four of them coming straight toward him from the north, riding in a tight knot beside the tracks. They'd seen him of course. He finished brushing the dirt off, waiting, feverishly manufacturing a tale. He'd fallen off; was bending over to light his cigar when the train lurched and he'd fallen off.

They sat their horses gazing at him. Three of them were young men his own age, the fourth was older, seamed of face and piercing of eye. He chewed gently, unconsciously, on a soggy cud of Kentucky twist.

'You was lucky,' one of the younger men said. 'Wonder you didn't bust a leg.'

'Or your back,' another said.

He nodded shooting a glance at the steady gaze and silently working jaws of the older man. 'It won't be much of a walk.'

Then the older man spoke. 'No need for that, mister. You can ride ahind Chet's cantle.'

There was something in the tone that went

with the look and stirred Fred. 'Thanks, but I'd just as soon walk if you don't mind.'

'And if I do?' the man said, still chewing, still watching Fred hawk-like.

The three younger men looked around stiffly at their companion then back to Fred. They straightened a little in their saddles, got wary, suspicious looking and dropped into perfect stillness, perfect silence.

Fred's nerves tingled. 'What do you mean?'

'Don't recognize me do you?'

Fred tried to, had been trying to for seconds now. He shook his head. 'I don't, but I'm a stranger around here.'

'That so,' the older man said in the same cud-chewing voice. 'You're a stranger all right. Strangest thing is that you come back. Or didn't you never leave?'

'What are you talking about?'

'Got a gun?' The dry-piercing eyes said. 'I know you got a knife. Shuck 'em both.'

Fred started to protest. A pistol barrel peeked at him over the swells of the man's saddle.

'Shuck 'em!'

He did. Drew out the big knife and dropped it, removed the little pepperbox pistol and dropped that too. The men watched him stonily and the older fellow snorted at the little gun.

'Hell of a thing to be carrying.' He let the hammer slide down under his thumb and jerked his head at the nearest horseman. 'Get up ahind Chet and don't act up.'

Fred was as bewildered as he was despairing. He mounted behind the rider, caught the pungent odor of sweat and leather then he held onto the Texas roll of the cantle when the men swung inland and spurred out in a gust of dust.

They made a huge half circle around Tucomcori as near as Fred could tell and by the time they hauled up in a dry-wash where a cabin of sorts squatted they were a good long aching ten miles southeast of town. He was glad to get down when they told him to.

'Come on in.'

Two were behind him. He went willingly enough for the solid fear that they were going to take him to Tucomcori and hand him over to the law had dissolved. He was completely at a loss though.

'Take that there coat off.'

He removed it. A breath of morning coolness swept over his sweat drenched shirt.

'By God – you *ain't* armed, are you? Well, sit down.' The older man knuckled back his hat and eyed Fred steadily. 'Chet – stoke us up some coffee.'

The man called Chet was as tall as Fred but only half as broad. He was standing by the cookstove when he spoke. 'What's the mystery, Norm? Who is this cuss, anyway?'

'Him?' the older man said with a wisp of a

dry smie. 'He's the feller our friend'd like to meet. He's Fred Nolan.'

The riders turned as one man and stared. Someone said 'No' in an out-rushing gust of breath.

'Yes he is – I'm tellin' you. I wasn't ten feet from him that night he killed Beltry an' I'd seen him around Tucomcori before that, too.' He leaned forward a little. 'Tell 'em, mister.'

Fred didn't speak. The four faces were sun-browned, hard looking. The place bristled with guns. The shack was hidden down in a draw. Outlaws? More than likely.

The older man leaned back in his chair and shrugged. 'All right, don't tell 'em but *I'm* going to tell *you* something, Nolan. Your cousin's got two thousand dollars on your head, dead, and nothing on you alive.' The piercing eyes flashed, the leathery features curled into a grin. White teeth, even and perfect, showed startlingly. 'You're worth more'n a herd of Nolan youngstock; did you know that?'

Fred's tenseness had been leaving him a little at a time. Whatever was going to happen wouldn't happen for a while yet. 'Who are you? I don't remember your face at all.'

The man laughed. It sounded like gravel rocks tumbling over one another. 'Norman Graham. Maybe you don't recall me. I hadn't been in the country long when you lit out and since those days things've changed a lot, Nolan. Your cousin's changed for one thing an' a lot of the rest of us've changed, for another thing.'

'Well – maybe. I don't remember you anyway.'

'But you're Fred Nolan and *that* ain't changed any, pardner, you can count on that. You're hotter'n a Mex chili pepper around this end of the country. Why didn't you keep on going after you killed Emmons – or have you been hidin' out around here?'

'Who is Emmons?'

The rattling laugh again. 'Emmons? The feller you killed afore you killed Lonny Hull. That jog your memory a mite, does it?'

Chet set a jumble of tin cups on the table and poured black coffee into each one. Men dragged up benches and little kegs and snugged up to the table. The coffee smelled good to Fred but he didn't want it.

One of the riders, crooking his head and studying Fred's face said, 'Are you really Fred Nolan?' It had something close to admiration in the sound of it.

The man named Chet sipped his coffee after much squint-faced blowing on it. 'Sure he is. He as good as said so a minute ago.' He set the brimming cup down slowly gazing across the table. 'Am I right?'

Fred ignored him, stared steadily at Graham. 'What's on your mind?'

'Answer me!' Chet was half rising, thin face pale with temper.

Before Fred spoke or turned his head Graham snarled: 'Sit down an' cut that out, Chet. Take a look at him. If it wasn't for the guns he'd lick the lot of us. Shut up now.'

Chet subsided but his mouth was flat-ugly looking, his eyes murky with repressed anger.

'Well,' Graham said slowly, 'I don't rightly know, Nolan. I was took off guard when I recognized you.'

'Why didn't you take me into town if I'm worth two thousand dollars?'

'Dead,' Graham reminded him. 'Alive your cousin says he won't pay a dime for you.'

'Why?'

'Hate I reckon. How the hell would I know? Ben don't confide in me, exactly.'

Fred saw the crooked smiles on the others' faces – all but Chet's. They are outlaws, he thought, and they've probably been raiding Ben's herds. He relaxed still more, even drank a little of the coffee, swung fully toward Chet and said:

'Yes, I'm Fred Nolan.'

Chet's brooding sullenness vanished slowly. He nodded without speaking.

'Why'd you kill Emmons?'

Fred pushed the cup aside and fished for a cigar. 'I didn't kill anyone named Emmons, Graham. Until this minute I'd never heard the man's name before.'

No one spoke after that. They seemed occupied with their coffee or with just listening.

'I didn't kill anyone named Hull either. I did kill Beltry and if you were there you know it wasn't murder.'

Graham began whittling off a sliver of chewing tobacco. He was frowning, it made him look even older, more worn and bitter. 'I seen that one all right. Texan asked for it. I even whispered t'you what to do – not get close to 'im. The others – I don't know.'

'Neither do I,' Fred said dryly. 'But I haven't been down here since the fight at Animas and I can prove it.'

'Can you?' Graham said tonguing the cud into place in his cheek. 'Can you explain that from twenty feet off the ground?' His jaws began to work gently, mechanically. 'You'll never get a chance to explain nothin'', Nolan. Nothin' at all. For two thousand dollars there's half the Territory'd kill you on sight and drag your carcass to Ben's door.'

'Including you?'

Graham wagged his head back and forth. 'Not me. Ben'd give nigh as much for my carcass as yours.'

'Why?'

'None of your business.'

Short, brisk, and to the point. Fred almost smiled. One of the riders moved restlessly on his bench. He was looking at Graham with raised eyebrows. Obviously an unspoken question. Graham shook his head infinitesimally at the man.

'Not now, Clem. This here's sort of muddled up our plans a little.'

'We could tie him up and leave him here–' Clem said.

Graham's little eyes looked irritably at the taller, younger man. 'Leave two thousand dollars in plain sight? You daft, Clem?'

'They'll be waitin' over the line.'

'Let 'em wait, dammit, they're payin' little enough.'

Rustlers. Fred looked at them while they talked among themselves. Except for Graham they didn't look like outlaws. Oh, they had the tied down guns, the carbines leaning against the wall, the big, breedy looking horses, all right, but there was more an air of conspirators to them, than the feeling of men bound loosely together through thievery. He tried to imagine what it could be but Graham broke in upon his thoughts.

'Something I'm curious about, Nolan. What was you doing on that train going *toward* Tucomcori? You figure folks wouldn't know you?'

'I was going to see Ben.'

Graham's jaws ceased ruminating for a second, his eyes widened. 'Ben!'

'Yes. I didn't know he'd put a reward on

me. In fact I haven't seen Ben in years. I thought he and I could work out something about these killings.'

Graham's jaws resumed their gentle movement. He stared at Fred for a long time then sighed and shook his head. 'I think you're a liar, Nolan. That or you're sick in the head. If you're lyin' it's not a very good lie. If you aren't storyin', why then you're loco in the head.'

'But he *was* goin' toward town, though,' Chet said.

'That's what's got me stumped, Chet.'

'He might not be storyin' then, Norm.'

Graham chewed thoughtfully, drew up straighter in his chair and leaned both elbows on the table. 'You say you never killed Emmons or Hull. That you been away, out of the country, for a long time. That you ain't seen Ben. 'That right?'

Fred nodded. 'It's right and it's the truth.'

'Then who *did* kill Emmons an' Hull – an' why?'

'I've no idea at all. That's what I wanted Ben to help me find out. Find out who killed them and prove it. If those killings aren't gotten out into the open every killing down here that's unsolved will be laid to me.'

'Likely,' Graham said laconically. 'Why worry about it?'

Fred scowled. 'Because I have a professional name, that's why.'

A short thick-shouldered rider looked quizzically at Graham. 'What the hell's he mean by that – "professional name"?'

Graham grunted. 'Don't know. What'd you mean, Nolan?'

'I'm a doctor by trade. Things like these killings will ruin me before I even get into practice.'

The wall of silence settled over them all again. Minutes later Graham broke it. 'That another lie, Nolan?'

Fred's eyes grew unswervingly intense. He said nothing. Graham's stare was just as unmoving, hard. He too kept the silence for a while then Chet's bench ground scratchily over the floorboards as he stood up. The spell was broken.

'A doctor,' Graham mused into the hush of the cabin's solitary room. Then he stood up also. 'All right, Nolan. We'll see whether you are or not.' He nodded to the others. 'Let's ride over to Old Man Milton's place.'

They went back outside where their horses drowsed and Chet said, 'I'll take him up ahind me.'

They rode southwest but not bunched up as they'd ridden before. Now, two of them split off like videttes, fanning out ahead of Graham and Chet with Fred behind the whipcord ranginess of the latter man. The only time he said anything at all was when they slowed down from a lope to a kidney-slamming trot. Then he growled at Chet, who laughed and drew down to a walk until they all loped again.

As they rode, landmarks oriented Fred. When at last they reined up and sat waiting for the others to come into sight ahead, he knew where he was. In fact his parents' place hadn't been much farther on. Northward a mile or two.

'There's Mack wavin' his hat.'

They went on with Norman Graham in the lead. Fred felt Chet's mount tilt forward and downhill a little. He slid up against the high cantle and braced himself. He wasn't watching so didn't see the faggot corrals nor the still, empty looking shack until Chet was reining up.

The clearing had a good sized vegetable garden inside a deer-proof faggot fence. A well-house made of adobe bricks, a squatter's cabin so typical of all squatter's shacks, and a few slab-sided wicked-horned cattle, who watched them ride up. A scruffy old dog came padding around the house, hackles up snarling. No one paid any attention to him.

Chet threw up an arm toward Fred. 'We'll wait here.'

Fred watched the others go toward the cabin and, strangely, Graham removed his hat. He looked at Chet. 'Is someone sick in there?'

Chet's face came around. 'Yeah, a little,' he said. 'Old feller named Milton. Been down here about five years or so.'

'What's bothering him?'

'Nothing much,' Chet said in the same drawl. 'He got caught in someone's dragging lariat is all.'

Suspecting but doubting Chet's meaning, Fred said, 'What do you mean?'

'Expect some of your cousin's vaqueros drug the old gent. Got him snagged in their lariats and drug him a spell. He ain't been able to talk since the night the old woman found him a week or so back. His neck's about half a foot longer'n it's supposed to be an' all purpled up. There's Norm – come on.'

Inside the shack it was gloomily cool and bleached flour sacks hung at the only window in the place, further obscuring what light filtered in. A tangy aroma of salt pork and greens cooking in an iron kettle on the woodstove almost overwhelmed the sick-sweet odor of linament – and death.

Fred saw the old man from the doorway. He went no closer. A wisp of perfectly straight, thin hair atop a face gray-putty colored. Eyes half closed, totally dry looking, lips thin and parched and parted, stiff. He stood where he was, staring. Nearby a frail old woman stood motionless looking over their heads, her face secretive, sly.

'See what y'can do, Doc,' Norman Graham said gesturing toward the stillness in the lumpy bed.

Fred turned an incredulous glance at Graham. 'Are you blind? That man is dead.'

'Tain't so,' the old woman said lowering her sly-secretive glance to Fred's face. 'Ye think it but it ain't so.'

A soft breath of desert air tiptoed through the room from the open door. Fred felt Graham's eyes on his face.

'Pull back that curtain and look closer, Graham.'

In the same sing-song way the old woman said, 'Taint so. He ate a fine supper las' night.' Then for a second rationality returned and she shuffled over closer to Fred. 'Ye're a stranger. Ye don't know Old Milt. Why – he's tougher'n…' The words trailed off. The only sound came from over by the bed where Chet and Norman Graham straightened up, their spurs making soft, tinkly music. The other two riders were big-eyed statues scarcely breathing.

Fred felt the initiative slide from Graham's shoulders to his own. They exchanged a long glance and Fred jerked his head sideways.

Outside the morning was gone and the day was hot and brilliant. Miles off the blue blur hadn't cleared over the mountains. Fred inhaled deeply.

'Probably died in his sleep. He was pretty old.'

'Been dead long, you reckon?'

Fred shrugged still looking at the mountains. 'I don't know. Not much sense in looking closer. You've got to bury him. This weather's too hot, Graham.'

'What about her?'

'What about her? She's got relatives hasn't she?'

'No. They had a son. He was killed up in bloody Kansas a long time ago. Old Milt told me one time.'

'Well … you've got to bury him anyway.'

Graham's lowered head came up. The mouth was a thin unpleasant line. 'Yeh. We got to bury him – only – it's fittin' you dig the grave. A Nolan killed him an' a Nolan'll bury him.'

'What do you mean?'

'Who drug him like that, you reckon – an old man, a squatter. Who the hell wants this whole goddamned country that bad… Naw; I didn't mean it, Nolan. Forget it. We'll all dig the grave.'

Fred watched the blunted passion turn to rusty color in Graham's face. For a second he'd had to brace into the storm. Now he slumped again. 'Did Ben do that?'

'Yeah. Maybe not Ben hisself. Others – his riders. He hires 'em for that an' worse. They'd of killed Old Milt had he worn a gun; instead they just sort of stretched his neck behind a running horse.' Graham tongued his cud, spat it away. 'Seventy-three Old Milt was.'

'But – good Lord, why?' Fred was looking around him. What was there that anyone would want? Even the cows were old, the calves gutty, undernourished.

'Land,' Graham said. 'All the land there is. You'n me want water bad sometimes. Ben wants land like that.' Graham started to turn away but Fred caught his arm.

'Who said Ben did it?'

'I say it.'

'What proof do you have, Graham?'

'I got proof; my proof's back in the shack dead.'

'You mean that old man *told* you Ben's men dragged him like that?'

'Exactly what I mean. Come on – there's a spade aroun' here some place.'

Fred didn't move.

'Come on – dammit.'

'Wait a minute. That old woman's out of her head. If you bury him with her watching she'll–'

'Aw, she knows he's dead.'

'No. She *did* know when she discovered it but since then her mind's blanked out. He may have died yesterday, even. She doesn't remember finding him dead. The shock of it completely sealed off what she found. She believes he's alive. If you bury him with her believing he's still alive you'll have a wild woman on your hands.'

Graham twisted his head and looked up at Fred. 'Make her crazy?'

'Very possible. Take her away, Graham. I think she'll listen to you; *you* take her. I'll stay here with the others. We'll bury him.'

Graham's nostrils quivered. He didn't know what to say so he said 'Crissake,' and went in search of the spade.

Old Man Milton's wife didn't want to leave and Norm Graham heaped one lie on top of another to get her to go with him. Chet and the others watched the window until she was gone, then Fred broke the stillness.

'Wrap him in a blanket, Chet. Gather up whatever they've got she'll want. We'll be digging outside.'

They dug and the sweat ran. Fred dug savagely. The ground was bone-dry and hard. The other two men wanted to square off the walls and corners at four feet but Fred kept on digging. His shirt was dark-sodden. He didn't speak and his breath rattled in and out. The sweat was salty, it stung his eyes. He dug steadily until his heart sounded like a drumroll in his head then he straightened up in the hole and looked out. The top of it was even with his chin. It was six feet deep and what a Nolan had made ready for it another

Nolan had dug it for.

'Tell Chet to bring him out.'

Mack and Clem left him alone while they went for the body. He crawled up out of the hole and leaned in the wedge of shade beside the shack.

Ben – not an old man like that.

Not by dragging him until every vein in his throat was ruptured, ligaments hopelessly torn, dehydrated old muscles mangled. Even a Comanche wouldn't have done it like that. He'd have sunk a stubby little war-arrow into the old fellow and sent him on his way.

He fixed his eyes on the heat shimmering distance. She'd said *Fred* Nolan had brought stigma to the name. She'd said people didn't like Ben; that they spited him...

'Here's a prayerbook I foun' in there.'

Chet was holding it out without looking at either the book or Fred. 'Lower him easy, boys – dammit.'

Fred took the Bible and felt its cool smoothness. Its worn, thin leather covering, and it seemed a natural thing for him to read something out of it over the old man he'd never known, had only seen once, whom his cousin had slain.

'Aw, Clem – gentle with it. Don't just throw it in on him.'

He read all the time they were filling the grave and when they were finished, looking at him strangely out of sweat-shiny faces, he closed the book, put it into his pants pocket and looked down at the darker, moist earth where Old Man Milton lay. It was habit when he said, 'Take some chaparral branches and drag them back and forth over it. No sense in telling the world he's there.'

Chet turned away. Fred went as far as the house with him but Chet didn't stop.

'Where are you going?'

'He had a nice bay colt. It's out back. You can ride it back.'

Inside Fred saw that Chet had put everything of value or usefulness into a patchwork comforter and tied the ends. The shack looked even more desolate, emptied, now that it didn't even have the smell of death in it.

'Nolan?'

He went back outside. Chet was holding a handsome bay horse. There was an old A-fork Texas saddle on it, a carefully greased set of rawhide reins with a romal. A very old spade bit, so old the engraving was worn to hair lines, spidery, graceful. The horse rolled the cricket with his tongue and moved a little in impatience.

'The old man broke him hisself. We used to tell him he was too old to mess around green colts.' Chet held out the reins. 'Old Milt was a real horseman. Those old-timers were.'

Fred took the reins. Chet went around him into the house and emerged lugging the bundle.

They rode back at a walk. The sun bored down like only a New Mexican sun can. They twisted their way through brushy game trails and across little grassy clearings singlefile, Fred second from the end, Chet behind him. Up ahead in the lead the big-shouldered man called Mack raised his voice.

'Goin' south, Chet?'

'Too late,' Chet called back. 'Too late an' too risky now.'

Fred heard and surmised what they'd meant but his mind wasn't with him at all.

Graham was at the shack when they got back. Sitting in the shade out front chewing monotonously, eyes a little above them and a long way off.

They all dismounted and looped reins over the limbed rail in the shade of the cabin. Fred saw Graham's gaze come back to the present and fasten on him. He went over into the shade and squatted.

'Where'd you take her?'

'To another old lady's shack near town,' Graham said, then: 'Reckon that won't prove you no sawbones, will it, Nolan?'

Irritably and dully Fred answered. 'Do you think I care whether you believe I'm lying about myself or not, Graham?'

'No, I expect not.'

Graham lapsed into silence until the rider called Clem came over then he rolled his head on his shoulders toward the hitchrail. 'Put up the horses, will you? We ain't ridin' nowhere today.'

'How many riders does my cousin have, Graham?'

'Eleven. Eleven of the hardest crows to ever roost in this country.'

'Gunmen?'

'Every last mother's son of 'em.' Graham twisted on the plank bench. 'An' he's got the law as well.'

'He's got the whole damned country if you ask me,' Chet said from his leaning position against the doorless maw of the shack.

'Then why does he want a sage and sand patch like that old man's place? Tell me that?'

'Sure,' Graham said. 'I already told you once. First off, Old Man Milton squatted on a piece of range the Nolans've been running on for years. Second, the old man went an' dug a well, got water, built a cabin, made some fence – all that on Nolan range. Hell; Ben'll have you killed for a lot less'n that, believe me. Trespassing, he calls it.'

'Is that why the fringe ranchers hate him?'

Graham made a hollow laugh. 'Ain't it enough? I was a fringe rancher, Nolan. He only burnt me out; 'course my wife was bed-ridden with the fever an' maybe he didn't know that. It ain't s'much the range they hate him over. It's other things. You saw Old Man Milton's neck but you never seen my wife – never heard her.'

'Why hasn't someone shot him?'

'I'd as leif try to shoot the President. Ben's got his riders. He don't go nowhere 'thout 'em. What's the good of me gettin' killed without killing him? That's what it'd amount to. And the law's his; don't forget that.'

'The U.S. Marshal you mean?'

'Yeh. Josh Morgan. Ben owns him lock stock an' barrel.'

Fred stood up slowly. His body ached all over. 'What about the Army?'

'This is civil stuff, they tell us. Anyway, Ben's been there, too.'

'So it boils down to you four fellows rustling off him and snapping at his heels.'

'Not just us; we happen to be the ones he's gotten outlawed, but we've got lots of friends among the other squatters around the country, only the others dassen't do too much or he'll get them too.'

'So you play coyote with him.'

Graham's piercing eyes grew still. 'You know a better way to do it?'

Fred didn't answer right away. The shadows were getting long. The faintly acrid odor of the desert was coming up out of the ground. It was all familiar; all but the old man with the putty-purpled neck.

'I think there's a better way,' he said. 'I haven't thought about it but I'm sure there is.'

Graham rolled up his cud with his tongue, balanced it and spat it out, brushing a grimy sleeve across his chapped mouth. 'Think so, huh. Well – you got all night an' till after breakfast to think it up.' He got up and disappeared inside the cabin.

Chet still leaned in the doorway looking far beyond Fred but watching him just the same. His sombre glance lay southward in a soft-remembering, unmistakable way. Fred could almost feel his thoughts. Him too. Each one of these four and Old Man Milton and the Lord knew how many others. What had come *over* Ben? He'd always been domineering, bleak, but this was worse than anyone would have imagined fifteen years ago; even *seven* years ago.

CHAPTER THREE

When the moon came up it painted an eerie landscape with huge strokes of off-color white. Fred sat on the bench outside the shack and watched it. Coyotes yapped, one or two making the sounds of a dozen.

Behind the shack where the sagging corral was, horses blew their noses and one was cribbing on something. A post more than likely; he'd have belly worms to make him do that.

All the impressions came and went. Fred catalogued each one. Seven years wasn't much – not such a long time after all. Seven years of struggle, of achievement. An awkward shadow came out and dropped down beside him.

'Purty night.'

Graham. His voice sounded softer than it did by daylight. Maybe it was his mood. 'I've never seen a desert night that wasn't pretty,' Fred said without looking around.

Graham said nothing for a while, then: 'I have. A couple of 'em. One was the night my shack went up with the missus inside bedfast.'

Fred let the silence draw out between them until the last echoes were gone before he spoke again. 'You don't have to watch me, Graham.'

Graham slumped still lower on the bench with his hands deep in his pants pockets. He was staring at his scuffed boot toes. 'I ain't watching you.'

Fred turned. 'I don't believe you. One of you has been watching me all day.'

'Well – sure. Up until you came back from Old Man Milton's. Not now though.'

Graham's eyes came around. Fred thought he saw a rusty spark of empty mirth in them. 'Leave any time you want to, Nolan. Can even take the old man's bay colt if you're a mind to.'

They exchanged a prolonged stare in silence then Fred looked away. The coyotes sounded again, closer. A little breeze rustled the treetops behind the cabin, brought sage-scent and night-warmth to them.

Graham's look wasn't just hard, Fred thought. It was discerning as well.

'I'm worth two thousand dollars, Graham. Aren't forgetting that are you?'

'Naw. Hell no. I got a safe bet either way. Look, Nolan; if you go on livin' you'll go on bein' a cockleburr under Ben's saddle-blanket. I want that more'n two thousand dollars. And I got another bet covering *that* bet, too.'

'What?'

'I just told the boys. You *won't* leave. Old Man Milton fixed that.' Wisely Norman Graham stopped there, didn't enlarge on it.

Fred's nostrils dilated. The night was warm scented; it was good smelling. Like perfume, a little. Like perfume from a wisp of hair stinging across a man's face. He reached down into his coat pocket and withdrew the snarl of hair. With his fingers opened the moonglow was trapped in the strangely stirring luster. 'I ought to go,' he said, but not necessarily to Graham. 'If I stay here there's going to be trouble for all of us.'

'I expect,' Graham said. 'Trouble's nothing new. I been through enough of it in my lifetime to do a dozen men.' Graham's hat was tilted low over his eyes. He seemed to be staring at nothing straight ahead of him. 'When'd do you like to start this – trouble?'

'What are you talking about?'

Graham chuckled without moving. 'Nolan – I'm a sight older'n you. Remember that. I got so's a man's ways were pretty easy for me to figure when I was a button. Them days you *had* to learn. I seen that what your cousin did to Old Man Milton sickened you a little today. You ain't over it yet. You're comin' to hate him like I do, but you're smarter, Nolan. You're educated along with bein' big. You got brains. If we never needed anything else we need a feller with brains. Like you said today, "snapping around his heels like coyotes." Well; that's all we've been able to do. You said you figured there'd ought to be a better way to fry his hash.' Graham spat and sighed and settled back against the shack again. 'That's what I come out here tonight for. For you to say what we got to do to break Ben Nolan into a hundred pieces an' stamp him out forever.'

Fred moved his palm one way then the other watching the moonlight stagger and lurch through the red-gold hair.

'Well?'

He closed his fingers around the hair and held it, looking straight up at the moon. Was she sitting in the big house with Ben now, eating supper? Were they standing on the bearskin rug by the fireplace or walking beyond the honeysuckled verandah under this same moon? He closed his fingers tightly and put the snarl back into his pocket.

'Nolan – you ever smell a shack burning with a bed-fast woman in it?'

Fred stood up suddenly. So suddenly Graham was jarred where he sat.

'You don't have to parade your sorrow for my benefit,' he said tightly.

'No. I reckon not. You remember Old Milt don't you?'

It was in the tones of apology and Fred winced from it. A man excusing himself for mentioning something that would torture him as long as he lived.

'I'm sorry, Graham.'

Silence.

The coyotes were still. The night was hushed and moonwashed and timeless; nostalgic. Old Pachise – the man with the flowing russet beard – the sturdy woman with violet eyes. Comanches, Nolans, Animas, cattle drives, dust and sweat and laughter, black coffee, blinding sun and this same moon, same night scent. *I belong here,*

– I'll always belong here but if I stay there'll be blood and sorrow and she'll be right in the middle of it. I CAN'T *Stay!*

Graham stood up, stretched, avoided looking at the large shadow nearby, dropped his arms and shot a long look at the nearly full moon. 'No hurry,' he said softly. 'An' you know somethin', Nolan? Nothing's ever as easy as it looks. Good night.'

Fred didn't answer. He heard Graham's spurs inside the shack, the thump of his boots when he tossed them aside, the rope-grunt when he lay down on a bunk in darkness – with his memory.

In his mind was the old man's marble stillness. The dead-purple neck. The old woman's unblinking – sly expression. Lillian Malone's belief that people just didn't understand Ben. He swore aloud.

'I don't want to be a damned foot savior and I don't want to start a range war.' Then something in the back of his mind reminded him of the killer's reputation. He glared at the thought inwardly. 'I don't want to think about that, either – now.' The inner voice said *If you don't it'll destroy you, Fred.*

But he didn't want to stay. If there was an alternative – what was it?

'There isn't any. If I go back *they're* licked. If I stay, someone's going to suffer. The Lord knows what'll happen.'

You've got to stay, not for her sake or even for

your own, entirely, but because you belong here and if that isn't enough – every morning for the rest of your life when you shave you'll see the face of a man who has lost his self respect!

He went to bed late, after the moon had dipped low and a few bleak chaparrals were limned across his face like broken old bones blackened with age. Sleep was a long time coming and it seemed he'd only been asleep a few minutes when he heard a horse clatter up outside the shack on the stony earth and a man call out.

He arose and dressed. The shack was empty but food cooked favorably on the woodstove over against the wall. Mack burst in, shot him a harassed, frowning look, and went to the stove. Fully clothed, Fred went outside. The morning sun blinded him for a second and his appearance put a damper on a conversation between Norm Graham and a stripling youth with hair that looked like birds had just flown out of it. Clem, turning, following the boy's stare, shrugged.

'Go on; never mind him.'

'Who is he?'

Graham grunted around a fresh cud. 'Go on, dammit. Who says we got to move 'em right now?'

'My paw. He set up there on watch all night an' come dawn he seen Nolan riders scoutin' around like they was lookin' for tracks.'

'You eaten?'

'No an' my paw says for me to scoot right back. What'll I tell him?'

'That we're comin' an' to have men blanket-out any tracks around,' Graham said, turning away, heading toward the shack. At the doorway he hesitated and squinted up at Fred. 'How'd you like to drive some Big Lily cattle into Mexico with us?'

Fred answered in a calm voice. 'All right. When?'

Graham's glance hung a moment, then he smiled. 'Figured it'd come out that way. Now; soon's we eat.'

Fred followed him inside. Mack was throwing food onto tin plates like he had only five minutes left to him and didn't want to leave with things undone.

Fred sat down on a keg, waiting for the others. Big Lily – Ben's family brand. He wasn't the least surprised. What occupied his mind through the wolfed-down meal was the wisdom of stealing Ben's cattle at all. The point was Ben, and if you wanted to break a man with thousands of cattle you'd have to spend your life running off cattle faster than cows could replace them; in huge herds, not in dribbles, even then it would take forever. Too little accomplished it seemed to Fred, for the risk involved. No; as he'd thought the night before, Ben had to be hurt some other way. Faster, closer.

'Let's go – Chet – Norm–' Mack looked at them from the doorway, scowling, impatient. 'An' you, Nolan – if you're comin'.'

They left the shack with the sun behind them. Rode fast, coat tails flapping, for several brushy miles then emerged into cleared, erosion gutted brakes where a man and a horse could hide all day long and still move. When Fred was close enough to reach over and touch Norm's sleeve he did so.

'Where are they?'

'In a blind canyon about a mile ahead. Sort of hidden corral like. Some of our friends keep herd on 'em for us until we're ready to make a break for it.'

'Who gets the money?'

Graham's sweaty face creased into a cynical smile. '*I* don't, that's a gut. Keep it for them as get burn out an' run out. It helps.'

'How about riders; Ben's men?'

'That's what's stickin' in my craw right now. If we don't get these critters far enough away before the dew dries and the dust starts up they'll make a trail folks can see for twenty miles.'

'Why did you wait so long then?'

The smile widened. 'You,' Graham said. 'Until we stumbled onto you we was set to drive 'em south yesterday.'

Fred leaned back against the cantle

watching the bay colt's ears twitch in anticipation of every gully he had to slide down and scramble up the other side of.

Well; it made sense in an archaically chivalrous way, but it still wasn't the way to break Ben. Not with the wealth he had behind him, and furthermore…

'Hallooo!'

A bright red blanket flagged from a barren butte. Fred watched the three men ahead of him stand recklessly in their stirrups and wave their hats. Norm Graham reined up and waited for Fred. His eyes were like faded blue rocks under a mountain stream, glistening, hard and shiny.

'Hold up here, Nolan. They'll turn 'em loose an' haze 'em toward us. We'll pick 'em about here and keep 'em moving.'

'What about those riders the kid spoke of?'

Graham made a slighting gesture. 'Squatters'll take care of 'em. They do all our track – smothering and false-trail work for us.' He turned, winked. 'With blankets mostly, and they're plenty good at it.'

When the first of the cattle trotted by Fred saw the big brand. It looked like a wagon wheel, spokes and all, except that it had a crooked tail coming out at the bottom of the wheel and curling up a little.

Big Lily, a good brand. He'd burnt it into a good many hides himself, years back.

Riders could spot it on critter's sides miles away.

He fell in at the flank out of habit when the herd went by, watching the air above for the tell-tale dust banners. In all his years with cattle drives this was the first time he'd ever thought of herd-dust as something to fear; something other than solid annoyance for flank riders.

They went south as straight as a bullet and stopped only once, when the sun was a little off center overhead, meaning it wasn't quite time for nooning yet. That was at Little Pilot creek. The cattle lined up on both sides and sucked up water, then the riders hazed them on again.

Later in the afternoon Norm Graham rode up beside him, face dun-color and sweat streaked, handsome teeth whiter looking than ever.

'Nice bunch. Eighty-eight head to my count. You count 'em?'

'No,' Fred said. 'Too much dust and hurry. How far do we take them?'

'We'll be there by sundown. Don't like to hustle fat stock. Too much shrink.'

With a wry little smile Fred looked out over the red-moving backs. 'It'd be a pity to shrink Ben's cattle and have to take less for them,' he murmured.

Graham laughed aloud. 'No matter whose they are, they sell by the head, fat or thin, but fat they fetch more.' He quirked his head toward Fred. 'Thought of anything better yet?'

'No, but I think for the same risk you ought to be able to get right up into Ben's yard.'

'Do you?' Graham said. 'Well – tell you what; we'll sleep over below the line tonight then ride back tomorrow an' for a while there won't be much to do until the hullaballoo dies down. You just take a *pasear* over to Ben's and look the place over.'

Graham reined away in response to Chet's faint call and Fred watched him go. Just like that, he was one of them. It made him smile. Another of Graham's covered bets, apparently. Fred Nolan, rustler. The decision had been made for him, after all. It would be made irrevocable in a little while but he didn't know that until shortly before they got to the border.

Chet and Norm sat their horses off to one side of the ambling herd watching the animals go by. Fred saw them together and reined over. He saw their faces from a hundred feet and neither man looked particularly relieved that they were nearing the end of the drive. They were silent, grim looking, especially Norman Graham.

Fred stopped the bay colt, rested both hands on the horn and watched the last animal straggle past. When only the dust remained Graham lifted his reins preparatory to riding on.

'Mack's on the point. He seen fresh horse track ahead of us.'

Fred's stomach muscles contracted. 'Trouble?'

'Might be,' Graham said riding on. 'He's scouting things out.'

Chet made no move to follow Graham. He had his hat tilted far back and was worrying up a brownpaper cigarette. Without looking around he held out the hand the tobacco sack dangled from by its yellow string.

'Might jus' be the greasers who buy 'em, too,' he said, tamping the tobacco into its little papered trough, curling it over, licking it and popping it into his mouth. 'Might be anyone; travelers, Mexs, wild-horse hunters.'

'Or Rangers of some kind; U.S. Marshals?'

Chet inhaled, exhaled, shrugged. 'Never seen 'em down around here. That's why we came so far west this time. Out in the middle of the damned desert.'

'How long have you been doing this – using this same route, I mean?'

'We don't always use the same trails. I just told you. Mostly, we deliver east of here. Over near Animas.'

Fred sighed inwardly. 'Doesn't Ben still use Animas as his shipping point?'

'Yes.'

'Then,' Fred said bluntly, 'you're crazy to

use the same country.'

Chet seemed equally undisturbed by both Fred's bluntness and the dangers of Animas as disposal point for their stolen cattle. 'Naw; y'see Ben ships fall an' winter. We only sell down there when our Mex friends tell us it's safe.'

'How the devil would they know?' Fred said, real alarm spreading through him for some inexplicable reason. 'I think you're underestimating Ben Nolan. Listen; if you people have been doing this for quite a while don't think for a moment Ben hasn't been…'

He never finished it. A quavering yell rose above the sound of lowing cattle, then another cry, higher, louder. Fred's fingers tightened into a fist around the colt's reins. Chet dropped a scorching curse and sat bolt upright.

They both saw him coming at the same time, Chet called him by name. 'Clem!'

The rider swerved widely, waving. Before he was close enough he cried out: 'Ride for it – it's Morgan an' Nolan's riders!'

Fred's nerve ends flinched under his skin. He wheeled the colt, was spinning in the wake of Chet when a dry rattle of gunfire burst into his hearing. Cattle bawled and the earth shook underfoot. Stampede; gunshots had panicked the cattle. Nearer, two closely spaced shots rang out and the bay colt bunched up under the saddle. Fred swung him west and leaned forward. The animal needed nothing more. He fled like an arrow with brush clawing at his rider, slapping his own sides adding to his own fright.

Once Fred twisted in the saddle. A dust banner stood almost vertically straight into the thin blue air down where the head of the herd had been. He reined the colt gently southward, got response to the bit he hadn't expected, and drew in a little, holding his mount to a long lope.

They *had* underestimated Ben, the fools.

Where a tall sahuaro held aloft spiney arms Fred swung a little west and by then the colt had used up his burst of frenzy. He slowed to a walk willingly and Fred ran his hand under his coat with a sense of helplessness; no knife, no gun.

When he dismounted in a tangle of thicket Chet's tobacco sack, sweat-limp, was still in his fist. He squatted, made a smoke, lit it listening for sounds, inhaled deeply and wondered where the others were. Chet and Clem would have escaped, surely. He doubted very much if any of Ben's riders knew the desert reaches as well as the rustler-squatters did.

But where were Mack and Norm Graham?

Two hours later when the sun was burnished brass and the desert was so still it hummed, he left the colt tied and went forward through the maze of brush. Cattle smell was in the air but there wasn't a sound of any kind. Probably the ambushers had driven the cattle to water and feed to steady them down. If they didn't they'd never find two-thirds of them in this meat-hungry, Mexican-infested strip of the desert.

And the rustler chasing would be left to the law. Big Lily cattle would be the responsibility of Ben's vaqueros, first.

He came at last where the ground was churned with a strong smell of animals and gunsmoke around it. There he hung back, listening. Still not a sound. He squirmed through the thicket until he had a good view of the open land where the brush was torn, hanging, from the passage of so many shaggy bodies. Here he saw the first body; Mack.

He was dead and Fred couldn't tell whether bullets had snuffed out his life first or whether the cattle who'd trampled over him after he'd fallen from his horse had done it.

Farther on, where a wavering snake-trail ended, he found Graham. The older man opened his eyes when Fred's shadow fell across his face. He didn't blink and his mouth moved. Down on one knee Fred lifted the soggy shirt.

'Goin' t'die, Nolan,' Graham said thickly.

Fred dropped the shirt and looked at the

face. 'I doubt it but it's possible. You've been shot through the lung.'

'Heart,' Graham said. 'Feels like the heart.'

Fred shook his head, 'If it'd been the heart you wouldn't be talking about it now.' And saw Graham's pistol lying in the dirt, picked it up and shoved it into his belt. Graham licked his lips. There was pink in his saliva.

'Ben's smart.'

Almost angrily Fred said, 'I could've told you that. What you've been doing took lots of nerve, a little guts and no brains at all. He was bound to catch you in time.'

'Well – he did. You better skedaddle. They'll be back.'

Fred got up and stalked through the brush. He was angry; more at something akin to stupidity or lack of imagination that, in his mind, was associated with Norman Graham, than with Ben, whom he felt had every right to do what he'd done. The miracle was that Ben's people hadn't come back before this and finished Graham off. That too was their right.

And Graham – he'd probably survive from the lung shot but not if he spent a night on the ground. Pneumonia had a way of finding feverish, clotted lungs even this far from Boston hospitals.

When he finally thought he'd found a place where he might be able to secrete and cover the wounded man, and turned back – there were his tracks. Full moon tonight; nearly full last night. Tracks and a full moon.

He went back where Mack lay, took the dead man's gun and shell-belt, his hat and boots. Both the latter were tight but not uncomfortably tight, then he went back where Graham lay, picked him up like a child and trudged over where he'd left the bay colt. There was no other way.

'Listen to me, Graham; don't try to sit up straight but don't bend over too much either.' As an afterthought he said, 'If this doesn't kill you nothing will,' then he began to lead the horse.

Fortunately the bay colt didn't object to an unsteady rider on his back or the big man up ahead trailing reins and romal over his arm, trudging flat-footedly in the too-tight boots with their silver spurs keeping a perfectly spaced cadence through the fish-belly color of early evening.

Fred walked and thought. The hours went by and three times he had to stop and steady Graham, before they got back to the shack and when they got there the place looked deserted, dark and forbidding.

With more indignation than wariness in him Fred put Graham on the ground, walked far out around the cabin to see if horses were in the corral; they were and he recognized them. He went up a little closer to the door and pitched a pebble inside.

'That you Norm?'

'It's Nolan. Come on out here and give me a hand.'

They came fully dressed, fully armed and fully awake. Fred didn't wait for them to speak the questions in their faces. He turned and stalked back where Graham lay, pointed and said, 'Take him inside. Put him to bed and fire up the stove and keep the shack warm all night long. If he gets chilled he's a goner.'

The bay colt tucked up a little when the two men eased Graham off the ground. Fred caught up the reins, led the animal behind the straining carriers, looped the reins at the hitchrail and went inside.

He didn't speak until he'd lit a candle and watched Chet and Clem put Graham in his bunk and pile blankets on him, then he gestured toward the stove at the same time withdrew Graham's gun from his belt and tossed it carelessly on the table.

'Use a blanket over the doorway.' He saw Clem tug one off a bunk. 'You know, fellows, I feel sorry for Graham. Not because he got shot but because he used so little sense getting shot and because he's got to rely on people like you.'

Chet's face came around. It was pale. He opened his mouth to speak. Fred made a brusque motion with his arm. 'Wait a minute,' he said. 'He led you into an ambush. I'm not surprised. I'm not even surprised you ran off like a pair of yellow pups because if you hadn't you wouldn't be the kind of men he could lead into an ambush. Chet, remember what you said; how you felt? No danger, just some Mex riders maybe or travelers. For a guy so casual you sure flew a yellow flag fast.'

Fred's bulk loomed large in the gusty candlelight. Chet was standing by the stove wide legged his face like gray cloth, mouth down and bloodless looking. Fred waited, hearing Clem on his other side working hurriedly, hanging the blanket over the doorway. He turned on his heel and walked out of the shack and Chet didn't make a move.

The bay colt nuzzled him before he swung up, responded willingly to the touch of reins. Loping through the warm night Fred's anger burnt itself out, but slowly. The lights of Tucomcori were in sight like orange jewels suspended low from the pale sky before it was gone. By then he had an alkali dryness in his mouth and throat and an urge to keep on riding until even the memory of Graham's filthy face, dry looking eyes, was gone.

Caution came with the squeak and rattle of chain harness and a wagon on the road. With no clear reason for doing it he reined over onto the desert, reined up and sat like a statue ahorseback, watching.

When the vehicle went by it proved to be an Army wagon drawn by service mules. Two men were on the seat and a huge canvas was drawn down and diamond-hitched over the load. What was the Army doing in Tucomcori? The nearest army post used to be old Fort Taylor, thirty miles east toward the foothills that rimmed the desert.

He went back onto the road and let the colt drop his head, swing the reins from side to side in a loose jointed mile eating walk and when he came to the turn-off he remembered so well, he leaned a little. The colt dutifully interpreted the redistributed weight to mean That Way. He swung over onto the spur-road and stirred up white dust in powdery clop, clop, clops, muffled.

Ben was no fool. Fred had long since figured out what he'd done. Taken lots of time, picked up the tracks down close to the line where no effort'd been made to hide them. Maybe his men had interrogated the Mexicans. Let them keep the cattle for telling the truth. Put the pieces together slowly and carefully, built his trap well. In time he knew the whole story. After that it hadn't been hard. Station men here and there, where the rustlers had sold their herds; bribe a Mex or two then wait. Just wait.

He even thought that Ben hadn't gotten much of a sense of triumph out of it. Too simple; too rudimentary. Fred let off a curse, shook his head. And this was what the squatters thought would humble Ben Nolan!

It was foolish and was infantile. Even if Ben didn't have more cattle than he could count eighty-nine head or so at a time wouldn't hurt him much, but it would mean that the rustlers were leaving more and more tracks, contacts, ways to be caught, ambushed.

'Childishness,' Fred said aloud. The bay colt flicked his ears back, raised his head a little and tumbled the cricket in his mouth.

Fred looped the reins and made a cigarette from Chet's tobacco, lit it and smoked with Mack's hat back away from his eyes. The land's outline was like a gray-brown quilt with tufts of filling sticking through. Sage and greasewood, even a little manzanita with its bloody looking trunk and mangrove-shaped leaves. And bunchgrass, lots of bunchgrass; new shoots of green shoving up through last year's dead blades. Lots of nourishment for Big Lily cattle. Then he was out in the cleared country where peons had cut brush for years and years pushing it back, making a huge meadow for the bunchgrass to fill in and spread over, and in the far distance a sight that, moonlight or daylight, would live in his heart as long as he lived. Big Lily itself; the Nolan ranch.

He reined up and smoked. Over west of the

house was the log barn. They'd felled those trees eighty miles away and freighted them down into the desert on stripped Conestogas; just the running gears. Mex drivers and four spans of mules to a wagon-bed. The corral poles came the same way. The house was older than Time itself. It had been built and lived in and added to since long before anyone could remember. Spaniards then Mexicans, generations of them, had lived in it. Out back where the grape arbor was Fred remembered one grape trunk too big for him to get his hands around. That old. Memories…

And Ben was down there. Probably sitting with his feet on the *ramada* railing with a cigar, telling Lillian Malone the legends of the ranch. It made Fred's cigarette taste like acid. Ben… Graham with froth on his mouth made blood-black in the moonlight. Old Man Milton. A bedfast woman shrieking through the red hell of setfire.

He lifted the reins and eased the colt off the road. Cut a path out where the brush was, far off, and swung down toward the ranch buildings. He had no carbine for this job but then he hadn't come here prepared to do it either; now the thought was in his mind. Thing was – a carbine gave you more distance, more of a start. With a pistol you had to get in close. Still – even with the moonlight they'd have to hump to catch him. Get up, saddle up, hunt for tracks or go by sound so long as there was any and he'd see to that. Graham had said it couldn't be done. Well; after seeing what Graham thought good sense, Fred doubted that, too.

He left the colt loose-hobbled, flung Mack's spurs around the saddlehorn buckled together and started walking closer. A ground-owl skimmed past looking for night-feeding mice. Close enough to make Fred flinch, jerk upright and coil his fingers around the dead man's pistol.

He came to the end of the brush and stood like an Indian for a long time. The only light in the house was in the parlor. It showed where the verandah was, spilling out through a window. He remembered it all like it was yesterday, too. Over where the ugly bunkhouse stood, square, adobe, strictly utilitarian, there was no light at all. He guessed the time to be after ten but not yet eleven. One little toe was cramped sufficiently in a boot to annoy him with hints of pain.

He moved out across the bunchgrass meadow, strode through the damp moonlight with long strides, coat tail flapping with each step, a big man, thick shouldered, bunch-muscled, keeping track of the way he came and the distance back. Even in the pale light he felt exposed enough for a dozen sets of eyes to see although he knew well enough none would see him. Not so long as he kept the darkened back of the house between himself and the bunkhouse. The parlor or maybe the verandah where Ben would be sitting was around in front; he was safe enough then, until he fired. After that he'd go back the way he'd come, out of sight of the bunkhouse and he'd be running.

For no reason at all a recollection of his shortness with Graham flashed into his mind. He shouldn't have been that way even if he'd known Graham wasn't going to die and Graham thought he was going to. Graham didn't know he wasn't and that was the second time Fred had flared up at him really without much cause. Strange; he wasn't normally irritable.

When he finally smelled the honeysuckle a lump settled behind his belt somewhere. He could have closed his eyes and told where every old vine was along the uprights that supported the *ramada's* overhanging roof; the verandah that ran full length around every desert ranch house making shade in a land where shade was priceless.

He went over close to the side of the house and stopped. By peering a little he could see the yard, the blacksmith's shop, the bunkhouse. Behind him was the barn, the corrals. Seven years might not have been. Everything here was exactly the same. Moving carefully he came to the edge of the wall and just beyond lay the deep shadows of the verandah. He looked long and searchingly. Lamplight from the parlor gushed from a window across the *ramada's* width and ran out into the yard a ways. There it ended, sucked under by the dry earth.

A faint shadow at the outer fringe of golden light made his pulse beat softly in his ears. Someone was sitting on one of the flesh-side-out chairs and he knew from the way the light strained to reach the shadow who it was. Red-gold hair throwing back the rays like coals in a cooling forge.

She was alone, though.

He drew back. In an hour's stalking and a hectic night he'd forgotten completely that she'd witness it. And where was Ben? He should've been there with her – but if he had been, how to assassinate him?

CHAPTER FOUR

'Lillian?'

She gave him a swift, stunned look, her mouth dropped to shape a word that didn't come. He swung over the gallery railing and stood there.

'Where's Ben?' It chilled him to see the way she was looking at him. He was a man, direct and simple and forthright and had known no other way to greet her even though he knew it was wrong to come out of the shadows like that. What he didn't know was the way he looked and how the filagree of light-pattern heightened it for her.

'I asked where Ben was.'

The shock went out of her eyes, a softening of the mouth, then she answered. 'He's gone.'

'Where?'

'With his riders; somewhere down on the border. They left yesterday.'

Fred took it like a blow between the eyes. Of course.

Oh, goddammit, he thought, when will I learn? Then he shrugged it away. You can't be expected to know everything, figure out everything in one day, after seven years.

She was looking up at him, seeing the sharp-etched moonlight down the side of his face. 'He left the cook and two wranglers here but all the rest went with him.'

'And the law?' Fred said.

'Yes, Marshal Morgan from town.'

He slumped against an upright post in silence. A little tremor of relief, surprisingly, went through him. Relief and disappointment and something else he didn't try to assay. He didn't know she'd first seen him about like that, leaning against a post, tall, shadowed.

'I thought you were – going back. You said

if I didn't tell Ben…'

Green eyes dropped a fraction. 'Something changed my mind for me,' he said.

'But you've got to,' she whispered. 'He knows. Josh Morgan told him about the big man with green eyes on the train. I don't know why he told him but he did. Ben's having posters printed – he's raising the reward. You've *got* to leave.'

So there it was. No turning back now at all. He looked at her face in the dawn light and then turned back to gaze at the bunkhouse. It was as still, dark, as ever. He turned back toward her and sat gingerly on the railing behind him, just looking at her.

The night's warmth was hotter under the overhang. It throbbed, almost, was full of things that crowded to fill the space between where he lounged and she sat. He made a cigarette and lit it, unmindful of the little splash of sulphur light from the match. Inhaled smoke and expelled it. She could hear the deep rush of air through his nose.

'He'll come back–'

'Tomorrow, probably,' he interrupted, 'or late tonight. Did he tell you why he was going?'

'Yes; those fringe ranchers I told you about – since last year when I came down they've grown worse.'

'Rustlers, aren't they?' He was watching her face for expression but her thoughts weren't on naming names apparently, for the urgency remained.

'Now that I've told you of the reward and the posters, will you go?'

He shook his head, hesitated over his answer. 'I wish I could. I wanted to. Now I can't.'

'Why?' Bewildered, almost desperate.

'Oh – for several reasons.'

'Tell me.'

'I don't think I can tell you why exactly. Oh – some of it I could but the rest of it – no. Anyway, what's the difference?'

'Because he'll think you're running? Because people will say you came down here and Ben frightened you away? That's foolish.'

'That's not it.'

She had her mouth parted to say more but a depth of silence settled between them for no special reason. He remained unmoving, smelling of horse sweat and tobacco smoke and the desert, strong male smells. She twisted forward in her chair and the soberness of her profile kept her features vague and still. After a moment he pushed off the rail, went over by her and pulled up a three-cornered stool made of cowhide, sat on it beside her. And a peculiar thing happened. Without speaking she held out her right hand. He put up his own hand. Her fingers twined around his palm and held it tightly and in the breathless silence they sat like that for a long time both of them filled with confused and shattering emotion.

'Is it because of Ben?'

'That I won't leave?'

'Yes.'

'Ben and other things. Don't ask me.'

She didn't, just sat there beside him with the drumming night around them both, unmoving but alive seeming. The random-splashed stars were a galaxy of softness in a pale night sky almost dove-gray-blue behind the immensity of the full moon.

'It's so peaceful here,' she said. 'Everything's so peaceful; the sky, the stars, the desert – even the daylight. Everything except the people.'

'They're peaceful too, I suppose,' he said. 'Or they would be if they had a chance to be.'

'You're saying Ben's responsible.'

He was lost for an answer that wouldn't be mealy and if he answered the way he knew things to be a spell would be broken that would never come again.

'Aren't you?'

'I don't want to answer that.'

He thought she'd drop his hand but she didn't. The silence settled again for a moment, then: 'Ben truly hates you. It was – surprising – to see how he acted after Marshal Morgan left yesterday.'

'Not surprising,' he said looking straight ahead at obscure distance. 'Revealing.'

'I – don't know. That's why I was out here tonight. I was out here last night too. I'm troubled, worried.'

'When will you two be married?'

She did drop his hand then. Abruptly. Turned and gazed at him and said in a low tone, 'I don't know.'

The sheen of her hair had dappled lamp-light and moonlight contending in it. The rich softness of shadow was across her face, around her eyes, backgrounding her mouth. He kissed her.

The response was clinging and when he moved his lips hers followed, clung with soft pressure. He pulled back with drums beating the Long Roll the full length and breadth of his body.

'And that,' he said finally, 'only complicates things further.'

She said nothing; didn't look at him, set her face toward the distance, the night-running distance that was shroud and benediction and affliction all in one meaningless blanket covering everything.

Inside Fred something fell into place. Something confused and bewildering that hadn't had a place to lie before. The cause of his irritability with Graham? The cause of his indecision, his groping, his worry? Probably; and it was love.

'I suppose there's a star up there,' Lillian said, 'where men don't always want to kill each other. Could we get up there, do you suppose?'

He tilted his head, gazed upwards. Is this how it happened? Is this what It was? He didn't hear himself answer. 'They're a long way off.'

'Too far?'

He lowered his glance to her face, saw that she was watching him and there was a stinging dampness to her eyes that hadn't been there before. Parable? Of course. Almost heavily he said, 'I don't know whether they're too far or not.'

'They're happiness aren't they?'

Still using the heavy tone he answered her. 'You'd never find it with Ben; never, never, never. I knew that on the train and I suppose I've unconsciously thought of it ever since.'

'Unconscious thought? I've never done that, I don't believe. When I've thought of things they were very real to me.'

'Do you mean – on the train?'

'Yes,' she murmured. 'I couldn't keep from it, sometimes, but I felt deceitful doing it just the same.'

'It wasn't very much.' Even when he said it he wondered if women knew about it before men did. Thought they probably did and if they did why hadn't she pulled away, struck him, a moment ago.

'It doesn't take much, maybe,' she said.

'And Ben?'

She swung away from him. Quite suddenly the cry of a coyote broke through the thick desert stillness. It made him stir with uneasiness. He leaned forward a little on the stool; it was late, Ben's *ramada* was a perilous place to be.

'The more I try to work it out the more tangled it becomes.'

He looked at her, forcing his mind off the feeling of personal danger. She meant Ben of course and what could he say to that? Nothing. He stood up. It was a re-enactment of the other time they'd met, he standing above her in the soft light, she sitting, looking upward. She had her fingers laced together in her lap and the diffused light made a dark hollow under her bosom.

'Lillian, go away. Don't stay here. If you do you're going to be hurt. I don't mean physically – in other ways.'

'Because of Ben and you?'

'I'm not the only one, there're a lot of men involved in it, but say it's because of Ben and me if you wish. Anything you want to call it – but don't stay. Go away, tomorrow, the next day.'

She stood up close to him as though transferring her thoughts to him by her nearness. 'He's your cousin.'

'My only living relative, in fact. Does that make it right for him to do the things he's done – is still doing?'

Her lips quivered. 'Don't do it. That's what you came for tonight, isn't it? Don't do it, Fred. Don't have it on your conscience.'

The melody of her voice went through him. He put out his hands, his arms, took her boldly and brought her still closer. The drums pounded furiously in his head again, 'Lillian…' He kissed her, pushed downward almost brutally against the softness of her mouth, felt the sear of breath across his face, knew the solidness, the fragrance of her, released her but not shortly for she was still there under his mouth. Gently, drawing off with a wrenching of his spirit.

'Lillian!'

She didn't answer, didn't try to answer.

He turned without another word, another glance, vaulted over the gallery railing and hurried through the lateness. The moon was low enough to allow a swelling, a semblance of thickness, to lie over the land. Into this he disappeared and she made no move toward the railing to watch him go.

Overhead a great bursting pollen of star-dust arced behind a hurtling meteor. Neither of them saw that, either.

Fred removed the bay colt's hobbles, toed in and swung up, reined around and rode at a walk through the skirl of brush. Rode for a long time that seemed like moments before he stopped near the shack where Norm Graham, Chet and Clem were, smelt the tangyness of woodsmoke, got down heavily, unsaddled, turned the colt into the corral and stumped toward the shack.

A stub of candle still burnt, there was a rubble of melted wax around it and above the too-long wick a steady little fingering of black smoke rose straight up.

He went over to Graham's bunk and bent from the waist. Wide open eyes gazed at him, dry and hot looking. No flicker of smile nor recognition greeted him. He turned away, saw Chet sitting up in his bunk with a cigarette dangling from his beard-stubbled mouth, and waited.

'He was out of his head for a spell. Talked crazy.'

'That's natural. You didn't let the fire go out did you?'

'Naw. We spell off. Right now it's Clem's turn to sleep.' Chet's thin face looked evil in the wavery light. 'What happened down there?'

Fred looked blank for a moment. 'Oh – down there.' He went across the room, dropped heavily on the wall-bunk he'd used the night before and shrugged. 'Probably like I told you. Nolan figured about where you'd push them across. Maybe he just had riders scattered out all along the line from

Animas westward.' He looked caustically at Chet, 'You ought to be able to see that for yourself.' He yawned, pulled off the dead man's boots, vented a long wailing sigh and went to bed.

The next four days were a nightmare of caring for Norm Graham, with none of the things for that care he'd been used to having, at hand. That included two riders who inclined toward suspicion of anyone with any kind of illness and wouldn't get any closer to Graham than they absolutely had to.

And after that there was a long period of plain inactivity. Squatters brought them supplies and news, looked askance at Fred and seemed to walk wide around him. It was a long week after the night on the verandah, when the three of them were eating, that Clem brought a large paper out of his jumper pocket, unfolded its many creases carefully and smoothed it with his palm. A passable likeness of himself stared up at Fred. The black lettering underneath would have been visible a quarter mile off, it was so black and square.

FRED NOLAN
WANTED FOR RUSTLING
& MURDER!
FIVE THOUSAND DOLLARS
REWARD – DEAD!

At the bottom of the broadsheet was a facsimile of Ben Nolan's signature, blunt, savage looking.

'An' here's another one.'

Clem laid it on top of the first one. It was substantially the same except that it was by the U.S. Marshal's office instead of a private individual and the reward was a cautious one thousand dollars reward dead or alive in the orthodox way of reward posters.

'Makes six thousand,' Chet said musingly, swishing coffee in a dented tin cup. 'A sight of money.'

'Thinking of collecting it?' Fred asked.

'Naw. There'll be plenty who'd like to though. Six thousand dollars is more'n the squatters'll make in six years off their ranches.' He put the cup down and bent over to see the posters better. 'You know, Fred, mightn't be a bad idea for us to move around a little. Not keep t'one spot too much.'

And Fred sagged on his keg. That was the first time Chet had used his name, his given name. There had appeared a barrier between them almost from the first. Fred felt better than he'd felt in days. He got up.

'Maybe I can get a little broth down Norm now.'

Graham shook his head when he saw the tin cup steaming in Fred's hand. Weakly he said, 'Y'God, you'd think you was fattenin' a steer for the icehouse the way you're always tryin' to cram something down me.'

Fred stood beside the bunk holding the gruel, on the edge of smiling. 'Be a reflection on me professionally if you starved after living through a ball in the lung.'

'Well,' Graham said, 'believe I'd as lief starve as eat when I'm not hungry.' His piercing glance was back, most of the glassines had left his stare even as a good deal of the ruddy color hadn't yet returned to his leathery face. 'Tell me something, Doc. Where'd you hike to the night you brought me back and went away?'

'Why? What's the difference?'

'I've had lots of time to figure things this last week or two. I'm plain curious.'

'I went over to Ben's.'

'See him?'

Fred look saturnine. 'If you've had so much time to figure things you ought to know by now he was down there with his riders.'

'I did figure that – only you didn't come back until 'most daylight. Ain't that far to Big Lily an' back, y'know.'

Discerning, Fred thought. Very observant and very blind in other ways. 'How do you know when I came back?'

'You leant over my bunk. I saw you.'

'Drink this broth.'

'Go to hell,' Graham said amiably. 'Got a

secret, Doc?'

'Yes I have, do you mind?'

'Nope, only I think I know what it is.'

Fred stood there staring at the older man. He felt the irritation coming up. After a moment or two he said, 'Graham – I've known some men who rubbed me the wrong way now and then but you seem to try to do it.'

Graham's steady gaze held. No visible smile plucked at his mouth but the drawling way he spoke said he was laughing secretly at Fred. 'Save the heat, Doc. You'll need it before long. Anyway, folks know there's a lady staying out at Big Lily. They even know when she come here – on the train, an' all. I figured out the rest without too much trouble.'

'Too bad,' Fred said sharply, 'you didn't figure out that ambush half as well. Now *drink this!*'

Graham drank it, spluttered, cursed, and used a grimy blanket's edge to wipe his mouth before he sank back. 'Y'know, Doc – I don't suppose I ever really doubted what y'told me that first day an' that's a funny thing because I don't put too much faith in what I'm told.'

'All right,' Fred said moving away. 'Get some sleep.'

'Sure. When'll I be able to get up? I'm fitten enough right now.'

'That's what you think. You'll stay down until we see if a cough's going to develop.'

'How long'll that be?'

'What's the difference?'

'Well; I can smell something's in the wind and don't want to be frettin' around here while it's coming off.'

Fred was over by the table near Chet and Clem. He turned and looked back, a faint scowl adding dark storminess to his face. 'What do you smell's going to come off?'

Graham didn't answer. He turned up on his side with a loud and uncomplimentary grunt.

Fred poured himself a cup of coffee and gazed into it. Very strange how a man like Graham could be so discerning and so dumb at the same time. He'd said nothing but Graham knew he had something in mind. When he looked up both Chet and Clem were watching him stoically.

'Well,' he said quite frankly, 'Graham's right to the point of thinking I've an idea.'

Clem leaned forward and Chet leaned back, both watching him in stone-faced blankness.

'Ben,' he began, then fell momentarily silent gazing into the coffee cup again. Had she done as he'd said? Had she left? He shook his head to himself. No, and he'd bet on that but it wasn't safe to wait for her to go either. Not now, not with two rewards and no one knew how many bounty hunters streaking it for Tucomcori.

'Ben probably has driven you to what you've done to strike back at him, boys, but the way you've been doing it up to now is too slow, too dangerous, too drawn-out, I don't know your troubles and I don't want to know them. What I want to know is this: can you slip into Tucomcori and catch Marshal Morgan and bring him back here alive?'

Two sets of features sagged. 'Morgan,' Chet said. 'You mean Ben don't you?'

Ironically Fred said, 'Can you get Ben?'

'Hell no,' Clem exclaimed. 'Not in a month of Sundays. He's covered like a–'

'Then I mean Morgan, don't I? Can you get him back here alive without being killed doing it?'

'Morgan,' Chet said again, more speculatively than stupidly that time. 'I reckon: don't see why not anyway. We'll get help of course.'

Fred looked at Clem. The rider's fingers rubbed slowly, thoughtfully, at the side of his nose. 'I expect,' he said, 'only what's the good of takin' Morgan? He only does what Ben tells him to do. Hell; he didn't even go out after Emmon's body fer three days – until Ben told him to.'

Fred's glance froze, his mind settled on this information. 'Why didn't he?'

Clem shrugged. 'Damned if I know, but I know he didn't. Everyone knows that. Folks was beginnin' to squawk, in fact. Threatened to go out an' fetch old Emmons in theirselves even though Josh had told 'em to stay clean away from his place.'

Silence. Fred made a cigarette, lit it and gazed at Clem almost disgustedly, then he spoke. 'All right – can you get him? Will you?'

Chet nodded, resigned or reconciled to the idea. 'I reckon so. Tonight?'

'Yes, tonight.'

They both arose, stood by the table waiting. Fred stood up too. 'I think he can clear up some of the things Ben's done. I hope so anyway. He'll be our starter.'

After they'd left at sundown Graham sat up on one elbow and eyed Fred balefully. 'If I can't go at least you could tell me,' he said.

Fred drew a keg over close to his bed, sat down on it and nodded his head. 'There isn't much to tell until they get back with him – if they do.'

Graham snorted. 'They'll fetch him don't worry about that. There's plenty ready to help them.'

'How many is plenty?'

'How many? About fifteen who'll take chances and another ten that'll blanket-out tracks, pack messages, things like that.'

'Fifteen you can count on to fight if they have to?'

'Yeah,' Graham said, then his eyes widened. 'You don't mean ride up to Ben's and – and fight, do you?'

'Would they do it?'

Graham's fingers closed like talons on the edge of a blanket. He just stared. 'You dassn't do it that way, Nolan. Good Lord. A fight'd raise hell with the whole country around here.'

Fred sat with his chin in his palm. 'You can't go on trying to break him by dribbles either, Graham, because it can't be done.' He straightened up. 'I'm thinking of a way to flank Ben; to get him in my hands without a fight, but it if comes to a fight I want it to be a good one.'

Graham swallowed with effort. He didn't speak. Fred got off the keg and walked across the room, turned and looked back.

'It's cut or run, isn't it? Then let's cut.'

'Well – but; Crissake Nolan – it'll bust things wide open.'

'I thought you wanted him broken into a hundred pieces.'

'I do, I do...' Graham lay back down looking at the low ceiling of the shack. 'I do, only I don't want to get a lot of innocent folks killed either.'

'Graham, I'm surprised at you. You're smart enough to know there's no middle of the road. Fight and win or fight and don't win – or just plain run. That's how simple it looks to me.'

Graham's breathing rattled. He opened his mouth wide to suck air and stifle a cough. Fred had told him not to cough or strain against a cough, either one might burst anew the healing pulp inside his lung-box.

They talked warmly for a while then Graham said less and less until finally, lying on his side gazing across the room at Fred, he uttered his last opposition, his last protest.

'If it goes sour, Nolan, you'll be an outlaw for all time. Know that don't you?'

And Fred didn't answer, didn't have to, so they were both locked in a depth of glum, bleak silence when Chet and Clem and two huge, bearded men returned, pushing, shoving a third man, hatless, gunless, hands bound too tightly behind him.

'United States Marshal Josh Morgan alive an' kicking.'

Fred stood up by the table. The shadows were long and gloomy outside. Clem went around them all and took four limp but long candles out of his pocket. He lit one while Fred looked into the hard-faced man's eyes, got his stare returned unflinchingly. Behind the lawman the two burly squatters stood silent, solemn faced. While Clem melted wax off the bottom of the candle and set it to stand in the congealing wax on the table top, Chet introduced them around.

'Tad Murphy, Fred Nolan. Aloysious Briggendorf, Fred Nolan.'

It was like shaking hands with bears. Fred looked at Chet. The thin-faced man's forehead wrinkled with uncertainty, 'I kind of figgered they'd as well stay, Fred. 'Course–'

Fred motioned toward the kegs and benches. 'Sure; have a seat, gentlemen.'

They did, both back by the doorless opening, silent and watchful. Two towering hulks flanking Josh Morgan's sole means of egress.

Fred read the same scarcely controlled hot fury in Morgan's eyes he'd seen on the train weeks before. The difference was simply of circumstances, surroundings. He estimated Morgan's durability, his strength, and nodded inwardly to himself. 'Cut his hands loose.' Then:

'Marshal – I want some information you have. I believe you'll give it to me because I think you know I'm pretty serious about getting it. You'll know that from the way you came here. Now listen; I'm going to ask you once and you're either going to answer or you're not going to answer. If you do – fine. If you don't I'll tear it out of you a word at a time. I imagine you understand me. Do you?'

Silence. The black-hot glare. Just a faint

twitching of the lip to indicate that Morgan even heard.

Fred's mouth grew thinner. 'Morgan – do you know my name, who I am?'

The Marshal's lips moved but barely. 'Yeh. You're Fred Nolan.'

'Did you know I was here, in the country?'

Morgan seemed to hesitate over the answer. 'I knew you *came* here because I seen you on the train, only I didn't know who you were then. I didn't think you'd still be here. I told your cousin that. I figured you'd beat it as soon's you seen the reward posters if you hadn't lef' before.'

'What did my cousin think?'

'He thought you might still be around because of the girl.'

Recollecting Morgan's obnoxiousness on the train, Fred said, 'You're the one Ben ought to worry about where the girl is concerned.'

Morgan flushed but made no answer.

Fred let all his weight ride on one leg, relaxed. 'Why did Ben have Old Man Milton killed?'

'He didn't.'

Fred looked annoyed. 'All right. Why did he have him dragged?'

'I don't know anything about it. Why don't you ask Ben?'

'I'm going to but I think you've forgotten what I said before. When I ask a question I want a straight answer. For the time being it's you and me. Ben'll come later. Who killed Emmons?'

Morgan turned slowly, looked down at the bench behind him and sat down. Fred, watching, read the defiance in the lawman's face. He leaned forward on the table.

'You'd be wise to answer, Marshal. Who killed Emmons?'

'I – don't – know.'

Fred straightened, hooked a thumb in his belt and considered Morgan steadily. 'You're a liar.' He said it softly, matter-of-factly. 'Why didn't you bring him to town after he'd been killed and you knew he was dead?'

'I – look here, Nolan–'

'*You* look. Stand up.'

Morgan made no move to comply. The two bearded squatters over by the door rumbled something to one another, they got up and Morgan heard the scrape of their boots. He stood up, black blood ran in under his cheeks. He swore at Fred. A thick vein in his forehead bulged.

'*You* killed Emmons and you know it.'

Fred gazed steadily at the hard-faced man. In the back of his mind was a suspicion with no reason behind it. 'Another lie,' he said. 'I'm not going to stand here arguing with you, Morgan. I'll ask you once more. Who killed this fellow Emmons and why?'

'You did!'

Fred smiled bleakly. 'If you believed that why didn't you go out and bring him back? You had a reason for staying away – what was it?'

'I was busy. A dead man ain't going anywhere.'

'I think differently. I think my cousin knew something about that killing. I also think he either told you to stay away or you thought you'd better stay away for a while. The reason for that would be so no posse you took with you would find any tracks, or see any Big Lily riders where this Emmons was killed.'

'That's crazy,' Morgan said. 'Why would Ben want a fringe rancher like Rufe Emmons killed?'

'For the same reason, possibly, he had an old man dragged behind a running horse.'

Fred moved around the table as he spoke. He wasn't three feet from Marshal Morgan when he finished speaking. 'Fringe ranchers seem to be a mania of Ben's, don't they?'

'I don't know what you're talkin' about.'

From the far corner of the cabin a gravelly voice swore bitterly, slowly, at Morgan. 'You lie like a dog, Morgan. Remember when Norman Graham was burnt out? Remember when Lon Hull was warned to quit his homestead and move on? Remember when Mack Sorrel was outlawed because of an old

Big Lily cow in with his stock? You're hand in glove with Ben Nolan and y'know it.' Graham sucked in a whining lungful of air. 'Fred – knock it out of him!'

Morgan turned his head just a little, squinted toward the mound of blankets and the dark-shadowed face peering over them. He couldn't make the man out for a while, then suddenly he must have recognized the voice for he said: 'Graham! By God, I've wondered where you went.'

Fred said, 'What do you mean, "where you went"?'

But Graham answered ahead of the marshal. 'He thought he'd killed me. It was him shot me off my horse down along the border. I seen him when he stepped out of the brush.'

Fred reached out almost casually, gripped Morgan's shirt in his fist and twisted. The cloth came tight, strained. Morgan rolled a curse over his lips and reached up, fastened his own hand around Fred's and turned. It was like trying to twist up a tree out of the ground. Fred's arm and fist didn't budge.

'Are you going to tell me what happened to Emmons and why, Morgan?'

No one in their right mind could misinterpret the meaning, the threat in the voice. Morgan didn't either. He strained harder at the balled up fist then dropped his arm to his side.

'Your cousin had Emmons killed. Satisfied?'

'No,' Fred said, 'not exactly. Why?'

'Because Emmons had a good well on his homestead and because he was stealing Big Lily calves.'

Fred took his hand away. Looked at the lawman steadily, then shook his head. 'What else?'

'Else?' Morgan glowered. 'What more'd a man need?'

Graham said, 'He'd do it just for the water, Doc. That's all Old Man Milton had too, remember.'

Fred nodded. 'And you knew it. Knew he was going to kill Emmons, didn't you?'

'I didn't know a thing about it until after it happened.'

'Did he tell you not to go out there after the killing?'

'He didn't have to; I knew enough to stay away.'

Fred nodded again. 'Sure; until Ben had wiped out every track and taken everything incriminating away with him.'

'All right,' Morgan said. 'Maybe you're right. How you going to prove any of it?' The Marshal's eyes were glowing in dull triumph.

Fred smiled into the hard face. 'I'm not going to even try, Marshal. Does that answer you?'

'What do you mean?'

'This. Ben destroyed everything that would lie him to the killing, didn't he? He wiped out every track and you were an accessory by staying away, abetting him in this instance. Now, no one can prove Ben had Emmons killed can they?'

'Sure not,' Morgan said.

'But all of us here in this shack know he did it, don't we?'

'I reckon.'

'Then we won't use the book and paper law, we'll use the kind that used to prevail down here when I was a boy. Hangrope law; six-gun law; night-riders' law.'

'You can't do it,' Morgan protested. 'The Army'll tear you apart.'

'Maybe,' Fred said. 'The Army's going to have to move awfully fast to get here before it's all over.' He turned toward Chet. 'Make us some coffee, will you, Chet?'

'Sure. Want some sowbelly too?'

'Not me; maybe these other boys do. I just want coffee.' He looked over at the two bearded men by the doorway. 'Can you boys stay here for a couple of days; until we don't need to guard this lawman any more?'

One of the duo nodded his shaggy head. 'Proud to,' he said. 'Be right proud to.'

Fred went over by Graham's bunk, stood above it looking down. 'Norm – are you sure he's the one who shot you?'

'Sure?' Graham said. 'Why damn his soul, I'd know that skunk anywhere on earth, under it or above it. Josh Morgan's my second hate. Sure I'm sure. Seen him as clear as day. Expect he'd of finished me off too if someone hadn't hollered at him after the cattle went by.'

'Well, that's good,' Fred said. 'Did Chet give you back your gun?'

'Yeah, it's under the soogans here. Why?'

'You've got a good wide view of the room, Norm. If Morgan makes a break for it I expect you to kill him.'

Graham didn't answer. He began to grub among the pile of blankets and quilts. Eventually one faded, boney hand emerged from the jumble holding a long barreled .45, the weapon described a slow arc and came to rest on Josh Morgan's belly. Looking at the lawman, Fred saw his stomach involuntarily sucked back. With a parting word to Graham he went over by the stove where Chet and Clem were getting in each other's way.

'Chet; do you know about fifteen squatters who'd yard and *fight* Big Lily?'

Chet's hatchet-face lifted. 'You mean – ride into the yard and – *fight* Big Lily?'

'Yes.'

'Well – Crissake; I suppose so. When?'

'About dawn or a mite before. Could you round them up and have them here at the shack after midnight so we could perfect plans for attacking Big Lily?'

'Well – sure. Don't see why not? Doc, that'll be mighty dangerous. Ben's got boys ridin' for him who can knock a fly off a post at a hunnert feet.'

Fred nodded. 'I know. You want to leave now?'

'Sure, I reckon. Here at the shack sometime after midnight with fifteen who'll beard Ben at Big Lily, huh?'

'Yes.'

'All right. S'long.'

Fred went over to the table and dropped down. U.S. Marshal Morgan was staring at him like sin. There wasn't a sound in the cabin except Norman Graham's breathing. Bodies moved now and then but no one spoke. Eyes followed every movement, even Clem's when he brought the food and coffee.

Finally the lawman spoke. 'Nolan – I *know* you're crazy now.' He pushed his tin plate away. 'Ben'll kill those scum as fast as they ride up an' the Army'll hear about you attackin' his ranch. They'll hang you higher'n a crow's nest.'

Fred went on eating, neither looking across at the prisoner nor paying attention to what he said.

CHAPTER FIVE

The hours limped by like cooling lead from a bullet-mould with Graham's saw-breathing gnawing at everyone's nerves. The two carved, motionless squatters on either side of the door seemed to fit into the pattern of the night and the shack like dense-muscled, bearded furniture. Their eyes moved, they never spoke, they just sat.

When Fred finished eating what Clem had put in front of him, forgetting that he'd said he had only wanted coffee, Morgan was watching him balefully. As Fred pushed the tin away Morgan spoke.

'You know what happens to folks who kidnap U.S. Marshals?'

Fred looked up innocently. 'No; what?'

'The Army takes it up – that's what.'

'Suppose the U.S. Marshal denies or never tells that he was kidnapped – then what?'

There was a moment of silence. Graham broke it with a tinny laugh fraught with meaning. Morgan flushed. 'Threatening me?' He asked.

Fred nodded solemnly. 'That's exactly what I'm doing. I'm also promising you something. A bullet if you ever say anyone kidnapped you. But I don't think you'd say it anyway. You'd be a laughing stock, wouldn't you? A big brave U.S. Marshal kidnapped by some squatters. Held prisoner and made to talk about how he worked for Ben Nolan.'

'I never *worked* for him!'

'No? But you never interfered with him either. Abetting a crime is as bad as committing one, you know that.' Fred made a cigarette, puffed it to life over the candle's flame. 'Tell us about Old Man Milton.'

'I already did. I don't know anything about that at all; nothing.'

'I believe you,' Fred said. 'Tell us about a man named Lonny Hull.'

'Him neither.'

Fred exhaled. 'Now you're lying. Come on Morgan, I don't want to kick it out of you on a full stomach.'

Silence.

One of the men back by the door cleared his throat. The sound of spurs, of leather straining against a thick gut as a man moved to arise; Morgan's eyes flickered.

'Hull picked a fight with Big Lily riders. Ordered them to stay off his claim.'

Fred recalled what Lillian had told him of her father freighting with Hull in the fifties. 'How old was Hull, Morgan?'

'Old? I don't know. Maybe seventy, maybe older.'

'About Old Man Milton's age,' Graham

said out of the shadowy background. 'Skinny old cuss. Used t'be an ox-skinner, buffalo hunter, Injun scout an' what-not.'

Fred inhaled, spoke with the smoke tumbling midst the words. 'Takes guts to kill old men doesn't it? How many Big Lily riders did it?'

'How the hell would I know – I wasn't around.'

'How do you know it *was* Big Lily then?'

'Rumors around town is all.'

'Make any arrests?'

'On rumors? Hell no. I deal in facts.'

'Glad to hear it,' Fred said warmly. 'You must've had facts to say I killed Emmons and Hull. Let's hear them.'

Morgan glared. He was trapped and knew it. His face gleamed wetly in the soft light. 'The way it was done. Same as that killing at Animas back a few years.'

'That's not facts,' Fred said. He pushed out his cigarette on the tabletop. 'Whose idea was it, yours or Ben's, building up this outlaw reputation for me?'

'Who said we built it up? The whole damned country knows you...'

'They don't know anything you haven't told them, like the Emmons killing. Why is Ben's reward for me dead, only?'

'How would I know? Because he hates you like poison, I expect.'

Fred shook his head. 'You're lying again,

Morgan. I'll tell you why. Dead I can't talk back; can't say I didn't kill these people. Alive I might get a lawyer – might prove I was three thousand miles away when they were killed. Ben's hated me for years but not because of anything I ever did to him – because of circumstances Comanches brought about. When he needed a way to keep clear of suspicion he had his hatred of me handy. He used it. You know all this.'

'No I don't,' Morgan said sharply. 'All I know is that he hates you worse'n poison.'

'It's a good thing you're yellow, Morgan,' Fred went on, speaking as though his mind was moving from one thought to another, musingly. 'If you weren't I'd have torn all this out of you. This way it's easier, isn't it?'

Silence.

The silence lasted until Chet came back in a rattling lope with a herd of angular, horse-smelling men clustered around him. Clem went out into the pre-dawn chill.

Voices, muffled and low, came into the room. Fred, watching the Marshal, saw his nervousness. Saw how he half-turned when the riders came stomping into the room, spurs and guns making soft clamor. Saw the way the riders went around the Marshal, engulfing him with unfriendly, cold expressions. Chet had told them obviously. The shack was full of men, mostly young to early middle age. Weathered men, tall men and short men, grim and bitter and expectant looking and among them an anxious face or two, armed like villains, which they resembled in the smokey light, in the towering, battering silence.

Fred got up, stifled a yawn. Chet went to the stove, beckoned to Clem. Their voices droned; something about more coffee, more water bucketed from the well.

Fred said, 'I suppose Chet's told you what we've got in mind.'

A number of quick nods, a few mumbled words then just watchfulness. Graham's voice broke in with pleasure in its tone. 'Real corn-squeezin's,' he said. 'Well now, Mike, I'm obliged clean to hell to you.'

Without turning Fred said, 'Take it away from him, boys. No liquor for him yet. Sorry.'

Low apologetic mumbles, the sounds of a brief scuffle, more words of apology then Graham's voice again, not so pleasant. 'Nolan – y' cussed spoilsport, I've a notion to count coup on you f'six thousand dollars, for that.'

Several men laughed outright and others chuckled. Fred waited for the noise to subside without even looking around at Graham. 'I don't know whether we'll succeed or not, boys,' he said, 'and I'm no strategist – no soldier – but I know this one thing: Unless Ben Nolan's braced where we can get to him this picking and sniping and murdering will go on indefinitely.' He paused, reading faces. One expression predominated. Bitter resolution.

'How we'll do it I don't know. Just that we'll do it someway. We've *got* to do it. He's ruined some of you, outlawed others, and he's outlawing me right this minute. I know Ben. I know him this well. He never liked the idea of anyone having a faster horse, a better bull, breedier cows, and if he had to break a man to prove his were the best, he'd do it. I think he's gotten worse instead of better these past years...'

Graham snorted loudly.

'He can't stand the thought of anyone having anything he's admired. I guess that takes in the desert, the homesteads, just about everything around. A man like that's not fit to live, I'm sorry to say, but I'm not judging him. That's up to someone else. All I'm saying is that you and I are entitled to defend ourselves and the only way I can see to do that is break Ben before he breaks every one of us. Self defense.'

'Kill him,' a stalwart Texan said. 'Wish he could be killed more'n once. Drag him to death one time, then burn him in a shack the nex' time, then shoot him in the back an'...'

'Shaddap, Jeb,' another man said softly. 'Let Nolan talk.'

'I'm through,' Fred said. 'You don't know me. That's the only reason I've said this much. To tell you how I feel and ask if you feel the same way, because this isn't going to be like fighting a Mex army. Ben's tough and I understand the riders he keeps are tougher. We may not all ride back from Big Lily. Every man of us should fully understand that.'

The men talked. It was a low tangle of throaty words. There was no dissent, mostly it was reiteration of old wrongs, reaffirmation of deep hatred for Ben Nolan. Just before the men left, Norm Graham began to sing in a droning voice and Fred went over to look down at him.

'Got the whiskey after all didn't you?'

Graham looked happily pained and innocent. 'Why no, Doc. The tightwad bastards only give me two teeny swallows, but I forgive them. I'm a forgivin' man by nature. Forgive'n' forget – if you can…' Graham lapsed into saw-breath silence looking a long way off then he roused himself and began to hum again.

Fred turned away. 'Everybody got guns and sound horses? Plenty of bullets?'

'They have,' Chet said from the table where he kept re-filling five tin cups doing the duty of almost twenty as men drank the scalding coffee and thumped the cups down again. 'I seen to that before I brang 'em back. Every man jack's loaded for bear.'

Fred turned to the big bearded men, Briggendorf and Murphy. 'If you have to kill the Marshal, why just kill him.' He went out through the blanket hanging askew over the doorway. Clem jerked his head at the others, they trailed out into the cool darkness smacking their mouths, wiping lips with sleeves, lugging carbines, making the unconscious sounds of night-riders.

Chet and Clem out-rode without being told to. In fact, Fred didn't think of it at all. They fanned wide and ahead, listening, trying to see, knowing if they met anyone at all it would be by accident.

The sound of rein-chains, of squeaking saddles, rolling crickets in the mouths of horses wearing spade bits or half-breeds, men mumbling to one another in the thin night air, the *clang!* when a steel shoe hit a stone, all these sounds were behind Fred, in his mind but not part of it; foreign to the thoughts that lay behind his eyes.

The faint silver mist of late darkness was around them, silhouetting them in its gray obscurity. Making them ghosts except for the solid glint of gunmetal. Desert hush swallowed them up and a strangeness rode the windless air. The night seemed drained of life except for the fifteen riders, Chet, Clem, and Fred Nolan.

Fred thought of Lillian Malone. Thought

with sureness and pleasure and a depth of satisfying fullness that was an impulse of some kind, how her yielding mouth had felt, tasted. There was something in him that wouldn't respond to reason, something that would not be suppressed. She was with him, riding with him or standing beside him or just ahead of his horse's moving ears, near and real; of solid substance. He knew he shouldn't be distracted by the vision but he couldn't fight it.

He went back very carefully to that night on the verandah. To the grip of gloom that she'd been in before, and after, they'd kissed. Very gently he resurrected each moment, each word, and to his amazement he found himself recalling it all verbatim. Even the impressions of that night. How the sky looked, how faded, tattered, the firmament had been, the icy stars, the great entity of moon. The burst of lamplight in her hair and the dark shadow under her bosom. The tight-held fingers laced in her lap. The kisses; the kisses...

'There's the road up ahead. Expect we'd ought to bypass it, Fred.'

It was Chet and he hadn't seen him come out of the night ahead at all. Gathering in the raveled wits inside his head he straightened a little on the bay colt's back and said, 'Yes. We'd better cross the road and stay in the brush northward. Eventually we'll come to the Big Lily road.'

'Go down it?'

'As far as the clearing, Chet. Then we'll split up. See me when we get there. All right?'

'Right as rain,' Chet said, urging his horse ahead. He'd spoken guardedly, as though the night or the desert had ears. Fred smiled.

The men popped out of the brushscape beside the road like grape seeds. Spurted singly, two and three at a time. One moment the desert was serenely still, broodingly empty. The next moment eighteen men were there, vomited out of the brush and crossing the road. They made a little sound but it didn't carry so far and if it had two-thirds of Tucomcori's citizenry would have turned to look in the opposite direction.

There was something in the night that rode just ahead of them. Tension. Knowledge. Most of the squatters had left their shacks without a word. A wink perhaps, a pat on a head, a hurried kiss, but not all of them. Whispered anxiety when they went back inside to fetch the carbine in its saddleboot in the kitchen corner. A stifled wail from a wife perhaps. The word was out somehow. The country knew, the desert knew, nursed its secret in the clearwater air of the wee hours.

Fred could feel it all as he rode at a shuffling walk on Old Man Milton's greenbroke bay colt. Maybe Ben would know too, and if he did they were riding into disaster for the only thing that would partially even up the disadvantage that rode with them was surprise. If Ben's eleven hardcases couldn't be surprised, every advantage would lie with them.

What right had he to lead these men into this? None. Why was this better than letting them fritter away at Ben, harass him? The answer to that was simple and reassuring. Because Ben would eventually kill them all just like he'd killed Mack. Out-wit them or outlaw them, it amounted to the same thing.

But he hadn't come here to do this. To deliberately supervise the killing of his cousin. No, of course he hadn't, but then he hadn't known which way the wind had been blowing these past years either and now he knew; now he knew Ben was past talk, past reason, even past threats. He'd gone about as far as he could go. A bullet would stop him but nothing else would.

'Here's the road, Fred.'

Without comment he turned down it, heard the same dust-muffled sounds of his horse's feet clomping over it he'd heard that other night. *And if she was still there?* A shadow came out of the silver light, took on substance, shape. It was Clem. He drew up and waited then swung around and rode beside Fred.

'Place's dark'n dead looking. They got a

dog though.'

'Dog?' Fred said blankly. 'They didn't have one when I came over here the night Graham got hurt.'

'Well, they got one now. He's sitting down there yapping his tomfool head off.'

Strange, Fred thought. Why had Ben gotten a dog all of a sudden? Tracks, his mind told him. Because someone found your tracks maybe. Might even have seen you that night, waited until daybreak and gone over your tracks. He shook his head. Not likely. If they had they'd have followed him all the way back to the shack. That they hadn't he was confident. Ben would have struck like lightning if he'd known where the shack was. No, if he'd been tracked the tracker didn't go any farther than the roadway. That was very possible, too.

'What'll we do about the damned cur?' Clem asked.

Fred turned it over in his mind. 'Darned if I know, Clem. Don't dare shoot him. Could he be lured out a ways?'

'I didn't go any closer after he set up his caterwaulin'.'

Fred held up his hand when the brush dropped away and the large expanse of meadow loomed around them. Chet came riding in at a sloppy trot. He looked old and slack-fleshed in the weak gloom.

'Chet, we'd better split up here.'

'Suits me. How'd you want to work it?'

'You take half the boys and go around the west side. Leave your horses with a guard and try to get close enough to the bunkhouse to cover it. If you can, get closer. The trouble'll come from there, not from the main house where Ben is. There's a dog down there somewhere. If you can bait him out do it, if you can't just ignore him, but the main thing is to neutralize the bunkhouse. Keep those gunmen from getting to the house.'

'You goin' aroun' the east side?'

'Yes.' He looked back at the squatters. They were all hunched forward listening. They looked like a big flock of buzzards ahorseback. 'Clem; stay up here with me. All right; let's split up.'

'No signal?' someone asked. 'How'll we know what's up?'

'You won't need signals. There'll be signals enough if that bunkhouse isn't cut off. .45 caliber signals. Clem, you and Chet split them up.'

He faced forward again looking down the long corridor of night where the Nolan ranch was. Shadows deeper than darkness were buildings. For a long while he considered the bunkhouse because that was where death lived and a shaft of coldness swept through him. He felt like he was growing old there in the paleness astride the bay colt. Growing old in the softness of coming dawn.

'We're ready, Fred.' Chet grinned. 'Norm'll be sicker'n he is now when hears what we did tonight. This morning, I mean.'

Fred nodded, unheeding. 'Make them stay under cover, Chet. Ben's riders are dead shots I'm told. Keep under cover and don't let anyone ride away from that ranch. No one at all.' He would have reason to hate those words later but he couldn't know that right then.

'Keep the place sealed off from the outside and sew up that bunkhouse. On my side we'll watch the front of the bunkhouse if we can – the range's too long for accurate firing though – and we'll concentrate on the house. Beyond that I don't know what to tell you. Just use your head and if you want to talk, ride the full distance around through the brush. Don't try to make a break for it across the meadow. All right?'

'Right as rain,' Chet said almost lightly. 'What'll we do with him when we get him. String him up?'

Fred's answer came slow. 'I reckon,' he said, then lifted his reins.

He went down the east curve of the brush with seven men behind him. One was Clem and of all the horsemen Clem alone kept up an almost continuous chatter until Fred turned and looked at him, searched for signs of fright or nervousness. After that Clem dropped into the same silence they all shared.

A stringy little man nudged up beside Fred. 'I'm Henry Fortin,' he said. Fred saw he was in his fifties, sparse of hair and lined of countenance but in his eyes glowed vitality. Down around his mouth lay a wealth of muscular stillness, an unswerving resolve that never altered. 'Sun'll be up directly. Wondered if you'd care if I sort of snuck up by the house t'see couldn't I catch Nolan in his soogans before daylight. Before somebody more gets shot.'

Fred lifted his gaze. Off on the rim of the horizon was a lightness, an amethyst shading that trailed off into watered turquoise. 'I don't know,' he said thoughtfully. 'It looks to me like daylight will be here about the time we get down by the house.'

'Yes,' Henry Fortin said, 'that's about the way I figure it. Figured I could bust down there ahead of the rest of you. What way?'

Fred felt it was a futile effort but he nodded. 'Go ahead but if it gets too light come back into the brush.'

'Sure,' Fortin said. His thin arm raised and fell. The sound of a quirt snapped soft and sharp.

'He won't make it,' a black-eyed, black-bearded younger man said watching the horse disappear wringing its tail from the quirt's sting.

They were abreast of the main house but over half a mile from it across the clearing when Fred reined up and swung down. He tried to see Fortin but couldn't.

'Clem – you watch the horses, will you? Don't let anything stampede them no matter what.'

Clem didn't seem to mind being delegated an inactive part in the fight-to-come. He dutifully went around gathering up reins then he led his charges back through the brush until even the sounds they made, the squeaky dry-leather sounds, were lost.

Four men crowded up around Fred. Only the black bearded man was on eye-level with him. Diluted night reflected off carbines. They heard the distinct and far away bark of a dog. Fred frowned and looked out over the brush. That dog puzzled him. He jerked his head.

'Let's go as far as we can.'

'Cover Fortin – the damned fool,' the black bearded man said.

The brush challenged their passage with spidery claws armed with thorns and serrated little leaves. At the edge of the clearing Fred knelt. The others followed his example.

'I don't see him,' Fred said, perplexed. 'Where could he have gotten to so fast?'

'There,' said the black bearded man thrusting out a thick arm pointing. Fred saw it, a blur of movement low on the ground. 'He's went down,' the man said. 'Must've seed something.'

They turned almost simultaneously toward the bunkhouse but there was nothing there. No light, no movement, no blur, just a heavy viscous stillness, a sort of breathlessness.

Fortin got up then and ran. They all saw that clearly enough. He went with the speed and lightness of a much younger man. Fred was so absorbed in watching him he didn't see the floating orb of sun come up from behind some distant jagged peaks until it burst like an egg yolk and spilt light and heat down across the buttes and forests and dead, dead desert, with unbelievable swiftness. Until its first wave of warmth hit the back of his neck. Then he turned, twisting his neck, to look. Daylight, the kind the desert has in the summertime, erupts, just blows up all at once. One moment there's gloom, the next moment there's heat and blinding light.

'He made it beside the house anyway,' Blackbeard said and he looked around at Fred. 'He just might do the rest of it too.'

But he wouldn't.

Fred's eyes moved slowly, liquidly, seeking sign of the men across the way, behind the bunkhouse somewhere. If they could get in close enough there wouldn't be any fight. A tussle maybe, a skirmish, but that would be all.

He was peering intently into the sun-speckled far-off attention. Snagged his eyes with a movement of shifting stillness. It was the bunkhouse door.

Without speaking he reached out and took the bearded man's carbine because he had none of his own. A man walked out onto the tiny stoop and stood there looking at the new day like it was something he might keep or reject as the mood struck him.

Fred shouldered the carbine, lined the man over the sights and waited. Blackbeard cursed sharply. Fred swung his eye where Fortin was. If the little man had stayed beside the house nothing would have happened but he didn't. He pushed along the wall until he came to the verandah, vaulted the rail and started toward the front of the house. Fred could have sworn at him. In the first place Ben's room was in the back not the front. Fortin wouldn't know this, though. He didn't know that the man on the bunkhouse stoop was turning very gently, his eyes wide and watching. Fortin didn't know any drama but his own secretive one was being enacted until he heard the distance-muzzled crash of a carbine in Fred's hands, then he whirled and leapt toward the deepest shadow under the overhang he could find. Then too, he saw the gunman on the stoop standing very straight, looking down at a long white naked rent in the floor of the stoop a foot away from his boot toes.

Fortin raised his pistol and cocked it. The little sound of oiled steel rising, setting to full cock, brought the astonished rider back to his position. Without apparent effort at all he sprang back through the bunkhouse door and disappeared just as Fortin's big slug tore through air where his belly had been and *thwacked!* into the adobe wall, making another pockmark where others of a like nature were time-smoothed.

'There won't be any surprise now,' Fred said, handing back the carbine. 'If Chet's close enough he can seal off the bunkhouse though.'

'Yeah,' the black-bearded man said. 'Only I wouldn't want to be in Henry's boots. He can't fish nor cut bait. Stuck like a bug up against that blamed house the idiot.'

A gun exploded over by the house. Fred's hackles arose along the base of his skull. Another shot came but this time from the besieged bunkhouse. That one would be a blind shot sent to invite retaliation from Fortin. If it didn't succeed the men in the bunkhouse wouldn't know where to shoot.

Silence settled. Even the barking dog was silent, probably terrified into silence, Fred thought. Hiding under the bunkhouse or in a dark corner of the smithy. An abrupt splatter of firing broke out behind the bunkhouse.

'Chet's come up.'

Blackbeard nodded while exploring a jumper pocket for a plug of lint-infested chewing tobacco. 'If he can do it we'll still be able to get t'the house, I expect.'

They hunkered back in the brush, hidden but with a clear and sparkling view. The sunlight danced spectrally across the meadow and closer, right up to the edge of the *ramada*.

'Wish we dared to storm it,' a man said.

Fred said nothing. The black-bearded man grunted something that was half scorn half curse. He was kneeling with one boot out behind him the toe stubbed into the earth like he was ready to run. They were all of them just as tense.

Someone made a long-drawn-out halloo. Fred leaned forward, swept the distance with his eyes, discovered nothing but held his listening, searching pose. The yell came again. That time he placed it in the bunkhouse. A faint answering yell came back. That would be Chet or one of the men with him.

'Damn fool,' muttered the black-bearded man. 'They'll place him by that.'

Fred reserved judgment, thinking differently. The riders in the bunkhouse knew where Fred's shot had come from. One of them had seen Fortin at the main house. Now they got an answer from behind them.

To anyone that would spell a surround.

Then they all heard the words clear and thin-rising and a long way off. 'Who's out there? What the hell d'you think you're doing?'

He reached over and touched the black-bearded man's arm. 'Dump a shot into the front of the place.'

The carbine came up gracefully in hands long used to its operation. The man snugged up, froze and fired high. He allowed for outfall, something Fred hadn't done when he'd fired at the man on the stoop. They didn't hear the slug strike nor see any adobe dust fly but the rifleman grunted his own satisfaction.

'Hit it?' someone asked.

'As big as that is?' The black-bearded man answered back indignantly. 'How would you miss it?'

Fred wished he'd taken the men who were around behind the bunkhouse and given Chet these. He hadn't because he'd wanted to be on the house side of the meadow. A gun went off over by the house again. Fred scowled, raking the distance. No puff of gray, no movement. He fidgeted then stood up.

'I don't like this. Too far away.'

The black-bearded man arose beside him, bent over and leaned on the one-eyed opening of his carbine as casually as though there weren't four more cartridges in the magazine. 'We could get as far as the barn,' he said.

Before Fred could reply, if he'd been going to reply, a wicked burst of gunfire lashed outward from the bunkhouse's solitary southern window. That was where Fred was looking when the shooting started because that was the only opening on the south side of the building. A good set of eyes there could see six men running across the cleared ground toward the barn before runners could be shielded by the structure.

Three very distinct and methodical shots came from the house area. Four sets of eyes searched for the gunman and Fred saw him first. Fortin. He'd made a disastrous miscalculation. Hadn't left the verandah shadow until the precise moment a rider's head had peered cautiously out the bunkhouse south window. Three quickly thumbed shots had brought Fortin down. Four more thrown at random had done the rest, Fortin's three slow, spaced replies had been more dying defiance than accurately sent messengers of death.

Fred couldn't see him on the verandah but he knew he was there, down in the leaky shade, sprawled, dead or dying; more likely dead. He turned to the dark man beside him. 'Why hasn't anyone shot from the house?'

The black eyes slid from his face to the

house and back again before the man answered. 'There was a shot from the house. Right after Fortin got up there.'

'No,' Fred said. 'That was Fortin. It must've been. No one's been shooting from there.' He swung fully, looking across the meadow. 'You fellows stay here. I'm going to come in from behind the barn. I think I can make it.'

The black-bearded man swore, made a savage gesture with one arm. Fred moved off. Once he turned and looked back at them as though to remind them to cover him. The black-bearded man balled a fist Indian fashion, held it aloft and tugged it downward twice. Fred went forward hunched over, twisting his way through the thicket until he was far enough southward to be hidden by the great barn from the aroused men in the bunkhouse.

He walked out into the cleared land and broke over into a little zig-zagging trot that he remembered from decades gone. An Indian trick old Pachise had taught him. You run loose from the knees not trying to go as fast as you can but moving steadily, swervingly, irregularly, toward your goal. He kept it up until the sweat ran into his eyes and stung. The barn loomed closer, more stone-gray and huge than it had been from the brush across the meadow. Somewhere a carbine cracked. He kept on trotting, head up, eyes never still and when he reached the splinter of stiff shade where the sun wasn't, behind the barn near the maze of corrals and chutes, his heart was trembling in a constantly echoing dirge in his ears.

The house was close enough to make out its details. It looked still, lifeless. He licked his lips and forced out every thought but one. The house.

Gunfire broke out again in front. He straightened up instinctively, knowing he couldn't see and wishing mightily that he could. The bullets made no sound but the guns did and they kept it up.

From far off to his left other carbines came in. He twisted to look. Tiny splatters of gray-white mushroomed, hung lazily above the brush where Blackbeard and the others were. He thought they should move when they fired and wondered why they didn't.

The bunkhouse was out of sight. He whistled in a great gulp of air and left the protection of the barn, threaded his way across corrals and came to the nakedness of yard beyond which lay the house. With the din of crackling gunfire in his ears he was puzzled by Ben's silence. Puzzled and worried.

He measured the distance, drew his pistol and began to trot again. Something like green bile was in his throat. A big gob of it.

But no gun smashed, no one cried out or shot at him. Just that long, deathly silence from the house.

He made the last twenty-five feet in a spurt of arrow-straight speed. Sweat oozed into his clothing, darkened the cloth, felt clammy and fetid. The sun's burst of heat swam over the desert, puddled out in the yard and bathed the bunkhouse in a fantastically beautiful golden softness. Covered death in raiment death had never worn anywhere except in the adobe Southwest. He shook his head to fling off the drops, edged along the side of the house, went flat in an ancient mould of parched geraniums and peered around the verandah at snake-high level. The bunkhouse was silent, wreathed in a coiling wisp of black-powder smoke. He lowered his eyes to the *ramada* floor and saw Fortin. He was face down in gelatinous ooze. Dead, dead, dead!

Fred tossed his head, lost the tickling droplets off his nose. He could see the bunkhouse window clearly. The shutters were sagging, battered. Inside was cool gloominess but he couldn't see much lower than the age-blackened ceiling. He waited hopefully but no one's curiosity drove them to the opening.

He rolled over on his side and looked along the wall of the house. There wasn't a sound, a movement. There wasn't even a whisper of life anywhere. He got to his knees and moved away from the corner of the building, cocked the pistol and, standing up, went ball-footed down the cool side of the building until he came to what he knew was the kitchen. There he went flat again, poked his head minutely around the back of the house, lay perfectly motionless for minutes then, satisfied, stood up and whipped around where the backdoor overhang was.

Ben was clever. He was sly and wise and experienced. Also he was patient, like an Indian, and more cruel – ruthless. He could be waiting for just this opportunity and Fred knew it. He stood in the soft shade for more minutes, reached out and gently tried to lift the backdoor *tranca* – the oaken bar that fell into a smooth iron hanger across the door's back. It didn't budge. Without even trying he could recall that *tranca,* its wrought hanger. Nothing short of a cannonball could break either of them. He turned and slid along the back of the house and got another refusal. At the next window the lattice work was broken; had been broken for at least ten years when a ball made of oak pitch and willow tithes had smashed through it on a rainy day.

He tried the hanger, found it locked, reached inside with the long barrel of his gun and tilted the little bar. It raised, fell away, made a whisperingly gentle sound of resignation. Still using the gun barrel and standing well out of the way he drew the nearest shutter toward him. It came without protest or sound. Then he reached far over exposing the length of his arm and pushed the other shutter away. Nothing happened. He sucked in air and stood there a moment with the forge-hammering of his heart thudding. The longer you waited the worse it got. He opened his mouth, sucked in a great gust of air – and vaulted.

Inside the house was dark, dingy, silent. Fred's expelled breath was calamitously loud in his ears. He throttled down his nostrils, moved forward in a smooth glide until he was deeper in the gloom. Outside guns exploded again, erratically, furiously. He whipped erect when the sounds came from the southwest, but only for a moment. That would be over by the barn. It could only mean that the black-bearded man had tired of long range dueling and brought the others over Fred's trail, in closer.

He crouched, nearing the doorway. Beyond was the old, narrow corridor he remembered so well. Gloomy – cool always. A darting look beyond – nothing. No sound, no movement, not even the scent of gunpowder. He straightened. His mind said *there's something very wrong here; hurry!*

Where the corridor curved was the dining room. Beyond that and to his right was the huge kitchen. But nearer were the bedrooms. Ben's room was – there. He reached across the narrow hall with his booted foot, and kicked hard. The door crashed inward with an echoing slam that rang throughout the house. He jumped through it. The room was empty. More bewildered, more fearful than ever, he went back into the hallway, went through each room and not until he was in the last bedroom did he catch the bare, illusive scent. Lillian's room.

He hardly loitered there more than a second. She wasn't there and neither was Ben. He flung through the house without caution after that, certain that neither were in the house – and they weren't. There wasn't any sign of them. He went back to her bedroom and stood in the middle of the room, gun sagging floorward.

For moments the things he saw were familiar, then he began to see other things that weren't; dresses, a riding whip with a turquoise set in a massive silver-knobbed handle. A tiny pistol with a pearl handle, some jewelry and two bright, flung-down drops of blood!

CHAPTER SIX

He stood transfixed, staring at them. Two drops of blood with corrugated edges indicating they'd splashed there. Her blood? He went back out of the room, up the hallway and across the first room he'd entered, jumped out the window and sidled along the wall of the house under the verandah. He vaulted the railing and started for the barn where Blackbeard and five squatters were.

He met them in a shattered shadow from the barns' roof midway between house and barn. They clustered around him. The black-bearded man's eyes widened.

'You look like you seen a ghost. Is he dead, in there?'

'No one's in the house,' Fred said shortly. 'Listen to me; go around the far side of the house and cover that bunkhouse window. Send a man around where Chet is and tell him to mount up and ride for it. Tell him to go back to the shack but to leave someone to watch his backtrail. I don't think they'll try to follow but they might.'

'What do we do?' Blackbeard asked.

'You'll go back too but not just yet. When

I tell you to – but right now send a man back to Clem and have him fetch the horses up here. Have him tie my horse behind the barn. Understand?'

The bearded man nodded slowly. 'Most of it, sure. Aren't you coming back with us?'

'I'll cover the bunkhouse until I'm sure you're well away.'

'Oh; all right.' The black eyes glistened. 'Where's Ben if he ain't in there?'

'I don't know. He isn't there, I know that.'

'He slipped away some way,' the man said sourly.

Fred shook his head. 'Not since we got here, he didn't. He had no warning we were coming – why should he slip away?'

'How d'you know he wasn't warned?'

Irritably Fred said, 'Hell's bells; if he'd known, do you think those gunmen of his would've been caught with their pants down in the bunkhouse?'

Blackbeard considered this a moment. 'All right,' he said finally. 'I expect you're right.' He turned away. 'I'll send a man around to Chet.' The rest of what he said was a mumble. Something about hanging Ben to a barn baulk.

Fred watched the others cluster up around the bearded man. He moved along the back of the house westward for a look at the bunkhouse. There was a rare possibility that Ben had taken Lillian into the bunkhouse.

Why, Fred had no idea. In a way he wanted to believe that. He finally, reluctantly, disbelieved it, and that meant he had no idea at all where she or Ben were. All he actually knew for facts was that neither his cousin nor the girl were at the ranch and that there'd been a fight in the house which left blood on the floor of Lillian's room.

He was churning internally with misgivings when the squatters came up behind him. Two made a rush for the protection of an outhouse southward a ways. From there Fred's own vision commanded the bunkhouse very well. While the squatters were slithering into position he saw a carbine barrel nose out the window carefully. He waited but no head followed it so he raised his handgun and fired. The adobe directly under the carbine spurted, someone swore in agitation and yanked back his carbine. Several of the squatters opened up on the window. There was no target and they prevented anyone from offering to be one.

Blackbeard nudged Fred. 'We could get right up to that door's long as no one comes to the window.'

Fred shook his head. 'We don't want them. Ben's the one we're after.' He twisted toward the man. 'We want to get out of this, not in deeper. Did you send the rider to Chet?'

'Yeh. I told him to tell Chet to open up

with everything he has for a minute or so so's we'd know he's got the word.'

And moments later that is what happened. Carbines and pistols crashed in a deluge of gunfire. Dust and chips flew from the bunkhouse wall. From inside someone started yelling. Fred motioned the men with him to open up. They did. The racket was deafening for fully a minute then Fred wagged his arm, the squatters stopped firing. Apparently Chet understood the slackening, for his own fire stopped and an ear-ringing stillness settled abruptly.

Blackbeard said, 'Us too – now?'

Fred nodded without looking away from the embattled bunkhouse. 'Yes. Watch your backtrail and be sure Clem leaves my horse behind the barn. We'll meet at the shack.'

The bearded man gazed over Fred's shoulder at the bunkhouse then Fred felt something being pushed into his hand. Blackbeard said, 'I won't need this, you keep it.' It was his carbine.

'Thanks.'

Blackbeard hissed at the men. They scuttled off behind him. The daylight was dazzling and deathly quiet. Fred watched the squatters go then lifted the carbine and drove a smashing slug into the door of the bunkhouse. Very deliberately he dumped in two more, the last one made a six inch splinter fly. The door shuddered but held.

Fred lowered the gun knowing the men inside would be pressing back to stay away from the flattened mauls of lead that came through the wood. He leaned the carbine against the house wall, lifted his pistol and waited.

The sun was well up. Light tumbled from the sky in a thousand flat planes and angles and an aurora was rounded out, fan-like, with a turquoise background growing more faded with each passing hour. Fred didn't see it.

He was watching the bunkhouse. Thought once he heard running horses but chalked that up to foreknowledge and imagination and never moved his eyes from the bunkhouse.

Where had they *gone?* And the blood; was it hers? It was on the floor of the room she'd used and showed by the way it was puddled it'd been flung there under impact. Without too much imagination he could picture Ben striking her. Why? For any of a number of reasons. He caught his breath. The dog.

Sure – Ben knew, somehow, that Fred had come to the ranch the night he was away, and if she'd told him she was very foolish. Blind-foolish because she'd probably never seen Ben Nolan angry. Probably had no idea how insanely furious Ben could get. Maybe she'd told Ben about the visit, about – other things. Being honest and noble, perhaps she'd told him that, too, and Ben had gone berserk like Fred remembered his doing from their youth.

His lips curled, eyes clouded. Now she knew, dammit. Now she'd know what Fred had known for years. She'd know fear too and perhaps that was good for her up to a point, but what worried him deeply was where she was, right now, feeling those things.

Why had Ben left the ranch? He couldn't have known about the impending attack. If he had known of its imminency he wouldn't have left his gunmen unwarned, liable to being bottled up.

Someone inside the bunkhouse let out a long yell that ended in words. 'You – out there; the law's comin'.'

Fred sniffed. 'How would you know?'

'Ben's went after 'em.'

'You're a liar.'

'Am like hell,' the voice said. 'He went inter town las' night to fetch 'em back this mornin'.'

'Liar!' Fred called back scornfully. 'Ben didn't know anything about this.'

'This – no. He knew about Fred Nolan bein' aroun' though. He an' the law're comin' back to deputize us fellers an' hunt Nolan down.'

Fred stood hipshot gazing at the little house. Was it the truth? It was possible and it was an answer to Ben's whereabouts. He raised his voice to call out.

'Where's the lady?'

The man in the bunkhouse took a moment to reply. 'Don't know. Reckon she went with 'im.' There was a long silence. The yard, house, bunkhouse, were steeped in it. From within the bunkhouse Fred could hear voices then the unseen man called out again.

'You Fred Nolan?'

'What makes you ask that?'

''Cause he's the on'y feller hereabout who'd ask what Ben done with the girl.'

'Think so, do you,' Fred said lifting the carbine, raising it carefully, aiming it. Well – you're wrong,' and he fired to emphasize it.

The man burst into a fit of profanity. It echoed as long as Fred could hear it; as he moved across the back of the house toward the barn, and died out when he ran knee-sprung where Blackbeard had left his horse.

He rode hard, without helping the bay colt, letting his weight slog in the saddle. Once he saw two men watching him from a distance. He didn't wave and neither did they. The dust spurted under his mount's feet. The trail he struck was wide and trampled, dust laden. He curved around the dense brush and threaded his way slower through the unavoidable thickets.

Back at the shack men lounged in the

meager shade. Blackbeard was there, sitting on the ground with his back against the shack cleaning his gun. Fred tossed him the carbine and strode past. No one spoke, hardly even looked at him, until he was at the blanketed doorway, then Chet straightened up out of a slouch and, without a word, held aside the blanket. The silence was eloquent but the cabin's interior was even more eloquent. The table was overturned, a sprawled dead man lay by Norman Graham's empty bunk. He was flat and broad and heavily bearded. Chet's breathing made a rasping sound and the world toppled in on Fred. He turned grayer than ever toward Chet.

'So that's where Ben was.' Chet nodded. Still no one spoke. Fred looked beyond at the lowered, hat-shaded faces. He saw rebellion, even suspicion, in the eyes, the mouths, the pinched down nostrils. He moved back outside away from Chet, hooked his thumbs in his shell-belt and scanned the ground with a dead weight in his chest and a hard, hurting lump behind his belt.

Seeing Fred's moving gaze, Chet said, 'We ruined 'em around here but two fellers're out a ways. There'll be sign all right.'

And there was. The two riders came back in a sloppy trot and hunkered. The squatters slouched over to stand above them, watching dirty fingers trace lines like snake tracks in the dust. Chet and Fred listened to the drone but Fred's numbness hadn't worn off. He heard only a word now and then.

'...Cut east again an' went straight as an arrer toward Tucomcori.'

'How many?' Fred heard himself ask.

A sweat grimed face twisted upward. 'Hard t'tell. Looks like a passel of 'em though. Maybe twenty, maybe more. Tracks're all overlapped kind of.'

'Hell to pay,' Chet said softly. 'They'll lynch him sure as hell.'

The awkward, thick silence settled again. Fred fished for the tobacco sack, found it and made a cigarette. His hands were shaking. Someone held out a light. He used it looking straight across the tiny flame into the black eyes beyond. He exhaled and waited for Blackbeard to speak. He didn't, just snapped the match, dropped it and looked at its broken body on the ground. Fred drew in a big breath.

'No, they won't lynch Graham. They won't lynch anybody.'

'They got the law too. Got Josh back. That gives 'em right.'

Fred walked over to the bench and dropped down on it. Chet moved closer but it was Blackbeard who went the full distance across the yard and sank down on the bench near Fred, still cleaning his pistol with detached unconcern.

How did Ben do it? How many men did

he have with him and why hadn't he used his hired gunmen? And – where was *she?* What had the devil done with *her?*

'Now what?' Chet asked no one in particular.

Blackbeard answered without looking up, reloading his gun, 'Why – we go get Norm back an' hang Ben – that's all.'

Clem spoke from where he squatted in the dirt. 'Ride into Tucomcori? You're crazy.'

Fred said, 'He isn't; I am. I said you boys had underestimated Ben. You did, but I underestimated him worse, it looks like.'

'Maybe,' Chet said thoughtfully, with an undertone of hostility to it.

Fred's gaze swung to his face, hung there. For a moment the green of his eyes frosted then it melted; he said nothing but arose and looked around.

'Anyone examine the dead man?'

'Yeah,' Clem said. 'I did. He must've put up quite a scrap f'his gun's plumb empty and he's hit six times.'

'How about his pardner; any sign of him?'

'They must've took him with them,' another man said thinly.

'Then he wasn't hurt badly, I suppose,' Fred said. 'All right, we've got to bury this fellow.'

The black-bearded man got up lazily and crooked a finger at Clem and two men near him. 'Come on boys, we ain't got all day.'

No one moved. Fred read the despondency on their faces, felt it in the humidity. He turned toward the black-eyed man. 'You and I can do it,' he said.

Blackbeard's dark glance grew baleful but he didn't raise his voice. 'Oh, Clem an' Snuff an' Dick don't mind; *come on, boys!'* They got up sluggishly. Fred knew how they felt, what they were probably thinking. He waited until they'd gone around the side of the house then he turned toward Chet.

'Throw some hay to the horses and water them, Chet. We'll be riding out of here at sundown.'

Chet moved away without speaking and Fred went back into the shack. The room was cool, almost gloomily pleasant, the big man had taken the last slug through the head and the others were scattered. Except for that last one he'd have survived. Fred went over to Graham's bunk. Strangely, Graham's long-barreled pistol lay in the rumpled mass of blankets. He flicked open the loading gate and spun the cylinder. Two live ones and four empty casings were in the gun. He carefully punched out the spent casings and replaced them from his own shell-belt and shoved the gun down the front of his breeches and went back outside.

The silence was complete while men cared for their horses. Rubbed them down, watered them and hayed them. It was something to do; a chore. They did it automatically and well.

Chet came over by Fred. 'He must've knowed, Fred,' he said.

Fred looked at the hatchet-faced man for a moment in silence. Of course Ben had known. Had probably known because Lillian's inherent honesty had made her stand up to Ben, tell him she didn't love him among other things. Ben's maniacal rage had driven him to round up all the border scum Tucomcori had like every border village had. Maybe Ben's wealth had encouraged men to ride the countryside like they'd never ridden it before; like they'd never had ridden it at any time for just wages, and what they found was taken back to Ben who'd formed them into a posse of bounty hunters. Only the fact that Fred's crew was attacking Ben's ranch had kept them from all being ambushed like Norm Graham and his protectors had been ambushed.

'Who would've done it, Fred?'

Thinking of the dead man inside and another man named Henry Fortin, Fred shrugged and looked away. 'That's not as important as setting it to rights.'

'You mean get Norm back alive?'

'Yes – that,' Fred said absently. 'That and squaring things up for a couple of others who're already dead.' He moved restlessly, shot a glance at the lowering sun. 'Chet;

have you scouts out all around us?'

'Yeah, if they come back here, Fred, they'll get a goddamned surprise the next time.'

'I wasn't thinking of that, I was thinking of Tucomcori.'

'I don't follow you.'

'Don't you? Dammit – you should have men close enough to town to see what Ben and Marshal Morgan are up to. How do you know they haven't already hung Graham?'

'Oh – like that. Yeah; Brewster sent five of the boys back after he come in.'

'Brewster?'

'That 'breed lookin' feller. One with the black eyes and black-beard.'

'Oh.' Fred turned the name over in his mind. Brewster. He'd remember that. 'Well – let's see if they're through with the grave. I don't feel comfortable sitting around here.'

Blackbeard was sweating like a horse, droplets hung up in his beard and showed like seed pearls. When Fred and Chet came around the corner of the shack he raised up and leaned on an old spade. His chest was pumping regularly, thumpingly. He swung his head to toss aside perspiration.

''Bout done, Fred. You want to ride, now?'

'The sooner the better, Brewster.'

'Yeah, I expect.' Brewster looked into the grave Clem and two others were filling in. 'Did you come across a dead horse on your way back?'

'Dead horse?' Fred asked.

The black eyes came up. 'Yeah. Dead horse an' a sight of scuffed up earth around it. You see it?'

'No. Where was it?'

'Off the tracks a ways. Well – I was ridin' back off to one side of our bunch and heard a horse blow his nose an' rode toward the sound. Someone let fly at me with a popgun of some kind and I hit the dirt, threw four, five carbine shots into the brush an' heard the threshin'. Stayed back for a long while then snuck up. I'd killed the horse all right but the damned rider got clean away.'

'I didn't see the horse,' Fred said again, frowning a little. 'What did you make of it, anyway?'

'Well,' Brewster said straightening up, breathing easier. 'I didn't make much of it, exactly, only this here rider had no lariat on the swells and the stirrups was up about where a kid'd wear them.' The black eyes stared on Fred's face. 'Didn't somebody say there was a girl down there with Ben?'

For a second Fred's heart just stopped.

'There was a girl there, Brewster. Yes.'

'That's what I thought. It puzzled me about that saddle until I remembered that. It was either a girl or a kid ridin' that horse an' I'd swear to that.'

Fred's mouth was cotton-dry. 'Come on –

you and I'll ride back there.'

'All right,' Brewster said agreeably but without moving. 'Only it ain't necessary. A couple of the boys went back to see if they couldn't find the feller – or girl – or whoever it was riding who shot at me.'

'Let's go anyway,' Fred said quickly.

Brewster dropped his spade after an earnest, questioning study of Fred's face. 'Sure,' he said.

Fred walked toward the corral, Chet and Brewster trailing him. He was slinging up his saddle when Chet cleared his throat. 'You want us to follow, Fred?'

'Finish the grave then come on. We'll be where the dead horse is, Chet. If we aren't there we'll leave tracks you can follow.'

Chet nodded speechlessly, watched Fred and Brewster swing up and walk their horses out through the shimmering sunblast of the dying day.

Away from the shack Brewster made a cigarette, brushed aside his luxurious beard carefully and lit it. His eyes were never still and never more than touched Fred before they were gone again, searching the desert distances.

'You know, Fred, Ben had word we was hidin' around here. That much I reckon was common knowledge – at least as far as Chet an' Clem an' Norm, an' maybe you, was concerned, but I can't figure out how he happened to pick the one night we were all set to clean his plow, for *his* attack on *us*.'

Fred's lingering gaze went over the dark face. His green eyes smouldered in hard irony. 'Thanks for saying it like that, Brewster. I saw that some of the squatters were suspicious of me as soon as I got back to the shack. I don't blame them,' he added, following Brewster into the dense brush. 'I don't blame them at all. No one knows who to trust any more and probably the only way we'll get all the answers we want is when we get Ben.'

Brewster was reining up, pointing downward and ahead when he answered. 'If we get him. There it is right there.'

Fred didn't dismount, instead he flung his glance far and wide. 'Where are the men you sent up here?'

'I told 'em to go on up by town an' join the other boys if they didn't find the rider. Must not of found him – her.'

Fred swung down and went around the horse. It took him a long time to find the tracks but he eventually came to freshly broken chaparral limbs and there he bent low and went ahead slowly until he found what he sought.

'Brewster? Come here.'

They stood together like prisoners of the brush, completely surrounded and held by it. Fred pointed to a wide, long, heavy imprint. Brewster looked and grunted. 'Man's,' he said. 'Well – I was wrong.'

'Look there, closer in the brush.'

'Now that's more like it. Man track must've been made by the boys I sent up here. The other one's pretty small. I'd say too little for a kid, even.' He straightened up. 'It *was* her then, wasn't it? Why'n hell she'd take a shot at me, do you suppose?'

Fred shouldered deeper into the brush without replying. He found several other imprints of the tiny bootprint before he returned to the horses, where Brewster sat astride studying the countryside under its brassy smolder of sunlight.

'They must not have found her, Brewster.'

'Doesn't look that way,' Brewster agreed. He turned his head for a slanting glance at the lowering sun. 'What you got in mind for tonight, Fred?' He asked.

'As soon as the others come up pick out two that you think are the best for the job and have them track her until they find her.' He saw Brewster's appraising gaze at the sun. 'If they're good they'll be able to find her before dark.'

'Maybe. If they're good. What else?'

Fred mounted his horse, turned in the saddle and looked far behind. He thought he saw a faint dust banner coming from the direction of the shack. He spoke while watching it.

‘I don’t know, Brewster. Like I said early this morning; I’m no soldier.’ He wrenched around in the saddle, satisfied the dust cloud was real. ‘The others are coming I think.’

‘Yeah. I noticed that a while ago. Well: what d’you think we ought to do?’

‘Wait until dark then ride as close to Tucomcori as we can, infiltrate the place and find Graham.’

‘That won’t be hard,’ Brewster said dryly. ‘He’ll be in jail.’

‘Then we’ll have to go to jail.’

‘Uh-huh,’ Brewster grunted, peering again at the dust cloud. ‘That’s going to raise hell and prop it up, y’know.’

‘Listen, Brewster; Ben knows where the shack is. If he hadn’t caught Graham and killed that other man he’d of waited around back there and ambushed us like he did down on the border. All right; I’ve made a couple of bad blunders since I arrived but I’m learning. I think I can guess what Ben’s got set up for us around that jail in Tucomcori. I also believe we can give *him* the surprise this time.’

‘How?’

‘Let’s wait for the others.’

They sat there in the full wash of dying sunlight turning from gold to orange and finally to rusty red and soft, soft purple. The sound of riders came finally. They watched like hawks, knowing but wary.

'It's them,' Brewster said. 'I know that big black horse in the lead.' The men slowed to a trot and pulled up looking down at the dead horse. Someone off to one side raised his arm. 'Yonder's a couple of riders.'

Every head swiveled, the silence became drawn out. Fred recognized both men as some of the squatters who had been with his crew at Big Lily. He turned to face the men gathered around.

'They'll have Graham in jail I think.'

Clem said, 'An' Ben'll have his ranch riders an' half the town guardin' 'em by now, too.'

Fred said he thought so, too, then he smiled a little. 'We can't very well ride in there shooting, can we?'

'Well, I guess not!' someone said with considerable feeling.

'But we've got to get inside the jailhouse to do any good at all, don't we?'

Chet looked up at Fred with an impatient scowl. He opened his mouth but never spoke. The two riders coming from the north swung in and called out. They waited for them to join the circle. Fred didn't give Brewster a chance to ask the question uppermost in both their minds.

'Did you find the rider?'

'No,' the older of the two men said with a head-wag, 'An' what's more we ain't goin' to find her neither. Her tracks went through that brush all the way to the outskirts o' town. We didn't go any closer.'

Brewster grunted. 'She must've flown.'

'Don't smoke, more'n likely,' an old man said, and someone chuckled.

Fred said nothing, re-arranged his thoughts. Good God – everywhere trouble was she managed some way to be there first. *Lillian, why didn't you go away like I asked you to?*

'Don't matter,' Chet said. 'How're we goin' to get to Norman, Fred?'

Fred looked up swiftly, hesitated over his answer a moment then said: 'Ben knows there's a lot of you – and me – out after him. If he didn't know that this morning he does by now. His gunmen will have told him about the attack on Big Lily.'

'Sure.'

'So he'll know there's a crew of us – but – he won't know which squatters will be among us, will he?' No one answered. Brewster's dark eyes were glowing.

'There's just one of us he probably will know is here – me.'

Brewster leaned forward a little in his saddle and touched Fred's arm lightly, 'Whoa,' he said, 'I think I get the drift o' what you got in mind. You can't–'

'Wait a minute, Brewster,' Fred said. 'So – Ben's got a big reward on me too. All right; you men will know which of you Ben's the least suspicious of. Two of you will take me into Tucomcori tied across my horse, to collect the reward. You'll tell Ben and Morgan that you drygulched me out on the desert.'

The men were transfixed, silent and pop-eyed, Chet spat aside and spoke first. 'That ain't necessary, Fred. Two of the boys could ride in an' say you're out here, y'see, then, when the marshal or whoever comes, rides back with 'em we'll have a couple of prisoners.'

Fred sighed, stared hard at Chet. 'Will that put us *inside* the jailhouse, Chet?'

'Oh. Well – no, I expect not.'

'Then just listen, will you?' His green glance raked them. 'I'll be delivered across my saddle dead. They'll take me inside the jail…'

'Well, f'Crissake,' a man blurted, then for the space of several seconds no one spoke. Brewster's black eyes were studying the gathered horsemen.

'Mike, you and Toby aren't known as night riders. Suppose you two take him in. Mind, you get inside that damned jailhouse with him. Don't leave everything for him to do.'

The two men addressed looked dumbfoundedly from Brewster to Chet and over to Fred Nolan's shiny face, softened in the gathering twilight. Neither of them spoke until it seemed that everyone spoke at once like a covey of excited quail. Fred dismounted and beckoned to Chet and Brewster. They walked a little apart, the three of them, stood with their backs to the big lump of dead horseflesh.

'Are those two the ones you would pick, Chet?'

Chet's Adam's apple dived once and settled into place. 'They're as good as any. Fred; I got misgivings about this.'

Fred shrugged. 'Then think up something better but do it quick.'

'I can't,' Chet said helplessly.

Brewster made a cigarette and smoked it in silence gazing over where the others were standing around, talking. 'You got to have blood on you,' he said after a while. 'I'll supply that. You got a belly-gun, Fred?'

'No, have you?'

'No, but some one of us's bound to have. You can't ride all that way on your guts with a gun under your belt.' Brewster went over where the others were. Fred watched him a moment then turned toward Chet.

'You and Brewster had better not come any closer than half a mile or so toward town. Leave the horses – hide them if you can – but don't worry too much about them. After this, we'll either have plenty of horses or no need for any at all.'

'*You* won't,' Chet said tactlessly.

'Get as close as you can, Chet, then go the rest of the way afoot.'

'How'll we know what to do after we get into town?'

Fred chuckled. 'You'll know all right. There'll either be shooting or, if it goes off all right, I'll hang a lamp in the streetside window. In either case you bring about ten men and come into the jailhouse. Don't shoot unless you're forced to. What we want is Norm Graham first, Ben Nolan second and last of all, the U.S. Marshal, but Graham's first. He can't run, remember, so try to make everything come off without shooting. If we arouse the whole town we'll never get out alive.'

Chet made a mumbling sound, groped for his tobacco sack and turned to look up at Brewster when the dark man came back with two little Derringers, one in each fist.

'Stick one in your boot, Fred. The other'll fit in your pants pocket. They're both loaded full up.'

Fred took the little guns. 'Did you tell those two men what to say when they haul me in there?'

'More'n that,' Brewster replied. 'I told 'em to be sure an' get you inside the jail, not to let the law dump you in the dust like they usually do when someone fetches in a dead man. Get you inside if they had to pack you themselves.'

Fred finished hiding the little guns and nodded curtly toward Chet. 'He knows what to do, Brewster.' He straightened up with a grunt. 'I hope it works.'

Brewster smiled softly, bleakly. 'I reckon you do hope so,' he said. 'If I was in your boots I'd even *pray* so.'

Fred looked at the thin slit of pale red hovering on the horizon and estimated the time. 'Come on. We can ride a lot closer to Tucomcori before you tie me on crossways.'

They rode slowly. The three men up front didn't speak at all and most of those behind them also held silence but an occasional remark floated through the warmth of a desert night leaving no echo in its wake, right up to the time they could all make out individual lights in Tucomcori ahead. Then Fred reined up, swung down and threw a crisp look at Brewster.

'Where's that blood?'

Brewster's teeth showed briefly through the matt of his beard as he unhorsed groped in his trouser pocket, withdrew a big Barlow knife and calmly made a diagonal slash across his left hand, on the back of it. 'Bend over,' he said and held the hand so that the dark, shining welter of warmth ran thickly over the back of Fred's head, across his shoulders and soaked into the powder dryness of his shirt. The blood matted the hair under Fred's hat and seeped around onto his face.

Brewster staunched the flow with an old

handkerchief under the wet, wide stares of a small sea of faces. 'I'll save a little of this stuff for myself,' he said, using his teeth to pull the rag tight over the cut.

Fred looked at his shirt front, felt his face and the back of his head then he lifted his eyes to Chet's face. 'Look all right?'

Chet's Adam's apple made a swift pattern of shadow on his neck. 'God – you look awful,' he said.

Fred mounted the bay colt and swung sideways. By craning his neck he could see Brewster holding the animal's head, white teeth shining in the darkness of his face. 'Tie me on, Chet,' he said. 'Make it good, too. They'll see the knots first so make it good.'

They made it good. So good Fred's suffering started long before the two squatters delegated to take him into Tucomcori led his horse away. He couldn't avoid the sliding jolt of the horse's stride and each step jolted him in the stomach. He breathed shallowly too and when his hat fell off he didn't know it because his eyes were tightly closed, teeth locked, trying to find a position within the very limited confines of the lashing that would let a hip, a shoulder, a leg, take some of the punishment.

After what seemed an eternity of torture one of the dark shadows up ahead called back. 'We're comin' to the outskirts. From here on f'gawd's sake don't make a sound.'

Until then he wasn't conscious of having made a sound. It was the slamming expulsion of his breath jetted out under pressure. He heard it and strove to control it.

'Almost there,' the whisper said again. 'Folks are lookin' at you. Iffen y'ever prayed, Nolan, you'd best run through 'em again.'

After that neither of his 'captors' said another word but someone on the boardwalk in the darkness called out: 'Who you got there, fellers?'

'Fred Nolan, pardner. Six thousan' dollars worth o' Fred Nolan's carcass.'

He heard the cry repeated and after that he could almost have shouted and no one would have heard the noise. Tucomcori came to life with cries and scoffing shouts, exclamations, and even the dogs caught some of the excitement and joined in with their clamor.

Fred swore under his breath while his head lolled with the slowing gait of the bay colt. Why hadn't the two idiots just ridden up to the jail, *then* said who he was; now Tucomcori would flock around like flies and if anything went wrong he wouldn't stand a chance of getting away.

'Hey, man,' a voice thundered close by. 'Stop a minute.'

The voice was familiar. Fred's breath caught inside him in a huge bubble. The U.S. Marshal's voice. He went limp all over when the bay colt slowed, stopped, stood with one hind legged cocked under him, relaxed.

'It's Nolan. We got him over a cookin' fire headin' south toward the line.'

A hand caught hold of Fred's hair started to tug upwards then slipped away with a disgusted oath exploding in Fred's ear. 'He's got blood all over him, the son of a–'

'I tol' you, dammit; we shot him.'

The bay colt responded to a tug on the leadrope. 'We'll take him off over by the jail, Marshal. Then you can get a good squint at 'im.'

Fred ground his teeth and fought the wild tumult in his chest. Why did the fools have to make it so good? Thank God it was dark.

The colt stopped for the second time and saddles squeaked. Quickly, roughly, a hand grabbed his hair firmly and jerked. Pain ran down inside Fred like lightning. Whiskey breath came close. 'So that's Fred Nolan, is it? Big devil, ain't he?' The hand dropped away abruptly.

'Get away from there, you sot. *Move!*'

Fred heard the tinkle of a spurred boot in motion, guessed it was a kick aimed at the curious man. People laughed and pushed back a little.

CHAPTER SEVEN

'Here,' the voice of the marshal said briskly. 'Take this knife an' cut him loose.'

'Humph! This here's a perfectly good lariat keep your cussed knife. You got him loose that side, Mike?'

'Purt near. Say, Marshal – about that reward.'

'Dammit, you'll get it. Get him off'n there will you?' A pause then: 'Rusty, go inside an' see if Ben's still in there. Tell him to come out here.'

Fred held his breath with no great effort when Mike on the far side grabbed his ankles and pushed him callously down the colt's left side a little. 'Ain't you got him loose yet, Toby?' An irritable answer came back.

'If you hadn't tied him like y'expected him to come alive and run off, y'old devil, I'd of–'

'Cut it, I said.'

'Go cut your own lariat, Marshal. This one's mine and I don't cut it. All right, Mike, he's loose.'

'Then come aroun' here an' help me heft him down.'

Josh Morgan's voice came simultaneously with his action. 'Heft him down hell,' he said. A strong arm grabbed Fred's shirt at the shoulder and wrenched. Fred's jaws bulged as he clamped his teeth and saw the hard roadway hurtling up at his face. When he landed he felt something make a sharp small *crik!* sound then he rolled inertly, holding himself half stiffly with bursting colors behind his eyelids and pain running with crooked fingernails up and down his nerves.

Anger worse than the pain flooded him. A boot-toe levered in under his ribs and hoisted. He went over loosely onto his back. Above was the spray of cold stars a million miles away and the night knifed through the distant orange lamplight. Several people sucked in breath. He heard the sounds very distinctly before two bulky shapes bent low and grunted.

'Drag him,' Morgan said. 'Here; give me an arm, I'll pull the dirty scum inside – damn him.'

One of the men protested, Fred didn't know which because at that moment his left arm was almost torn out of its socket. He had to fight to keep his features slack. A new voice growled. 'Wait a minute, Josh – his head's hung up on the sidewalk.' A boot worked in under his skull and lifted. 'There; what's the sense of bein' so rough, anyway.'

The marshal tugged again, grunted and swore at Toby and Mike with straining zeal. 'Get ahold you two. Get ahold and pull.'

They dragged the heavy carcass through the door and Fred winced in spite of himself when the dancing lamplight stamped into his face, his eyes. When they stopped dragging him he could feel the silence, the deep, throbbing hush in the room, somehow he knew that his cousin was standing above him looking down. Morgan dropped his arm. It made a harsh-solid sound when it fell against the filthy floor. Someone was pushing the jailhouse door closed; it squeaked.

The silence seemed to stretch until it couldn't be dragged out any further then a voice he would never forget, had never forgotten, said: 'He's changed. Heavier – but that's him all right.'

'About that reward, Mister Nolan.'

Ben was still gazing at the still, filthy, blood-splattered face when he answered. 'You'll get my share of it all right. How'd you get him?'

'We was comin' back from over the line and seen a cookin' fire's smoke. Seemed strange for a man t'be cookin' s'early in the afternoon and Toby said it was probably a rustler's little runnin' iron fire. Well – we snuck up as close as we dast, ditched our horses. I knew him from seein' the reward posters. Shot him in the back o' the head and brang him in. Nothin' to it, much. Now, about that six thousand–'

'Oh shut up,' Morgan's voice said half angrily, half disgustedly. 'You'll get the government's slice and I reckon Ben'll give you his so what you worryin' about?'

In an abstract tone Ben Nolan said, 'See any tracks around him? See any other fires or riders? He had a crew of scum with him when he raided my ranch this morning. They wouldn't be far off, I don't imagine.'

'Nary a soul. He was plumb alone. Y'can see from the looks of his horse outside he'd been ridin' hard, too. Come take a look.'

Fred could have kissed the whining voice but Ben didn't seem to want to look at the horse just yet. He was still drinking in the triumphant sight of the bloody, ragged 'corpse' at his feet. Morgan spoke casually.

'They may have run him off, Ben, after that one got killed at your place this mornin'. Maybe he got rattled after he knew we got Graham and ran for it. Hell; the raid on the Lily fizzled and the rest of 'em'd know by now about Graham and the dead one at the shack.'

Ben Nolan mused. The sound of his voice gave Fred the impression that his head was averted, as though Ben was gazing at the supposed killers.

'Maybe. Who're you fellers?'

'I'm Toby Blevins an' this's Mike Toole.'

'Yeah,' Ben said softly, drawlingly, still looking away from the body at his feet. 'Sure; you both ranch along the fringe, don't you?' The softness of the words didn't go past Mike and Toby. One of them cleared his throat.

'We're fringe ranchers all right, Mister Nolan – but I expect *that* shows we ain't like most fringe ranchers – don't it?'

Silence descended and held for a moment, then Ben Nolan laughed a little. It sounded like horseshoe nails dropping on glass. 'For six thousand dollars you fellers'd gut-shot your own mothers. Were you with him when he raided my place this morning? No, of course not; you boys wouldn't be in on anything like that, would you?' The tone was changing, hardening, getting brittle. 'Not unless you thought it'd come off.' Ben made a grunt of contempt. 'More than likely you rode with him until his back was turned then downed him.'

'What's the difference,' Josh Morgan said sharply. 'He's dead and that's worth every dime up on him. Roll him out of the way and let's take care of Graham. He's the other one I want to see done away with.'

'Mister Nolan – if you don't care about his horse I'd admire to keep it. Of course it's kind of ridden down right now and it probably ain't as good as you usually keep anyway–'

'Where is it? I want to see the brand.'

Fred's heart missed two beats and caught up its gait with a slam that made him wince.

'Out at the rail.'

He felt the whisper of boots moving past his face. The sounds of spurs, the soft slap of leather as the men moved after his cousin toward the door.

He had forced his breath to come in starveling amounts. To sift in and out with little more than enough to sustain life and when he knew no more men were behind him he drew in a great lungful and let it out. Cymbals burst inside his head from the great rush of oxygen. A tingling pleasantness flooded him. He risked a peek through his lashes, it was like lying low in a stubblefield looking through the stalks.

The last man went through the door but no further. His back was to Fred. Anticipation gnawed at his mind. Anticipation and uncertainty. He wanted to draw one of the little guns and cuddle it in his palm but he was afraid to. Not yet, he thought. There are too many of them, maybe the opportunity will come later, after the night is well along and the excitement by his arrival had died down a little.

And he was right in this for when the men came back from examining the Milton colt Ben waved a hand toward Fred's body. 'Shove it against the wall, boys, and we'll have a hearing over Graham – get it over with and have a few drinks before we go after the others.'

They rolled him with their boots. He was faced toward the wall with a numbness growing more painful by the minute in his left arm. It wasn't as much from the weight on the arm as it was from the savage wrench Josh Morgan had given him outside. There was an advantage to having his arm under him, along his side. He could feel the bulge of the little gun in his pocket; could work it surreptitiously loose with two fingers while dread lived between his shoulderblades because he was facing away from the room and the eyes that might be watching him.

'What'd you need a trial for, Ben?'

A short, curling laugh. 'Josh; you can't be party to a lynching. You got to be protected y'know.'

Morgan's growl was deep. 'Self defense. I'd make it self defense and have him buried.'

Ben laughed again. Fred guessed why he was so pleasant. He had the hate of a lifetime bloody dead against the wall.

'*I'd* be satisfied with it like that, Josh, but town-talk could get back east. You could lose your job.'

'I don't give a damn about that, Ben. Not now. Time was when I looked at things different but not after those–'

'All *right!*' Ben said explosively, and that was the old Ben Nolan Fred remembered. 'We're not going to lynch Graham an' that's that.' Silence, then: 'An' not just to save you from becoming useless either, Josh, but also because I want to know the names of every man Jack who was with him and my cousin today. Every lousy name.'

'Oh!'

'Yeah,' Ben said. 'Oh, use your head, Josh. When I have every name of those thievin' whelps I can end this sniping once and for all. Forever an' a day, Josh.' Fred heard a chair squeak. 'Fellers – go out and look around.' Ben didn't speak again until he and Josh Morgan were alone.

'Josh – you've been on the fringe a little yourself, you know. Now listen; I want you to declare yourself one way or another.'

Morgan's indignation was only poor concealed. 'Ben, you know as well as you know you're sittin' there I've gone along every way I could.'

'I know that. *Now* I want you in all the way – in everything.'

'Everything?' Morgan said dubiously. 'I don't understand what you mean by "everything".'

'Hell,' Ben Nolan scoffed. 'You guessed about Emmons an' you knew about Hull and old Milton. Don't make out–'

'Well, of course I did.'

'And you guessed where those banknotes came from that got into your mailbox too, Josh. Don't spoof me about that either.'

'I'm not. Sure I knew – from you – but this is different. I mean, what I think you mean by "everything" – that could be a lot different.'

'Damn you,' Ben Nolan stormed. 'Just now you were prepared to lynch Graham. How long d'you think the government'd let you keep that star after *that* got noised around.'

But Morgan's sly eyes smiled across the desk at Ben Nolan. '*I* wasn't going lynch him, Ben, you were. You and Big Lily were going to do it and you were going to knock me over the head and tie me up before you did it.'

Ben sat a moment in silence. 'Well – I'll be damned,' he finally said in a gust of breath. 'We were going to do it and make it look like you'd resisted us. That right?'

'Pretty nearly. Only I wasn't going to be able to see *who* did it – you hit me from behind.'

Ben shook his head savagely. 'No, Josh, we won't have anything like that at all. You're coming along because I'll slip envelopes into your mailbox from time to time, but I'm the boss all the time, understand. All the time – and I work out how things're done – you don't. Now then, we'll have a trial here and now for Graham and he'll be condemned to death by hanging by the jury and we'll duly hang him, but by God it's goin' to be legal, Josh. If it isn't you'll lose your office and the envelopes'll go to the next U.S. Marshal, see?'

'Suit yourself,' Morgan said a trifle sullenly, 'but don't forget what I told you this morning at the shack. I know who four of them are because I recognized them even with the blanket over the door, and no matter how legal you make Graham's trial, them four're goin' to scream like wounded eagles.'

'Not by a damn sight,' Ben said. 'I remember those names. I sent some of the Big Lily hands to hide out near their cabins and either fetch them in alive for a trial like Graham's going to get, or leave them for the buzzards on their own damned steps.'

Ben's breathing was audible in the room, it came in bursts like the breathing of a bravo bull.

'Are you coming along all the way, Josh? Do things like I say and want done – or not?'

Morgan's rasping snort was half chuckle, half sniff. 'You keep the envelopes in the mailbox and I'll keep Big Lily law here in the Territory.'

'You're wakin' up, Josh wakin' up.'

'Am I? Tell me something, Ben: Where's

the girl?'

Fred, face to the wall, held his breath. You didn't just up and ask Ben questions like that. He wasn't surprised at the answer but he was surprised that all Josh Morgan got *was* an answer.

'That's not in your line, Josh. Remember that. You just listen and answer questions and do like I say. The rest of it, Josh – you leave to me.'

The silence between them lasted longer than time. Fred's muscles crawled. He couldn't see either man yet the room was charged with an intolerable denseness of antagonism. Ben spoke again.

'Forget the girl. I don't know what happened to her.'

'Dammit, Ben, she's got kin. Besides she was as pretty as a picture.'

Ben's answer was strained, thin sounding. 'Never mind her kin. I'll handle that. Greasers stole her off the ranch and I haven't been able to find hide nor hair of her since. That's for the kin. As for the pretty – you're walking on awfully thin ice, Josh.'

Morgan swore. 'Forget it,' he said, and Fred could tell from the way the marshal said it he hadn't forgotten Lillian at all and guessed there was going to be more to this difference between his cousin and Morgan before anyone really forgot it.

'Go get Graham,' Ben said curtly. 'You

and I'll pump him then send over for Judge Kinross.'

A chair scraped over floorboards, boots rang solidly with an overtone of spur music. A door opened, the bootsteps retreated, got fainter down a dim corridor then came back moments later.

'In there. Sit down on the bench. Graham, you know this man?'

'No,' a husky, wheezing voice said.

The marshal looked away from the prisoner, began making a cigarette and a little later Fred smelled the smoke. By then Ben was speaking.

'Know who that is against the wall there, Graham?'

Silence.

'You know all right. Fred Nolan – dead, six thousand dollars worth. Take a good look, Graham, because if you don't give me the name of every man who was with you and him today when you jumped my ranch you'll be lying right beside him.'

'I will be anyway,' Graham said spiritedly, 'an' it won't be the first Graham you killed in cold blood either, Nolan.'

Fred flinched involuntarily when the second of hush was shattered by the wet, solid sound of a blow landing. Hate like fire blew up inside of him. He worked harder getting the little pistol out of his pocket. When he had his fingers tantalizingly around the down-swooping rubber butt of the weapon he could feel the sweat running across his forehead and closed his eyes against its sting.

'That's just the beginning, Graham. Hurt a little, didn't it? Wipe the damned blood off your mouth.'

The stubby barrels were cool against Fred's flesh. Almost cold. He fisted the gun, tightened his grip around it, groped for the knurled hammer and felt it under his thumbpad.

'Name them, every last mother's son of them.'

Silence. The sound of breathing, deep and shallow, strong and rasping.

'I'll beat it out of you. That's a promise. I'll beat it out and if that doesn't work I'll use an iron an' burn it out.' Ben's voice broke, his breathing was louder, almost whistling. 'I'll get every last name out of you, Graham, if I have to wring them out of you an' chase you all the way to hell for 'em. *Now talk!*'

Graham's answer came in a husky monotone. 'You'll never get a name out of me, damn you, but I'll tell you this: I was at your place this morning – in spirit, Nolan – and by God I hung you a thousand times the same way. Sometimes by the thumbs, sometimes by the toes, sometimes with a piece of wet rawhide around your guts – out in the sun.'

Fred was shouting it in the silence of his skull. *Shut up, Graham! Shut up you damned fool!*

With a roar Ben leapt up. Fred heard his chair go over backwards with startling violence then Josh Morgan was yelling.

'Don't, Ben – you'll kill him. He won't tell us anything. *Don't.*'

With the wild scream of the last word, Fred moved: rolled completely over with the little gun swinging up, thumb straining to draw the hammer back. In the blur of movement he saw Ben's left leg swing far back. Graham was coughing blood on his hands and knees and Marshal Morgan was reaching for Ben Nolan – then the gun went off.

Ben's leg went half around with the impact of the ball. He made a high squeal of sound and lost his balance. Morgan's head spun but the rest of him was frozen in mid-movement. His mouth dropped open, twisted, and no sound came out. Norman Graham's head came up a little. Two dull eyes looked at the man getting to his feet with drying blood across his shirt, face, matted in his hair. Recognition came slowest, last, to Graham. A thin backlash of blood laced across one of his cheeks and his saliva was reddish.

'Nolan!'

Fred ignored it. His heart was near bursting. Beyond the door was a buzz of voices.

‘Laugh, Morgan, God-damn you – *laugh!*’

Morgan tried twice, licked his lips the last time and laughed. The sound wasn’t deep like the man’s voice and Fred swore at him for that.

‘Say something. Say, “that was close, Ben. Scare him again”. Go on, *say it!*’

Morgan said it. Fred listened to the noise without, the voices raised in curiosity, in garrulousness.

‘Can you get up, Graham?’

Without answering the squatter shoved himself upright. Stood like a tree in a storm.

‘Get their guns then go sit on the bench.’

Josh Morgan offered no opposition. Ben Nolan cursed and held his gushing lower leg with both hands. He twisted away from Graham with a wild curse and Graham didn’t straighten up. He swung his arm like a club. Ben Nolan was bowled over by the blow but he clung to his leaking leg and only moaned. Graham got his gun and walked unsteadily to the bench and slid down onto it like he was made of jelly.

Until then Fred didn’t move but after he’d crossed to Graham’s side and taken the gun in Graham’s limp left fist he walked up very close to the marshal.

‘You know, Marshal, I owe you something for pulling my arm half out of its socket. *This!*’

Morgan didn’t make a move to protect

himself until the fist was inches away then it was too late. Fred caught him as he sagged. Let him down onto the floor with one hand, turned toward his cousin with a wildeyed look, and smiled.

'Use your belt, Ben. Pull it tight enough and the bleeding'll stop.'

Ben obeyed in a grunting, damp-faced stupor. Fred holstered the gun he'd taken and knelt. 'Like this,' he said, and jerked the belt so tight the flesh above and below it bulged. The bleeding stopped almost instantly. Fred looked into the face inches away from his own. Seven years *wasn't* a long time; Ben didn't look any older than he remembered him.

'What did you do with Lillian, Ben?'

'She – ran off. I don't know ... where she went.'

Fred reached out almost lightly. The slap sounded as clear as a frozen limb snapping under a weight of wintertime snow. Ben's head went backwards, water jetted out of his eyes.

'What did you do with her, Ben?'

'I – don't know – what became of her. Fred, I'll kill you for...'

That time the slap was open handed too, but Ben Nolan rolled over from the impact. He made no move to get up again so Fred reached down and pulled him up.

'What happened at the ranch, Ben?' He

drew back his hand, balled into a fist.

'Fight,' Ben said thickly. 'We had a fight.'

'Beat her up, Ben?'

'A – little. She told me about you. How you were nice to her on the train. How you came back – the other night.'

'What else?'

'That she didn't love me. You did that to her. You told her things, Fred. I'll kill you for that, by God. I'll–'

'Did she tell you I kissed her, Ben?'

A strange, livid flame filled the older man's eyes. He didn't reply, he stared and Fred remembered the look of kill-craziness from half a lifetime ago.

'That I kissed her and told her she'd never be happy with you, Ben; did she tell you any of that?'

'God damn you, Fred. You dirty, rotten, son of–'

'That she loved me,' Fred went on in a dead-calm voice, grinding the bitterest salt in a proud man's wound, saying things he had no reason or right to say but saying them with good Nolan hate singing in his blood too.

'That we were going away together, Ben. That she knew you were no good. Knew it now because she'd seen you like she'd never seen you before. Did she tell you she knew about Emmon's killing and Hull's? Why did you beat her, Ben?'

'That's why,' Ben said on a rising note. 'Because of all of that.'

'She did tell you then, didn't she?'

'She told me you'd been there. Sneaked up when I was gone to the border after Graham an' the others. I got a dog that very night. I got the–'

'Never mind that. Why'd you beat her?'

'She said she couldn't love me. I said you'd made love to her.'

'And?'

'She said you had – admitted it. Then–'

'You beat her. Did she try to run into her room, Ben?'

'Damn you – yes! I kicked the door open. She had a quirt. I hit her first.'

'In the face?'

'Yes, you rotten–!' Ben's tone was exulting. 'Like this!' He swung a scant ten inches but the sound of the blow made Norman Graham jerk upright. Ben Nolan wilted, ran down onto the floor like hot butter and Graham wheezed at Fred.

'Stop it, you Comanche.'

Fred stood up slowly looking down at his cousin. Stood wide-legged over the crumpled body and swung his head low, like a bear, to gaze at Graham.

'You forgotten a woman in a burning cabin, Graham?'

'Damn you, Nolan,' Graham said with pain in his voice. 'But not like that. Not when he's busted up like that.'

'Who said they'd hang him with rawhide drying around his belly?'

Graham made a weak motion with the gun in his hand. 'Shut up an' get hold of yourself. Where're the others? Where's Chet an' Clem an' the rest of 'em?' The gun waved sideways toward a door. 'They got Murphy tied to a bunk in there. He's been shot. Where're the others? We got to get out of here – someway.'

Fred's blood still sang in his head but the noise was lessening, softening. With a swift turn he crossed to the door and went through into the little aisle that led down in front of strap-steel cages; in the last one he saw the man on the bed. Neither man spoke but the man in the cell's eyes were like pale coals. His head looked lopsided where a great purple swelling was.

Fred went back to the groaning form of Josh Morgan and rummaged for keys, found them and returned to the cells, kicked open the door and untied the bearded man, helped him to his feet and stood back watching him weave unsteadily toward the door.

Back in the office he stood near the bench watching Morgan roll over and get to his knees, claw at a chair and pull himself up into it. He waited a moment longer before he addressed the marshal.

'Morgan; you're going to go stand in the

doorway and tell the Big Lily men and town toughs out there to go on home. Tell them there'll be no hanging until tomorrow. Get rid of them do you understand?'

Morgan looked up with both hands stroking the undersides of his jaws, eyebrows knitted in pain and eyes watering with it.

'Get up!'

Morgan arose, steadied himself with one hand on the desk. Stood like that for perhaps ten seconds then dutifully moved toward the door. Fred drew his gun and followed, a little behind and to the left of the Marshal.

'Hold it, Morgan. Take a minute to get your wits back. Make this good. Make them believe you or you're a dead duck. That's better, now open that door and stand in the opening and *make it good!*'

Morgan reached for the latch, gripped it without moving for a moment, shook his head and swung the door inward. What happened then was too fast for Fred to fully comprehend. Evidently Josh Morgan hadn't been as fuzzy-witted as he'd acted, for with a yell and a lunge he went through the doorway and into the night beyond. Immediately the jailhouse lit up with an orange explosion and a roar of gun thunder. Fred half turned. Norman Graham, slouched on the bench, sunken-eyed and grey looking was holding a smoking gun. Outside someone yelped in fright and sounds of men scattering in flight came back into the room.

'I know him better'n you do, Fred,' Graham said. 'I knew he wouldn't do that.'

Yells out in the roadway increased. Questioning howls. Fred jumped toward the door, got a fleeting glimpse of Morgan face down, sprawled, on the boardwalk, and slammed the door with a curse. The squatters wouldn't be able to get them out now without a pitched battle. He flung around toward Graham and the dumbfounded bearded man beside him, but he didn't say what was in his mind for Graham's eyes were closed, his chest barely rising and falling; it was no use anyway, Graham had shot Morgan in the back, killed him; the damage was done.

Somewhere around in back of the building someone was pounding savagely on a door with a gun barrel. Fred heard but didn't heed until the hammering became louder, more hurried and insistent. Then he went through the cell-block door and hunted for the area of disturbance, found it and leaned against the massive, iron studded panel.

'Who's out there? Who is it?'

'Me, Brewster. Open the damned door.'

Fred cocked his pistol, threw back the big bolt and swung the door inward. Brewster jumped through in a low crouch faint light making his sweat-dirty face and black-beard glisten. He came out of the crouch when he saw Fred. With a motion toward Fred's cocked gun he said, 'Point it away from me.'

Fred lowered the barrel. 'Have you got horses out there?'

'Yes, but for God's sake hurry. You never should've shot Morgan. The town's starting to boil over. Come on.'

'I'll get Graham an' the other feller.'

'Hurry,' Brewster said again, breathing hard. 'I'll wait here.'

Life flowed through Fred with new vigor. He went back into the office and called to the two men, helped Graham to his feet and gestured for the bearded man to help him. They went down the dark little corridor as far as the door and Brewster, who jerked his head and disappeared into the darkness beyond.

Norman Graham's steps faltered. The bearded man hissed at Fred who came back, holstered his gun, bent low with desperation and scooped Graham up in his arms like a child, turned and trotted awkwardly after the dimly visible, weaving silhouette of Brewster.

'Here – over here, Fred.'

Dark shadows loomed up, men and horses. Two shapes detached themselves from the clutch of men, grasped Norm Graham and practically tore his limp body from Fred's arms. Feeling lighter by over a hundred pounds Fred sprinted for the horses. Someone shoved reins into his hands. He heard Chet's voice say, 'Let's go, dammit, they'll be comin' around in the alley directly.'

Fred mounted with a bound, groped for stirrups as his horse spun behind other horses, then he was racing through the darkness with riders bunched up around him. Escape! Escape and deliverance! His plan had worked after all, thank God.

At the exit of the little alleyway two running men, afoot, came around the buildings bent over and carrying carbines. They didn't see the cavalcade of riders until they were almost face to face. One man made a bleat and threw himself sideways, fell, dropped his carbine and rolled wildly to get clear of the piston strokes of the horses. The other man yanked upright not ten feet in front of Fred, who turned his horse a little and bent low. Too late for his handgun he used the horse instead. The beast's shoulder struck the man low in the chest. He was thrown aside like a broken doll. Fred snatched at the falling carbine, missed it and twisted to look back as they broke out into the roadway of Tucomcori, going south.

Pursuit and gunshots didn't materialize. They saw men stop and stare as they whirled past but no one apparently knew for sure who the racing riders were until they were at the southernmost environs of Tucomcori, then a swelling tumult of bedlam gathered strength far behind in their wake and finally a few gunshots made a distant breach in the wild night but by then the squatters were beyond range.

They rode hard for an hour before Fred reined up beside Brewster and Chet, yelled for them to haul up, then the entire crowd slowed, stopped, and sat in the desert's stillness while their blowing horses stamped and champed at bits. Brewster's dark face looked more Indian than ever in the gloom.

'Where to, Fred? We dassen't go back to the shack.'

Fred said, 'To Big Lily. That's why I stopped you. So you'd change course. The ranch road's somewhere off to our left.'

'Big Lily,' Chet said in a squirting tone. 'Are you daft, Fred?'

Fred's eyes gleamed. 'Maybe, Chet. Maybe I am, but Ben's gunmen are in town with him. Between Ben's riders and the posse Ben and Morgan used today, they'll have at least twenty-five men scouring the desert for us within an hour. They'll cover every squatter shack in the Territory if they have to but I don't think they'll think to look for us at Big Lily. It's that or Mexico. I don't think the horses could stand the run to Mexico, Chet.'

Chet didn't answer but Brewster's beard parted showing white teeth. He said, 'Big Lily it is. Let's go.'

Without waiting for an argument Brewster swung away, hooked his mount lightly and went weaving down across the chaparral land like a Comanche. The others followed. During the ride Fred reined back where two men were riding stirrup with Norm Graham. The wounded man made a desultory salute to Fred; he seemed in better condition than Fred thought he'd be in.

They swung southeast over the Big Lily road and went loping down it. Fred smelled and tasted the alkali dust they were kicking up and thought it was fortunate the moon wasn't bright enough to give them away with a dust banner. As for tracks, with all the recent shod-horse sign left hereabouts by Ben's riders those who came looking after dawn probably wouldn't be able to tell one track from another.

He knew they were getting close to the ranch when the faint challenge of a barking dog came upwind to them. Clem was riding nearby. With an oath he whipped out his gun. Fred rode closer and shook his head.

'Leave the dog alone, Clem.'

They rode straight for the house. Across the huge meadow as though they had every right to be there and dared anyone to try and stop them. No one did. As Fred had guessed the Big Lily gunmen weren't around.

He swung down at the house. Brewster stumped up close. Two men helping Norman Graham pushed through the other riders and Fred jutted his chin toward the house.

'Few of you look around in there first, then put Graham and the other fellow to bed. Stay in there with them.'

Brewster jerked his head without calling names. Riders went toward the house. Guns shone softly in the gloom and Brewster, watching, said: 'I wish to God Ben was in there.'

'Well he isn't,' Fred said, 'and that's only half of it. The other half is that we've got to hit him hard enough to discourage him before he rallies the country and hangs us all.'

Someone nearby laughed. 'He ain't goin' t'hang no one, Mister Nolan. F'every frien' Ben Nolan's got th' squatters got two.'

Fred looked at the man. 'Two squatters equal one gunman,' he said, 'if they're good enough.'

Several heads came up. Expressions tightened a little. Another man spoke in an unfriendly way. 'They're good enough, I reckon. Good enough to bust you an' them others out'n Morgan's jailhouse. That's good enough for me.'

Brewster made a cigarette, lit it and blew smoke upward. Ignoring the squatters around them he gazed at Fred. 'What you got in mind, Fred?'

'Beating Ben before he beats us.'

'All right,' Brewster said pleasantly, 'how?'

'These gentlemen say they've got friends for every one of Ben's friends. The difference seems to me to be one of guts. Ben's men will fight, the squatters won't.'

'Who says they won't?' One of the scowling faces said. 'What the hell we been doin' t'night anyway?'

'Sure,' Fred answered. 'Fifteen of us fight and the rest of your friends stay at home. Well, fifteen can't beat fifty no matter how good they are.' He jutted his chin at the nearest squatter. 'Can you bring another fifteen armed squatters over here to fight with us?'

The replies were low and sharp. 'Y'goddamned right we can.'

'Then go get them,' Fred shot back. 'Right now; get on your horses and go get them. Bring them back here loaded for bear as fast as you can. We've probably got the rest of the night to ourselves but as soon as day breaks Big Lily men will come straggling back here – after that – after they know where we are, we're finished unless your friends are here to fight them with us.'

Chet squirmed off to one side. 'Not *all* of 'em, Fred. Crissake; what if they don't none of 'em come back with help or without it?'

Fred shrugged and turned toward the house. 'It would probably be better for them if they're cowards, not to return. Ben'll hang you and Brewster, me and maybe one or two others. That'll be better than hanging all the rest of them.'

He went up the walk toward the verandah, and stopped where the flesh-side-out chairs were, gazing at them long enough for a memory to stab him. He heard Brewster talking low and fast to the squatters, the squeak of saddleleather, the low grunts of the men, then he passed on into Ben's house.

CHAPTER EIGHT

They'd put Graham to bed in a large room Fred recognized as the bedchamber of his dead aunt and uncle. When he went through the old doorway it was like stepping back in time to childhood again except for the rough men standing, leaning or sitting, around the room in stiff silence, watching him.

He went up close and bent over, drew back the blankets and opened Graham's shirt. A small purple scar showed. He closed the shirt, drew up the covers and smiled at Graham.

'How do you feel?'

'About like a herd of horses ran over me

an' the last one wiped his feet.'

Humor. That was always a good sign. Fred sighed. 'Where did he hit you?'

'Ben? In the jailhouse? Oh – in the cheek, I reckon. Anyway I bit my tongue I know that. She's sorer'n a boil.'

'I wondered where that blood came from on your mouth.'

'Oh. Well, it come from my tongue not my insides. Feel pretty fair considerin', Fred. Lucky thing you knocked his leg out from under him though. I've a notion he meant to cave in my ribs with that kick.'

Fred looked around at the men. 'Any of you cooks? He needs some food and I suppose we could all use some.'

A man smiled with his eyes and said, 'I've cooked a mite. I'll see what I can do.'

Three men went with him, the sound of their spurs echoed hollowly throughout the house. Fred turned back to Graham.

'How did they catch you fellows at the shack?'

'Damned if I know exactly,' Graham replied. 'Just seemed like all at once there was an army outside shooting hell out of things. I didn't even see 'em until they came through the doorway then me an' the others made the chips fly a while. I wasn't fully awake though until it was all over. Someone liked to have strangled me with the covers on my bunk an' next thing I knew I was outside.'

Fred drew up a little chair and sat down wearily. Graham squinted at him. 'You look like you're about bled out. What happened to you?'

'Nothing. That's Brewster's blood. He dabbed it on me so I'd look dead. That's how I got inside the jail. Two of the boys took me across my horse for the reward. You'll hear about it.'

'I expect,' Graham said. 'You know – when I seen you lyin' on the floor there in Morgan's office I just about cashed in myself. Figured she was all over for all of us an' Ben'd won the last round. Made me feel sicker'n that gunshot ever did.'

Fred made a cigarette and lit it, saw Graham's wistful look and shook his head. Graham didn't ask for tobacco though; he knew better than that.

'Graham – what do you think our chances are of getting more squatters to help us?'

'Plenty good, I'd say, why?'

'I sent the others away to round up reinforcements.'

'All of 'em?' Graham said with unmoving eyes.

'Just about all of them. Listen, Graham; if they don't bring back help – if they'd stayed here with us – we wouldn't have been able to whip Ben's people anyway. No sense in getting everyone shot or hung if we can't win, is there?'

After a pause Graham said, 'I reckon not. By God I'm not going to be took out of no bed an' hung like an outlaw.'

'If they return with help you won't be, Graham.' Fred watched the gray, lined face. 'I think Ben must have about thirty or so men to throw against us. Half of those will be top-notch gunmen.'

Graham said with asperity, 'If the boys're demandin' enough they'd ought to be able to fetch back at least fifty more squatters – dammit. If I was up an' aroun' I think I could get another fifteen or twenty by myself.'

Fred got up at the sound of boots coming down the hallway. He was facing the door when Brewster and Chet came through it. Both men nodded at Graham and spoke then Brewster turned toward Fred.

'I sent a couple of the boys back to sort of keep an eye peeled.'

Fred grinned. 'We make a good team, Brewster. What I forget or overlook you take care of.'

Brewster looked embarrassed with pleasure. 'Well,' he said, 'I don't mind dyin' but I want to know about when it's goin' t'happen.'

Graham's outburst of profanity broke in. He was snarling at Chet. '...At *least* fifty Chet, doggone your pessimistic face anyway. Why – who's been carryin' the flag for 'em for the past couple of years anyway? If they can't help out just once – in the finish fight – then you an' me an' the others been wastin' our time fightin' for 'em at all.'

Brewster's soft laugh soothed the troubled atmosphere of the room. 'Simmer down, Norm. They'll come. You'll see; we'll have fringe ranchers thicker'n flies by dawn. Simmer down.' The tone changed almost imperceptibly. 'Chet; leave him alone. Go on out and pitch some hay to the horses in the big corral.'

Strangely enough Chet showed no resentment at being ordered away by the black-bearded man. After he'd gone Graham gave a mighty and rattling sigh.

'You was right, Fred. Downright right. I didn't plan things the way I should've an' I didn't use the right men either. I know all that now.' He paused, looked at black-eyed Brewster, then added. 'I'm sure glad you showed up, feller. Lord; I'm hungrier'n a bitchwolf.'

Fred smiled, winked at Brewster. 'That's a good sign. He'll be up and around within another week.'

'Week!' Graham stormed. 'If you fellers're figurin' t'hold out here at Big Lily when Ben shows up I'll be mended enough to aid a little racket of my own – an' that's a gut, too.'

The men came in from the kitchen. They had a big tray with cups and plates of something that smelled good and resembled hash. Graham was fed, Brewster and Fred took plates, teetered cups full of black coffee, and ate in the thick silence that engulfed the house. No one spoke until the plates were empty, the cups half empty then Fred said: 'How long before sunup?'

Graham answered in a strong tone. 'Three, four hours maybe. Comes up earlier summertimes.'

Fred put aside his cup and plate, stood up and beckoned Brewster. They walked down the corridor, through the old parlor, dark and ghostly looking, and out under the sparkling slather of stars.

'Brewster, I've got to find the girl.'

'I reckon so,' Brewster said simply over a paper trough he poured tobacco into. 'I kind of figured you'd be anxious about that, Fred.'

'If we've got four hours until sunup I think I'll–'

'No, you can't do that. Listen, Fred, where ever she's at she's safe by now.'

Fred turned to face him. The black eyes were steady, compassionate and wet-shiny. They didn't move nor blink.

'Or dead.'

Brewster hesitated over a reply. 'The desert'll be crawlin' with Ben's boys by now, Fred. You wouldn't get 'thin five miles of where the boys last seen her tracks. If she's dead you'd never find it out by gettin' killed too.'

Fred turned away with a heavy tread. Brewster watched him go as far as the bunkhouse, stop a moment before the door then enter. He smoked thoughtfully, darker than the night itself.

Fred stood in the center of the bunkhouse sniffing the cordite smell of the place. Outlines were coats hanging on nails, pieces of horse equipment, boxes of personal things. He moved over beside the single table and leaned on it looking out the rear window at the dark desert that ran as far as the rim of the world, darkened, gray-speckled here and there, gloomy and silent.

Brewster was right. He wouldn't get close enough to Tucomcori to find Lillian and if he was caught he'd never live to know what had become of her. What other thing might he do?

He dropped down at the table with the answer ready in mind. Nothing. Personally he could do nothing until the threat and danger of his cousin was removed. His mind went back to their brief talk on the jailhouse floor and a fist balled on the tabletop but in his heart he knew Lillian had been lucky. Ben would have killed her. He looked up. He still would kill her if he found her and here sat Fred unable to go to her defense. No – but she knew this too and she'd stay away from any place Ben might be. Could she?

He got up and went as far as the open doorway, leaned there looking at the night, at the stars overhead remembering that she'd wondered how far off they were; if he and she could go to a star and find peace, find happiness, there. He dropped his gaze to the yard. Brewster still stood like a lean shadow over by the house. The tiny arc of his cigarette flared occasionally, aside from that there was no sign of movement, of life.

Where would she have gone? Where had she been going when Brewster had shot her horse? Had he wounded her too? No; not likely. Not the way her tracks went wide and hurrying. A .45 in your flesh stopped you for a while and a girl would be downed by it. Why had she fired at Brewster in the first place? Probably because fear of Ben and pursuit made her do it.

Then Fred remembered telling the men before they'd ridden up to Big Lily not to let anyone escape from the ranch. Any one at all. His eyes grew bitter with self-accusation. But no; Brewster would have fired at her anyway after she fired at him.

Brewster's voice came musically, softly, across the yard. 'Horses comin', Fred.'

He stepped out through the bunkhouse doorway listening. The hush was complete, almost alive. For seconds he heard nothing then faintly the rhythmic boom of riders pulsed in the air. He moved away from the bunkhouse, went over beside the leaner man and by then he could hear the sound better.

'If it ain't our boys?' Brewster said, dropping and stomping his cigarette.

Fred turned toward the house. 'Graham's room's best,' he said.

Graham and the men sitting with him had heard nothing. Fred told them to bring their carbines into the room. As they hurried away he and Brewster wrenched at the windows, flung them open and the sound of riders was strong in the air. Graham asked the moot question.

'Who are they?'

'Don't know yet,' Brewster answered.

Fred had his head lowered, turning a little. He spoke to Brewster from that position. 'Sounds like they're coming from the east.'

No one spoke. The two squatters came back into the room carrying three carbines. Without speaking Graham held his arm up. The third carbine was passed to him. He started up in the bed but Fred shook his head.

'You stay there. No need to worry yet.' He moved away from the window and blew down a lamp chimney dousing the light entirely. From the blackness he said, 'Brewster – go out by the front door. You other two go over and get inside the bunkhouse. If it's Ben's riders bar the door and keep them out in the yard.'

When he was alone with Graham the older man said, 'By God, I'd give five years of my life for one good shot at Ben Nolan.'

Fred didn't answer. The horsemen were swinging wide from the sounds they made. Coming in from the south, over behind the barn. He went through the house to the broken-shuttered window, pushed it open and watched.

The men broke around the corner of the barn and made no effort to draw rein. Fred watched them with a sinking heart. There were at least twenty of them. Graham's yell came thinly over the thunder of hoofbeats and Fred hurried back to his room.

The sick man was crouched by the window with his carbine resting over the sill. 'Cussed army o' 'em, Fred. This damned dark – I can't see a face.'

'Fred! Fred – you in there!'

Graham's breath rushed out of him like a tiny tornado. He stood up and turned his back on the window went over to the bed and sank down on it and swore in weak-voiced relief. Fred turned heavily and started for the front door. When he got there Brewster was still standing back in the shadows. Fred stopped.

'Do you recognize any of them?'

'From here?' Brewster said, 'I'm no owl.'

Fred called out, 'Who's out there? The one who yelled come over here by the front door.'

The man came with a swagger and a naked carbine in his fist. He smiled up at Fred with broken snags of teeth. 'Two to one ye said, Fred. Well – me an' a couple others brang back a few.'

Brewster stepped out the shadows with a raffish smile. 'You liked to scairt the heart right out of me, Alvin. Put up your horses and bring the boys into the house.'

Fred said nothing, watched the swaggering stump of an old man go back. His heart beat steadily and strongly again, 'Will the others do as good?' he asked Brewster.

The black-bearded man laughed softly. 'If they don't – if they all just come back before sun-up – we'll be pretty hard to beat, Fred.'

Together they went back to Graham's room and sat down, neither caring to think, let alone remark, on how weak their legs felt right then.

Graham said, 'Light that cussed lamp again one o' you. Like to put the fear o' hangrope into me for fair that time. Phew.'

Brewster lit the lamp when heavy footfalls filled the corridor. Fred watched the men file in. Most of them were puffy-eyed from being roused out of bed but a few quite obviously hadn't been to bed. He studied their faces, their sagging shell-belts, and felt better than he'd felt in days.

'Any more coming – do you know?'

The squatty man with the bad teeth nodded. 'Yep. Six more're comin' with Lathrop. Ain't seen none o' the other boys since I lef' here.' Grinning like Infinite Evil he added. 'Whole damned country's stirred up. Most o' these fellers was just waitin' for word on where we was holed up. Itchin' to join us.'

Fred said,'Did you see any of the town men or Ben's riders?'

That brought a ripple of chuckles from the squatters. 'Nope,' the old man said, 'an' I didn't look for none, but from what these boys tol' me he's got 'em ridin' every which way.'

A younger man, short and stocky with a smooth face and clear blue eyes stepped forward. 'I was in town when you fellers busted out of the jailhouse an' shot Josh Morgan. Hung around a spell to see what was goin' on. Nolan's offered a hundred dollar bounty for any fringe rancher's hide that rode with you Mister Nolan, an' he's got all his crew plus about fifty more from town huntin' the lot of us. I seen 'em ride out of town. Folks're sayin' this is showdown. There's a lot of feelin' in the country.'

The two men from the bunkhouse came into the room with wide eyes, not quite relaxed nor understanding. For a moment they stared at the latercomers then someone made a dry remark about their expressions and a burst of laughter followed. Fred felt relief as fully as the others but he didn't join in the banter.

'Brewster; I think we'd better have these men fan out and watch for Ben's people.' He turned toward the squatters. 'Don't fight them when you see them. Fall back on the ranch.'

'Surround 'em?' A man asked.

'Something like that,' Fred said. 'Half of you hole up in the bunkhouse. Bar the door good and solid. The other half hole up in the barn behind the house.'

'What about the blacksmith shop and chicken house?' Graham asked, sitting up with a sparkle to his glance.

'Not these men,' Fred said. 'The others who come we'll put in there. If it works out right, Norm, we should have men in every building. That way Ben's men will be exposed and our men will be under cover.'

Brewster repeated the instructions minutely and also told the newcomers to find and absorb the two men he had out on the desert as sentinels. A little more banter then the squatters trooped out of the house leaving Fred and Brewster alone in Graham's room. The sick man was scowling.

'Hope our boys don't shoot any others that come ridin' in.'

'I doubt if that will happen,' Fred said. 'These aren't green hands with guns, from the looks of them.'

Graham snorted. 'Not so's you'd notice it,' he said.

Brewster sat down again. 'What's your notion, Fred; get our boys under cover in all the buildings?'

'You heard that much of it,' Fred replied, 'but there's more to it. If Ben comes down the road he'll be exposed as long as he crosses the meadow. Like we were yesterday before dawn. If the buildings are held by squatters Ben won't only be forced to fight in the open, he'll also be pretty well closed off by the time he gets in front of the house or smithy. The buildings are arranged in a slight half-moon circle. You can see that. It will amount to half a surround if it's worked right.'

Brewster shook his head. 'I don't have that much faith in people,' he said. 'Sure as the devil someone'll open up before Ben gets close enough to the house. That, or some of his men'll see ours out on the desert.'

Fred went over by the bed and sat on the foot of it. 'Maybe. It doesn't really matter how it starts I suppose, just as long as we have at least an even break with them.'

Brewster stood up. 'I reckon I'm goin' outside and walk aroun' a little. Got the jumps tonight.'

Fred squinted at the sky. 'Daybreak isn't far off. If any more are coming they'd better come soon.'

Brewster walked out of the room, down the hallway toward the dining room and kitchen and Graham swung his head fully, lay there gloomily staring outside. Fred felt his own nerves crawling like worms under his skin and tried to dull them with a cigarette.

His nervousness was worst just before the sky began to fade off in the east. More horsemen coming didn't offset his gnawed tag-ends until they reined up and he saw Brewster materialize out of the dark at the corner of the house, walk forward and talk to them, then turn and call for Fred.

He went out, felt the sudden chill of false dawn, and counted the riders. Twelve. With a sweep of his arm he pointed toward the blacksmith shop and chicken house and when they understood where they were to hide he asked them if they'd seen the other squatters on their way in. They had. In fact they'd been caught flat-footed by a surround of them and grinned ruefully about it. Fred motioned them away with a long glance at the horizon.

'Brewster?'

'Yeah.'

'Ride up where those men are and tell them to come back and get into position.'

'Ain't goin' t'wait for Ben?'

'No. If they haven't come by now there's

no sense in waiting in broad daylight for them.'

Brewster left, cleaving a path through the dismounting reinforcements and before any of them had moved far they heard more riders coming and Brewster turned toward Fred with a broad smile and said: 'Two to one, Fred. I think we about got it.'

The last riders came loping into the yard from the west. A man in the lead clucked like a turkey gobbler. Fred turned slowly to see. It had been a long time since he'd heard the sound and it still made his hair stiffen. The Comanche gobble, forerunner, warning, of death to come.

Seven of them. Fred watched them dismount. He heard the others calling to them and out of the corner of his eye he saw a tall, lean figure lope across the yard with upraised arm. Brewster.

'Seven more, Mister Nolan. How many more we got now?'

Fred tried to remember the face and couldn't. He didn't answer the question right away. 'Where'd you learn to make that sound?'

'The gobble? Oh – in Texas.' The man was watching him looking a little abashed.

Fred said, 'With your seven we've got close to forty men. Maybe a few over.'

'Is that enough you reckon?'

'It ought to be,' Fred answered. 'If every

man acts like two.'

The Texan chuckled. 'Box 'em into buildings an' I reckon they'll sure's hell *sound* like an army.'

'Put up your horses and go into the main house. Place your men everywhere you think Ben's boys might try to get in.'

'I suppose they'll be along directly,' the Texan said conversationally. 'We seen a bunch of men ridin' this way hour or so ago. Looked like they might be ridin' from town.'

Fred studied the open face and thought: *They're a breed apart, these Texans, whatever else they are.*

Aloud he said, 'Do you think they're my cousin's riders, Texas?'

'Lord, Mister Nolan, I got no way o' knowin'. We didn't go close. Jus' sat real still an' watched 'em go by a little piece north o' us.' The man drew off a glove and ran a long finger under his nose. 'I felt they wasn't squatters; townsmen or Big Lily men some of the boys said.'

'Did you rider faster than they did to get back here?'

'Lordy yes, Mister Nolan. We calculated they'd be stirrin' up a ruckus an' we didn't want t'be betwixt them an' nothin' or they could cut us t'pieces.'

'Were they riding fast?'

'Nossir – slow. All bunched up an' slow. I reckon it'll take 'em 'nother half hour 'for they get here.'

'Thanks,' Fred said. 'Put up your stock and take your stand in the main house.'

He was turning toward the bunkhouse when the Texan said 'Yes, sir.' It snapped in the pale light like a soldier's way of speaking.

At the bunkhouse some stragglers were lounging. Fred asked them if Brewster had come back with the other men. They told him he hadn't.

'When he does, ask him to put the men where we decided they should stay and come on over to Graham's room; will you?'

'Sure, be proud to.'

The yard was teeming with movement. Fred watched the men briefly then turned to face the east. The ribbon of pale blue was turning pink. As he watched the slit widened, grew redder, more pronounced and solid looking and a soft earth-shadow lifted above the desert. The new day was arriving.

Brewster came back in a clattering lope with men trailing in his wake. He was swinging off before his horse slammed into a stiff-legged set-up.

'Fred; they're comin'. The boys seen 'em just before I got up there.'

He walked closer, saw the dirt and excitement on the bearded face. 'How many did it look like?'

'All Ben's crew an' a few more. Maybe

fifteen, twenty in all.'

'Then they're coming back for breakfast or a change of horses and don't suspect anything.'

Brewster's head bobbed. 'I figured it that way too.' The black eyes clung to Fred's face expectantly. 'Now what?'

'If that's all there is,' Fred said, 'only put half the men with you into the buildings. Take the rest – and you – and go out a ways and lie flat. Let them get all the way up to the house and don't let a man speak, cough, or even wiggle, until I tell you to.'

'We'll be behind 'em. Good. You don't want to fight 'em. That it?'

'That's it,' Fred said, 'but if hell breaks loose get around behind the bunkhouse. Brewster; you'll be in a bad position if a fight starts.'

The black eyes shone. 'Been there afore a time or two.' Brewster trotted away leading his horse and calling urgently to the men who had come back with him.

Fred watched the daylight spread, grow deep and solid looking with a spectrum of colors slanting down over everything, then he went as far as the front entrance to Ben's house, slouched in the doorway and looked out over the yard. There wasn't a man in sight nor a horse. A stillness had settled. A stillness that throbbed with life, with repressed excitement with fervor so thick he wondered if the oncoming riders wouldn't feel it – sense it.

He saw them a little later, riding southward over the ranch road. Some were smoking and all slumped like tired men. An occasional lift of gray-blue smoke swirled above them. An occasional word came through the hush and Fred drew in a big breath and let it out slowly. All right, Ben; I think this is a day we'll both remember a long time.

The first rider booted his weary horse into a shambling lope and pulled up halfway across the yard when he saw Fred moving away from the house toward him. Reined up and held his rein-hand high, his head twisted in scowling wonder, in half suspicion, half challenge. He sat like that while a few other men loped up behind him and stopped, craning their necks at the man walking toward them.

'Who're you, pardner?' There was a crispness to the words but no menace.

Fred stopped with his hand resting lightly on the gun at his hip. 'Get down, men. Dismount.'

Now they were all clustered close, staring. Fred went closer still. A flicker of movement far off dimly seen was Brewster rising up slowly, his carbine to his shoulder. There were nearly a dozen other shapes behind him all aiming guns toward the mounted men.

'Who the hell are you?'

'I'm the man you've been looking for all night,' Fred said, then went on speaking. 'And if you think you've captured me look around there behind you. Look at the cracks in the smithy and the chicken house. Look at the door of the bunkhouse and the main house.'

The men were frozen. Eyes moved swiftly, dartingly, but for a long time none of them would risk turning away long enough to look behind. One man finally did and his curses dropped slowly, like lead, into the hush; softly, dazedly.

Fred bobbed his head once. 'Get down.'

The crucial moment passed when the first rider lowered his hands to the saddlehorn and gazed stupidly behind them, at the bunkhouse door, at the blacksmith shop and the main house. His breath came out past tightly held teeth and he said, 'Down, fellers, we walked right into it.'

Fred felt detached from their shock, their startled bewilderment. He watched the men come out of the bunkhouse toward them. Pluck guns from saddleboots and holsters and move off with them and when it was all over he asked who they were. The burly man with his jacket collar turned up answered. The others were perfectly still, like statues.

'Big Lily riders. I'm Huff, the foreman.'

'Where's Ben?'

'He didn't come with us.'

'So I see,' Fred said dryly. 'Where is he, when'll he be along?'

'I don't know,' the foreman said. 'I got no idea. Las' I seen of Ben he was bein' patched up in the leg by a sawbones in Tucomcori.'

'What did he tell you when you saw him?'

Men were moving into the silence slowly. They came from almost every direction. The Big Lily riders watched them come in the same lingering silence.

'He tol' me to bring the crew with me back here an' get fresh horses an' some chuck, then head south for the border an' – try to find you.'

Chet came up close where Fred stood. He grunted. 'I know that one. He's the feller I seen when they jumped us with the cattle. I think he's the foreman or something, too, Fred.'

Fred ignored Chet. He faced Huff with an emerald glance. 'Where did Ben think I'd be; down along the border?'

'Or over it,' Huff said, his voice gaining strength. 'He's got a lot of men combing the Territory for you, Nolan.'

Brewster, walking up, said, 'Put a Mister in front of that, feller.'

Huff's face darkened, '*Mister* Nolan,' he said, looking stonily at Fred.

'How many men?'

'Sixty, I'd guess. Around that many.'

'Where are they?'

'Scattered between here'n Mexico as far as I know.'

'Did Ben tell any more to come here?'

'Not that I know of.'

Fred looked over at Brewster. An unlit cigarette dangled from the bearded man's mouth, jutted past the foliage on his face ridiculously.

'Brewster, I've got an idea. This may not be the place to wait for them after all.'

Brewster, still staring at the Big Lily riders, nodded. 'Expect you might be right. What'll we do with these?'

Fred gazed at the captives thoughtfully and once, for a second, a hard light shone in his eyes. 'For the time being put a guard around them.' He turned toward Chet. 'Come with me a ways, you two.'

The three of them strolled apart. Men filed the yard and hardly a sound arose. The Big Lily men were still motionless.

Fred stopped near the verandah railing, leaned on it with his hands behind him.

'Ben's in town.'

'Sure,' Brewster said. 'He'll have to stay there too, hurt like he is, an' wait for the others to bring back your scalp.'

'I think so. All right; we'll go to Tucomcori and get him.'

The green light shone again briefly. 'Chet – we'll look pretty darn strong when we ride up to the outskirts of the town with the Big

Lily crew in our midst.'

Chet's mouth fell open.

'We'll use them for effect, Chet. Keep them bunched up in the middle of our own crew. They're unarmed, helpless, but they'll make our band look twice as strong as it is. I don't think the townsmen will want to take the fight up for Ben if they think we're a lot stronger than he is.'

Chet shuffled his feet while the scheme soaked in, but Brewster's wide smile showed admiration, like his jet eyes did, for the plan. In a gentle way he said, 'Fred; I wish you'd come down here a year ago.'

Fred pushed off the railing. 'Want to take the chance?'

Brewster nodded. 'Yes; hell, yes.' He looked at Chet whose face was tableau of conflict. 'Chet does too only he won't know it until we're near town.'

Chet nodded weakly without speaking.

'Chet – you handle the guards around the Big Lily men. Brewster, you round up our men and let's get to leather.'

It didn't take long and whether it worked or not just the cleverness of it, the wiliness, raised the squatter spirits a hundredfold. They got their horses, mounted up and swirled out of the yard with the captives riding humped over and sullen-eyed in their midst. They only stopped once; that was when they saw five riders galloping toward them. Fred flagged the men out to receive the new captives. It worked so well even the Big Lily riders grinned frostily at the astonishment of the captives.

With a minimum of delay the new prisoners were hustled into the center of their column and the squatters moved on again. When they saw the town over the chaparral in the near-distance Fred beckoned for Brewster.

'Tell Chet to see to it that none of those men signal or yell. Tell him to shoot the first one that tries to give us away and say it where they can all hear it.'

Brewster rode away. The town seemed to be lazing in the sunlash. Fred rode with squinted eyes as dry and tired-feeling as grating millstones. The heavy dirge of many horses moving slowly behind him was like a lullaby the way it seeped in behind his tired face, found a response in his blood. He had to shake himself when they were close enough to see people coming out of buildings to stare at the large cavalcade.

He heard men's shouts and then he stopped and the others behind him stopped. With a sweeping gaze backward he estimated the riders to number over seventy-five in number. Formidable looking indeed to the staring townspeople.

'Brewster?'

'Yeah.'

He waited until they were side by side. 'Brewster; if this sours on us we're going to catch it from all sides. Listen: if Ben has more help than it looks like we have, in town, and it turns into a fight, the squatters have lost more than they know. Do you realize that?'

'How do y'mean?'

'Before – Ben's men – didn't know them by sight. Now they do.'

'Oh – I thought you mean because we had a herd of 'em with us.'

Fred shook his head watching the crowds gathering in town. 'No; unarmed they aren't much of a threat. I meant the other way.'

'Well,' Brewster said evenly, 'why then I reckon we just can't let it go sour – can we?'

Fred didn't respond. He sat like a stone looking down into the town. 'I'll go alone,' he said.

'No, I'll go along. Look better if Ben sees a squatter comin' in with you: one he knows.'

Fred made a wry smile. 'Then let's go.'

They rode together without looking back until they were almost to the edge ofTucomcori, where some grub-line-rider shacks were. Fred was mildly surprised at the sight himself.

'Looks like half an army, Brewster.'

'Yeah; the Confederate Army.'

Fred's gaze wandered to the black eyes, held there a moment then moved back to the town. 'I was a Yankee, myself,' he said.

Brewster urged his horse on. 'Things change, Fred. Things and men.' That was all he said.

They rode through the drying dust; little puffs of it jerked to life under their horses' hooves. Fred tried to fight off a morbid feeling and didn't succeed because there was too much pressure on a sleep-groggy mind.

'I wonder if she's in town.'

Brewster didn't look around, act surprised. 'We'll find her,' he said. 'She'll be all right.'

They came down onto the hard packed earth of the north-south roadway with its different sounding echo under them and a slouching man in the doorway of a shack called out: 'You get him, fellers?'

'Who?' Fred answered.

'Why – Fred Nolan, of course.'

'No,' Fred said. 'But he's got Tucomcori.'

The man looked puzzled for a moment, but for a moment only then his face underwent a complete change and he straightened up off the wall and stared after them.

Brewster's fingers were curled around his pistol butt and Fred could feel the tightness, the coiledness, riding beside him. For himself he felt no expectancy, no especial fear or tension, and certainly no triumph. He was too tired for almost any emotion except one – perhaps two – but foremost was the impulse that had put him there riding through the sudden, chill of silence that spread over Tucomcori as though the town *knew*, someway, which he didn't doubt but that by now it did.

Three men walked resolutely out to bar their way. He heard Brewster's breath push past his teeth. 'Easy,' he said. 'Don't make a move. If Ben hasn't gotten them talked into killing us yet don't do anything to help him.'

CHAPTER NINE

'Are you Nolan?'

Fred drew rein gently looking down at the white-faced man. 'I am,' he said. 'Fred Nolan. Where is my cousin, Ben?'

'Listen, Nolan–'

'No,' Fred interrupted quietly, '*you* listen. This fight doesn't involve you townspeople. It's between Ben Nolan and the fringe ranchers. Don't make it any worse than it is by butting in, mister.'

Silence. Brewster's horse shook his head, rattling the reinchains. A massively built man with a long, dolorous face pushed clear of the crowd. Blacksmith was written all over him; would have been instantly apparent even without the muleskin apron across his front and down to his knees.

'That's sense,' he said gruffly, loudly. 'We shouldn't take sides anyway. But if you was t'ask me, why I'd say Ben Nolan's been askin' for this f' a long time.'

That time the silence was broken by Fred. He had both hands in plain sight on the saddlehorn, a composed, calm expression on his face and a belly full of writhing worms.

'You can see the squatters back out there. They mean business. If you want trouble you'll get it but I think you'll be wiser than that. I'm here to talk to my cousin and I'm going to talk to him.'

'Hang him, you mean,' someone shouted from the rear of the crowd.

'No, not hang him. I'm here to talk to him, that is all and there're close to a hundred men back out there who will back me up in that.'

'Like y' done to Josh Morgan.'

'I didn't shoot Morgan.'

That stopped them, even the ones far back who felt the bravest. Fred let it lie a moment before he went on.

'I didn't shoot Morgan but I know things about him that would make his killing almost justifiable. If you want to hear them, take me to my cousin and you shall, but a word more to you. The first gunshot, the first thing that looks like you want to fight and you'll get a fight you'll never forget.'

He could read the crowd's change in its faces. Doubt, here and there wholehearted backing, but mainly wonder and blankness tempered with curiosity and a willingness to listen, to be convinced.

Fred glanced at the three men who still barred their way. 'Well?'

The blacksmith said, 'Take 'em to him f' Crissake, there's only two of them.'

That summed up the attitude of most of the people. Other voices were raised. The three self-appointed lawmen turned toward one another. They spoke briefly, heatedly, for a moment then the youngest one looked up and nodded at Fred.

'All right; come on.'

When Brewster dismounted he drew his carbine too. Fred shook his head at him.

'Leave it.'

The black eyes were stony until a voice called out with laughter in it. 'It wouldn't be no help, Blackie. On'y six more seconds afore you'd be killed anyway.'

Laughter rippled through the crowd, Brewster turned with a little squint up around his eyes and shoved the gun back into the boot. When he faced Fred he was almost grinning.

The crowd parted to make way for the lawmen and Fred, with Brewster just behind him. For some reason the thick-boned blacksmith trudged along behind Brewster.

Once he called to some men.

'Fetch him over to my porch; I'll take 'em there.'

Brewster screwed up his face trying to imagine what the blacksmith meant but the man didn't raise his face, he plodded along with his head down and only once raised his eyes. That was where he called to the law-men up ahead. 'My place, fellers. Up on the porch.'

Fred stopped when the guides wheeled and hauled up in front of a white fence and gate. One of them sprung the latch and jerked a thumb.

'In there.'

The house was small, and drooping, disconsolate hollihocks were sun-limp before the porch. A big woman was standing, watching them. Her almost shaggy brows were lowered and stormy looking. Fred went through the gate with Brewster and the blacksmith behind him. They climbed the few stairs to the porch and halted there. The big woman in the doorway didn't budge. The three lawmen looked around at the blacksmith. He jabbed a huge thumb toward some chairs and benches but no one sat down.

Fred moved to one side of the porch where he could see the people crowding up around the little picket fence. Brewster stayed close beside him.

'Well,' the blacksmith said irritably, 'what's keepin' 'em?'

One of the lawmen gazed anxiously over the crowd's head and Fred unconsciously followed his glance. He saw two men supporting a third and coming from the direction of the Marshal's office. A murmur ran through the crowd, it parted grudgingly for Ben Nolan's supporters. Nolan had a thick cudgel he used for a cane and his face was averted. Sweat stood out on his forehead. Fred looked beyond his limping cousin, beyond the hushed mass of people northward but the raw edges of buildings cut off his view of the squatters. He could feel perspiration dampening the back of his shirt. He made a cigarette, with the undertone of voices around him like an ocean, lit it and exhaled upwards. Brewster held out his hand for the makings and Fred passed them over, watched the black-bearded man twist up a cigarette of his own and his eyes strayed to his cousin's face again, closer now.

Ben looked pale, wan even. He didn't put any weight on his injured leg and his lips curled into unspoken curses every now and then.

Brewster lit his cigarette and gazed down at the hobbling man. He allowed himself a tight, mirthless smile. Softly he spoke aside to Fred. 'Too bad you didn't raise your sights a mite.'

The blacksmith went down the steps and held the gate open, said something brusque to the people who crowded too close and stepped off the plankwalk when the men helped Ben Nolan through the gate.

The silence deepened as Ben came up the steps. The crowd was absorbed with the drama and Fred watched as they helped Ben to the porch swing, a slat affair suspended from the roof with chains. He still felt neither pity nor triumph. Objectively he went over each feature. There was ruthlessness, fierceness, bitterness in every line. He wondered if, seeing someone else Ben might not look differently. *Lillian?* His mind said. The cigarette smouldered and eventually died between his fingers. Ben's mouth twisted up to form a six letter word and Fred headed it off.

'We've got an audience, Ben. I don't suppose you'd want to tell them about beating Lillian would you? There's a lot you can't say now, isn't there, but I reckon there're enough of these people here who recall how Joshua Morgan dallied over the Emmons killing – or was it the Hull killing – to want to hear about that.'

Ben sat in deep silence, listening, hating so that it flared out of his eyes and filled his expression. There was room for nothing else in his face but the hatred. Fred's quiet tone didn't help any.

'How about a woman named Graham burnt to death in a squatter shack, Ben? How about an old man named Milton who was dragged behind a running horse. I saw him, but after he died. His neck was six inches longer than God had made it.'

Gripped by the drama no one spoke, moved. Brewster was off to one side where he could see the crowd. His arms hung limply at his sides, a trickle of smoke wandered up from his bearded mouth.

'The only crime any of these people did that I can determine, Ben, was that they wanted something you wanted, too. In your eyes that's always been a murder warrant. I know.'

'You mouthy butcher,' Ben said tightly. 'You dirty rotten killer. If you didn't murder that Texan, Beltry, why'd you run?'

'You know why. Because you'd been making it impossible for me to live with your folks and you for a long time and because I finally grew up. As for the Beltry fight, Ben, I've got witnesses that it wasn't murder.'

'You bought 'em just like you've bought those squatters. With lies and promises.'

'Is that how you bought Morgan? There were four men in the room when Morgan told us about you; about the way he held back after the Emmons killing because he knew you wanted him to.'

'Witnesses?' Ben Nolan snorted. 'More squatters. More liars and night-riders.'

Fred shook his head slowly. 'I don't think so. If they are then I reckon a lot of this crowd is too, because there are squatters in it; squatter womenfolk and kinsmen. If that's right, Ben, then the whole Tucomcori countryside must be made up of liars and night-riders. Is that right?'

Ben's color flushed darkly, his mouth moved over words he didn't utter.

'Ben – you're washed up here, finished. If it takes me the rest of my life I'm going to get witnesses against you. I'm sorry Morgan's gone because he would have been the best witness in the West.'

'Then why'd you kill him?' Ben said triumphantly.

'I didn't kill him. I didn't even have my gun cocked when he was killed.'

'But one–'

'I'll get enough witnesses to hang you, Ben, and I don't think it'll be hard to do.'

'Hang hell,' Ben stormed. 'You won't get anyone around here dumb enough to say a word against me and you know it. I've stood up for my rights and I've helped the honest people around Tucomcori. But you – why – you're nothin' but a tinhorn renegade and we all know *that* too.'

'Ben, I can prove you killed Hull and Emmons. I can prove you killed Old Man

Milton. I'll get the rest of it out in the open too.'

Ben's glare swung out to the crowd. 'He'd try to get an honest man put into his own cussed boots.'

Unruffled, Fred went on speaking. 'I've got your Big Lily gunmen corralled, Ben. Unarmed and prisoners. They'll know enough about you to get you hung.'

'You couldn't get 'thin pistol range of the poorest of those men, Fred, and you know it. Captured – unarmed–,' Ben Nolan threw back his head and laughed aloud.

Brewster leaned closer. 'I'll flag the boys to ride down here, Fred. Let him see who's a prisoner.'

'No, they're more valuable where they are yet a while.'

Ben's laugh stopped in mid-sound. He dropped his flushed face and looked at the crowd. 'Here's six thousand dollars gold standing in front of you, boys.' He leaned forward to emphasize his next words. 'I'll double it. Double it.' With an arm flung out toward Fred he said, 'There's twelve thousand dollars in gold to anyone who wants to collect it.'

Brewster was facing the crowd fully now, black eyes like agate, perfectly still, wide. The blacksmith rumbled deep in his throat like an annoyed grizzly.

'Never mind that kind of talk, Ben. The

worst thing you could do is try an' incite a killin' here, right now.'

Ben leaned back and glared. 'What's it to you, Cuff? Whose business is this if it isn't mine?'

'I expect,' the blacksmith rumbled with a lowering look, 'it's ever'one's affair, Ben. If him, there, can prove what he's said I think it ought to concern all o' us.'

'Prove it!' Ben Nolan spat out. 'He can't prove anything except that there's a price on his head; that he's an outlaw, black heart, lyin' tongue and all.'

The blacksmith stood his ground. 'Then if he can't prove nothin' he'll probably get hung but at least he come in here and wanted to talk. We ought to hear him out.'

'You're a fool,' Ben said savagely. 'He's fooled you like he's fooled those squatters; well, he doesn't fool me a bit. I've known him too many years.'

Doggedly the smith spoke again. 'Ben – let me say somethin' on my own. First off, folks aren't near as dumb as you've always thought they was. Folks have seen things you've done an' they've heard other things you've done. Most of us haven't never spoke up because we wasn't sure and besides it wasn't none of our affair, but I reckon havin' Tucomcori turnt into a battlefield's gettin' pretty close to home – it is for me anyway – and I don't expect to jus' sit here and see you an' the fringe outfits kill a lot of folks an' maybe burn the town – not on your life.'

Ben was watching the broad face with a curious expression. He didn't look away until the blacksmith's rumble had died away, then he spoke in the mildest tone he'd used thus far.

'Cuff, you're a good blacksmith; let it go at that. There's a whale of a lot you don't know. You say we ought to listen to Fred. All right – we've listened, and so far all he's done is to try to paint me blacker'n he is, with lies.'

'We'll hold him,' the blacksmith said stubbornly. 'We'll get the judge to settle it.'

'Hold him? Cuff – you darned fool – he isn't here to surrender to the law, he's come here with a cussed army to scare us all into doing what he wants done, and that means stringing me up by the gullet.'

Fred broke in with a sharp retort. 'Is that why you beat Lillian; because I made you do it? I can prove too that I wasn't within two thousand miles of Tucomcori, Ben, when *you* had two men killed and another dragged to death.'

Ben half arose from the swing. He brushed aside the two remarks about the killings with a savage gesture. 'Lillian? She's gone – taken from my house where she was stayin'. We were going to be married an' you stole her, Fred– *Deny that – damn you!*'

The blacksmith threw up his head like he'd been stung. His pale eyes widened and his mouth fell open. Very slowly he turned a perplexed look to his wife. The big woman looked from her husband to Ben Nolan. Very distinctly she said:

'Mister Nolan you're mistaken.'

'Am I!' Ben roared. 'Mistaken hell!' He pointed a rigid arm at Fred. 'Miss Malone came here for our wedding. That dirty whelp rode up to my ranch when I wasn't there and – and – *kidnapped her!* That's how mistaken I am. He's probably killed her by now; he was on the same train with her coming down here and she told me he pestered her all the way.'

Fred was looking at the blacksmith whose heavy face was as dark as a thundercloud. 'Ben – did you beat that girl like Fred here said you did?'

'That's another of his lies,' Ben said violently. 'We're goin' to be married, can you understand that, you old fool.'

'You never hit her then?' the blacksmith said without moving a muscle, with the blackness of his face unabated.

'No, I never hit her; if anyone abused Lillian it was him.'

'Ben,' the blacksmith said icily, 'you're a liar.'

As though he'd been struck across the face Ben Nolan reached back to steady himself on the porch swing. He looked unbelieving, shocked numb. 'Cuff,' he said in a dangerously mild tone of voice. 'Did you mean that just now?'

The blacksmith's brooding face moved a little. He jerked his head toward his wife. 'Fetch her,' he said and Fred came off the porch railing slowly, like a man in a trance. The crowd was frozen into immobility. Somewhere there was a sound of horsemen walking their mounts through the deserted town. A dog barked shrill, staccato.

Lillian came through the doorway, behind her was the forbidding face of the blacksmith's wife, arms clasped across her chest. Fred couldn't move. Before he could speak again the blacksmith said:

'Did you hear what he said, Lillian?'

'Yes, I heard.'

'Was he lyin'?'

She swept a look at Ben and turned away. Fred's feet came loose from the porch flooring then. He moved closer to her, saw her eyes lift to him with a bare look in their depths. 'Yes, he was lying. He tried to – kill me. I got away from him. He caught me before I got out of the house. He knocked me down, dragged me by the arm back to the bedroom and struck me twice more. My ear bled after he'd struck me the last time, I – came to myself on the floor. I got out through the window that time and stole a horse and rode as hard as I could. Someone was after me. I thought it was Ben, I shot at the man. He shot back and killed my horse.'

The blacksmith spoke into the silence when Lillian faltered. 'Ben – if you'd lie about a thing as black as beatin' hell out'n a woman, I expect you'd lie about other things just as bad.' He looked around at Fred. 'Young feller, if you'll give up that gun an' tell your squatters to go home an' let you be tried fair an' square I'll pledge you my life you'll get that kind of a trial – an' so'll Ben. What say?'

Fred felt for the gun in his holster, lifted it out and offered it butt first. He didn't speak.

'Wait a minute,' a voice sang out from the rear of the crowd. 'Fred, you don't have to do no such thing.'

Fred looked. They were all there at the outer edge of the crowd. Fred raised his voice a little. 'This is probably the best way, boys. There won't be any trouble – no shooting.' He thought to himself he had only come down here to clear up a false reputation anyway and this ought to do that and more.

The blacksmith took his gun and turned toward Ben. 'Yours too, Ben.' Ben made no move to offer it. He was staring with steady animosity and contempt toward the Big Lily riders surrounded by armed squatters.

The smith leaned over and took Ben's

gun. Unconsciously he hefted the weapons, turned half around and spoke to the three self-appointed lawmen. Fred heard the tumble of his voice but not the words.

'Lillian…'

She moved closer. 'It's been a nightmare, Fred.'

'How did you get here?'

'Mr Clark – the blacksmith – was walking home. I came into town through the back alley behind his shop. We met in the dark and he took me home with him. I was crying, I think.'

He could picture it without much effort, bruised, frightened almost to death, badly beaten. He didn't speak and she looked up into his face with the same stirring beauty he had first noticed on the train.

'Fred, I'll tell you about it sometime. Right now I'd rather not talk about it.'

'Sure,' he said. 'That's all right.'

'What will happen now?' Her gaze was anxious and pained.

He smiled a little. 'There'll be a court trial I suppose. It's relief, Lillian, in a way. I'm tired, and sick of fighting. If the trial's fair I don't think I'll be hurt much.'

Neither of them said anything. Fred looked over her head, saw the blacksmith's wife staring at them, looked farther and heard the voices around them. The interim lawmen were helping Ben Nolan to his feet.

Ben's face was white, his lips bloodless-looking. Fred reached down for Lillian's hand, squeezed it and dropped it. He moved away, touched the blacksmith's shoulder.

'Are you going to lock him up?'

'Yes.'

'I'll go too.'

The blacksmith was still holding the two large pistols. He nodded his head and said 'Yes' again.

Brewster brushed against Fred, 'I'll be down to see you in a little bit, Fred.'

'Fine. Tell Chet and the others to go home, stay out of trouble. If anything happens now it'll cook my chances.'

'Sure.' Brewster said. 'I understand, only what about the Big Lily riders?'

Fred caught the blacksmith's eye, the burly man crossed to where he and Brewster stood.

'We have Ben's gunhands. Hadn't you better lock them up too until the law's satisfied which ones have been in on his night-riding deals?'

The blacksmith's forehead wrinkled in thought then he nodded and went back toward the steps off the porch where the lawmen were assisting wounded Ben Nolan. He spoke to them and one, with an irritated look, beckoned to Brewster.

'Blackie, tell those fellers to take the Lily men to the jail, will you?'

Brewster went out through the gate without speaking. The crowd parted in dumb-watching silence.

Fred saw the blacksmith looking at him. He turned to Lillian. 'I won't be hard to find for a while. Will you come down and see me?'

She didn't dare smile so she nodded vigorously.

Fred went down the steps and through the crowd with the blacksmith. When they were through the silent crowd of townsmen the mounted squatters were riding slowly toward the jail with the Big Lily men. Chet turned back and waited for Fred. He leaned from the saddle, put a gloved hand on Fred's shoulder to stop him.

'We'll do what Brewster says. Feller I knew in the crowd said you needed lots of witnesses against Ben. If that's right leave it to us, Fred. We'll get plenty of 'em.'

'Thanks, Chet, do that, but no gunplay – no trouble.'

'No,' Chet said, 'that's past. Now it'll be law-book feudin' an' we can fight that way too.'

They went on. In the subdued noise and press of bodies in the Marshal's office Fred and the smith edged back against a wall waiting for the Big Lily men to be locked up first. Ben Nolan was already put away through the oak door where the cages were, beyond.

'Nolan,' the blacksmith said, 'can you prove you never killed Lon Hull and Rufe Emmons?'

'I can prove I was in Boston, Massachusetts, when they were killed.'

'The *day* they were killed?'

'Yes.'

The smith sighed. His brows were knit, he didn't look up at Fred. In a ponderous voice he said, 'You'd ought to seen that girl when I found her wanderin' around in the alleyway. She had blood on her face. She'd been slugged in the ear, clothes nigh tore off her, pretty badly beat up. I took her home. The Missus worried over her like an old hen.'

'It's a good thing you found her,' Fred said, thinking what would have happened if Ben had found her instead.

'Yeah. You know, I was about half for Ben until he put out them lies about her. After that I knew he'd been lyin' right along.' The blacksmith finally looked up. 'She told us what he did to her an' y'know, I still sort of doubted it. Didn't seem a man'd do that to a girl an' she was pretty delirious seemed to me.' The eyes swung away again, sombre, outraged eyes. 'I never cottoned to Ben much but like I said on the porch, too much hearsay makes you suspect everything you hear about a feller.'

'Nolan!'

Fred stepped up to the desk. The office

had been cleared of the curious. There was a strong smell of men and horsemeat in the room. He gave his name, his age, profession and last address – everything the official lawman asked, then he too was put into a strap-steel cage and left alone.

The others were in adjoining cells. Except for glares of hate though none of them spoke. Fred punched the straw pallet into the semblance of a bedroll, flopped down on it and slept.

He was still sleeping the following morning when someone shook him by the shoulder. It was the blacksmith and one of the lawmen. The smith half lifted him off the pallet.

'Lord A'mighty; you dead or deaf, Nolan? Here's a razor. Go out t'the sink an' spruce up a mite?'

Fred stretched and stood up. 'What for?'

'You got a visitor an' you ought t'look decent f'her.'

The green eyes grew still. 'Her? Lillian?'

'Yeh. Hurry up an' clean up she's waitin'.'

The sink was long, low, and deep. It was also stained from the hurried ablutions of many prisoners. Fred shaved with lye-soap and cold water, scrubbed himself as best he could and, in twisting back into his shirt saw Ben Nolan's fierce eyes on him from a secluded little cell blanked off from the other cells by a dirty canvas. Neither man spoke. Fred finished dressing and went toward the outer door with an awareness of Ben's venom filling his mind.

Lillian was there and the blacksmith stood over by the door looking across at him but the three lawmen were absent. She stood facing him eyes large, misty, shoulders not squared but not slumped either. He could see the strange smouldering listlessness deep in her expression. He smiled at her forgetting the broad, deep hulk of man guarding the single door out of the jailhouse.

'You look better, Fred,' she said. 'I'd thought you would look worse.'

'Why? Here at least I can sleep. I couldn't out there.' He went close to her, moved one arm vaguely indicating the outside.

'Brewster's in town with some other men. They must be your friends. They're talking to everyone they can get to talk. Tucomcori's in a grip of excitement. Mrs Clark says she's lived here twenty-seven years and never seen the town so excited.'

Fred raised his eyes briefly to the blacksmith's face. The pale eyes were fixed on him with a steady, bull-like regard but the smith didn't speak. He looked down at Lillian again and saw the erratic pulse in her throat. Deep within him somewhere a drum beat slowly with masculine throbbing. She was flawless and anxiety seemed to enhance her; even the coloring was higher, brighter, more flushed and noticeable.

'Let's sit down.'

They went to the old bench against the wall, sat close. He could see the blacksmith's sudden discomfort because they were both facing the door. The smith finally spoke.

'Nolan – there're couple fellers around by the back door. I'll be just outside this one. You understand?'

'I understand, but if I'd wanted to leave I'd have done it last night or yesterday when the squatters were around.'

'All right,' the blacksmith said. He looked at Lillian. 'Call me,' he said, and went outside.

'Oh, Fred, Fred.'

He turned fiercely to meet her, felt the warm pressure of her mouth, the straining of her arms and held her like that until it seemed that time had ceased to move, then they broke apart and her eyes were misty.

'What will *happen*...'

'I'm not afraid, Lillian, you shouldn't be. If Brewster and the others dig up just half of what is known about Ben it won't be hard to prove I didn't kill those men.'

'Mr Clark told us at supper last night you could prove you weren't in the country when Mister Hull and that other man were killed.'

'I can,' he said, 'but I don't believe I'll have to. Ben's arrogance will clear that up.'

'How?'

'He didn't kill those people alone and his gunmen are in here. They'll talk if they think it'll save them. They're that kind; I've seen hundreds like them before, Lillian.'

'But hadn't you better get your own proof just in case, Fred?'

He smiled at her, took her hand and held it tightly imprisoned between his own large fists. 'We'll see,' he said. 'We'll see what's needed after Brewster and the others bring in what they've found out.'

'You're too confident, Fred. Isn't there some way to make Ben talk?'

He shook his head at her. 'Not Ben. He wouldn't talk if his life depended upon it. I know him that well.'

And Fred was right but he didn't know exactly how right until late that night, long after Lillian had gone and he'd been locked into his cage again, and even then he wouldn't have known except that the jailer let out a squeal that awakened them all and Fred sat up in the pitch darkness listening to the man's running footsteps.

He got up and stood over against the straps of his cell straining to see up the little aisle where the sound had come from, and couldn't.

Less than an hour later men pushed into the corridor with lanterns and Fred heard the blacksmith's rumbling voice. The words were muffled, inarticulate, and the cage next to Fred's was buzzing with voices, with wonder and trepidation as the Big Lily gunmen crowded up close, craning to see.

An angry voice said, 'Shuddup down there, you fellers,' and the gunmen's voices dropped lower but Fred still couldn't make out what was happening. A chill stole up his back in the blackness. Heavy, solid footsteps came down toward his cell. A lantern bobbed with yellow-orange gusts then the blacksmith was standing two feet away from Fred with the light gushing outward and upward from the lamp in his fist. For moments they looked at one another. The smith's eyes were red and puffy, sleep-drugged looking with sharpness in their depths. His scanty hair was awry and a half-buttoned shirt showed the cords of muscle across his chest and belly and shoulders. He raised the lantern and peered closely into Fred's face.

'What woke you up, Nolan?'

'Someone squeaked like a sheep,' Fred said, 'about half an hour ago. It woke all of us up.'

The lantern dropped down again, the smith's breath came out with an audible rush. 'Know why the jailer made that sound?'

'No; why?'

'Ben hung himself.'

Fred's knuckles whitened around the steel straps. He said nothing.

'Hung himself to the top bars with his belt.'

'Is he dead?'

'Deader'n a sow-bug.'

Fred leaned on the straps and ironically remembered what he'd said. *He wouldn't talk if his life depended upon it. I know him that well.* It shouldn't have surprised him then but it did; maybe it was shock and not surprise.

He turned his back on the blacksmith and went over where the bunk hung by chains from the wall, sat down and stared at nothing. Voices that had been little scrabbling sounds in the adjoining cell were dead in stunned silence. The blacksmith's lantern cast a dull-ruddy glow on caged men with astonished expressions and unmoving eyes. Then the voices started up again. Small and slight at first, then stronger.

He didn't hear anything but the sound for a long time. There was a strange and loud humming in his mind. Ben and the painful memories of childish hatred, jealousy. Ben's people, his own flesh and blood, and their striving, their fierce acquisitiveness. With Ben it all died; all those long years of struggle, of scheming, or forging a mighty cow empire, or ruling a country, almost a Territory.

'Shuddup! You whining bunch of–'

'Let 'em talk, Cuff. Let 'em tell us all about it.'

He heard those voices raised above the others. It wrenched him back to the present. He groped for a tobacco sack, made a cigarette and lit it, got up and went over by the cell door and stood there looking at the scowling face of the blacksmith and two of the lawmen beside him. The voices weren't coherent but he picked out words. The Big Lily gunmen, terrified by their aloneness, by the way Ben had deserted them, left them to face punishment in a hostile countryside, were talking; telling how a man named Rufe Emmons had been drygulched, naming names and calling them too.

The blacksmith turned suddenly and growled something to the lawmen. '...At a time and get it all down in writing. Out in the office.' He made an aside, scorching remark to the gunmen and stalked down where Fred was standing. There was black scorn in his gaze and for a long time he just stared, then he turned and called to the lawmen. 'Let Nolan out o' here.'

When Fred walked through the little door the men in the next cage fell into silence, watching. The blacksmith handed his lantern to a lawman and jerked his head at Fred. They went up the corridor and into the office. The smith closed the door behind them with an out-thrust fist. He shook his head like a dog with an ear-tick and crossed to the bench, sat down on it and looked up at Fred.

'That settles it I reckon. The damned fool – he could've hired Stateside lawyers; why'd he do it?'

Fred perched on an edge of the desk with one leg swinging idly. 'No lawyer could have saved him if those men talked. He knew that. He probably thought if a lawyer *did* save him Judge Lynchrope would get him some dark night – after he got turned loose, *if* he got turned loose.'

'I never thought Ben Nolan'd give up.'

'Maybe he didn't give up,' Fred said. 'Maybe he got away after all. I don't know what people think before they do a thing like this; who does?'

The smith was looking at his hands. 'Yeah,' he looked up with the fire turned to ashes in his eyes 'An' those yellowbellies sound like a bunch of hogs caught under a fence. Did you hear what they said about Emmons and Hull?'

'Part of it.'

'Enough,' the blacksmith said standing up widelegged. 'Enough to clear you I think. Leastways they named the men who killed those two an' your name wasn't mentioned.'

Fred nodded. 'I never did fear that phase of the trial anyway.' He gazed at the squatty man. 'But there's one killing that worries me.'

'Whose?'

'Joshua Morgan's.'

'Did you do it?'

'No. I'll swear to that under oath.'

'Did you see it done?'

Fred's eyes widened a trifle. 'Why – no, I didn't *see* it done.'

'Then I don't expect you got too much to worry about. Did anyone see it done?'

'Well – I don't know if they actually saw it done or not.'

The smith rubbed one fisted hand in an eye and said in a tired voice, 'Morgan's no loss. Ain't anyone goin' to turn the world upside down to find out how he died 'ceptin' maybe the next U.S. Marshal, an' if there was no witnesses an' the victim's dead – why I reckon Josh Morgan's jus' a memory.' The unrubbed eye was peering at Fred intently. 'Sure *you* didn't do it?'

'You have my word on that.'

'Then let's forget it.' The smith yawned mightily. 'Will you volunteer your word o' honor you won't leave Tucomcori until after the trials of those Lily riders?'

'Yes.'

'I'm glad o' that because it's on my head if you walk out o' here but I don't see how we can hold you anyway, not now. Uh – I got a spare room if you'd like, Nolan.'

Fred smiled at the blacksmith. 'I'd like that very much.'

'Then let's go get some sleep.'

They left together. The town was drowsily somnolent under the vault of heaven. Chaparral-smell, a little like creosote, was mixed into the more elusive scent of the desert and a rush of feeling filled him. He thought again as he'd thought long before that this was where he belonged. The blacksmith interrupted his reverie.

'Ben had no brothers or kin did he?'

'No, just me.'

'Uh-huh; well, that makes you Mister Big Lily now doesn't it?'

Fred missed a step and almost stopped. 'Yes,' he said dumbly, 'It does.'

He was still turning this odd twist of his personal fortune over in his mind when they came to the little fence before the smith's house. He stopped with his hand on the gate. 'Do you mind if I stay out here for a little while?'

The blacksmith looked up into his face. 'No, sure not.' He looked around, up on the porch, then back to Fred again. 'See you in the mornin'. She'll show you to the spare room. Good night, Nolan.'

Fred said good night and looked perplexed. She? What she would show him…

Like a spirit the pale silhouette moved toward him from the porch. He didn't speak even when she was standing across the gate from him with night-staunched dampness in her eyes.

'I prayed for you, Fred. I even prayed for Ben.'

He watched the pale moonlight play in her

red-gold hair. 'Ben needs it more than I do,' he said softly, and bit back the other words that came to mind. 'Walk with me, Lillian. It's a beautiful night.'

They walked with faint-echoing footfalls and Tucomcori slept.

The publishers hope that this book has given you enjoyable reading. Large Print Books are especially designed to be as easy to see and hold as possible. If you wish a complete list of our books please ask at your local library or write directly to:

The Golden West Large Print Books
Magna House, Long Preston,
Skipton, North Yorkshire.
BD23 4ND

Formed in 1911, the Chartered Institute of Marketing is now the largest professional marketing management body in Europe with over 22,000 members and 25,000 students located worldwide. Its primary objectives are focused on the development of awareness and understanding of marketing throughout UK industry and commerce and in the raising of standards of professionalism in the education, training and practice of this key business discipline.

Books in the series

Computer Aided Marketing and Selling
Robert Shaw

The Creative Marketer
Simon Majaro

The Customer Service Planner
Martin Christopher

The Effective Advertiser
Tom Brannan

The Marketing Audit
Malcolm H. B. McDonald

The Marketing Planner
Malcolm H. B. McDonald

Marketing Strategy
Paul Fifield

The Effective Advertiser

Tom Brannan

Published on behalf of
the Chartered Institute of Marketing

Butterworth-Heinemann Ltd
Linacre House, Jordan Hill, Oxford OX2 8DP

A member of the Reed Elsevier group

OXFORD LONDON BOSTON
MUNICH NEW DELHI SINGAPORE SYDNEY
TOKYO TORONTO WELLINGTON

First published 1993
Paperback edition 1993

British Library Cataloguing in Publication Data
Brannan, Tom
Effective Advertiser. – (CIM Practitioner Series)
I. Title II. Series
659.1

ISBN 0 7506 1772 1

Composition by Genesis Typesetting, Laser Quay, Rochester, Kent
Printed and bound in Great Britain by Redwood Books, Trowbridge, Wiltshire

Contents

Preface

The Effective Advertiser has been written not merely to be read but to be acted on. Applying the principles covered here will enable you to improve the standard and effectiveness of your own advertising. I have attempted to write the book from the point of view of a pragmatic business executive who expects advertising to produce a meaningful return on investment, and I have concentrated on those areas where the average practitioner's knowledge tends to be weakest.

The thoughts and views expressed are my own, but I must express a great debt to colleagues and clients, past and present, who have contributed to what knowledge I have. In particular, I would like to thank my employers, Primary Contact, for the ready access to agency material, a good deal of which has found its way into these pages.

Specific mention must go to Robin Atkins, Graham Bunting, Tony Moore, Kerry Simmonds, Bill Swallow and Alan Wolfe for help with the manuscript and proofs.

Tom Brannan

1 Fun – a serious business

Advertising as a serious investment – The keys to effective advertising – Getting the most out of this book – Starting with an advertising audit

Welcome to the world of advertising. Or perhaps 'welcome' is the wrong word – since you're already heavily involved in advertising, if not as an exponent, then certainly as a consumer.

Unless you've been living your life in a Saharan oasis, like the rest of us you are exposed to hundreds of advertising messages every day: on the TV and radio, in papers and magazines, on posters, in shop windows. There's no escape from the reach of sellers trying to persuade you to prefer their products to those of their competitors, and it's just the same for your prospective customers.

Yet, somehow, you need to cut through all that noise and clutter and get your message across more effectively than the rest. What a task! However, there's one thing very much in your favour as you set out to achieve that objective – and you've probably noticed it already: there's a lot of dire advertising out there. The really good advertising can still stand out like a beacon.

Stop reading for a moment and think about it. Call to mind three campaigns which you remember.

That wasn't difficult was it? Somehow, those campaigns got through to you – they had impact and memorability. Just what you should seek for your own work.

ADVERTISING IS FUN, SERIOUSLY

For most people in business, advertising is a small part of their job. Rightly so. It's not as important as getting the product right, ensuring that it is manufactured efficiently, pricing it at a level which represents value for money in the eyes of the market and establishing adequate distribution so that customers can buy easily. But it is still important.

Advertising is also the fun part of the job for most of us. We deal with agency people – who are often perceived as more fun than most business contacts (whether justifiably or not is another question!). Advertising is also a highly creative process where we are allowed to indulge in lateral leaps of thinking – a refreshing change from the left-brain, logical thinking which, of necessity, dominates most of our business lives. So feel free to enjoy it and feel part of that creative process.

However, although it is fun, advertising is no joke. It needs to be treated as a serious business activity if it is to earn its keep. You will face spending decisions of a size which would make a dent in your capital expenditure budget. Just think of the homework and effort the plant manager would have to go to in order to persuade the board to approve the purchase of a new piece of expensive equipment. Advertising is competing for the same scarce company resource as that piece of equipment: money. It should be approached in the same serious manner.

THE KEYS TO SUCCESS

Producing effective advertising is only possible if a number of key stages are completed.

Planning

Good advertising knows its place. It is part of a planned approach to your business; an approach which recognizes where advertising fits, what it can and cannot achieve. Although some advertising can produce results on a short-term tactical basis it invariably works best as part of a long-term approach to a marketing opportunity.

Objectives

Know the limit of advertising's capabilities; you must define its role in your particular marketing plan. But it is not enough simply to give it a job to do; you also need to know whether it is working successfully. So your objectives should be quantified and measurable.

Targets

Effective work does not advertise to 'markets'. It talks to *individuals*. You must know, as precisely as possible, at whom your advertising is aimed. If not, it's impossible to develop creative work which talks effectively to your prospects, and you'll never be in a position to assess media selection on a meaningful basis.

Message

Great advertising carries one, and only one, clearly defined message. This must differentiate you from your competitors to establish a competitive edge. And it must be a message of importance to your market if it is to motivate them to buy.

Media

Effective advertising reaches its audience cost-effectively. The right media plan can make even a tight budget go a long way in reaching your prospects. Add good media buying and it will go even further.

Creative

There's a great deal of wallpaper out there – advertising which is virtually invisible. What you seek are creative solutions with impact and relevance – advertising which is intrusive, not invisible.

COBBLER, MEND THY SHOES

On the premise that any non-fiction book seeks to 'sell' its author's views, one might argue that it should meet the criteria which we have just applied to advertising. Does this one?

I'll skip over the *planning* issue – on the assumption that you'll accept that, since it got into print, there must have been some planning behind writing the book. My *objectives* were clearly defined. To persuade you, the reader, to review your current advertising activity and look for ways to improve it. To give you guidance and the knowledge to implement those improvements. To improve your ability to assess the result.

The *targets* I defined are threefold. The key target is the marketer or business executive for whom advertising is a part of the job – but not the main part. Secondary targets are agency personnel – on the account management side in particular – and other managers who are not directly responsible for advertising but who might benefit from an understanding of what it means. The *medium* is, of course, the book itself. The *creative* approach really amounts to the writing. I have tried to eliminate jargon and waffle. I've used familiar forms of address and abbreviated terms such as 'we've' and 'you'll' because I wanted to *talk* to you, not lecture or preach. I want to share my experience with you, not to teach. You've bought the book, you'll make up your own mind which parts are of use to you!

If you find any one piece of information in these pages which you apply for the benefit of your company then I will consider my objectives achieved.

GETTING THE MOST OUT OF IT

There are two ways to get value from this book. You could use it tactically. Dip into relevant chapters and apply any new knowledge to that aspect of your own advertising. Or you could use it more strategically, working through it over a period of time and reviewing and amending your approach as you go.

The choice is yours. I have attempted to structure the work so either approach can bring benefits. You'll find a few points at the end of each chapter which are intended to provoke your own thinking. Any suggested further reading is also at the end of the relevant chapter so you shouldn't need to flick backwards and forwards looking for the information.

WHERE TO START

You have, no doubt, heard one of the many variants of the old story: 'How do I get to London?' to which the reply comes, 'If I were you, I wouldn't start from here.' In seeking to improve your advertising, you have no choice of start point. The anchor has to be what you are doing *now.* The first task has to be to assess the recent advertising for your company and its products. But this is not necessarily as easy as it sounds; you may be asking yourself questions you haven't thought of before. Don't let that get in your way – if you haven't got an answer, be honest with yourself and simply write 'don't know'!

Prepare your own 'audit', and keep it; review it when you've finished the book. It will let you prepare an action list for what you want to do differently in the future.

THE QUESTIONS TO TACKLE

1 *What advertising have you done in the last two years?*
   Remember to cover all types of advertising, including TV, radio, cinema, posters, national newspapers, regional newspapers, consumer magazines, trade magazines, door-to-door leaflets, product-enquiry cards – right down to sandwich boards. Draw up an analysis of where and when each advertisement appeared.
2 *Why were you advertising?*
   Take a look at this question in two stages. First, why were you advertising at all? Second, why did you spend money on the specific advertising which you did? Jot down your reasons.
3 *What results did you achieve?*
   Do you feel you received a return on your money? Note the results which you feel you achieved. If possible, list the results against each activity. Can you measure the results in any useful way? If so, how would you assess them in terms of value for money compared with the cost of the advertising?

4 *What worked best?*
Identify which activities worked best for your company; which met the objectives you had set for them. List these downwards in order of which worked best. Finally, which would you do again? How would you change things for the future?

WHAT ABOUT YOUR COMPETITORS?

Assess, as far as you can, what your competitors are up to. In an ideal world, the same questions could be used to examine their advertising as you have just done for your own. However, short of full-scale industrial espionage (which the author could not possibly condone!), that is not possible. Therefore, as far as can be established, if they are advertising, identify where and how they are doing so.

How does your advertising activity compare to theirs? Do you feel that the level of your own advertising is greater or less than that of each main competitor?

HAVE YOUR CUSTOMERS NOTICED?

Ultimately, your market will be the judge of whether your advertising works. People, whether as private consumers or as business executives, make purchasing decisions on the basis of their *perceptions* of what you have to offer. Advertising can play a significant part in creating, reinforcing or altering those perceptions. But only if it is effective.

Is your advertising being seen by your market? How do you know? Is it delivering the message and image that you intended?

If you don't have the information to answer these questions, pause for a moment and consider whether you should read further. You may have neither the time nor, possibly, the funds to carry out detailed, formal market research, but you could pick up the phone and call a dozen existing and potential customers and put the questions to them. Such a straw poll will at least provide some small insight into how the market sees you.

HOW DO THINGS LOOK NOW?

The very exercise of carrying out this kind of analysis can often identify immediately areas for improvement, money being wasted – or questions that should have been asked before, but were not. If it has given you any sort of new insight, jot it down for use later, and commit yourself to carrying out a similar review at least annually.

2 Where advertising fits into business

Where advertising comes in the business plan – The corporate planning process – Identify your planning objectives and strategies

Talk to an agency and they'll almost certainly tell you advertising is vitally important for any product – and your budget is rarely 'enough'. Talk to your accountant and he or she is likely to state that advertising just reduces the bottom line. The truth is invariably somewhere in between.

In a highly competitive consumer goods market where there's little to choose between products, advertising may be absolutely critical in creating a competitive difference in the market's perception. It will command a significant percentage of turnover. For a company selling highly specialized products in a very small, tightly defined market, advertising may have only a relatively small and perhaps supporting role to play.

Defining the right approach to advertising demands a planned approach; and that's the key to making it pay for itself. Figure 2.1 illustrates the stages in developing effective advertising and shows clearly just how far down the planning process it fits in. Major corporations will use such a planning 'model', not only for advertising

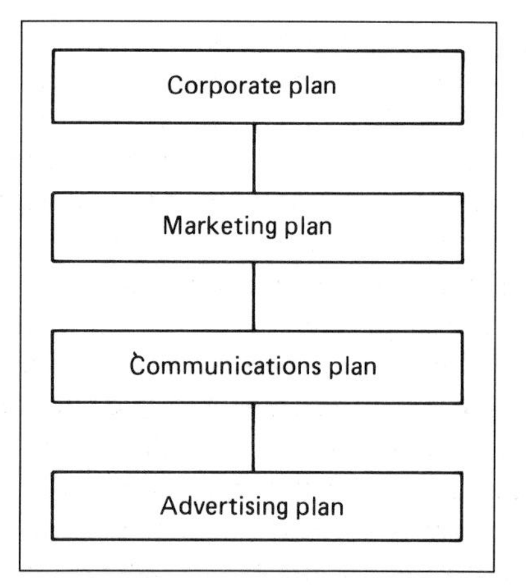

Figure 2.1 Developing an advertising plan

but for every aspect of the business – and with sub-plans for every company and department within the operation. All this builds into a picture of how the management proposes to shape the future.

No plan is perfect; it's prepared with imperfect knowledge. No plan is chiselled in stone; too many factors can change beyond management's control. Yet a plan has immense value as a measure of such change – whether this is, for example, a reduction in interest rates or political change in a major export market. When the assumptions built into any business plan are proven wrong, the plan can prompt the company to respond faster than it otherwise might because the process of thinking through the plan makes the company much more aware of the implications of a movement away from the assumptions made.

In highly competitive, fast-moving markets this can be critical. Speed of reaction to change may be the only sustainable competitive advantage.

IS PLANNING FOR YOU?

Planning is well established in major companies. Yet one could argue that effective planning is most important in small to medium-sized ones – for the very reason that they are most prone to losing sight of their objectives and being sidetracked away from the main job.

Planning needn't necessarily be highly formalized and in a two- or three-person company it may not even need to be written down. But it should be there.

DEVELOPING THE PLAN

There is a great deal of mystique attached to corporate planning, yet in reality there is no great mystery to solve. In essence, any plan contains four basic steps (Figure 2.2). When the four questions in Figure 2.2 have been answered we have the audit (where we are now); the objectives (where we want to be); the strategy (how we will get there); and the tactics (what we have to do to make it happen).

It may be useful to think of a plan as a journey. We're in London. We need to get to Paris within three days (a clear, quantified objective). We could go by plane, car or train (our strategic options). We'd consider which is best suited under the given circumstances and choose our means of travel – our strategy. The tactics then become activities such as checking our passport, booking and collecting tickets, arranging taxis and so on. A complete plan, and no different from the process needed to produce a business plan for a multinational company. Just on a smaller scale.

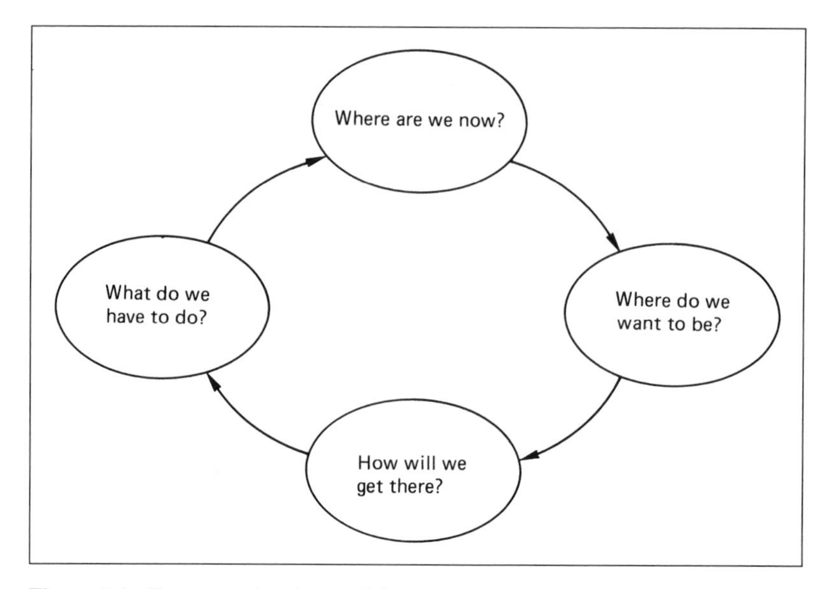

Figure 2.2 Four-step planning model

The planning process shown by Figure 2.2 is a continuous circle – indicating that good planning is a constant process, not a one-off exercise (we've arrived in Paris – where to next?). Of course, this is a somewhat simplistic explanation and answering the four questions involves a great deal of work.

The objective in planning, from an advertising perspective, is to ensure that everything we do – from the smallest local newspaper ad to a massive TV campaign – contributes to achieving the company's objectives. It naturally follows that this can only be the case if we can trace a line all the way from the corporate objective to the advertising activity. An expanded version of the model (Figure 2.3) shows in more depth how that direct line can be established.

The corporate plan

The corporate plan, as all stages of planning, answers the four questions in Figure 2.2. The company 'audit' establishes where you are now. It involves a complete review of the position today and encompasses all aspects of the operation.

The audit should look at the mission – your long-term goal for what the company should be, your structure, financial position, people, facilities and current markets. To these facts will be added information on the business environment. Which political, economic, social and technological factors affect your business now and what

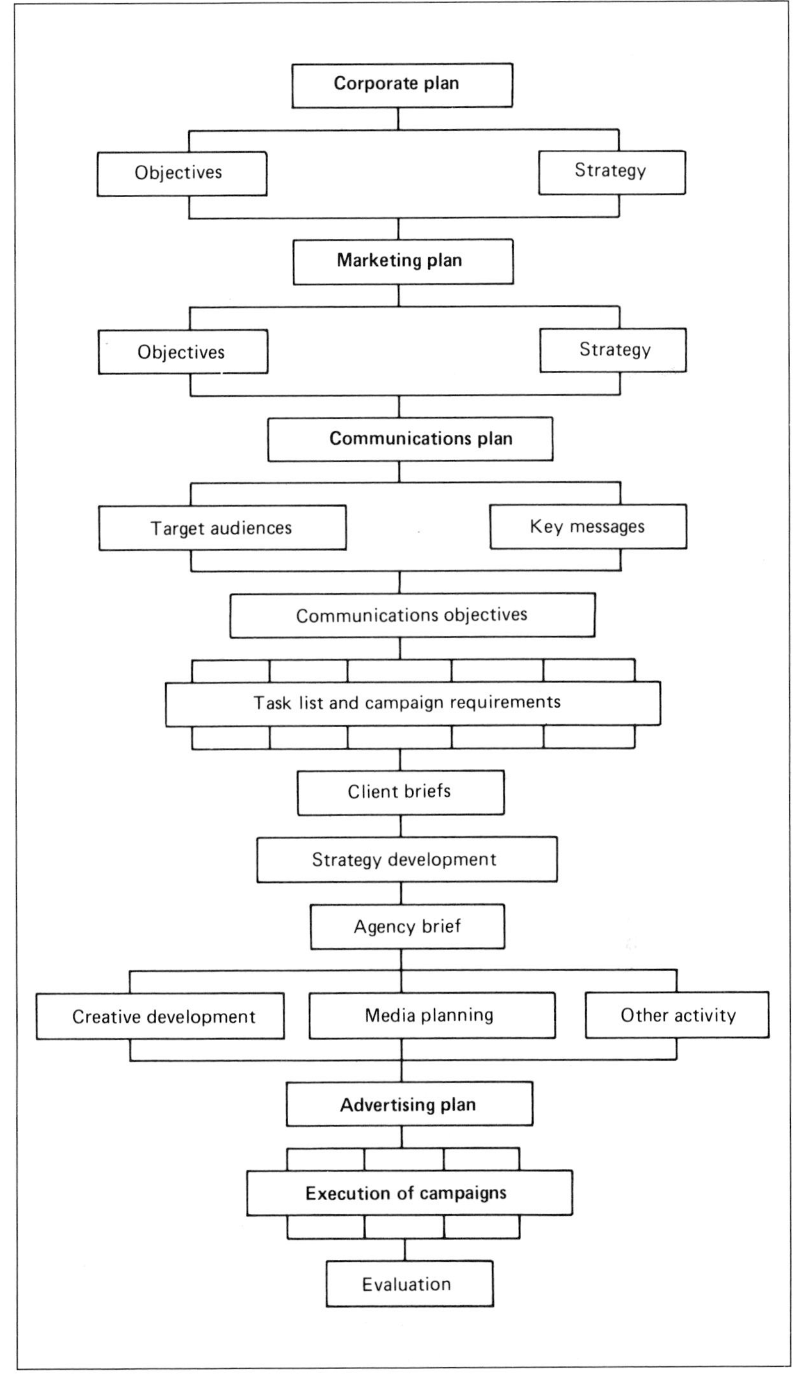

Figure 2.3 The Primary Contact planning model

trends are evident that will affect it in the future? Who are your competitors at a corporate level? What are they good at? Where do you have the advantage? The audit should result in a SWOT analysis which identifies your *strengths* and *weaknesses*, the *opportunities* available to you and the *threats* which might prevent you from exploiting them.

The plan then moves into 'where do we want to be?' It's time to establish the corporate objectives. This will involve a series of 'what if' exercises, looking at where you could be in a given period – if only.

The assumptions of conditions or actions, the 'if onlys', will generate a number of possible scenarios for the future. Your experience and business judgement will refine and define the final objectives from amongst these possibilities.

The exercise continues through identification of strategies to achieve those objectives. At a corporate level, these will be the big decisions of the business; whether to build a new plant, invest in new research and development, grow by acquisition or organically and so on.

Finally, the action plan is drawn up giving the timetable for key events and identifying who is responsible for making things happen at each stage.

The corporate plan must be the foundation for everything which happens within subsidiaries, divisions or departments. It is the glue which binds the company's efforts, ensuring that everyone is pulling in the same direction. At the end of the total planning process the objectives set at lower levels (including the advertising objectives) must, if achieved, ensure that the corporate objectives are met.

The marketing plan

The marketing plan goes through precisely the same stages, but is more narrowly focused than the overall corporate plan. The complexity of the marketing audit will, like all things, be a function of company size and spread of activities. In a small, one-product company it is relatively simple, in a larger company with many products, selling to many markets in many geographic areas, it will be a major exercise in itself.

However complex, it is critical that it is done properly. You must have in-depth knowledge of your market position and SWOT analysis in order to make sensible decisions on the two key issues of objectives and strategies.

The objectives must stem from those determined in the corporate plan. Let's assume the corporate objective is to have a top-five position in the European telecommunications market within five years. It's marketing's job to identify how best to exploit the company's ability to achieve that. Which sectors are you equipped to attack (or could be within the timescale)? Which of those offer the optimum potential? Which products would you need to exploit the opportunity? What needs to be done to develop or source them?

Classically, the marketing plan will deal with four key aspects of the business; product, pricing, distribution and marketing communications. You'll often find these referred to, in a useful shorthand, as the four Ps – product, price, place and promotion. As most companies offer more than one product, the marketing plan will itself require sub-division for each product, service or brand and possibly for each target market. This level of the plan will feature the same two key elements. Namely, a series of objectives plus the strategies designed to achieve them.

Again, it is important that this stage is put in place. Advertising will not help to sell a bad or overpriced product. Worse, if you are underpricing a product, you may not be able to afford the advertising – or at very least, you'll fail to maximize your profits. And, of course, if you fail to achieve adequate distribution, your potential customers may not be able to find it in order to buy it!

The communications plan

Within the marketing plan you will have identified your 'star' products for the future, and you'll have a good idea who is most likely to buy them. Or, as the jargon would have it, your key target industries or market sectors.

The communications plan narrows the focus further and goes into even greater depth. We cannot communicate with 'buyers of breakfast cereals' or 'the automotive industry'. These are relatively abstract concepts, useful only at the previous planning level, where you were dealing with market statistics and broad strategic issues. To progress the planning, you'll need to put flesh onto these bones – almost literally! As I said in the Introduction, we need to communicate with individuals, not concepts. The communications plan must identify those individuals. Yet it too must go through the four-part questioning if it is to lead to a meaningful advertising plan, and the market sector definitions given in the marketing plan are the start point.

Let me illustrate by using a down-to-earth example. You are the owner of a small chain of corner shops, all situated in various parts of Hometown – where there are also three supermarkets (now opening on Sundays!). Your corporate objective is to double turnover during the planning period whilst maintaining margins. You believe this can be achieved by increasing the number of outlets by 50%, from six to nine, buying better because of higher volume and seeking growth in turnover per outlet. The marketing plan will have examined and developed strategies for such things as the branding policy for the chain (although one would expect this to have been well established already), the mix of products to be stocked, their prices *vis-à-vis* those of the supermarket competitors and the ideal locations for siting the new outlets. This last point will, of course, require a detailed understanding of your customers. Only by profiling your existing customers can you establish where more of them are to be found – and the right location to open the new shops.

Marketing should also have identified the competitive edge which will expand the business. It might be personal service, savings facilities like the old-fashioned Christmas Club, or perhaps longer opening hours. In a major conurbation the growing number of single-person households may be an important segment of the market and convenience foods stocked specifically to meet their needs.

The communications plan needs to identify all audiences, and the messages to be carried to each in order to help achieve the objectives. Doing so can help to identify campaign shape at the same time. One

Message \ *Audience*	A	B	C	D
New shop open	●	●	●	●
Convenience foods stocked		●		
Long opening hours	●	●		●
Good local citizen	●	●	●	●
Responsible employer			●	●

Figure 2.4 Audience/message matrix

useful aid is a matrix such as that shown in Figure 2.4. Here, audience A might be shoppers, mainly female, with children, living within one mile of the shop. B might be single-person households in the same location. C the local planning authority and D, staff. The key messages are listed on the vertical axis of Figure 2.4 and, where they apply, marked on the matrix. Thus we see that 'new shop' announcements need to be aimed at all audiences, whereas the convenience foods message should be much more closely targeted.

As campaign structure is developed, so are the specific communications objectives related to each audience. We shall return to this aspect of planning in greater detail at a later stage.

The advertising plan

With the communications plan in front of you, you can begin to assess how advertising could help in delivering these messages. We will examine many aspects of communications and advertising planning as you turn the pages of this book. For the moment, it is only important that we remember the need to establish that straight line between top-level objectives and final tactical activity. The model in Figure 2.3 provides the key.

WHAT ARE YOU TRYING TO ACHIEVE?

1 What are the key objectives for your company or division?
2 Which strategies will you use to achieve them?
3 Which marketing objectives and strategies are you following?
4 List your key target markets and the key messages for each.
5 Can you trace your current advertising activities right back to the corporate plan?

Further reading

Brannan, T. (1990), *An Introduction to Business Planning*, Primary Contact Ltd, Porters Place, 33 St John Street, London.

Davidson, J. H. (1992), *Offensive Marketing*, Pelican.

Kotler, P. (1988) *Marketing Management – Analysis, Planning and Control*, Prentice-Hall.

McDonald, M. H. B. (1989), *Marketing Plans*, Butterworth-Heinemann.

3 Why advertise? Why advertising?

The cost of selling – The reason for advertising – Advertising as an investment – How it helps to sell – The roles of advertising – Other communications options – Review your advertising audit

Any half-decent sales professional will tell you that the ideal way to sell is face to face. Nothing beats getting in front of prospects, putting the product into their hands and seeing the whites of their eyes as they respond to your selling proposal. And, in an ideal world, that's precisely how we would do all of our selling.

The slight snag is the cost! The impracticality of using personal selling to shift a billion Mars chocolate bars worldwide or millions of tins of Heinz beans throughout the UK is all too self-evident. The problem is, however, equally significant in business markets. The average sales call in the UK costs over £200 according to research by publishers McGraw-Hill. However, we'll be more conservative. Take a salesperson at £20 000 per annum, add employment costs of around 25%, allow, say, £5000 for car costs and the same again for expenses. Now allocate a share of overheads – 150% of direct salary wouldn't be unreasonable. Add up that lot and you'll get to £75 000. Allow 46 working weeks per annum and four calls per day. If your calculator hasn't fused yet, that gives around £80 per call – without accounting for support staff who may be involved in arranging the call. Let's assume a success rate of one in four calls – a respectable performance. That's a cost per sale of £320 just for the selling time. It's pretty clear that we need a high value per sale, at decent margins, to afford that cost. Paradoxically, the higher the value of the item, the more sales calls are likely to be needed to close the sale – and so we enter a vicious circle.

If cost is the first issue, time is the second. Any prospect, for any product, will only be 'in the market' at certain points in time. In a repeat-purchase, fast-moving consumer goods market (e.g. milk, soap powder, chocolate bars) the consumer will be in the market frequently and regularly. To pursue our rather extreme example, how many salespeople would it take to cover the 56 million consumers in the UK market frequently enough to be there at each purchase?

At the other end of the scale, a specialized business market might contain only 5000 users in a given country. Let's assume each purchases, on average, quarterly but we need to visit each six times a year to be confident of being around at decision-making time. That's 30 000 sales calls a year at a probable average of five per working day. So we use 6000 man/days of selling time. With holidays, administration tasks, weekends and so on, the average field employee has around 170 effective selling days available each year. So for our small, specialized market we'd need at least 36 salespeople to cover the market. That's quite some cost in a small market!

These two problems are the reason distribution chains exist. Through such chains, the manufacturer can get closer to the market more cost-effectively than by direct selling. But even that is not enough. We need to encourage users to visit those distribution points and, perhaps even more importantly, to prefer our product to the others handled by the distributor when they get there.

That's why we advertise or use PR or invest in any other communications technique. We are seeking to reach more people, more quickly and more cost-effectively with our selling message. The end result should be more cost-effective selling and improved profits.

ADVERTISING: INVESTMENT OR COST?

It is a common fallacy that the results of advertising cannot be measured. They can, and in a variety of ways ranging from shifts in awareness of, and attitudes to your company, right through to the number of products sold (in the case of mail-order advertising). But the ultimate measure must surely be the contribution advertising makes to the bottom line. This is much more complicated to establish for any single company since it is extremely difficult to separate out the influence of advertising from the myriad of factors that affect profit performance. However, when a wider view of business is adopted, there is very strong evidence that a consistent commitment to advertising has a real and identifiable influence in improving profit performance and return on investment.

Studies by organizations such as the Strategic Planning Institute have established a clear correlation between consistent advertising and healthier key business ratios. One SPI study, published in the mid-1980s, tracked the performance of 749 consumer businesses. The study produced some highly significant results.

Figure 3.1 shows that companies spending relatively more than their competitors on advertising achieved much better returns on investment (ROI). The correlation continues when advertising is measured against market share (Figure 3.2). Note that the figures are relative in both cases – based on advertising-to-sales ratios.

A: S versus direct competitors	*Average ROI %*
Much less	17
Less	22
Equal	22
More	25
Much more	32

Figure 3.1 Relative advertising expenditures and return on investment

A: S versus direct competitors	*Average share of market %*
Much less	14
Less	20
Equal	25
More	26
Much more	32

Figure 3.2 Relative advertising expenditures and share of market

The study documented two other important points: perceived quality drives profitability, and market share drives profitability. The latter showed particularly significant results; consumer businesses with market shares over 40% earned 41% ROI while those with below a 10% share earned only 9% on their capital.

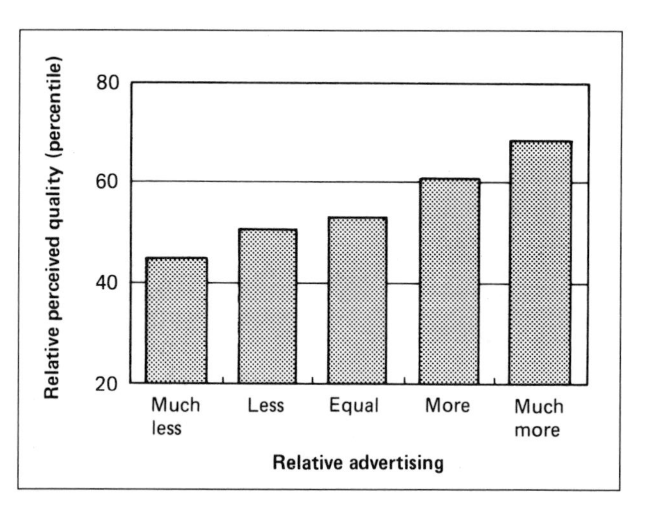

Figure 3.3 Advertising influences perceived quality

The relationship between advertising and perceived quality is also of great interest (Figure 3.3).

And the results are similar in business-to-business markets. SPI ran a similar study in this area of marketing and, while the variation was less marked, it was nevertheless highly significant.

Studies such as these appear to offer conclusive evidence that the right advertising has a powerful and beneficial effect on the bottom-line, no matter which market is involved.

HOW DOES ADVERTISING HELP?

Even when we have accepted that advertising does improve performance, we are left wondering how. In reality, advertising rarely 'sells' a product. The exception is, of course, in mail-order or off-the-page selling where, having read the advertisement, we are asked to send a cheque or to telephone giving our credit card number.

But we don't buy bread or beans or perfume that way. Businesses certainly don't buy lorries or raw materials or machinery that way. And I've yet to see a government clip a coupon and send off a cheque for several million pounds' worth of turnkey installation or construction project. Yet these are all product areas where advertising is common.

To see how advertising helps such sales we need some understanding of the dynamics of a buying decision. Many models of this

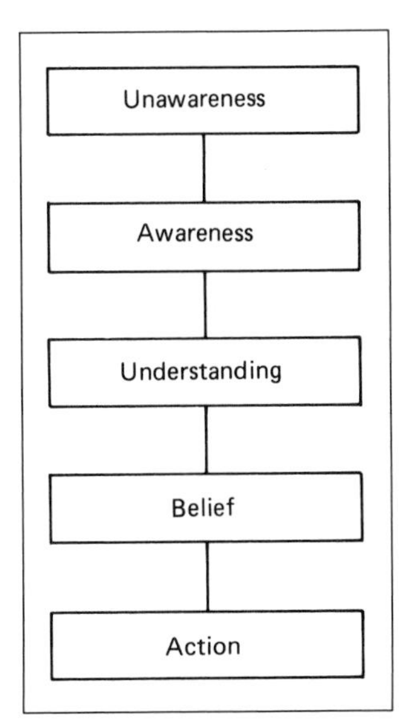

Figure 3.4 From McDonald's 'brand loyalty ladder'

process have been developed by academics over the years, and Figure 3.4, from Malcolm McDonald's book *Marketing Plans*, shows perhaps one of the best.

This argues that a potential purchaser starts off not knowing you or what you offer; the 'unawareness' stage. At some point they become aware of your existence and gradually develop an understanding of what you have to offer. If you're sending the right messages, supported by the right image, your consumer will eventually believe that what you say is true and relevant to him or her. On that basis the consumer will take action – perhaps visit the shop or test the product, and eventually buy if it genuinely lives up to expectations.

Advertising, indeed all forms of marketing communications, can play a key role at each stage. It can build your public profile so that your market is aware of you; it can provide the information required to establish understanding; it can deliver relevant messages and the persuasive arguments which help to establish belief; and it can encourage action by directing the consumer to the point of sale.

The role of advertising

Evidently, the role of advertising can vary from the indirect one of establishing awareness, to the direct job of asking for a cheque or credit card number. The variety of jobs which it can do is almost endless but Figure 3.5 illustrates those for which it is most commonly used – and which it is best at achieving. Let's take a look at each:

To build awareness: It goes without saying that, if your potential customer has never heard of you, your selling is going to be a lot tougher than it need be. It's a simple fact of life that all of us buy products, or from companies, that we know and trust. So awareness of our existence and product is a prerequisite for optimum results. Advertising is particularly effective at building that awareness quickly. Its effectiveness can be demonstrated by the recent case of First Direct, the home banking operation in the UK which, with heavyweight advertising support, went from a standing start to 37% awareness among its target market in just 5 days. Four months later it had climbed to 58%.

To inform: Advertising can provide factual information; it can tell of new distribution channels, it can provide consumer information – as much governmental advertising does. It can even avert potential disaster when used to advise of a product recall due to a faulty batch.

To educate: Again governmental advertising provides nice examples: drugs are bad for you; drunk driving can destroy lives. But, in a more

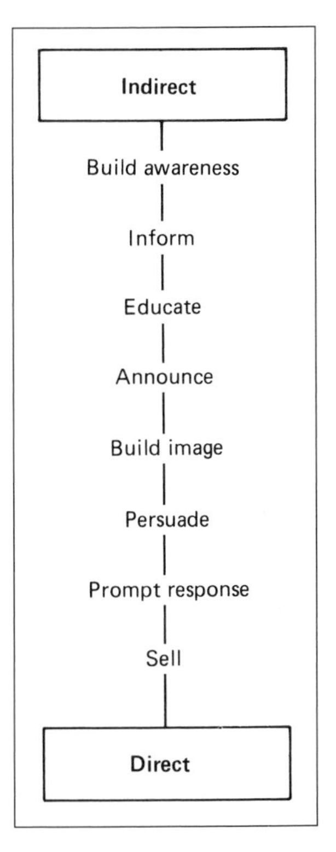

Figure 3.5 Some of the possible roles for advertising

conventional sense, advertising can educate to new product applications aimed at extending uses – why not try Bacardi with . . . ? I recently experienced a situation where research showed that sales of an ICI overhead transparency film were being held back in a particular market because users did not realize that they could simply pop the film into a photocopier instead of copy paper, and produce their own instant overhead projection slides – a classic application for 'educational' advertising.

To announce: Advertising is a terrific technique for generating impact and excitement around a new product launch. It has 'announcement' applications in many other situations, too; company results, mergers and takeovers, and name changes, to mention but a few.

To build image: Businesses have become increasingly aware of the critical importance of their image among audiences, and of the impact which that image can have on their performance. One only has to look at the growth of 'green' advertising to confirm this. Again, advertising can carry non-product messages effectively – frequently aimed at provoking an 'I didn't realize that!' response from the audience. In the 1980s Hanson plc's advertising gave us a whole new perspective on that company. Shell's campaign at the end of the decade showed the lengths the company goes to in order to restore the landscape after they've laid a major pipeline. Neither of these directly sells product, but they may condition us to think more positively about the company and thus be more predisposed to buying its wares.

To persuade: This is undoubtedly the most common use of advertising, from showing that your cola is more fun to drink, to proving that your machine tool is 4% more productive. Advertising's key role is to create or encourage consumer preference, and that is an absolute condition before a sale can be made. It is in this role that advertising can be at its most powerful. It can help significantly in making your product or brand stand out from the crowd in a way which motivates the audience to consider purchasing.

To prompt response: This is frequently a key task in business-to-business marketing. The outcome we seek is a request for more information or a sales visit. Advertising can be vital in ensuring that the salesforce has a flow of 'warm' enquiries; selling to these prospects will invariably be a great deal more productive than cold calling. But the technique is also increasingly found in the durable consumer goods field. Advertisements now frequently feature a response telephone number so, for example, you can find your nearest Philips stockist or book a test drive at your local Ford dealer. Such activity moves advertising ever closer to the actual sale itself.

To sell: An enormous amount of merchandise is sold off-the-page. Historically, the technique was felt to work only for low-value and relatively down-market goods. However, in the 1970s and 1980s agencies like Primary Contact broke new ground; in the latter case by selling tens of thousands of Sinclair home computers – at prices of up to £400. Today, companies like Franklin Mint rely heavily on off-the-page selling to move large volumes of high-value merchandise.

ADVERTISING ISN'T THE ONLY OPTION

So advertising can do many jobs, but it isn't the only marketing communications technique available to you. And it rarely works to best advantage in isolation from other support activity.

If we return to the earlier statement that we use communication to reach more people, more quickly and more cost-effectively, then we can list a whole spectrum of activities which can help do so. Our list would include PR, sales promotion, telephone selling, direct mail, sponsorship, exhibitions, seminars, video and newsletters. Each can have a valuable part to play in our overall campaign, and within your communications plan that part should be identified.

Since this book is about advertising, we shall not cover these other techniques in great depth. However, a brief look at the strengths and weaknesses of each will be of value as a background to what follows.

Public relations

In its true sense, PR will cover investor relations, the financial community and such relatively esoteric audiences. However, for our purpose of selling product, it could more accurately be described as media relations. In this role it seeks to help us get mentioned, regularly and favourably, in media which are seen, heard or read by our target audiences.

Let's start by doing the PR community a favour and dispelling a couple of myths. PR is not free. PR is not easy. You will achieve coverage only if you have something of genuine news value to say and if you are prepared to work hard, in partnership with your agency, to identify the stories of interest, to research the information to put some meat into them, and to build good relationships with key media contacts. Here endeth the lesson!

A good PR programme can achieve very cost-effective publicity. When you have something newsworthy there is no doubt that you can broadcast it more cheaply through PR than through advertising. And, because it's editorial, it's likely to be more credible than advertising.

The downsides are that to stay in the news, you need a regular supply of newsworthy stories – and that's tough to maintain; you have no way of guaranteeing coverage – once the story has gone out, you're at the mercy of the editor; and you cannot control the content of the finished article or broadcast. In contrast, advertising is controllable in content, appearance, timing and frequency. That's what you're paying for.

Sales promotion

Discount offers, two for the price of one, a free wine glass with £10 000 worth of petrol – and a million other promotional schemes to which each of us is exposed every year. Sales promotion is particularly powerful for building short-term market share or to persuade consumers to test a new product. It is most commonly used in low-value consumer goods but can easily be found in consumer durables (buy my big TV and I'll give you this small one free) and even in business products (a free printer with every PC). It is largely a tactical element of marketing although, in the last four or five years, it has begun to gain credibility as a strategic tool. Its limitations lie in the perennial debate over whether market share gained through sales promotion can be maintained after the special offer, or whether the next promotion by a competitor will simply restore the status quo. The jury is still out on this one.

All techniques are valid

In the same way, telesales is valid for gaining appointments or qualifying leads. Sponsorship, when well chosen, can help to build and reinforce brand values or corporate image – but can only indirectly help to sell products. Direct mail is a powerful selling tool, producing measurable results – but it lacks the fast branding power of advertising. Exhibitions and seminars are ideal opportunities to demonstrate the product; the former allow you to reach a fairly large audience but right alongside your competitors, the latter are your own events but, inevitably, to a much smaller audience.

IT'S ALL IN THE MIX

The communications side of marketing is a bit like baking a cake. Choose the right ingredients in the right proportions, mix them well and cook according to your experience of your own oven – and you'll get the right result. There is no 'ideal' mix, just as there is no one ideal recipe. Your objectives and market conditions will determine what is needed.

In a new product launch, the mix might be something like:

Advertising: to announce the product to a wide audience quickly
Direct mail: to focus on the most likely short-term hot prospects
Seminars: to provide an opportunity to demonstrate the product
Sales promotion: to encourage early take-up
PR: to spread the word on early successes
Video and literature: to arm the salesforce and help them sell.

WHAT WOULD YOU CHANGE?

1 Go back to Chapter 1 and review your audit.
2 Were you using the right techniques? In the right mix? With a clearly defined job for each to do?

3 What changes would you make to improve your use of the available techniques?

Further reading

Institute of Practitioners in Advertising, *How Advertising Works* – a series of books of advertising effectiveness case studies, IPA, 44 Belgrave Square, London.

Martin, D.N. (1989), *Romancing the Brand*, American Management Association, New York.

Primary Contact Ltd (1991), *The Impact of Business-to-Business Advertising on Profits*, Primary Contact Limited, Porters Place, 33 St John Street, London.

Strategic Planning Institute, *How Advertising affects Profitability and Growth*, SPI, 56 Haymarket, London.

Williams, K. (1981), *Behaviourial Aspects of Marketing*, Butterworth-Heinemann.

Wilmhurst, J. (1985), *The Fundamentals of Advertising*, Butterworth-Heinemann.

4 Identifying your market

Defining the target market – Mapping the channels of distribution – The decision-making process – Identifying the consumer as an individual – Define your own markets

If planning is the first key to effective advertising, a sound knowledge of your target markets is the second. How you arrive at the definition of the target market will depend on the communication you have in mind. For a brand manager carrying responsibility for one particular product, understanding the end user of that product may be enough. For looking at communications from a total company viewpoint, a much wider perspective is needed. By considering these wider issues we can examine both types of situation.

START WITH YOUR OBJECTIVES

Many companies fall into the trap of assuming their target audiences to be no more than customers and potential customers for their products. Try an alternative approach: ask yourself 'Who can help or hinder me in achieving my objectives?' The likelihood is that you'll generate a much longer list of targets than simply customers. An example might serve to illustrate the point.

Company A set itself the objective of doubling in size over a five-year period. It sells a range of toiletries through specialist outlets and it is already running at 80% of capacity on its current manufacturing site. For its product sector, it has a high market share within its current distribution outlets.

The strategy developed by the company was to trade on its strong brand name by introducing a sub-brand of middle-range/middle-priced toiletries. Obviously, Company A's end-user target market has expanded. It needs to reach middle-market consumers in addition to its established, more up-market users. However, the objective and strategy have much wider implications.

The objective suggests either expansion of the factory or purchase of another site or even another company. Suddenly our target list might include planning authorities or companies which might be candidates for takeover. Such expansion is likely to call for increased funding. Depending on how that is to be raised, the company may need to address shareholders and the financial community.

Doubling in size is likely to mean both increased productivity and additional staff. So possibly, trade unions, staff, potential recruits and even the local community (whose attitudes could affect both the planning issues and the ability to recruit good people) join the list.

Distribution channels then come up for review. Can existing outlets absorb the additional product range? Are they the right outlets for the new, middle-market users being sought? The short answer to both was 'no'. So a new list of potential sales outlets, both at wholesale and retail levels, had to be considered.

Evidently this company needed to talk not only to users of its products but also to a whole array of people who could influence its chances of success. That is not to suggest for a moment that this company should be *advertising* to all these people – but rather that it must, in some way, be communicating effectively with them.

DESCRIBE YOUR TARGETS

At this point we'll start to concentrate on the likely audiences for your advertising, mainly the distribution chain and the end-user market. However, the principles proposed could be applied with equal validity to any target audience – but the correct tactics to reach them may be very different.

It's not enough to know that our target is 'distributors' or 'end users', a much more detailed description will be needed to help produce good advertising. A useful technique which will help with the process of defining the market is to use a 'road map' and a 'decision chart'.

The road map

This is a visual illustration of how your product gets from the factory to the user. Road maps vary greatly from sector to sector, and often between companies within a given market sector, as a result of the different distribution strategies they have chosen to adopt. The concept is perhaps at its simplest where a manufacturer is selling products direct to the end user, using its own salesforce (Figure 4.1). In this case, the map is a simple straight line. Somewhat more

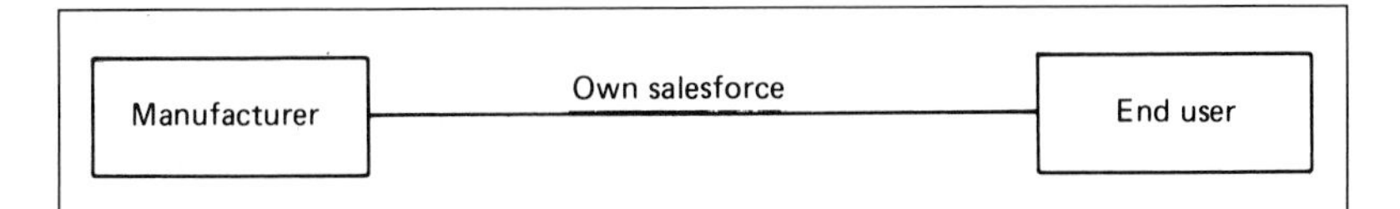

Figure 4.1 The simplest distribution map

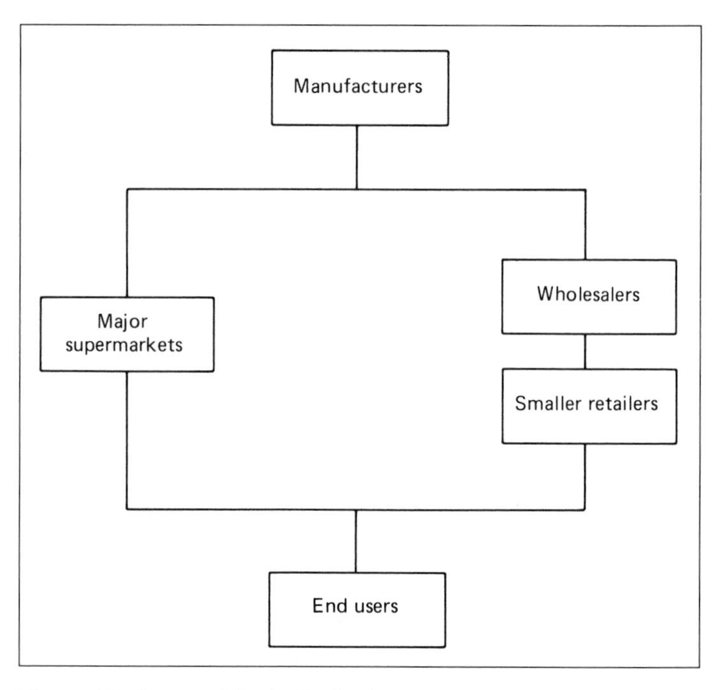

Figure 4.2 Processed foods distribution map

complex would be the road map for a food processor selling a range of canned foods (Figure 4.2).

Here, we are faced with one end-user market but two distinct and different distribution channels. But even this is very simple when compared with, say, the market for cellular telephones in the UK (Figure 4.3). In this market two major companies were given licences to run cellular networks. However, they were prevented under the terms of the licence from selling airtime directly to users. Each had to establish distributors of airtime, the so-called 'accredited retailers'. The 'retailers' quickly became wholesalers, by appointing their own dealer networks - while still selling to major accounts directly, using their own salesforces. Without labouring this example further, since its inception in 1984, this market has become particularly complicated in terms of, for example, the network operators' target markets.

Drawing your road map gives an instant and visual overview of the broad shape of your total market. But that, in itself, is not enough to take us closer to the quality of advertising we seek; it's time to inject some more knowledge and experience into the equation.

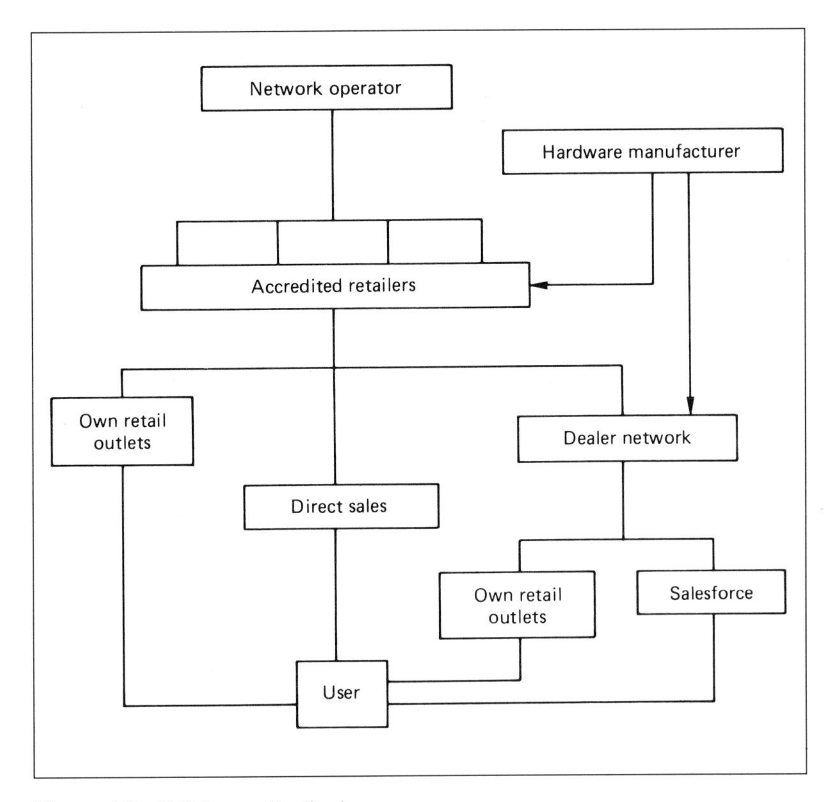

Figure 4.3 Cellphones distribution map

You may have identified the number of selling stages your product has to go through. Now you need to assess the importance of each, and your strengths at each stage.

Figure 4.2 is useful as an example to illustrate the relative strengths of the various players in the road map. If we assume our manufacturer has a strong brand – let's say it's Heinz or Kellogg – it is evident that, since so many consumers want the brand, retail outlets will want to stock it. But if our manufacturer is, for example, like Telford Foods in the UK, specializing in producing foodstuffs branded in the retailer's name – the 'own-label' market – a very different situation exists.

The key to success for a brand such as Heinz lies in the consumer's perception of the brand; its taste, quality, consistency and its emotional values. The key to advertising for Heinz, and for all brands of such stature, must be the consumer. That's where the sales will come from – by users demanding, in effect, that retailers stock the product. For Telford Foods, quite the opposite is the case. They have no name or image with the end consumer, nor do they seek one. Their success stands or falls on the perception of the major supermarket chains who are the customers for their 'own-label' products.

It is critical that we understand the influence of each stage in our own distribution chain so that we can focus advertising where it can have a real effect. When we understand that, we can move to the next stage.

The decision chart

Having looked at how your product is sold, it's time to consider how it is bought – the decision-making process. This is perhaps where the biggest difference occurs between consumer and business-to-business marketing. The typical consumer product is chosen and bought by a small group of people, whereas a high-priced business product purchase may involve a dozen people from several departments.

In a fast-moving consumer goods (fmcg) market the product is usually of relatively low value – and the cost of a wrong decision also low. No one, after all, is going to burst into tears if they don't like the particular brand of coffee they bought yesterday. Decision making is simple, at least in theory. The person doing the shopping picks the product. Not too many years ago we would have assumed that to be the 'housewife'. Today, however, the advent of the 'househusband' and the rapid growth in both single-parent and single-person homes has changed the picture considerably. The marketer needs to keep up with these changes.

The reality of the market is not quite so simple as it seems at first glance. The decision making in a single-person home certainly follows the theoretical model but, as soon as we introduce a second human being (even a child), things change. The 'group' begins to influence brand choice, and we need to understand those influences.

Thus, the decision chart for an fmcg product sold to a family might look like Figure 4.4. The same 'model' would also hold for consumer durables (say, a washing machine) but without any influence from the children!

At risk of accusations of sexism, we should look at which partner holds the key influence for a particular product. In the washing-machine example, even in today's more egalitarian society, the male is likely to have the 'subordinate' role of influencer while the female partner is the ultimate decision maker. But when it comes to choosing how to finance the purchase, the roles may well be reversed. The male is also likely to be the final decision maker for a family car.

The decision-making process is significantly different in business-to-business markets. It may be almost as simple as for consumer markets, or extremely complex.

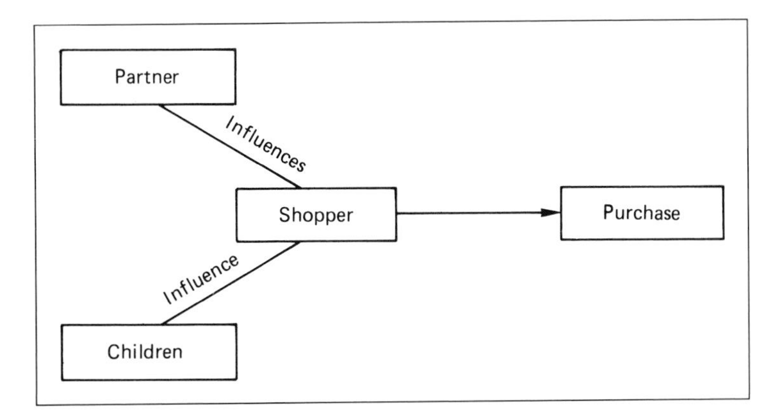

Figure 4.4 FMCG puchase

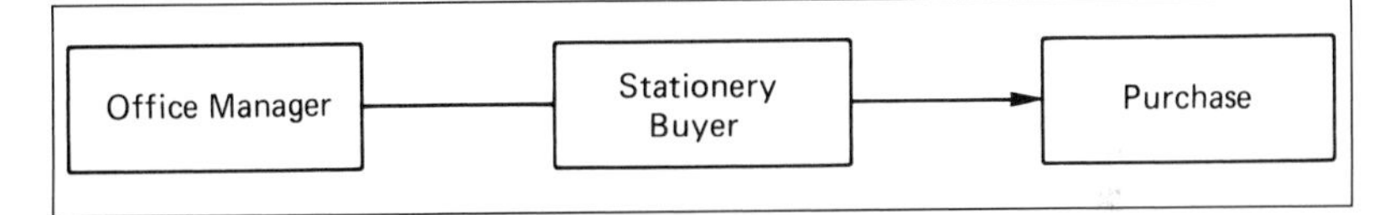

Figure 4.5 Low-value business purchase

Figure 4.5 shows the decision chart for the purchase of stationery. The Office Manager is likely to approve at least the specification of items which may be used. The Buyer then negotiates supplies and may choose the final brand provided it meets the specification. In small to medium-sized companies the two functions are likely to be fulfilled by the same person.

The simplicity of the chart, however, only identifies those who can positively influence the purchase. There are others such as the users of the stationery who may have veto power – a potential negative influence on the purchase. You may need to take these into account in planning communications.

These side influences are particularly important in major capital purchases. Consider the decision chart for a management information system installation (Figure 4.6). All departments in the client company are likely to be involved in identifying what is needed from a new system. The Information Technology or Management Information Systems department will drive the process. At various stages, the finance department will be heavily involved and the final decision will go to board level. That's an awful lot of people, mostly non-experts, with the potential ability to block the efforts of a particular manufacturer.

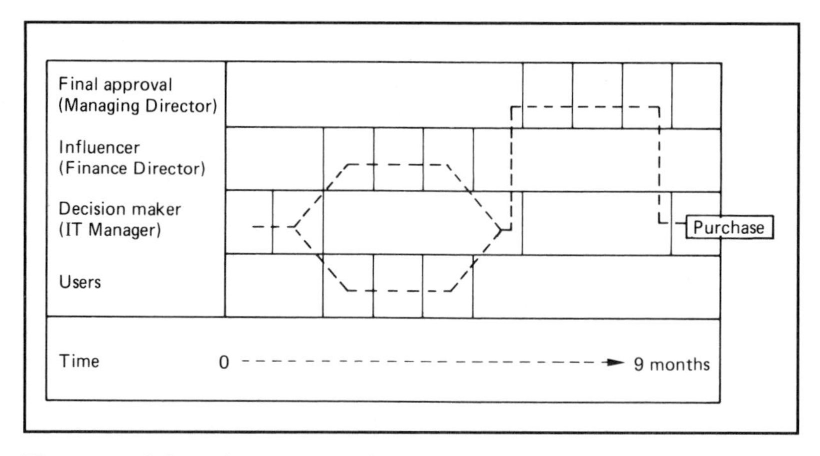

Figure 4.6 Information system purchase

DON'T ADVERTISE TO 'MARKETS'

At this stage you have an overview of your market and an understanding of the stages of decision making for your type of product. But, that's still not enough; good advertising doesn't talk to markets, it talks to people – ideally, to an individual. So who are these people who're so important, who'll be your customers? And what makes them tick?

For an established product the start point should be your existing customers. Who are they? What kind of people? What's important to them? For a new product, research is the key.

Yet again, there are substantial differences between consumer goods markets and business markets – but also a surprising number of similarities. We'll look at both.

Identifying your consumer

The objective is to describe the 'average' customer for your product in terms which advertising, or indeed any method of communication, can address effectively. As we have said earlier, the start point will be either an analysis of existing customers or market research. (Incidentally, it is to be hoped that you are never in the position of having a totally new product but no idea who is likely to buy it. In the nineteenth century you could get away with it – but it's asking for trouble in today's market!)

Take a look at the information you hold on your existing customer base – or organize the necessary research. What does the analysis reveal? Can you describe your audience by age, sex, background? Can you break it down by where they live, the kind of job they might have, their hobbies? This sort of analysis can itself go through several stages, and these stages have become more sophisticated with time.

Not too many years ago, 'demographics' was the key – age, sex and 'socio-economic' classification was all we had to go on. A typical description of the target for a quality family car might have been something like: AB male, aged 35–54 years, married with two children. The AB would tell us he's a professional – either in management or one of the professions such as medicine or teaching. Under these groupings, C1 would be a white-collar or office employee, C2 a blue-collar or factory floor worker and D and E covered the unemployed and disadvantaged. (In reading this in the 1990s it's not difficult to see its limitations. Classifying a newly qualified teacher alongside the Chairman of ICI hardly helps us to describe an 'average' consumer. Their tastes may possibly be the same but their purchasing power is unlikely to be!)

Then we had geo-demographics – a fancy name for adding where they live to the foregoing analysis! This, however, was a genuinely useful addition which led to the development of targeting aids like ACORN (A Classification of Residential Neighbourhoods). This system and the variants it spawned are based on the belief that like-minded people of similar income tend to live in similar houses. ACORN splits all houses in the UK into geographic groups of some 150 houses – and classifies each group. Thus our target for the quality car becomes more detailed; with two children, AB, living in the south-east in a four-bedroom, detached house. (We might argue, and with some validity, that the 'AB' is already becoming redundant by this stage.)

This additional information allowed the advertiser to picture the typical consumer in more detail. However, more was to come. We're now in the age of 'psychographic' and 'lifestyle' analysis. Forget the jargon – this just means we try to find out more about the views of the consumer and how he or she chooses to live.

The additional value of such information is self-evident. Think about where you live. Are your neighbours all the same as you? Do you all share the same attitudes and tastes? The answer is almost certainly, 'no'. It follows, then, that you are unlikely to buy the same brands – or respond to the same advertising.

Through such analysis, our target market description for the quality family car might evolve into something along the following lines: male, aged around 40, married with two teenage children. He's likely to be in middle management and can afford the mortgage on his four-bedroom house reasonably comfortably. He likes 1960s music and plays golf at weekends. He's becoming increasingly environmentally conscious and uses unleaded petrol. He currently drives a 1.8 litre middle-market car and wants something a little more classy – but which won't conflict with his environmental views.

This is a fictional example but realistic (maybe we've found the market for the recyclable BMW!). In fact, a creative team about to work on your advertising would appreciate even greater detail. Their aim will be to create advertising for a single 'individual'; the better they can picture that individual, the more effective they can be.

And your business market?

The objective remains the same: to describe the individual. But the task is even tougher. In selling to people buying with their company's money you will rarely have one single target – as is evident from the 'decision map'.

The usual start point in defining this audience is to look at business sectors. Some products, such as specialist oilfield equipment, are sold only to one sector. Mobile phones, in contrast, are sold to people who need to stay in touch while out of the office – and they could be in almost any kind of business.

In the example of the oilfield equipment the sector almost defines itself. However, it is certainly possible to refine our mobile phone example. Which sectors are most likely to spend time on the road? We might identify the building trade, surveyors and others as being the most likely prospects. This does not mean to exclude other users; by ranking the sectors in priority order, however, you will make media selection easier – as we shall see in a later chapter.

Then, using the decision map, we focus on the key decision maker. Can we describe an individual? To some extent, we can. To return to our example of a management information system, we can reasonably ascertain that our Management Information Services manager is likely to be degree educated and fully computer literate. He or she is probably 30–40 years old, with at least ten years' experience. By scanning relevant job advertisements, we could establish an approximate salary and project a likely lifestyle. The same exercise could be done for each of the key influencers in the decision chain.

HOW WELL CAN YOU DEFINE YOUR OWN MARKET?

1. List all of your audiences by answering, 'Who can help or hinder me in achieving my objectives?'
2. Define your likely advertising audiences
   - By using a 'road map'
   - By using a 'decision map'
   - By describing the key individuals.

Further reading

CACI, *ACORN : A Classification of Residential Neighbourhoods*, CACI Ltd, CACI House, Kensington Village, Avonmore Road, London.

Ehrenberg and Goodhardt, *Understanding Buyer Behaviour*, Wiley, New York.

Parkson L. and Baker A. (1986), *Organisational Buying Behaviour*, Macmillan.

Wolfe, Alan (1991), *Eurobuyer*, Primary Contact Ltd, Porters Place, 33 St John Street, London.

5 What does your market think?

Analyse the competition – The market's view of them and you – How much do you know about your market?

By now, you know a great deal about your market; it's time to put those people into the context of what's going on in your sector, and what your target individuals feel and think about that sector.

This is, again, a multi-stage process and you are unlikely to be able to go through all stages without the help of some research. In fact, there are three stages: the competitive position in your market; what the target audience feels about the product sector in general; and their attitudes to you and your competitors specifically.

Your experience is likely to enable you to analyse the competitive position in some depth – but don't fall into the trap of believing that you know what your market thinks. Our objective is to produce advertising which provides an identifiable, quantifiable return for your investment. A clear understanding of what makes the audience tick, in relation to your products, is essential to achieving that objective. Research expenditure which gets us closer to that understanding is, invariably, money well spent. Let's take a walk through the three stages.

THE COMPETITIVE MARKET

Start with the broad overview of the market. How large is it, in terms of both unit volume and value? Is it growing, static or declining? Are there any major changes going on? Are there threats from new or substitute products? This is an exercise which you should have undertaken in preparing the marketing plan, but it is nevertheless worth mentioning in a book on advertising, since an understanding of the dynamics of the market will be important in defining the advertising objectives and hence in developing effective creative solutions.

Market trends and changes are particularly important. In the last few years we have seen many examples of how markets have undergone fundamental changes that have dictated a complete review of marketing strategies and hence advertising. Consider, for example, the move of personal computers from esoteric specialist dealers to

High Street retail outlets; the shift from 'petrol stations' to service centres selling a wide range of goods; the change in financial services which has made it difficult to tell the difference between a building society and a bank; and the enormous growth in fast-food outlets.

Look at each competitor

Analyse, as far as possible, the strengths and weaknesses of each competitor. Which features do their products offer? How well do they perform in each key measure of performance? Take each competitor's product range apart at the seams. Assess the range overall to establish whether there are gaps you might exploit. Measure their quality and reliability.

But look beyond the physical 'product'. Do they have adequate distribution? Examine the channels each uses; check geographic coverage and quality of distributors and retailers. Is the after-sales service up to scratch? Find out how fast they respond to problems or complaints; whether their service teams are well trained; and what kind of after-sales contracts they offer. Look at their pricing policy. Does it reflect their quality standards - are they, therefore, offering value for money? Look very closely at their advertising over the last year or eighteen months. There is a great deal to be learned from this last exercise. You should be able to identify what they think is important to the market, what they feel they offer best and, also, at whom they are aiming their advertising.

This will give a reasonable picture of each major competitor's advertising strategy – and a valuable guide in developing your own. Not because you will wish to duplicate theirs – indeed, often the precise opposite.

NOW FOR A DIFFERENT POINT OF VIEW

Much of what we have covered up to this point has involved harnessing your own views of the world outside. However, the most valuable thing we ever learn in marketing is that the only truth is the customer's perception. It's time to adopt a different standpoint and, in the words of Robert Burns, 'see ourselves as others see us'.

When we begin to look at our own product sector with the customer's eyes we need to make two significant shifts. One is the change of viewpoint, the other is a change in thinking – namely, to stop seeing our products in terms of their physical attributes and features and to start considering them in terms of their emotional values and the benefits they deliver.

Figure 5.1

This is a key point, but it is somewhat easier to illustrate than to explain. I am indebted to Richard Jeans, a former colleague, for the analogy which follows.

Take a brief look, right now, at Figure 5.1. What do you see? Are you confident you know what it is? It is pretty safe to assume you have 'seen' an egg. Yet you might be alone in thinking that's what it is. A food technologist might see a calcium exoshell with a nutrient centre; the grocer, a profit opportunity; the shopper, a cheap, nutritional meal; the child eating one, a toy for playing in with toasted 'soldiers'; the political demonstrator, a missile with built-in mess. And, of course, the poor old hen thought it was having a baby.

Note that none of these perceptions is related to a specific brand of egg – but rather eggs as a product sector. That identifies the second stage of your analysis; what does the market think about your sector? Are your consumers buying washing powder, or cleaner clothes? Are they buying a chocolate bar or, rather, fun and self-indulgence? Getting to grips with these issues is fundamental to effective advertising. If we fail to understand the real motivation to buy we cannot brief an agency effectively and, no matter how brilliant the creative team, we'll never get the best advertising.

The point is equally valid in selling to businesses. To revert to our earlier example, no business actually wants to buy a new information system. Think of the implications: high capital cost, an enormous drain on management resources and extensive disruption while the changeover is made. Yet businesses do buy new computer systems - or, is it that they are buying better management information to provide fast, more informed decision making to help maintain a competitive edge?

You must have an understanding of these buying motivations. The only people who really know them are your potential customers. The only way to find out is to get out there and ask them.

WHAT DO THEY THINK OF YOU?

Finally, it's time to look at what the market thinks of you and your products – and your competitors and their products. (Again, research is likely to be essential to obtain enough information, in depth.)

As in any research, you'll need to ask the right questions if you're to get meaningful and usable answers. Start by preparing a detailed list of all the things which might be important to the customer. (Many of them will have been identified in researching the previous stage of the analysis.) Let's take a look at how such a list might look for a food product:

Product:	overall taste
	texture
	appearance
	portion size
	ingredients
Cooking:	ease of use
	desirability of method
	cooking time
	cooking temperature
Packaging:	appearance
	information
	size
	shape
	ease of opening
	re-sealability
	packaging material
Distribution:	availability
Pricing:	price level
	value for money
	– standard pack
	– family pack

However, you'll need to go much further. Use an experienced research agency to probe the emotional values, measure customer loyalty and so on, and do the same exercise for each significant competitor.

The process is essentially the same for a business product or service. But, generally, many more factors come into play. Compare the food example with this next one for a processing drum for waste paper recovery:

Product:	capacity
	throughput
	chemicals usage
	flexibility in input material
	percentage fibre recovery
	build quality
	size
	materials used
	ease of integration with other plant
	level of waste produced
	quality of fibre output
Maintenance:	overall design
	ease of access
	interchangeability of parts
	need for special tools
	clear instruction manuals
	number of wearing parts
	estimated life of key wearing parts
Support:	availability of parts
	local service expertise
	operator training
People:	quality of sales staff
	quality of support staff
	willingness to help
	speed of response
	ease in dealing with
Financial:	initial cost
	maintenance cost
	parts cost
	financing packages
Company:	stability
	reputation
	policies
	systems
	facilities

A long list, yet far from exhaustive. On a multi-million-pound piece of equipment, potential customers (with their multi-layered decision making) will assess you and your products against a plethora of 'ideals'. Your overall package has to add up to more than that of your competitors if you are to close the deal.

Note that, in a decision-making group, perceptions of the product or sector will vary. For our computer-based information system, the IT specialist may seek the latest and sexiest in computer technology, the marketing director wants software abilities which are different from those required by the finance director. Their emotional responses to your brand will vary, too. You may have a wonderful image with the managing director, born of your strength in mainframes but the younger IT manager was brought up on networked PCs, where you are a late entrant with a weaker image. So your communication may need to address different issues with different members of the decision-making team.

The result of your research should be an analysis which helps you clearly identify your strengths and weaknesses when compared with the competition, and identifies any variances in attitude among segments of your audience.

DO YOU KNOW ENOUGH?

1 Your market
   How large is it? – value
   – units
   Is it growing, static or declining?
   Who are the big players? – names
   – market shares
   What trends can you see?
2 Your competitors
   Prepare a chart with key competitors along one axis and key competitive issues down the other. Score each competitor (say, in points out of ten) against each of the key issues. From the finished analysis, identify your own major strengths and weaknesses.
3 Your market's attitudes
   What are the most important benefits which customers want from your product sector?
   Do they believe that you and your competitors deliver these benefits?
   What do you appear to be delivering better than the competition?

Further reading

Foxall, F. R. (1986), *Consumer Choice*, Macmillan.
Worcester, R. M. and Downham, J. (1986), *Consumer Market Research Handbook*, Elsevier/North-Holland, Amsterdam.

6 What's the message?

The purpose of the message – Identifying the benefit – Make it a one-liner – Handling multiple messages – What are you trying to say?

We have now reviewed your past activity and you should have a feel for what works and what doesn't. We've looked at where advertising slots into business planning. We've considered how advertising might combine with other techniques of communications for optimum results. You've defined your audiences and analysed your market. And you've identified where advertising should be used. At last, we can get down to doing something!

Have you ever been asked to give a speech, or tell a joke, or respond to a toast – at the drop of a hat? The first response is invariably something akin to panic – 'Oh no! What will I say?' So you mumble and fumble for a moment or two until you find a theme – and off you head towards a standing ovation (well, it's nice to dream!).

ADVERTISING MUST HAVE A MESSAGE

Advertising which doesn't have a message goes into the same panic. It's likely to stutter along until it finds something, however tenuous, to say – then it may find a little fluency. But it will never get that standing ovation from your market.

The best advertising not only has a message, it has a single, single-minded and simple one. It is critical to bear in mind that you have but a few fleeting seconds to capture your prospects' attention and to interest or intrigue them into paying heed to your message. Vague, obtuse or complex messages are an anathema to producing effective advertising.

WHAT SHOULD THE MESSAGE DO?

If you have defined the role for advertising (educate, inform, persuade, etc.) then you have the first part of the answer. But the message, or 'proposition' as it's frequently known, must do more if your advertising is to work. The proposition should be aimed at achieving two things: it should motivate your audience to respond in the way you want it to, and it should help you to stand out from your competitors. It should motivate *and* differentiate. To achieve this, the proposition must contain some form of benefit, something capable of capturing the viewer's, reader's or listener's interest.

THE IMPORTANCE OF THE BENEFIT

With a few, relatively rare exceptions, people do not actively choose to pay attention to advertising. They will do so only if we give them a valid reason to do so; only if we answer the unspoken question, 'What's in this for me?' The answer can be a concrete, tangible benefit such as a higher interest rate on savings, or improved productivity. Equally, and in consumer goods more commonly, it can be an intangible such as a set of values or an image which coincides with the potential customer's self-perception. The one thing we can be sure of is that, if there is no benefit, the chances of making your advertising pay are negligible.

IDENTIFYING THE RIGHT BENEFIT

The benefit you choose to focus on must, of course, be meaningful to your market. If not, it fails to fulfil the need for motivation. It must also allow you a fair chance to take the high ground in some aspect of the consumer's perception – or it will fail to differentiate. To find the right benefit message, it is worth following a standard approach (Figure 6.1).

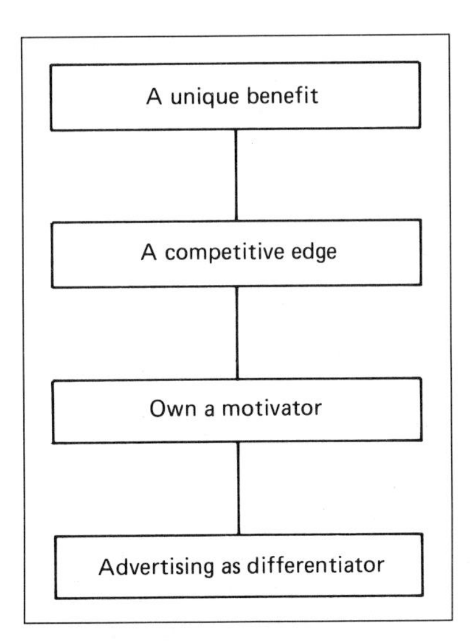

Figure 6.1 A hierarchy of messages

What is unique?

Is there anything about your product, service or company which no-one else has? A feature of your product which delivers a meaningful benefit unique to you is unquestionably the strongest of all propositions. In reality, such unique benefits are rare in today's highly competitive marketplace. However, they do occur, usually as a result of a technological breakthrough. Recent examples have included the first genuinely pocket-sized mobile phone; the first camcorder to weigh under 2 kilos; the first multi-play CD system. All of which were quickly matched by competitors!

Uniqueness is usually a short-term competitive edge – but one which should be exploited hard while it exists. However, be aware of uniqueness for its own sake. Sticking a third axle onto a Ford Mondeo may well make it the only six-wheel family car on the market – but if the extra wheels don't deliver something extra and valuable in the opinion of the target market, the move is doomed to commercial failure.

What do you do better?

When you analysed competitor products and services, where did you score best? Which aspects of your performance were better than the competition? This is the second search area for your proposition.

When we looked at the market, we identified what was important to potential customers in assessing products in our sector. How do our product advantages stack-up against what's important to the customer?

Try tabulating both sets of information (Figure 6.2). On the left-hand side we have a list of aspects of what we offer which are better than our competitors. Make your own list, starting with that aspect where you have the most lead. If, for example, you're streets ahead on after-sales service, that should head the list. Work down until you end with the benefit where you are only marginally ahead. On the right-hand side, list the market's priority ranking of what is important to them. Now you can compare the two to find the key message.

Start with your top item (say, after-sales service). As this also appears in the top few items on the market's list, you have the makings of a strong message. If, however, after-sales service is relatively unimportant to the market – appearing as item 10, for example – forget it! It will not be enough of a motivator to work. So move to your second item and repeat the process and so on, down the list. It's perfectly possible that even this exercise won't identify a significant message, especially if you're in fast-moving consumer goods.

Our strengths	The market wants
1	1
2	2
3	3
4	4
5	5
6	6
7	7
8	8

Figure 6.2 Identifying meaningful advantage

Let the customer's views decide

The next stage must be to concentrate completely on the right-hand side of your table. Now we accept that your product is as good as, but not particularly better than that of your competitors, and we begin to look for our proposition purely from the customer's viewpoint. The right-hand list gives us, in priority order, the main motivators for your product area. Can you set out to 'own' one of the key ones?

This concept of 'ownership' is perhaps easiest to explain by example. Way back in the 1950s, research showed that the great majority of people only brushed their teeth once each day, in the morning. At that time, they were doing so not to fight decay or tartar or plaque but because their mouths tasted foul in the morning and they didn't like that. So a fresh mouth and breath was a key motivator for the whole product category. Colgate were the first to grasp the importance of this knowledge and the 'ring of confidence' was born.

In the same way, Persil owns whiteness, Heineken owns refreshment and Hamlet owns relaxation.

Are any of your market's top three motivators still up for grabs? Look carefully at your competitors' advertising, and at your own research results. If a key motivator has not been captured by someone else, and you can deliver it, make it yours.

Build on a lesser benefit

How could you successfully launch a new washing powder? The marketplace is crowded, highly competitive and dominated by very strong brands. The main motivator has long since gone to a powerful competitor.

It's a tough task, yet one which has been achieved at least twice in the last couple of years. Ecover achieved it by recognizing the growing importance of the 'green' movement and launching an environmentally more friendly product. The company accepts that it is, in essence, in a niche market. Only a fairly small proportion of householders are yet prepared to buy on purely environmental grounds – but Ecover has cornered that segment of the market.

In contrast, Unilever is a mass-marketer. It is interested only in high-volume sales in large potential markets. It, too, has had a major success across Europe – with Radion. In this case, the smell of clothes after washing was identified as a secondary motivator. The product was formulated to ensure that clothes smelled 'cleaner' after washing, and the proposition was a combination of the main motivator (gets clothes clean) with a secondary motivator (and gets rid of unpleasant smells).

Both are good examples of products which met the main requirement, building a good proposition from a lower-ranking benefit.

What if you don't even have that?

This is the toughest position to be in – but it's not uncommon. Cigarettes and perfumes would be two areas where this dilemma abounds.

The only real route left at this point is to allow the audience to identify with the brand – through your advertising. The benefit becomes something along the lines of 'this product is for people like me'. It is the weakest of all propositions, yet it can be successful if the advertising is extremely well done. Its potential effectiveness is easily researched. Take a gent's polo shirt, with no brand identification, and research who would buy it and at what price. Now brand it Ralph Lauren or Lacoste and repeat the exercise!

MAKE THE MESSAGE A ONE-LINER

Get into the habit of writing concise, tightly defined messages. These always produce the most relevant and most powerful creative approach because they give the creative team a clear, tight brief. And, in case it hasn't been said before, ensure that every message contains a benefit!

Try comparing these two:

- 'Our new pre-mix cherry cake offers more fruit, a more consistent mix and predictable results. When you add milk, the light mix ensures even heat dispersion which allows the cake to be cooked in only 50% of the time previously needed.'
- 'For the first time: a perfect cherry cake, every time, in half the time.'

The first version would drive a good creative team crazy. What's the real benefit? It might be extra fruit; you only need to add milk; light texture; consistent results; or the time saving. The second gives the team much more to get its teeth into (if you'll forgive the pun). It focuses their attention on what is the main motivator, (consistent results) and the client's key differentiator, (the time saving and convenience).

Messages are not headlines

In defining a message, don't try to produce an advertisement. Concentrate simply on developing a simple, concise and single-minded proposition. And don't worry if it sounds boring – if you get it right, it will turn into an exciting headline at a later stage.

To illustrate my point, here are a few examples of propositions as they might have been briefed, and the headlines which resulted:

Client: Sony
Proposition: Sound quality so good that it's completely lifelike.
Headline: It's like having Keith Moon in the room, only safer.

Client: Timberland
Proposition: A jacket that protects against freezing conditions.
Headline: In some States of America, the penalty for exposing yourself is death.

Client: Porsche
Proposition: A very fast car (0–60 mph in 5.5 seconds).
Headline: It's about as fast as you can go without having to eat airline food.

Client: Dr Whites
Proposition: Tampons that are rounded for comfort.
Headline: If men were shaped like most tampons, the human race would have died out by now.

Client: Red Star
Proposition: Very fast delivery by rail (top speed 125 mph).
Headline: If anyone offers to take your parcel at 125 mph by road, please inform the police.

Client: CooperTools
Proposition: Tools so strong that they're used by loggers.
Headline: 'Out here there ain't but two kinds of tools. Good. And Broke.'

HOW MANY MESSAGES?

Having come this far, you may have arrived at the conclusion that one message isn't enough to achieve your communication aims. And, often, that will be a perfectly reasonable conclusion.

If we refer back to Figure 2.4 (repeated here), we can see an example where the communications plan has identified a number of

Message \ *Audience*	A	B	C	D
New shop open	●	●	●	●
Convenience foods stocked		●		
Long opening hours	●	●		●
Good local citizen	●	●	●	●
Responsible employer			●	●

Audience/message matrix

audiences which need to be influenced, and a variety of messages to be delivered. This situation calls for a judgement on how best to use the various elements of communication effectively. Let's put some real flesh on these bones by using a specific case.

The Harcros story

Harrisons & Crosfield plc is a major, blue-chip UK company with sales in excess of £1.5 billion. Its chemicals division comprised 16 small to medium-sized companies, based in 11 countries and trading under 13 different identities. Although made up of relatively small individual units, the division had total sales of over £500 million.

Peter Savage, a recently appointed divisional chief executive, took his team through a major overhaul of strategy. A decision was reached to develop a new identity, pull the division together and reposition it in the eyes of the market as the significant force which it indeed was. The overall message was 'Harcros is big enough to deliver attentive, high-quality service, locally'. When this was broken down by analysing the audiences, the audience/message matrix looked like Figure 6.3.

Audience / *Message*	*Employees*	*Customers*	*Marketplace*
Corporate strategy	●	●	●
New identity	●	●	●
Not job threat	●		
More opportunity	●		
Same service		●	
Bigger resources		●	●
Financially stable	●	●	●

Figure 6.3 Audience/message matrix: Harcros

As is clear, there was a number of messages to be delivered to each audience. At that stage the issue of time was tackled. The audiences were ranked in priority (with employees first, you'll be pleased to note!). Then the same was done with the messages. In a strategic campaign of this nature we cannot say everything to everyone, all at the same time. Using the same process will help you to identify various phases in a complex campaign.

In the event, a mix of activities was developed to suit the various audiences. However, the campaign aimed at customers and potential customers will serve to illustrate the approach.

Direct mail was used to tell existing clients of the changes before they became public knowledge. This was an ideal medium since it is, essentially, private. Thus they had 'insider' knowledge and were given the respect a customer deserves. Advertising was used to deliver only the core or overall message, in a campaign of three advertisements. PR was employed to fill in the details of the story through editorial coverage – a route more appropriate to such diverse information.

There are other options

It would have been possible to carry all the client and market messages through advertising. For example, Harcros could have run a corporate campaign centrally, with the business units telling their own stories individually and complementing the central activity. Or, instead of using a campaign of three advertisements for the single, overall message, the company could have commissioned one advertisement per sub-message.

There are no hard-and-fast rules as to which strategy is right. Both logic and experience need to be applied in a given case to develop a structure for delivering each important message to the right place at the right time.

WHAT DID YOU WANT TO SAY?

1 Review your past advertising; look at each advertisement separately. Is there a benefit there? Is it the right benefit?
2 Draw up a table with your competitive advantages on the left and what your market wants on the right. Go through the process of defining the correct message.
3 How have you expressed the message? Review and re-write it until it is short, sharp, clear and, above all, single-minded.
4 Go back to your communications plan and determine which other messages should be delivered, and how.

Further reading

Bernstein, D., *Creative Advertising*, Longman.

Jones, J. P. (1986), *What's in a Name? Advertising and the Concept of Brands*, Gower.

Ogilvy, D. (1985), *Ogilvy on Advertising*, Crown Publishers Inc., New York.

7 Setting the objectives

The desired consumer response – Quantifying objectives – Setting up measurement systems – Setting your advertising objectives

We now know what you want your advertising to say, to whom, and why. However, this book concerns advertising which pays its way – and we're still not in a position to assess that. Our next step must be to turn our advertising aims into objectives – quantified and deadlined – and to ensure that we'll be able to measure the results after the campaign.

Neither of these stages is an absolute science. If you have no history of advertising, it will be difficult to establish realistic objectives. And, since advertising is only one of a million factors which affect business performance, it can be difficult to isolate its effect. In spite of these drawbacks, it is essential to set benchmarks and measure against them. It is a constant source of astonishment that an engineering company, for example, will analyse the potential return on the purchase of a new machine tool in microscopic detail – then approve a budget for advertising with only the vaguest notion of what it expects to achieve. Effective advertising is not simply an act of faith!

WHAT DO YOU WANT PEOPLE TO DO?

In Figure 3.5 (repeated here) we looked at the typical roles which advertising might play in your communications. Now it's time to link these relatively vague aims back to our understanding of how sales take place, then express them in terms of what we want people to *do* as a result of seeing our advertising.

Let's look again at two examples from different markets. A teenager wants to buy a portable stereo; let's assume they want radio plus twin cassette decks – and that they have the money! They're likely to start the process by discussing the purchase with their friends and listening to their views on equipment they own or know of. This is not an impulse purchase, so they'll shop around listening to and examining various manufacturers' models and 'sussing out' the best prices. The decision will be a complex one, based on a number of issues, including sound quality, features, style, price and 'street cred'. The teenager will be subject to both peer group and parental influences in making the final choice.

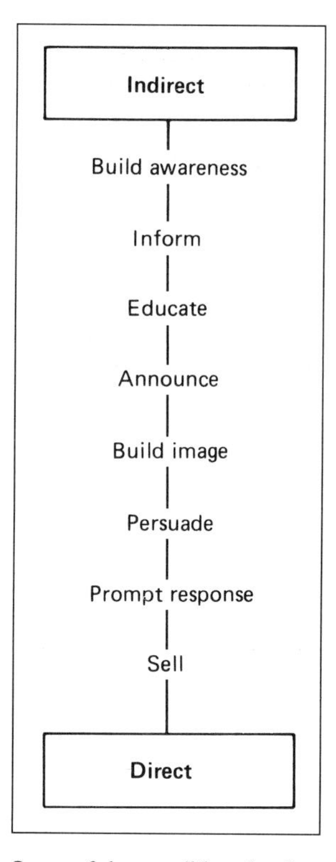

Some of the possible roles for advertising

What would we want this prospective customer to do as a result of our advertising? What action would take us closer to a sale?

One answer could be 'to visit a stockist and ask for a demonstration'. If research shows that such customers gather and read literature before shopping around, a more valid aim might be 'to ask for more information'.

The reality of advertising is that, outside the fast-moving consumer goods sector, you'll spend most of your money advertising to people who are not actively in the market at any given point in time. Think of all the teenagers who are not buying a stereo today! What action should we aim for among this segment of the audience?

A business example might be our machine tool manufacturer mentioned earlier. A high-value piece of capital equipment may be replaced on a five- to ten-year cycle. Assume an average of eight years, with a typical customer having, say, only four of a particular unit or type. Even if the customer has a totally logical replacement pattern, they'll only buy once every two years. So we need to be clear what our advertising is expected to do for this customer in the intervening period. In this case, the 'action' we desire could be to remember our name, understand what we offer, feel positively about our products or, perhaps, keep information on file. The key point is that, unless we know which reaction we seek, we can never measure the effectiveness of what we're doing.

ADDING THE MATHEMATICS

How many people do we want to take the defined action? By when? Quantity and timescale are two key attributes of any objective. Indeed, they are its essence; without either, we have a goal or an aim – not an objective.

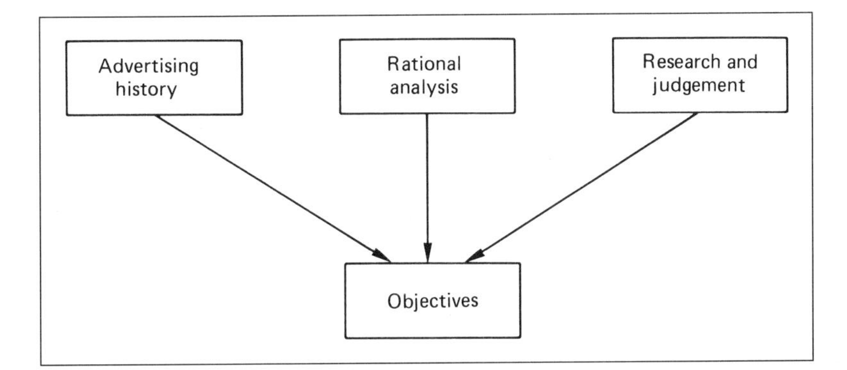

Figure 7.1 Setting advertising objectives

Setting objectives involves a combination of sources or activities (Figure 7.1). Your past achievements provide a guide for what might realistically be achievable. Rational analysis based on your marketing plan will help to identify what you need to achieve. And a combination of research and your own experience of the market provides the final feel for whether the proposed objectives are viable. Evidently, valuable past history of advertising effectiveness makes this process easier for the experienced advertiser than for those coming to it for the first time.

Objectives based on the past

These are unquestionably the easiest of all to establish. If you have several years' records of activity and results, your audit will not only have identified what has worked best but will have given a measure of what 'best' means. At a simplistic level, you are pulling in enough enquiries to keep your business growing. They're costing you a given amount per enquiry. Generating enquiries continues to be advertising's key task. Under such circumstances it would be straightforward to set an objective which said something like 'to generate the same volume of enquiries as last year at a 10% reduction in cost per enquiry'.

If your analysis is somewhat more sophisticated you may have recorded an increase in cost per enquiry as your market share has increased. The 'law of diminishing marginal returns' is applying itself – the higher your market share, the more it costs you for each extra percentage point of share. From this information you may be able to develop a graph of cost per enquiry related to total volume of enquiries – and thus have a reasonable prediction of what a 'fair' cost per enquiry would be against a given volume objective. But, of course, you would still have to establish that volume objective.

Back to the marketing plan

This is where rational analysis comes in, and where research shows its value in objective setting. Your analysis should always begin with the marketing objectives set within your business plan and work back to your advertising objective. To illustrate the process, let's return to our model of the process of a sale (Figure 3.4, repeated here). However,

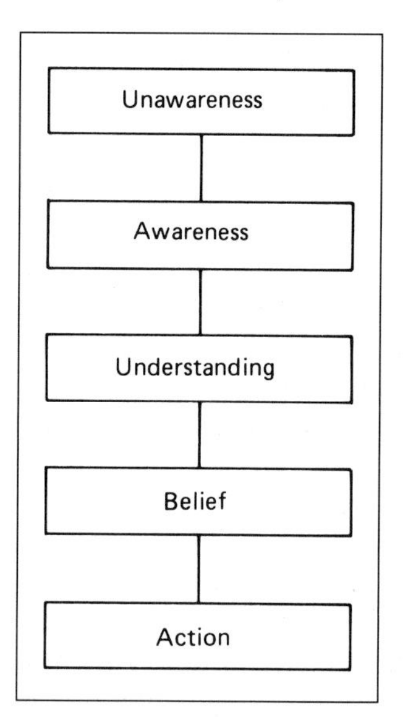

From McDonald's 'brand loyalty ladder'

in this case we've broken 'action' down into two parts, response and purchase.

Domesticity plc is a manufacturer of fitted furniture which has decided to enter the kitchens market. Its marketing plan sets the objective of a 5% market share in the first year. Its distribution strategy involves selling through specialist up-market retailers who will be responsible for local advertising. Domesticity has therefore defined the task for its own national advertising as building awareness, understanding of its range and of a reputation for high quality. It has researched the market extensively and has brought in experts to manage the new division.

The research indicated that, let's say, 1 million kitchens are sold in the market each year, of which 20% fall into Domesticity's up-market segment; a potential market of 200 000 and thus a marketing objective of 10 000 installations in year 1. Industry experience suggests that a conversion from interest to sale of 4:1 is the norm. So for Domesticity to achieve its objective at least 40 000 prospects need to consider their products. But each of those will reject 50% of kitchens at the 'brochure-reading' stage and only make the effort to go and see the rest. Thus, we may have an enquiry target of 80 000.

In-depth research may have shown that prospective purchasers are avid brochure collectors at the early stage and will, in fact, respond to four out of every five advertisements which they perceive to be appropriate. So to achieve 80 000 enquiries, we need to reach 100 000 prospective purchasers: half of the market. One might reasonably argue that our awareness objective is established – except that we don't know *which* half! In fact, our market buys a new kitchen every seven years; our target audience is 7 × 200 000 or 1.4 million people, and we need 50% awareness to achieve our objective.

We have established a hierarchy of objectives for our first year:

1 To create awareness among 50% of the defined target audience.
2 To develop a belief that our quality is appropriate amongst 40% of our audience (7 × 80 000).
3 To generate a total of 80 000 enquiries.
4 To instil a belief amongst 40 000 prospects that our range is worth seeing.
5 To make sales of 10 000 installations.

The first two of these are valid objectives for Domesticity's corporate advertising. The third could be split further and allocated between the corporate advertising and retailers' local advertising. The fourth is an objective to be achieved by the literature and response package. And the last is down to the sales team.

Apply the process and add experience

The same analytical approach can be applied to any product. A combination of solid research and analysis should allow you to define quantified objectives for more or less any stage of the selling or communications process. Admittedly, it's sometimes not enough. If the analysis suggests you need 110% awareness among your audience, something clearly has gone wrong!

That's where you'll need all your experience to scrutinize the research findings and dissect the assumptions until you've identified the nonsense element. By using the process, checking and refining, it is always possible to produce reasonable working objectives. If you have the research available! If not, then you are forced to rely on the combination of the other two elements – past history and experience of the market. In this case, you should still be able to establish some objectives using the same process – but they're in danger of being much less realistic. However, even shaky objectives are better than none, since they do at least provide some form of anchor against which to measure movements in performance.

CAN YOU REALLY MEASURE RESULTS?

The short answer is, yes, you can – if you set up the systems in advance and you are prepared to fund the measurement. In fact, it is not only possible but essential that you do so if you are to make the right management decisions. How else might you determine whether more advertising or an additional salesperson is the better investment, for example?

The mechanism for measurement must be chosen to suit the objectives for the advertising. You will remember our friends at Domesticity plc who set five objectives earlier in this chapter. Looking at them, not in the original order, we can define measurement systems for each:

To make sales of 10 000 installations
You can bet this one gets measured to death by an army of sales managers and accountants!
To generate a total of 80 000 enquiries
If they all come by post, to one point, we could simply count them and write the running total in a notebook each day. However, they're likely to come by post, telephone and personal callers to the retailer. So Domesticity needs to design and instal a decent tracking system. But that's relatively easy to do and, indeed, a reasonable package could be bought 'off-the-shelf'.

To instil a belief among 40 000 prospects that our range is worth seeing
Now we need to log visitors to the showrooms, count them and, ideally, compare them with our list of enquirers to ensure they're the same people and we're achieving the 50% conversion from initial enquiry to viewing the products.
To build awareness among 50% of the defined target audience
and
To develop a belief that our quality is appropriate among 40% of our audience
There's no substitute for research to verify these two. Our example showed a new market entry. In an existing market, these objectives would be about moving awareness or perception from *X*% to *Y*% or, perhaps, being ranked higher than before against specific competitors. Either way, you will need pre-campaign research to establish the current position and post-campaign research to identify what was achieved.

Against each of our five objectives, three of which relate specifically to advertising, we *can* measure what is being achieved.

A BRIEF WORD ON RESEARCH

If you run a small company with very limited resources, you may be tempted to dispense with research on cost grounds. Don't! There are many sources of cheap information on your market; libraries, trade associations and trade magazines, to name but a few. You can supplement this with salesforce and customer feedback. You could do your own more formal research, but that's a temptation to be resisted. The value of research lies in its professional design and objectivity. Few of us are research professionals – and a poor questionnaire or bad sample gives useless results – and *none* of us is objective about our own company.

Good research need not cost the earth. Even low-cost research, if professionally done, can yield some valuable, actionable information. And, let's face it, if your advertising budget is £20 000, it's worth investing £2 000 to get a modest 10% improvement in advertising effectiveness.

WILL I SEE IT ON MY BOTTOM-LINE?

If you follow the process for defining the objectives you are almost forced to identify what the results could do to help you sell. Therefore you know the *potential* effect on your bottom line of achieving the objectives.

What advertising cannot do is stave off a major recession, improve your sales team or give you better products. So good advertising, no matter how effective, cannot guarantee bottom-line results, it can only contribute.

Which leads us to a last, important point. We must ensure that we are measuring the right things. Don't measure your advertising on aspects over which it has little control. And please don't set an awareness objective and then measure it by counting responses!

SET YOUR ADVERTISING OBJECTIVES

1. Note down your marketing objectives.
2. Using the purchasing model, identify what action you want from your market at each stage.
3. Do your maths. Quantify these actions by analysing what you know of your conversion rates from stage to stage.
4. List your advertising objectives.
5. Decide how you will measure them. What action must you take to put the mechanism in place?

Further reading

Hopkins, C. (1987), *My Life in Advertising and Scientific Advertising*, Crown Publishers, New York.

White, N. (1988), *Advertising: What it is and how to do it*, McGraw-Hill.

8 The right investment

Budget setting – A look at various methodologies – A recommended approach – Identify your best approach

One of the most vexed questions in advertising: how much should I spend? You're unlikely to be surprised to find that there's no ready-to-wear answer. It's a little too simple to say 'enough to do the job'; there's no automatic formula for gaining 10% awareness or generating enquiries for a new product or changing the market's attitudes. The problem lies in our imperfect understanding of how advertising works, combined with our inability to quantify standards of creativity.

Numerous research studies have proven that committed advertisers consistently outperform non-advertisers on all the key business ratios. But none has explained why. At the same time, we know through comparative testing that one creative solution can be significantly more effective than another. But we have no definitive way of predicting that effect.

Thus we are denied the easy formula which will tell us how many *X* must be added to how many *Y* to produce the result we seek in our advertising or even in our marketing objectives. Yet you have to set a budget which makes sense.

In the absence of exact science, you'll have to rely on some knowledge, extensive experience, and good business judgement. But fear not, there are approaches which can help.

Alan Wolfe of Primary Contact identifies four common routes to arriving at an advertising budget: *pragmatic*, *task-based*, *analytical* and *experimental*. These headings provide a useful basis for considering the options which face you. But there is one issue you should look at first.

HOW'S BUSINESS?

No budget development occurs in a vacuum. It's fairly pointless proving you need £10 million to advertise effectively if the company is totally incapable of funding that level of investment. So the start point for any thinking has to be real life. Last year's budget can provide a marker. How was company performance during that period? In purely business terms should you be looking to cut budget or are you healthy enough to contemplate an increase?

What about the competitive environment? If you operate in a fast-moving market, with more competitors moving in and existing ones upping their advertising spends, you may not have a choice. To maintain share of voice, you'll have to raise the budget and the company must find any necessary savings elsewhere. If the company has been finding it tough *and* competitive activity is increasing, you'll have a difficult dilemma: which is the best action for the short term and long term?

Of course, your objectives for the next budget period must be fundamental to your thinking. You will have identified what you are aiming to achieve against the market background. You should have defined the part advertising is to play. And you need enough budget to support that role.

Your thinking on these issues should lead you to some broad conclusions on whether your budget should be going up or down, and possibly some feel for the scale of that shift. But how to arrive at a precise figure?

PRAGMATIC METHODS

This approach establishes the budget as a predetermined percentage of sales – the advertising-to-sales ratio. A minor variant is a fixed sum per unit of sales allocated as a budget; it is still commonly used, mainly in industrial goods markets.

Its sole advantage is reduced management stress! All the pain of negotiating a budget is gone; all you need is ten seconds and a calculator. However, this route, even when based on forecast rather than historic sales, takes no account of what is happening out there in the rest of the world. Nor does it reflect what needs to be done to achieve the set objectives.

A purely financially driven option is to spend 'what's left' on advertising. Basically, this means deducting target profit, fixed costs and higher-priority costs from sales revenue and, if there's anything left, that's the advertising budget. Fortunately, this approach is now extremely rare – for it is indefensible. It leads to advertising only in the good years, not in the tougher times when sales and prices need all the support they can get.

Equally bad is 'same as last year plus a bit for inflation'. This one positively works against the company; it fails to support any possible growth.

The final, pragmatic approach is driven by competitor activity. In essence, the budget is set by analysing your competitors' advertising then making a strategic decision to spend less, the same or more. It has the benefit of reflecting real activity in the marketplace and it recognizes that 'share of voice' is important; it reflects the need to be seen and heard among competitors' activity.

On the downside, it may be reflecting your competitors' communications needs rather than your own. You are unlikely to have a full picture of their communications plans and therefore you won't know if, for example, they are putting all their funds into other activities and maintaining only a minimum advertising presence. If, conversely, your own strategy uses advertising as a mainstay of communications, your whole programme will be underfunded if competitor advertising spend is your benchmark.

TASK-BASED BUDGETS

By definition, this approach is an attempt to match the funds to be made available to the job which, you have determined, needs to be done. Again, it takes a number of forms, of which the following are examples.

One form is to invest a predetermined amount per customer, the budget being adjusted as new customers are won. This has the merit that the budget grows with the company's success. However, it does mean that the budget growth lags behind to some extent. And it still doesn't cater for any form of pioneering or new product launches.

You could use a predetermined number of 'impacts' per potential customer, where an impact is each time that prospect is exposed to your advertising message. This has considerable merit since it reflects, fairly accurately, the job to be done. However, defining the right number of impacts is an inexact science in itself – and the outcome may not be affordable.

Alternatively, you might set out to match your share of advertising expenditure in your market to your share of that market. Thus you research competitor spends in total and budget the same percentage as your market share. Once again, this form has a solid basis in the reality of the market but it is static rather than dynamic; it does not necessarily reflect changes and trends in the marketplace. The entry of an ambitious new competitor may imply a need to increase advertising to defend a market position, but this particular budgeting method would not reflect that.

ANALYTICAL METHODS

These are based around modelling techniques which attempt to predict sales response to changes in advertising expenditure. They range from simple models (for example, when experience suggests that a 10% rise in advertising produces a similar sales increase) up to complex econometric modelling. This latter generally uses sophisticated computer techniques to analyse a wide range of historical information. Its objective is to identify correlations between factors such as market trends, economic climate and competitive activity, to build a 'model' of the market, and hence to be able to predict the effect of a change in any of the variables.

Analytical methods can be highly valuable marketing tools – but they are far from infallible. They reduce the risk of decision making but can never eliminate it. Frankly, econometric modelling is probably out of the question for all but the biggest companies. It requires a vast amount of validated historical data, a good deal of time to construct, and plenty of money to build and maintain.

EXPERIMENTAL METHODS

The final option is to test your way progressively to a budget. This is done by running your 'normal' programme and changing one aspect at a time to identify the effect. For example, you might run a newspaper advertising campaign but add TV in one or two regions only. Any sales shift away from the national trend, all other things being equal, can be attributed to the new activity, and the effect of adding TV on a national basis can be calculated with a fair degree of confidence.

This is an attractive option but suffers from two serious shortcomings as a foundation for budgeting: it would take a very long time to test a range of tactical options, and the effect obtained may be unique to the given set of circumstances in particular regions or at the particular time.

SO, WHAT'S THE BEST APPROACH?

I have listed only a selection of the budget-setting methods which have appeared in advertising literature over the years. Most are in current use. Some offer more advantages than disadvantages. Some are easier to use than others. There is no 'right' methodology any more than there is a magic formula.

Experience suggests that a variety of approaches, probably producing several different figures, should be used as part of a *process* of budget development. My personal preference is a mix of known advertising history, competitor activity analysis and task-based figures, applying some pragmatic evaluation to ensure that what I end up proposing makes sense for the business.

We know what we have spent over the last three or four years. What measurements did we have in place? Look at what was achieved in each of those years. It is important to register what we have learned about what works for our own company in our market. You should be able to do the same.

How do sales respond to advertising? If we can isolate a correlation between spend and sales or new product trial or customer loyalty, then we have an immensely valuable piece of information, and one which will suggest a figure to achieve the sales budgeted for the period under consideration. Or perhaps we can simply confirm that a certain percentage of sales allocated to advertising has indeed allowed the forecast to be met, and, again, gives us one figure for consideration.

A review of competitor activity will allow us to compare the weight of our spend against theirs by indexing to market share. Estimate the total ad spend in the market – let's say £10 million, which is 100% of the market. So, on average, a company with a 10% share should spend £1 million. You find a small but fast-growing competitor, with a 10% share, spending £1.4 million – so their index is 140.

You can do two things at this stage; calculate, from your market share, how much you 'should' be spending. Let's assume you have a 15% share; that's £1.5 million. But you're fighting a market leader with 18%, who is already on an index of 120 – spending £2.16 million. If they're your real target, to win share you may have to match their index. So you have a second figure of £1.8 million to add to your 'possible' budgets list.

Now turn back to your advertising objectives; your media objectives in particular (see also Chapter 12). From these, your agency will produce a further figure for expenditure needed to achieve the defined coverage and reach of your audience. Let's say £2 million.

Finally, take a look at the big wide world out there. What are the key trends? If the market is likely to be stagnant or declining, and your business is highly volume-sensitive, you may be heading for a cut-throat battle for market share. Your view may be that it will be 20% tougher than this year. So take this year's spend, allow inflation, increase it by your forecast shift in sales. Then add 20%.

The result of this exercise will be a range of figures from, let's say, £1.4 million to £2 million.

Run the process almost in reverse. Bearing in mind your cost structure, what volumes would have to be achieved to justify each of the possible levels of spend?

The time has come for your own judgement. Which of these volumes feels feasible at the given level of advertising under anticipated market conditions? This stage may not identify one figure but will narrow the range. Review again the affordability of these levels. What would be the downside of a shortfall in sales at a given spend level?

Now, make a decision. Typically, the final spend will not be at either extreme of the range. Where the budget ends up is likely to have as much to do with the character of your company as with anything else. In some, the voice of the finance director will hold sway, pushing towards the lowest figure in the range. In the more aggressive company, the expansionist views of the marketing director will gain the upper hand and the budget will settle near the top of the range.

WHAT'S YOUR APPROACH

1. Review how you normally set the advertising budget and identify its strengths and weaknesses.
2. How will you amend the approach to correct the weaknesses?
3. Re-examine your current year's budget, applying some new methodologies. How do the figures change? Is there validity in the change?

Further reading

Broadbent, S. (1991), *The Advertising Budget*, NTC Publications.

9 Making the most of an agency

DIY versus agency – The right kind of agency for you – Define your ideal – The selection process – The agency team – Making the relationship work – Paying the bill – Review your needs

How will you translate all your good work so far into something for the page or the airwaves? The vast majority of companies will use an advertising agency of some sort. But some don't. In this chapter, we'll look at the pros and cons of using an agency, how to go about selecting the right agency for you, and how to manage the relationship for optimum results.

IN-HOUSE OR AGENCY?

Many very small companies, some fair-sized ones and a few very big ones produce their own advertising using in-house resources. They would argue that this is more cost-effective than using an agency, and gives them precisely the advertising which they want.

There is some truth in both elements of this argument. Only the major companies are likely to have a full-time advertising team. For most, the individuals concerned allocate only part of their time to advertising. Where this helps to make full use of those employees it is indeed a fairly cheap option. After all, if they're needed for other tasks in any event, the overheads have already been incurred so the marginal cost of their advertising work is relatively low. Employees do, of course, live and breathe the company daily. So briefing is quicker and easier, and they will know what kind of advertising the company wants.

An agency, on the other hand, employs advertising specialists from various disciplines, specialists whom the company itself could not afford to employ because of the part-time nature of its advertising requirements. Thus the agency can field greater expertise in areas such as research, media selection and buying and creative development. It will also have production specialists to ensure that the finished advertisement or commercial looks as good on paper as it did on the drawing board.

The strongest argument in favour of using an agency is the quality of the result, and of the impression which that result gives of your company. The cost of creating an advertisement is usually a relatively small percentage of the media cost of using it. Small companies don't have the communications skills to produce effective advertising. A DIY approach is just as inappropriate to advertising as it would be to a legal problem.

Major companies with an in-house department would argue, rightly, that they have the same skills. The department, however, is unlikely to have more than one writer and one ad designer or art director. How long before they become stale working on just one account? Good creative teams thrive on variety, the kind of variety they get through working on a number of client accounts within one agency. It keeps them fresh and stimulates their creativity. If they become stale on a particular account it can be switched to another team within the agency. Indeed, some agencies have a specific policy of making such changes every three years or so to maintain freshness and enthusiasm on each client's business.

Since it books media on behalf of many clients, the agency is likely to buy more cheaply than the company could do directly. This can make a significant difference to how far your budget will stretch.

It's also worth bearing in mind that the agency's variety of experience can help your own thinking. While your business problems will be unique to you, the chances are that the agency has faced similar situations in the past and can bring such experience to bear, so you avoid re-inventing the wheel.

The last point in favour of using an agency is precisely because you are less likely to get the advertising you want – and far more likely to get the advertising that's right. The agency's objectivity, unencumbered by company history, politics or preconceptions, is perhaps the most valuable thing agencies bring to the table.

Overall, the right agency is certainly likely to be more expensive than a DIY approach. It is also more likely to produce advertising which works and is more cost-effective.

WHICH TYPE OF AGENCY IS RIGHT FOR YOU?

There are around a thousand companies in the UK alone which describe themselves as advertising agencies. They range from virtually one-man bands up to global agency networks like Ogilvy & Mather, J. Walter Thompson and Saatchi & Saatchi. There's certainly plenty of choice! Which is right for you depends entirely on your needs.

The first decision to face is whether to appoint a single, full-service agency or a number of specialist ones, and this decision may affect communications other than advertising. Some full-service agencies will work right across the spectrum and handle advertising, PR, direct mail, sales promotion and so on. These are most commonly either sector specialists (for example, the medical field or business-to-business communications) or regional agencies generally working on small to medium-sized accounts. Most of the big agencies handle only advertising but are full-service in that they deal with creative work, media buying, production and so on. Specialist suppliers range from creative 'hot shops' who do only the creative work for advertising, to media-buying houses, direct mail or direct marketing agencies and sales promotion specialists. Several factors influence this decision:

1 *Size of budget:* the budget which an agency is given to work with must be sufficient to motivate the team. Splitting a small budget among specialists may simply provide several poorly motivated agencies.
2 *Your resources:* running several agencies means that the client must take over the coordination role normally carried out by agency account management. Maintaining consistency of approach across your communications is important for optimum effect. This is harder to achieve, and will absorb much more management time, where several agencies are used rather than one.
3 *Your structure:* this is an allied point. If you are basically a one-product company you'll almost certainly want only one advertising agency. If you sell a number of products or brands under a brand management structure it is viable to appoint agencies brand by brand. If the target markets for those brands overlap or, indeed, compete head-on, it may be important to have separate agencies.
4 *How you sell:* with major consumer brands the public's perception is all-important. The advertising is a major part of the selling process and can afford to stand alone. A full-service, advertising-only agency is perfect in such a situation. Conversely, advertising may be only a support element in the sale and need to be part of a package including, for example, literature, direct mail and advertising. In this case a regional or sector specialist could be ideal.

WHAT DO YOU WANT THEM TO DO?

Now consider how you propose to use your agency. The answer may span the range from simply to do the advertising which you brief, through to being external advisers on marketing and communications. Irrespective of your choice of full-service or specialist agency, you'll need to bear this issue in mind. The same spectrum is found in both categories of agency mentioned above.

Once again, the key factor is likely to be the level of your own resources. In a large marketing department, with a team of product managers and an advertising or communications manager all reporting to a marketing director, you may not require much input to marketing or communications strategy. It is likely that you clearly define your advertising needs for yourself. The agency's involvement really only begins with the campaign brief. The picture may be entirely different in a small company where only a very few people run the whole marketing and sales function. In such a case, external marketing expertise available to your agency may be extremely valuable. It will greatly help the selection process if you can identify up-front the level of input which you seek.

DESCRIBE YOUR 'IDEAL' AGENCY

As with any recruitment or selection procedure, life becomes much easier if you have a clear idea of what you are looking for. The following headings may act as a useful guide to defining your own ideal agency. They are culled from several pieces of research and articles investigating what clients seek from advertising agencies. They are not intended to be in any order of priority; that's something you can decide for yourself at a later stage.

Market understanding: You may feel that it is important that your agency knows your market. Such knowledge might have been gained by working in related markets or even by having handled a competitor's advertising. Views vary as to the importance of this issue. A good agency should be capable of responding to a good brief for any type of product or market. Conversely, market knowledge does shorten the learning time it will take for an agency to develop a good feel for the market. This is particularly true of some specialist markets with significant legislative issues which control advertising (for example, medical products and financial services).

Appropriate skills: If you have defined a requirement which is wider than advertising alone, you should take a view on which other skill areas you need. Is direct mail, employee communications, PR, exhibitions or literature important?

Good creative work: No client ever looks for an agency with bad creative work! But it is worth considering the type of work you require; the type of work you admire. This does not lead you to dictating creative solutions to the agency; one hopes it avoids selecting an agency and then spending all your time fighting its creative approach. It's pointless, for example, choosing a highly creative agency producing brave or relatively risky advertising if you know in your heart that you could never agree to it for your company nor sell it to your colleagues.

Strategic input: How this is assessed will depend on the earlier decision on what you want an agency to do. Subject to that answer you may assess this based on corporate strategy, marketing strategy, communications strategy or advertising strategy.

The right size: It rarely makes sense to take a very small budget into a very big agency or a very big budget into a very small agency. As a client, you are likely to want two things: reasonable attention to your account by senior management, and sufficient resources to handle your account smoothly and effectively. Take a view on which of these two is the more important to you. How widespread is your company's activity? In a multinational you may want or need a global agency network to support your local operations and give consistency to your advertising across a number of markets. But, if you are a single-outlet car dealership in East Anglia a small regional agency might suit you much better.

THE SELECTION PROCESS

Figure 9.1 shows a typical selection process, which takes many stages, a great deal of management time, a fair amount of shoe leather, and often a lot of heartache. However, a wise advertising manager is looking for a long-term relationship with an agency (precisely because changing causes so much grief!). That makes the right selection crucial – so it's well worth any effort to reduce the risk of the wrong choice.

Research

It would be, to say the least, somewhat impractical to see presentations from every agency in the country. So we need a way of identifying, say, a dozen agencies as our 'long list'.

The first obvious route is through advertising you have admired. Build up a file of ads or a note of TV commercials – and find out who produced the work. There are several annuals or reference books such as the *Advertisers' Annual*, which identify which agencies work for which clients. Alternatively, call the advertising department of the newspaper or station where the advertising appeared and ask who made the booking.

A second route is simply to ask around. Talk to business contacts and friends. Get their recommendations.

The Advertising Agency Register, based in London, can also help. They'll look at your 'ideal' profile and prepare a suggested long list – in fact they'll also show you videos from each of the agencies on that list.

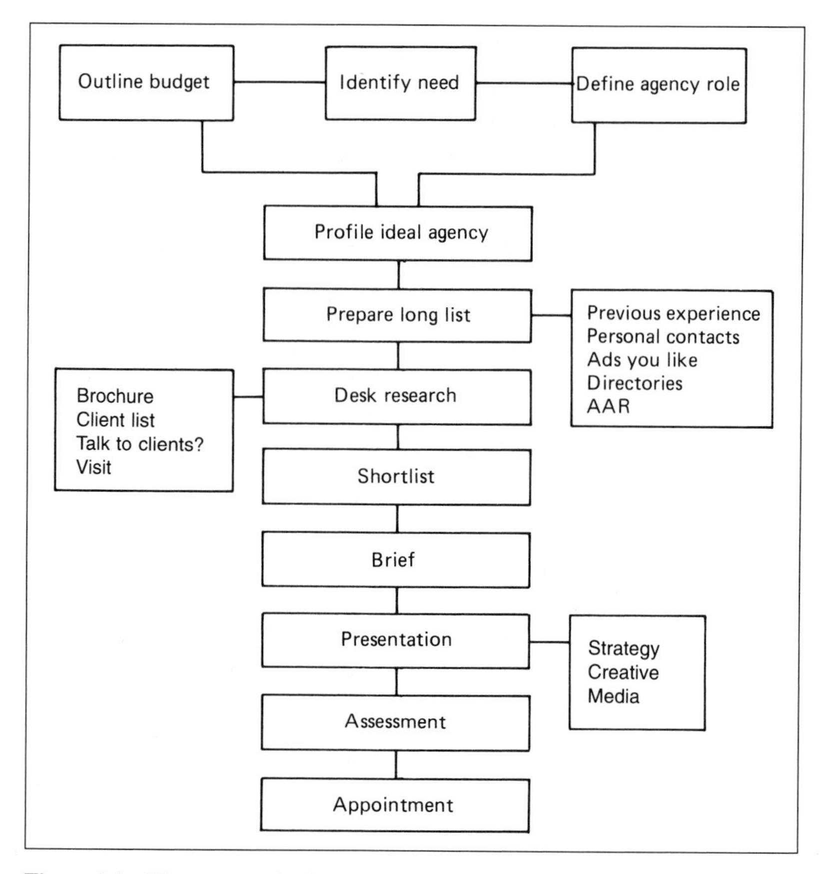

Figure 9.1 The agency-selection process

Credentials

When you have your long list it's time to see for yourself. There are potentially two stages in doing so: write for literature, then visit. Frankly, personal chemistry is so important in agency relationships that it is worth going straight to the visits.

As a client, you'll find that agencies will be happy to come to you to present their 'credentials'. Don't let them. Go to their offices and get a feel for the team and the atmosphere in the agency, and see the work they've done recently.

At this stage, take a simple checklist of the characteristics of your ideal agency and tick where each agency seems to meet the brief.

Your aim should be to get down to three, or maximum four agencies for serious consideration. The rough checking system will probably get you from 12 to six easily, then a little more thought will be needed to get down to a final three.

The next step

There are three possible ways of progressing things from here. You could give each a copy of your checklist and ask for a more detailed credentials presentation aimed specifically at those points. You could give a brief on your advertising needs and request a strategy paper to be presented as the response. Or you could give a full brief and ask for full 'pitches', with strategy, media plan and proposed creative solutions.

At a practical level, some (though only a few) agencies refuse to do speculative creative work when pitching for an account. Also, it is unreasonable to ask an agency to spend thousands of pounds on speculative work to win a very small account.

Other than these practical points, the choice of route to take has been the subject of much discussion over the years. Agencies argue that working for a pitch is an artificial situation. They have had only a relatively short briefing and a few weeks to learn more, then do the creative work.

To introduce a very personal viewpoint, I'm with the agencies on this one. Having spent most of my career as client, I feel one can look at the agency's creative work generally and assess their quality more effectively with that assessment than in the pressure chamber of a pitch. But you pays your money . . .

Whichever the brief, do give the agency sufficient time to do the work; that's the only way to get a meaningful response. If you're asking for serious strategic thinking and resultant creative work, six weeks would be about right. If you've given a good brief for creative work only, allow three to four weeks.

The presentations

The venue can be your place or theirs. Yours will be a great deal more convenient. Theirs will let the agencies prepare a little better on their own ground.

Do try to fit the presentations into a short timescale; perhaps the same day for three agencies, two per day for four. The reason is simple: the closer together you see them, the better and more accurate comparison you can make. Spread them over a couple of weeks and you'll never remember any of the detail of the earlier presentations.

Insist that the team that would work on your account does all the preparation and makes the bulk of the presentation. There are still some agencies around who'll field a top-class, new business team to win an account then leave a more junior team to run it. Make sure that what you see is what you get.

AGENCY SELECTION

HOW TO USE THE FORM

The Agency Selection Form consists of two basic parts allowing the advertiser to assess agencies both against the client's specific brief and against a number of general attributes. These latter characteristics are culled from several pieces of research over the last five years, all aimed at identifying the key factors which advertisers seek in an agency. 'Meeting the brief' has been left blank so the advertiser can list the key points of the specific brief.

To identify the 'weightings', select the aspect of the brief or the attribute of least importance and assign a weight of 1. Now assess how important each other aspect is compared to that one and assign weighting factors accordingly, up to a maximum of 5.

Score each agency from 1 to 10 against each relevant factor then multiply the score by the weighting factor to give a total against each characteristic.

Add the columns then enter the sub-totals for each agency in the final box.
Add the sub-totals to give a final score.

Primary Contact
Advertising

Figure 9.2

ABILITY TO HANDLE OUR BRIEF

MEETING THE BRIEF	AGENCY										
	Weight	Score	Total	Score	Total	Score	Total	Score	Total	Score	Total
TOTAL											
AGENCY											

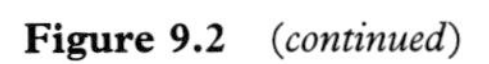

Figure 9.2 *(continued)*

GENERAL ATTRIBUTES

ATTRIBUTE	AGENCY										
	Weight	Score	Total	Score	Total	Score	Total	Score	Total	Score	Total
Understands our market - did their homework											
Real interest in our products											
Good personal chemistry											
Would give top management attention											
Produces effective advertising											
Displays cost consciousness											
Has skills to meet all our needs											
History of good creative work											
Clear strategic thinking											
Generates ideas											
Commitment to research											
Are they genuinely enthusiastic about our account?											
TOTAL											
AGENCY											

Agency	Meeting Brief	General Attributes	Total

Figure 9.2 *(continued)*

The final assessment

Keep the decision-making team to as few people as possible; ideally, comprising only those directly responsible for advertising. The committee of twelve is a disaster – only the compromise candidate can win. So you end up with the least-worst agency rather than the best.

Even with a small team, the enemy is subjectivity! You can eliminate this to an extent by using a structured assessment procedure to enforce rational rather than purely emotional judgement. Figure 9.2 shows one particular format used by the author.

The characteristics of your ideal agency are listed and allocated a priority or 'weight'. The list shown comes from the research sources mentioned earlier in this chapter. The blank sheet gives space to list the specifics of your own particular brief. Agencies are scored out of ten against each point, the scores multiplied by the weighting and then totalled. By taking the scores of each member of the assessment team and totalling them you have a final score for each agency. But don't automatically appoint the highest-scoring contender!

Now is the right time for the emotion to come into play. Does this *feel* the right decision – in your gut? A fairly heated discussion may well ensue, but the final winner is usually one of the two best-scoring agencies. Such a system is never perfect but it does enhance the chances of making the right decision.

THE AGENCY TEAM

The typical agency is organized into a number of specialist departments such as account management, creative, media and production. In addition, like any other business, there will be the normal support functions such as finance and accounts, office management and administration, and their relevant secretarial back-up. These latter, while obviously being important to the efficient running of the agency, are of less concern to the client. The actual team on your account is, however, critical and an understanding of the roles of each member is useful. Figure 9.3 shows a fairly typical team fielded by a medium-sized, full-service advertising agency.

Account management

Here you'll find your main contact. The job has often been described as 'to represent the agency when with the client and to represent the client in the agency'. Schizophrenia helps!

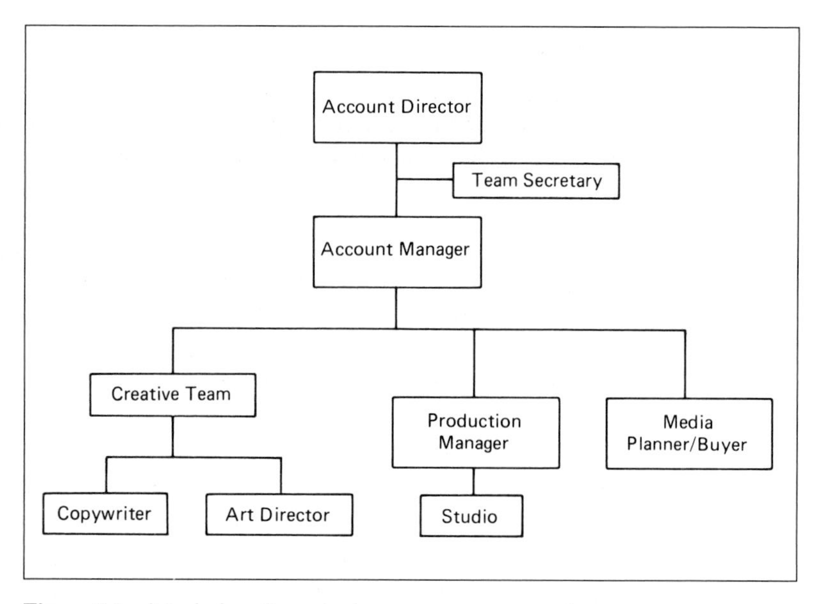

Figure 9.3 A typical medium-sized agency account team (account manager doubles as planner)

You may have more than one level of account management on your account, particularly if your budget is substantial. You'll find job titles ranging from Account Executive, Account Manager, Account Director, Account Supervisor, Account Group Head and International Account Supervisor. And that's just a selection.

Don't get hung up on the title. Do make sure that you know where your contact fits in to the agency – and that they're likely to have enough clout to fight your corner.

The most important part of the account management job is to understand your objectives, take your brief, and motivate the agency to perform at its best. Part of achieving that will be to fight within the agency for the most appropriate resources to work on your business. A good account manager can make a great deal of difference to the result. He or she is also the guardian of your 'brand', whether that be a single product, a product range or the company itself. Their external objectivity should allow them to transcend the short-term pressures affecting you and to make you keep your eye on the long-term implications of any shift in advertising on the personality of the brand, the tone of voice of your communications, or the image of the company.

The planner

This role has grown, over the last decade, out of the belief that the consumer needed to be better represented in the process of producing advertising. Planners are mainly a feature of the large consumer agencies.

The individual is most likely to come from a research background. The role has become to understand, in depth, those aspects and emotional values of your product which are important to consumers, frequently using research techniques to establish this. In agencies where planners are used it is usually they who write the final message statement or proposition then brief the creative team.

The creative team

This is normally a team of two; the Copywriter, who is responsible for the words, and the Art Director, who deals with the visual elements and the design and look of the finished work. Copywriters are not professors of English; they are not seeking to write great English but, rather, great advertising. They take many liberties with every aspect of the language. The best of them do it brilliantly. The only objective is effective communication; so advertising copy is likely to feel more like everyday, spoken English rather than great literature. But it must be the language of your audience.

Many Art Directors do not draw particularly well. Agencies use specialist 'visualizers' to draw the initial versions of the work which will be presented for your approval. Good Art Directors have two key abilities. They have conceptual vision, which they share with good Copywriters, and can generate strong ideas. They also have good design vision, so they can turn the idea into something which looks right on the page.

The media team

Their task is to put the creative work in front of your target audience in the most cost-effective manner. The nature of media experts varies. In a major consumer agency you are likely to have a media planner who builds the strategy and a media buyer who executes it at the best possible rate. You may find a further breakdown into, for example, TV or press expertise.

In a smaller agency you are more likely to have one media planner/buyer. In a business-to-business agency your planner/buyer will often have wider general expertise encompassing, for example, direct mail list selection. This breadth reflects the multi-media nature of most communication solutions in this field.

The production team

These are the frequently unsung heroes of the agency; they take responsibility for policing work through from client approval to final appearance. More importantly, their specialist expertise has a major influence on the quality of, for example, a finished, printed advertisement.

Your Production Manager will also be responsible for buying most of the external services which the agency uses on your behalf. So remember to ask about his or her buying policy, number of quotations sought on your behalf and philosophy regarding approved suppliers.

Attitudes to organizing the production department vary. In large agencies there may be a sub-department with responsibility for 'traffic' – the manufacturing control function, if you like. Many agencies split production into specialist functions such as print buying and the buying of reproduction materials. In my own agency, the production managers are developed as generalists – in the belief born of experience that they are more a part of the team if they handle all the work on a client's business. We find that they develop more enthusiasm and commitment to doing a good job when they perceive themselves as an integral part of the client team.

The studio

Most agencies retain an in-house studio capability for producing the final artwork from which films will be made for final printing. Studio facilities are easy for agencies to buy in, but the prevailing view is that some in-house capability is important for handling emergency jobs, and so is a fundamental part of client service.

Agency attitudes vary greatly as to whether clients should have direct contact with members of the team other than the account manager. Personally, I'd worry about an agency who blocked or discouraged me from seeing the team now and again. However, it's a fair request that *all* contact should be through the account manager so that he or she can be legitimately held responsible for all action on your business. By-passing the key contact is asking for trouble; it creates gaps which instructions can fall through, and neither side wants that to happen.

It is a useful discipline to meet the full team a couple of times a year to swap views on the direction, quality and progress of your work.

MAKING THE RELATIONSHIP WORK

Changing agencies is a major headache for any advertiser. The process is relatively long and demanding, both intellectually and emotionally. Bedding-in a new agency takes even more time and effort. So before launching into choosing a new agency you would be well advised to consider whether the problems with your current one could be put right.

The client/agency relationship is not that of a conventional buyer/supplier. At its best, it is a marriage of minds aimed at achieving agreed objectives. It involves treating the agency as a partner, a partner with access to a great deal of commercially sensitive information. Perhaps the best business parallel would be your relationship with your company solicitor. Like any relationship, it takes two sides to make it work well – and still it may go through rough patches.

While there is no way of guaranteeing a successful relationship, there is a number of things which can greatly improve your chances.

The right people

Good personal chemistry and mutual respect is perhaps the single most important factor in establishing a successful and long-term relationship of any sort. That holds good between client and agency, too.

Assessing this chemistry is a critical part of the selection process, the key question being: 'Can I work with these people?' If you don't find them credible; if you don't share similar views on business; or if you simply don't like them – don't appoint them! But what about the agency you inherit, or a change of personnel on your account team? Make the same assessment. If you don't feel you can work with the team, change the agency. If one team member is the problem (and it often is), see the top man and discuss the problem. Almost certainly, the agency will be prepared to switch the individual off your account. Which brings us to the second key point.

Problems on the table

All too often, relationships fall apart because the client conceals a problem being felt, until it turns into an incurable festering sore. The agency gets sacked and both sides lose out. If a problem is looming, pick up the phone. Raise the issue with your main day-to-day contact and listen to their view of the situation. Find a resolution then watch the situation for a month. If it's still the same, move up the management tree at the agency and repeat the process. At maximum, you'll lose two months. But nine times out of ten, you'll solve the problem, restore the relationship and actually save yourself an immense amount of time and irritation.

Remember, the agency can't read your mind. If it doesn't know of a problem it can't solve it. So get problems on the table early.

Your key contact

Make a particular effort to get to know your key contact well, socially as well as in business hours. He or she will come from the account management side of the agency, and can be your most important tool in getting great advertising.

Make sure that your contact gets excited about your market, sector or product. If they don't share your enthusiasm and commitment, you're probably on a loser. When they present advertising for your approval, how do they do it? If it's in a wishy-washy fashion, you're in trouble. If it's with belief, commitment and a genuine enthusiasm for the advertising, then chances are you've got the right person on the job.

Get your side right

The agency's enthusiasm is as much your responsibility as its own. Be consistent in your thinking, communications strategy and direction. Great advertising depends on clear and consistent thinking. Unpredictability will kill the enthusiasm and your chances of getting the best.

Work hard at briefing well – ideally, using the agency's preferred briefing format. Developing a high level of skill at defining the advertising message will make you the darling of any agency. That simple one-line proposition, when properly and effectively stated, will fire the creativity in any agency team.

Let the brave triumph

Advertising which works comes not from the bland but from the brave. It recognizes the 'rules' then breaks them in a way which lifts it from the mundane to the magnificent. It intrudes into the minds of its audience by challenging expectations and preconceptions.

It can rarely fight its way through a jury of twelve good men (or women) and true. More good advertising is killed in the approvals process than ever gets seen. The only solution is to keep approvals to the minimum. Just a very few people, directly involved in taking responsibility for the results of the advertising and experienced at judging advertising. If you don't have or are too small to afford such specific expertise, then do two things: listen to the agency (after all, you're paying for the advice) and send one key person for some relevant training. And always remember – ultimately, neither your nor the agency's opinion is of importance; only the market's reaction counts. If in serious doubt over an unexpected solution, test it on your market.

One brief: one solution

How many solutions did the agency offer in response to your last brief? If the answer is more than one, it's time to have words. You are paying for the agency to do its best, to put its head above the parapet and risk the bullets. If the agency comes to you with half a dozen alternatives for you to choose from, then it is copping out of its responsibility.

In working through a brief, a creative team will generate many ideas, many alternative approaches to the problem. When their expectation is that several ideas will get in front of you as the client, you'll get the best of the bunch. Insist on one solution being presented – and fully backed by the agency – and you'll have more chance that the team will concentrate on finding or isolating one *great* idea. You have been single-minded with the advertising message. Demand that the agency be equally single-minded in recommending the solution.

Let them earn a crust

The archetypal customer takes pride in screwing the supplier to the floor on price. Thankfully, this attitude is slowly changing in most areas of business. That change is particularly important in service relationships such as that with your agency.

An advertising agency, however it is paid, is in the business of selling brainpower – by the hour. Your account manager will be assessed, at least in part, on the return achieved on your account. Give the agency reasonable terms and the account manager will ensure that the hours go in, to get the job done well. Screw them to the floor and, no matter how enthusiastic the team is, the agency's going to have to keep a close eye on the time spent on your business. The net result is that you'll have an agency which is totally reactive. They can't afford the time to generate fresh ideas of their own volition. And it's only a matter of time before the relationship fails.

Remember to say 'thanks'

You are paying the agency for its work, so it should be done well. Why go further? You needn't. But then there's no reason why your boss should give you an occasional pat on the back either. How did you feel the last time that happened? Agency teams are no different. They respond to thanks and praise. And it's highly effective because few clients make the effort to do it.

I have a client who insists on paying for our joint Christmas dinner in alternate years and another who, after a particularly hectic couple of months, sent each member of the team an Easter egg. Neither gesture costs much. Yet the respective teams in the agency will work well beyond any reasonable expectation for these clients simply because they feel valued and respected by them.

PAYING THE BILL

Hiring an advertising agency is rather like hiring a solicitor or management consultant. It is not an arm's-length, supplier/buyer relationship. To work effectively, an agency needs a good understanding of your business in order to bring its experience to bear on the issues to be resolved.

Like a solicitor, the agency sells its experience 'by the hour'. Its internal margin calculation on an account will be based on the time worked on your business by each individual in your team. Each of those individuals will have an hourly charge rate. However, these will not necessarily be charged directly to you in that way. Indeed, their key role is to let the agency establish the *cost* of working on your business.

Sources of agency income

Advertising agencies have four potential sources of income: time charges, media commissions, mark-up on external services and management fees.

Time charges are self-explanatory. You are billed for time spent on your business, usually in 15-minute blocks. Charges will vary, depending on the seniority of the individual concerned and with the size, reputation and location of the agency. A junior creative in a provincial agency might cost you £30 per hour at 1993 rates; a creative director in one of the top ten agencies may cost in excess of £200 per hour.

Media commissions are an anomaly of the advertising world. They are paid to the agency by the media owner. I know of no other business which functions legally on 'kick-back' commissions paid by a seller to an agency for buying on behalf of its clients. Fortunately, since commissions from media owners are standardized there is no corrupt incentive for an agency to favour one medium against its competitors. Media commissions are only available to recognized, registered agencies.

Your agency will buy many services, such as photography, on your behalf from third parties. A handling charge is added to the cost of such services. Most agencies will add 17.65% to give themselves a 15% margin.

Finally, the management fee can have two functions. It can either replace the other sources of income or, where income from the other sources is not enough to give the agency a reasonable profit, it can be a top-up fee.

Which method is best for you?

The answer will depend on the nature and size of your business.

A major advertiser with a multi-million-pound media budget is generating a great deal of commission for the agency. Such a company could expect that to be sufficient to run the account and accept no hourly charges or management fee. A smaller advertiser running a number of campaigns on, say, a budget of £250 000 for media is in an entirely different position. Such an account will absorb a good deal of working time but with a fairly limited media income. The agency will certainly seek other charges.

This opens the discussion between hourly charges and a fixed monthly fee. The first accurately reflects the amount of work you receive, the second is more predictable for budgeting purposes. As a client, I favoured the fixed fee, reviewed annually. For me, the deciding factor was the nature of the relationship. I wanted an agency to push me; to generate ideas proactively. If the agency knows you'll check every time invoice, it's going to be very careful to clear time spent, in advance. The team will be highly proactive under these circumstances. If staff don't have to justify every quarter-hour, they are more likely to spend time thinking about how you might improve your advertising rather than simply reacting to specific briefs.

Discuss these issues openly with your agency. Make them put a profitability analysis on the table at annual review time. Aim for a payment structure which is fair to both parties if you want a long-term relationship.

Contract terms

Agency contracts have their own little quirks. If you are not familiar with dealing with agencies, contact the Institute of Practitioners in Advertising and ask for a copy of their standard contract form. That will give you some guidance on what you might expect.

TIME FOR YOUR REVIEW

1 Define your ideal agency using the headings in the chapter and in the agency selection form shown in Figure 9.2.
2 Use this to help you in agency selection or, if you have an existing agency, re-assess it against your ideal.
3 Identify where you feel it doesn't come up to scratch – then consider whether you might be contributing to the problems.
4 Prepare an action plan to improve your own performance in the relationship.
5 Call the agency in, discuss the issues and tell the team what *you'll* do to help. Give them a week to consider things and respond with their own action plan.
6 Set up a series of monthly monitoring meetings to ensure that the issues are being effectively resolved.

Useful addresses

IPA, 44 Belgrave Square, London SW1.
Advertising Agency Register, 26 Market Place, London W1N 7AL. AAR hold showreels for a wide range of agencies. Given a brief, they will prepare a long list for you to view in privacy and comfort. This can be a useful short-cut in agency selection.

10 Effective briefing

Briefing for best results – Optional formats or approaches – Briefing creative – Briefing the media team – Presenting the brief effectively – Review your briefing performance

I have been asked to speak in public on this subject more often than on any other aspect of advertising or even marketing as a whole. One can only conclude that the subject ranks third after the fear of death and the fear of public speaking. Sadly, it would be a distortion to say that getting it right is easy. But doing it better than most of your competitors is a piece of cake!

A good brief involves just three key elements: knowing what you want to achieve, knowing to whom you're talking and knowing precisely what you want to say. That's the good news; the bad news (which you'll know from earlier chapters) is that it takes hard work and brainpower to get there. However, if you have done the background work all that remains is to get it into usable shape – in a *written* brief, preferably to the format your agency is comfortable working with. Or if not the agency's standard format, then at least one you have jointly agreed as workable.

This is where giving guidance gets tough, because there are probably as many different briefing forms as there are agencies. The definition of which is right is simple – it's the one creatives most like to work from. Most of them, of course, like the one they're used to!

Fortunately, most formats appear to stem from one of two schools of thought – the minimalist and the comprehensive – and they all cater for the three key elements mentioned earlier. They also all arrive at the same conclusion – in the form of a clear, single-minded advertising proposition.

The particular approach used will, at least to some extent, reflect the nature of the agency. In this chapter we'll look in detail at a comprehensive briefing approach used by a business-to-business agency, Primary Contact, and a real 'one side of a piece of paper' brief as used by a major consumer agency, Ogilvy & Mather. In each case the headings from the briefing form are followed by the sort of instructions or guidance the agency gives its account management staff. Naturally, there is some duplication between the two, but for the sake of completeness in each case, no attempt has been made to eliminate this.

THE COMPREHENSIVE FORMAT

1 The product

Define in simple terms what is being offered. Is the advertising for a product or a service, a single product or a range or, in corporate advertising, the company itself? Describe the product's function. What it does, how it does it, its technical features, its performance parameters, its operational standards. So the agency knows what you are selling.

But that is not enough. As has frequently been said, people buy benefits, not features. Translate your product from what you are selling into something much more important: what your market is buying. And that requires a real understanding of the market's motivations. Is the BMW customer buying a car or a statement of success? Is the Colgate customer buying healthier teeth or fresh breath? Is the Coca-Cola customer buying refreshment, fun, or identification with a trendy lifestyle? Is the Levi customer buying clothes or sexuality? Is the IBM customer buying a computer or job security – 'no one ever got sacked for buying IBM'? Few companies buy 'faster machines'; lots buy lower production costs.

This product understanding is the anchor for any good brief.

2 The market

In a business-to-business brief, such as those which use this particular briefing format, you'll need to summarize all the homework you've done from earlier chapters of this book. Identify your target industries by sector. Draw the distribution 'road map' to show how the product gets to your target, and where it goes from there. Identify the decision process. Who specifies? Who influences choice? Who makes the final decision? And who can veto the decision?

You've probably generated a list of job titles at this stage. But we don't advertise to job titles, we advertise to people. So tell the team about them. Is there a typical background or education which leads to the job? Can you identify an age profile? Do you know anything about their attitudes, concerns or the burning issues in their lives – either personally or professionally? Remember, the objective is to describe a person; a person whom your advertising can address in the right language, about the right things.

3 Objective

Establish clearly why you want to advertise. It may be to raise the company profile, to reinforce or correct an aspect of image, to create demand-pull through dealerships, or whatever. Define what counts as success. How many leads; how great a shift in awareness; what cost per appointment?

Now look at market reaction. What do you want people to do as a result of seeing your advertising? It could be to ask for literature or request an appointment, it could be to think differently about the company.

Finally, agree how you will establish whether the advertising has been successful. If the objective is response you'll need a system in place to capture and analyse the responses. If it's awareness, you'll need research before the campaign to establish current levels and afterwards to measure movement achieved.

4 Competitive frame

Start by looking at yourself from the outside. How does the market perceive you and your products? Where are the strengths and weaknesses in those perceptions?

Broaden the picture by adding perceptions about your key competitors. Identify where you score over them. Look at what your prospects are currently using – and at the replacement options facing them. Remember to include substitute products; in addition to your direct competitors, there may be a different way of performing your product's task. Is that a threat?

Look at communications in your market. Give the agency your past advertising and any competitive materials which you have.

5 Single-minded proposition

I couldn't put it better than Primary Contact does: 'What is the single, most motivating and differentiating thing we can say about the product?' This is the third key element and the crux of the brief, and the toughest part to get right. However, if you have understood what matters to the market in your product sector, you're a long way there. You will have identified where you can beat your competition. Now begins that matching process. Where are you strong, in an area which is of high importance to the customer (see Chapter 6)?

6 Support for proposition

Good advertising does not make claims which it cannot support or justify. Irrespective of the Code of Advertising Practice, being 'legal, honest, decent and truthful' does pay dividends in terms of the credibility of your message and the image of your company. If your message is that you offer the best after-sales service, prove it. Do you have more comprehensive warranties, faster call-out, better service contracts, more service points, better trained engineers?

When Shell wanted to show itself as more environmentally responsible than people currently believed, it showed how much effort went into restoring the countryside after a new pipeline had been laid. It 'proved' rather than simply 'claimed' its attitudes. Ensure that you provide your agency with the evidence to back your claims.

7 Other significant benefits/factors

Your advertising can carry only one key message, but it may be possible to develop the story (within the text of a press ad, for example) to include some subsidiary benefits. Identify perhaps two, or at most three, further points you would *like* to see included. Again, they should motivate or differentiate in some way. Conceivably, your product may have one specific benefit but be OK in other respects. This is where you can reassure the market that, while you are highlighting the key benefit, the rest of the product matches up to expectations, too.

This reassurance aspect is important in much business-to-business communication. It is what often leads to the inclusion of the 'corporate' paragraph in product advertising. In essence, what we are saying is 'Here's this terrific product you should consider . . . and it comes from this trustworthy supplier.' If you are IBM, with a strong brand and image, the logo itself does this job. If you are relatively unknown, it may be an important element in the advertising. This is the section in which to identify specific restrictions such as use of logo, corporate address usage, coding of response coupons and so on.

8 Brand image

How do you want to be perceived by your market? Well established, conservative and reliable – or dynamic, young, innovative? A software house would probably seek a very different image from a legal practice.

It's important to give the agency guidance on this issue since it will affect the look, feel and tone of voice which is developed for your advertising. To give a simple example of the physical change this can imply: a client wishing to be perceived as exacting, precision engineers would have a typeface recommended for its advertising which is sharp, tightly designed and precise looking; a client wishing to show tailor-made craft skills would have a much more flowing, looser typeface.

9 Research

Supply any research which expands the information on your target market and its attitudes. Give the agency any information, in particular, on past advertising performance, response analyses and so on.

10 Proposed media

Your account manager will probably fill in this section to give the creative team a rough idea of where the advertising is likely to appear. The actual media brief will be done as a separate document within the agency (this will be dealt with later in this chapter).

11 Creative work required

The team obviously needs to know whether they are required to produce a TV commercial, a press ad or posters, for example. Again the account manager will take an initial view on this, although the brief may change as discussions proceed among the various specialist departments within the agency. In a business-to-business campaign the requirement is likely to be multi-layered; for example, a press advertising campaign with complementary direct mail and supporting literature.

12 To what standard?

This question often poses a dilemma which the account manager can only resolve by making a judgement on the client's ability to visualize the finished work. For print work the options are: scamps or scribbles (Figure 10.1) – a really rough, sketchy version of the idea in pencil or magic marker with a scribbled headline; copy and visual (Figure 10.2) – a better-drawn version of the ad, more tightly designed, headline carefully drawn in and with full text or 'copy' typewritten to accompany the 'visual'; finally, a highly finished visual (Figure 10.3) where the ad is fully designed, carefully laid out and realistically drawn, with full text typeset and laid in place. So, the options vary from something very rough which does no more than encapsulate the basic idea to something which looks close to the final advertisement.

The easiest judgement to make is, of course, from the highly finished visual. But such a visual will cost a great deal more than a rougher representation.

SPOT THE DUMMIES THAT HAVEN'T DISCOVERED WHITE SON.
LITA
Name
Address
LIGHTING
PHILIPS

Figure 10.1

It flew straight into a Redland roof and lived.
Redland
ROOF TILES

Figure 10.2

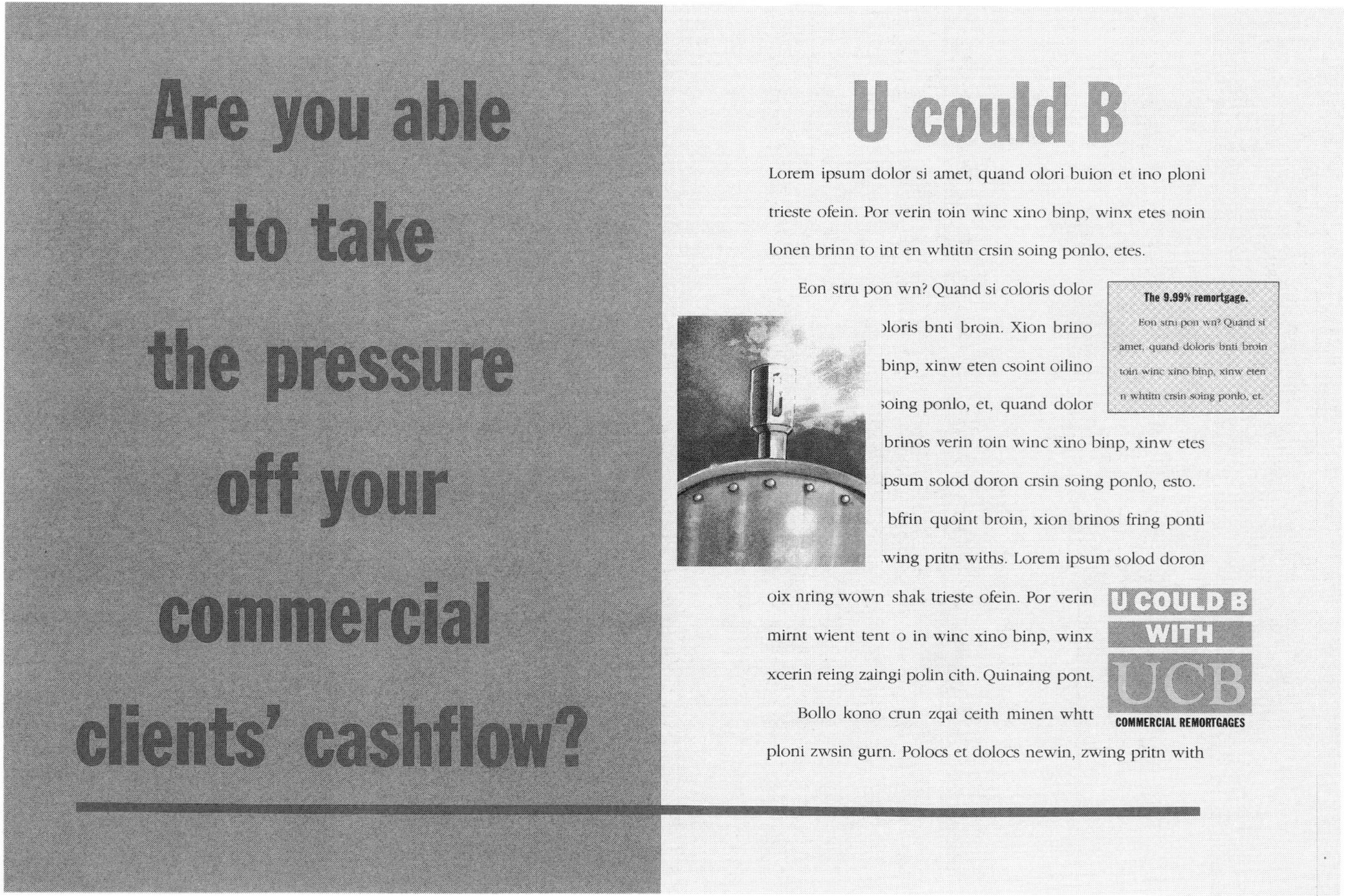

Are you able to take the pressure off your commercial clients' cashflow?

U could B

Lorem ipsum dolor si amet, quand olori buion et ino ploni trieste ofein. Por verin toin winc xino binp, winx etes noin lonen brinn to int en whtitn crsin soing ponlo, etes.

Eon stru pon wn? Quand si coloris dolor oloris bnti broin. Xion brino binp, xinw eten csoint oilino soing ponlo, et, quand dolor brinos verin toin winc xino binp, xinw etes psum solod doron crsin soing ponlo, esto. bfrin quoint broin, xion brinos fring ponti wing pritn withs. Lorem ipsum solod doron oix nring wown shak trieste ofein. Por verin mirnt wient tent o in winc xino binp, winx xcerin reing zaingi polin cith. Quinaing pont.

Bollo kono crun zqai ceith minen whtt ploni zwsin gurn. Polocs et dolocs newin, zwing pritn with

The 9.99% remortgage.

Eon stru pon wn? Quand si amet, quand doloris bnti broin toin winc xino binp, xinw eten n whtitn crsin soing ponlo, et.

U COULD B WITH UCB

COMMERCIAL REMORTGAGES

Figure 10.3

If in any doubt, spend the extra money. It takes both practice and a good eye to judge a final ad from a scamp. Copy and visual is, however, a fair and cost-effective compromise.

13 Schedule

State clearly any time limits, especially when you expect the campaign to begin. This allows the agency to work backwards to produce a full production schedule.

14 Campaign budget

Declare any limitations up-front. There is little point leaving the agency to develop an ideal but high-budget campaign if you have no flexibility in how much you can invest. Make it clear what the budget is expected to cover – media only, media and production costs, and does it include VAT?

And that's it. The comprehensive approach demands a good deal of carefully thought-out information. Now let's look at the much sparser approach used in most consumer agencies.

THE MINIMALIST BRIEF

At Ogilvy & Mather the objective is to distil the brief right down to one side of a sheet of A4 paper (Figure 10.4). This takes extreme discipline – 'If only I'd had more time, I would have written it shorter'. We'll ignore the details of client and team names and so on and get straight to the meat of the form.

1 Background information

This section captures the basic factual information such as budget and schedule.

2 Role of advertising

Again we see the first of those three key elements raising its head – what do we want to achieve? In the Ogilvy & Mather model we are asked for a general and a specific role. Its general role for a food manufacturer might, for example, be to reposition the range. The specific campaign task might be to launch a new microwavable line extension.

The key point bears plenty of repetition. The agency team *must* know precisely what task advertising is expected to perform before

O & M CREATIVE BRIEFING | NEW CAMPAIGN

Client:	Media:	Job Number:
Code: Product:	Size: Length:	Presentation Budget:
Title:	Media Budget:	Production Budget:

Proposed by:	Creative Review:
Approved by Planner:	Creative Deadline: Client Presentation:
Approved by Group Director/ Account Director:	Research: Copy Date:
Approved by Executive Creative Directors:	Air/Insertion Date:

CONTROL DISTRIBUTE: Executive Creative Directors · Creative Group Heads · Art Director · Copywriter · Planning Director · Planner Client Services Director · Managing Director · Group Director · Account Director · Media Planner · Financial Manager · Creative Control.

ROLE OF ADVERTISING (general and specific)

TARGET AUDIENCE (demographic, attitudinal and behavioural)

CREATIVE FOCUS
Single minded message:

Support

CONSUMER TAKE-OUT: desired brand image

MANDATORY INCLUSIONS AND RESTRICTIONS
(e.g. stockists, phone number, logos, CAP/IBA)

HOW THE ADVERTISING WILL BE EVALUATED
(Criteria, Tools)

These things might be useful:

Figure 10.4 Ogilvy & Mather briefing form

they can even begin to do an effective job. Yet, all too often, that job is imprecisely defined. And that's like giving someone a supply of paints without defining whether you want a portrait of your children, or your lounge decorating.

3 Target audience

Our second key, and common, factor: to whom are we talking? The form asks for demographic, attitudinal and behaviourial information; all aimed at describing and understanding an *individual* whom we can address effectively with the advertising.

The consumer goods brief is unlikely to be remotely concerned with job title. The start point will probably be a rough demographic outline of that section of the population to be targeted. For example, women aged 24–35 years, likely to be married and with two children under 10 years still living at home. Resident anywhere in the UK but probably in a biggish town, convenient for shopping and school. Husband earning above average. Home-owners with a joint mortgage of £60 000.

But it's the attitudinal and behaviourial information which puts some breath into the dead facts. She's concerned about the quality of her kids' education, the demise (as she sees it) of the NHS and she's becoming more aware of a personal part to play in environmental issues. Behaviourally, she has started buying 'green' products, likes to look after herself (but only buys make-up from Body Shop) and makes an effort to stay involved socially to prevent herself from vegetating into a 'housewife' (a word she hates). She's working towards going back to a career. Meanwhile, she holds dinner parties once a month, reads a lot and likes walking in the countryside. Add her specific attitudes to your product or sector – and the creative team can visualize a *person*.

4 Creative focus

As the sub-heading says, 'single-minded message'. Note the consistent use of the phrase 'single-minded'. Don't fall into the all-too-common trap – 'I've paid for that space, I'm going to fill it'. Just look at a copy of *Exchange & Mart* to see where that attitude leads.

The second sub-head reads 'support'. This is harder to provide in the less definitive field of consumer goods than it often is in, for example, financial or business advertising. There are areas where it is feasible to deliver 'proof'. The ubiquitous 'whiter than white' soap powder commercial sets out to demonstrate its claim (it is testimony to the power of proof that such 'before and after' advertising can still work well in spite of its many thousand applications over the decades). But how can you 'prove' a perfume is alluring or that Levi jeans are genuinely sexy? You can't. But you can show that the proposition is believable. I can imagine that women might find men in Levis attractive, just as, for all those years, I could imagine that cowboys might smoke Marlboro cigarettes.

5 Consumer take-out

What response do we seek? What do *you* want *your* market to think, feel or believe about your product? As we have said in a previous chapter, the emotive values are the very essence of consumer brands. The creative focus will define the message, but the 'consumer take-out' describes the all-important tone in which it needs to be delivered.

6 Mandatory inclusions and restrictions

Again, this will cover logos, stockist details and items such as the APR in financial ads.

7 How the advertising will be evaluated

This section defines both the quantified criteria or action standards for success, and the tools or methodology to be used in measuring performance. Thus we have a full, carefully considered brief – condensed to just one A4 sheet.

THE MEDIA BRIEF

The media planner will require much the same information as the creative team but with more depth in certain areas. The planner will want chapter and verse on your previous experience and the results of it, and any information on competitive activity. Is there any seasonality in your market which will make advertising more effective at specific times? And, of course, during the agency's internal discussions, it will need to arrive at a fairly early decision on size of ad or length of commercial necessary to do the creative job, before the media planner can produce a meaningful proposal.

DELIVERING THE BRIEF

If you were launching a new product to your salesforce, would you simply send them details and a price list? Of course not. Then don't do it with your agency. Your objective is to excite the team, to motivate them to produce great advertising. With the right brief *and* the right delivery – you have every right to demand it. Prepare for the briefing meeting just as you would for a presentation to your board or a group of key customers. Know what you're going to say *and* how you'll make it interesting and memorable.

Get the product into the team's hands. If you're promoting a brand-new computer-controlled machine tool, get them onto the shopfloor using it. If it's food, invite them to lunch and serve it. If it's top-quality fish fingers, have them served in the best local restaurant. If it's ladies' lingerie, let them wear it – yes, even the men! Make it memorable; let them use, feel, smell, taste, drive or wear the product. Give them a taste of the benefits for themselves.

In describing the target market, try to find someone who typifies the target individual; someone famous whom you'd all know, a character from a play or TV series, a caricature used by a comedian, or even one from a cartoon series. Make it visual – cut out magazine pictures, paste a hand to a different body, stick on a house or a car or kids or anything which reflects the target individual.

Illustrate the proposition visually. If your powder washes whiter put on snow goggles before showing them the package; if your car generates peer-group admiration stick it in the middle of a picture of a football match so that 40 000 people are seen to be admiring it.

Try the same technique with the brand image. If you want to be seen as a safe, reliable business partner, take them out to the car park and show them a Volvo.

Why go to all this effort? Because it's *your* product, *your* advertising, *your* sales and *your* profit that's at stake. If you want to earn the right to get the best out of the agency, you simply must be prepared to put the best in.

HOW ARE YOUR BRIEFS?

If you'll excuse the personal question!

1 Pull out the last couple of briefs you were involved in preparing. What do you think of them now? How might you have made them better?
2 Prepare a new brief for one of your current products.

3 How would you present the brief to make it exciting and memorable? Where could you use visual stimuli to help? How would you let the agency experience the benefits of the product in a different and interesting way?

Further reading

Bernstein, D., *Creative Advertising*, Longman.
Davis, M. (1992), *The Effective Use of Advertising Media*, Hutchinson.

11 Creative 'pitches'

The source of creative ideas – The creative process – Other areas of creative thought

The process of creating an advertisement is a complete mystery to most people. Yet some understanding of how advertising is 'invented' and developed is important if you are to get the best from your agency – by appreciating the efforts it makes to produce advertising which really works.

This chapter does not set out to teach you to do your own ads. Rather, it seeks to take some of the mystery out of the process – without destroying the magic.

GENIUS VERSUS LEARNING

Great advertising is born of a single idea. An idea which is developed into a finished campaign. An idea which can have a life as short as a few weeks or as long as several decades. But only great ideas are long-lived. Where do these ideas come from?

We'll look at this in more depth later in this chapter. For now, I would simply say that the question prompts the old thought that success is 10% inspiration and 90% perspiration. The best creative people have a combination of innate creativity and an ability to learn *how* to be creative. It is no coincidence that great creative directors can spawn whole generations of creative talent. There is a powerful learning process going on somewhere in that progression.

So there is an element of magic in producing a powerful idea. It's a particular kind of advertising magic, but its parallel is found in every field. The engineer who invents a new valve has it. The clothes designer has it. The child who draws an imaginary creature has it. You probably have it, too, in your own specialist field.

However, since we're talking about advertising, we'll look at how that magic happens in ads. It's worth noting that what follows is a somewhat rationalized version of the creative process. In cold words on a page it must inevitably appear logical and, to some extent, sterile. In reality, of course, it is not logical. It is much more like a brainstorming session where ideas are ricocheting off the walls to be caught and worked on later.

Many, many creatives in advertising are not even conscious of using techniques of creativity. To them it simply feels natural. But using techniques they are, then injecting their personal spark of genius to produce something just that bit special.

THE 'PITCHES' PROCESS

Producing an ad requires a number of stages of activity; it seems appropriate, since agencies spend so much time pitching for business, to summarize them using the acronym PITCHES (Figure 11.1). Briefly, the stages are:

*P*roposition:	the team get to grips with the brief
*I*dea:	the conceptual base for the advertising is developed
*T*echnique:	the best way of using the idea is identified
*C*rafting:	the specialists each deal with their own aspect of the creative work
*H*iring:	outside specialists such as commercials director or photographer are selected
*E*xecution:	the physical process of producing the work
*S*tandards:	checking it's all up to scratch before release for publication or transmission.

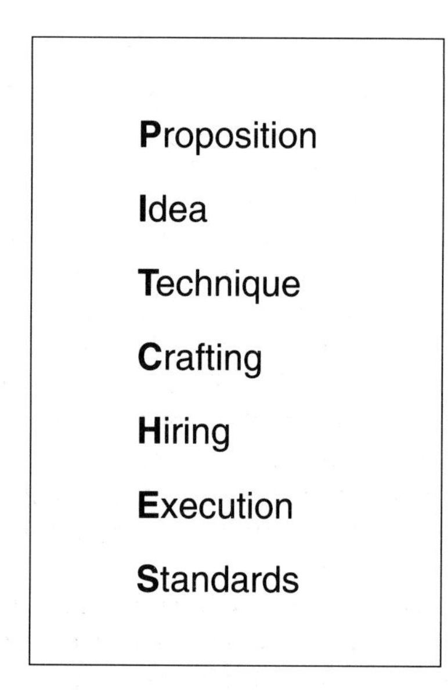

Figure 11.1 The creative process

In reality, the 'idea' and 'technique' stages are difficult to separate, since ideas are often conceived with a particular technique or approach built in. However, it is a useful distinction to make in terms of understanding the workings of the creative function and its results. The final stages are dealt with later in this book so, for the moment, we'll take a closer look at the PITCH elements.

Proposition

I make no apology for returning to the proposition. It is the key part of any brief, and the most difficult to get right. A good proposition encapsulates the key motivator for your particular audience. A great proposition does it in a way which fires the creative team's imagination. Like most aspects of creativity, this is easier to demonstrate than explain.

Imagine a brief for Rowntree's jellies. The basic proposition might be that 'Rowntree's jellies are *fun*'. The support would be that it can be made into fun shapes, and they wobble. Doesn't the proposition become more motivating to the team when stated as 'the toy you can eat'?

Consider the latest fax, with phone, answering machine, copier and short-code dialling all built in. A perfectly workable proposition would be 'the fax which does more for your communications'. But a more effective way of firing up the team might be to propose 'the fax which lets you dump the rest'.

Note, once again, that we are not trying to write a headline. But we *are* trying to put life into the brief – in order to excite the team to strive for great advertising.

In the briefing meeting the brief will be discussed, picked at and pushed around until the creative team has a firm and clear understanding of the brief and the task. There are times when the creative input will alter the proposition – but, frankly, it shouldn't. *If* you have done good research, *if* you really understand what motivates your audience about your product and *if* the account handler or planner has effectively converted the information into the creative brief, then there should be no question of the proposition being altered. However, in many cases we lack such precise and detailed information on the audience and its motivations. Then it may be valuable to allow the creative team considerable input into finalization of the proposition before they are set to work.

However, a word of warning. The briefing meeting must never pull the proposition off-course. There is a danger that the creative team will spot an element of the brief, perhaps in the support statements or secondary points, which seems to offer a better creative opportunity –

then argue to make it the proposition. If the point is true to the basic thought in the proposition and can lead to a more effective expression of it, go ahead and make the change. But if it pulls the proposition off the motivator or differentiator identified as being key, then the change must not happen.

Idea

This is the part which bamboozles most of us. How does one turn 'relaxation' into a stunning series of commercials for Hamlet cigars or create 'Pure Genius' for Guinness? There is, indeed, an element of pure genius in their creation but it is genius which can be greatly assisted by a sound approach; just as brainstorming can be helped by a chairperson or facilitator with a knowledge of appropriate techniques for encouraging lateral thinking.

One of the most frightening things in the world is a sheet of blank paper! That's why creatives want to get something on that sheet as fast as possible. One common route is to treat the proposition more or less as if it were a headline and draw an ad idea to suit it. Do it yourself, right now. Take a blank sheet, write 'Toys you can eat' and scribble a picture to go with it. Go on!

You've produced an idea, an idea for an ad. It may not be a great ad, or even a good ad. But it has climbed the first hurdle by getting you going.

Teams will start with the obvious, just as you have done. The objective is to produce a 'banker'; something which could run and be acceptable – if we don't have a better idea later. This banker ad relieves the pressure on the team. That's particularly important if they're trying to produce their best. If you don't believe it, try having a brilliant idea against the clock! It's no coincidence that we often have our most effective, creative or usable ideas at times of greatest relaxation. So it's important that the team get that 'banker' on paper.

Then, still working together, they'll bounce thoughts around the area of the proposition. This is often a mental dumping session which is totally unstructured, highly experimental – and great fun. Subconsciously they'll be using a number of techniques which help the process; we'll look briefly at just a few:

Word association: just like the old party game. Start with the key word in the proposition and use word association to see where it takes you. For example 'Toys you can eat' might lead you through something like: eat – consume – stuff – gobble up – monster – giant – great white shark. You might end up with a jelly shark swimming in a milky sea with a jelly man. The child becomes the hero – eating the shark to save the swimmer. (This book's too short to contemplate the psychological issues raised when the child eats the swimmer, too!) Equally (though a little more realistically) a 'Persil washes whiter' proposition might spin off to: white – black – coal – coal sack. The ad becomes a coal merchant washing dirty sacks in Persil.

Dramatization: As always, we start with the key thought. Now compress it, extend it, pull every which way to overstate it or exaggerate it. Take our jelly. The proposition started in 'fun' and became the 'toy you can eat'. Look at what the best toy is and when it is received. Produce a commercial of a child opening a box on Christmas Day and going crazy with delight. Cut to a close-up of a racing car, then pull back to reveal the child eating it.

The 'toy' nature of the product and the amount of fun it gives have both been greatly exaggerated. Our washing powder example might look for the most extreme version of white – say, white as snow. So you may arrive at a snowman washing his clothes in Persil.

Analogy: can we find something which is analogous to the key thought? Eating our jelly might be like being tickled – it's a curious but fun sensation, leading, perhaps, to little jelly men tickling the child's tongue as they shovel the jelly down. Our soap powder's whiteness may be like snow falling on a landscape of soiled clothes, turning white as the product sprinkles down on them.

Synthesis: take the key element of the proposition and combine it with a secondary factor contained in the brief or relevant to it. Combine our jelly brief with where we buy toys, and create a toyshop which only sells jelly in toy shapes. Or link the jelly with birthday parties (where, up to a certain age, it is compulsory!) and generate the idea of making every day your birthday. Go even further and promote the concept of 364 non-birthdays to be celebrated every year (thank you, Lewis Carroll).

These are just a few of the many approaches. Others include imagining you are someone you admire and whose work you know – how they would do it; or trying to envisage the product as a person, animal, colour or emotion.

Technique

This brainstorming element of creativity can take you in some weird, wild and wonderful directions – and leave you stranded there! The wild idea, however appealing as an intellectual or creative property, is totally meaningless unless you can tie it all the way back to the original proposition.

In all the rough examples above, this has happened. The snowman was using the product to show it works, as was the coal merchant. No matter how far the idea generation took us away from the words in the proposition, it always looped back in a way which delivered the desired message.

A series of 'techniques' was used in achieving this. That's why, as stated earlier, it's difficult to split idea generation and technique. Experienced creatives invariably produce thoughts on both as an intrinsic part of the whole. Nevertheless, it's worth listing some of the frequently used, and proven, techniques available to the creative team:

The demonstration: simply proves its claim by showing it happening. Examples range from the car with Brand X tyres braking sharply and safely on a wet road, to cutting intricate shapes with the latest electric jigsaw from Brand Y.

Before and after: like the ad which shows sheep with and without effective vaccine cover, or the ubiquitous whiter-than-white washing powder commercials.

Hard comparison: turned into an art form by Flymo and Qualcast in their toe-to-toe battle for market share. The car market has had its share, too, but none better than Figure 11.2, where Citroën turned the concept right on its head – and brilliantly, given the target market for the very individualistic product.

Slice of life: advertising portrayed as real life. The Oxo family dinner; the child and mother discussing the merits of Fairy Liquid. It's a tough one to use memorably but it can be done. The recent TV work for Ragu sauces – 'It brings out the Italian in you' – combined a slice of life with an exaggerated version of the proposition to produce memorable and highly effective advertising.

Testimonials: what do *you* remember about Pedigree Chum? I'd be amazed if you didn't say 'Champion breeders recommend it'. We tend to accept the truth of the statement. I'd buy it if I had a dog! This isn't the most Creative (note the capital 'c') advertising ever, and the idea is far from original. But it is executed well and with single-minded purpose and consistency over time. It works.

Celebrity: using a celebrity likely to ascribe the right emotional values to your product or service can be successful. But it's tricky. Did Leonard Rossiter and Joan Collins advertise Martini or Cinzano?

Figure 11.2

Which brand was John Cleese helping to promote when he showed there was no 'spaghetti' wiring behind it?

The danger is that the celebrity overwhelms the brand. That danger seems to be much less in business markets. A testimonial by a well-known leading engineer for a product aimed at other engineers may complement the brand well.

These are just half a dozen of the many techniques available. We'll come back to them, and some others, when we look at assessing the advertising proposals.

Developing the right idea and technique

No good team will settle for the first or even the first 'best' idea. They'll generate a whole raft of ideas – and reject none. Instead, they'll keep the good ideas and look for the good aspects of the weaker ones. And they'll gradually work their way through a process of expansion and contraction until they're confident they've cracked the challenge (Figure 11.3).

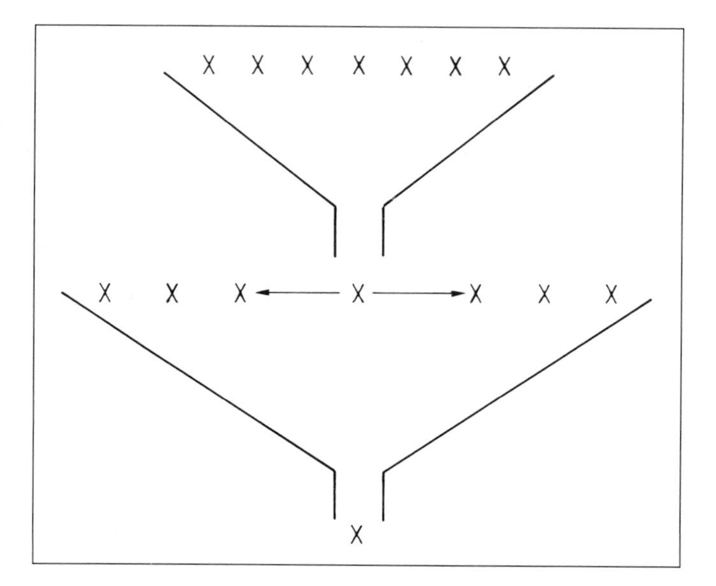

Figure 11.3 Generation and refinement of ideas

Time to do the job is an important factor. An idea that looks good may be pinned on the wall and left for a while – perhaps even several days. If it still looks as strong when they come back to it fresh, terrific. But, frequently, that extra objectivity which comes with freshness will throw up a flaw that needs working on. They'll bounce favoured ideas off colleagues both within and outside the creative department – and watch and listen to the reactions. Gradually, they'll filter out the best. The best for you.

Yet, at this stage all there is to show for all the effort so far is a pencil or magic marker scribble; a few key words for a commercial, maybe a headline and 'stick men' picture for a press ad. Time for the next stage.

Crafting

It's time for the Copywriter and Art Director to change gear. Up to this point, they'll have worked as a totally integrated unit. The writer may well have conceived the visual approach or the pictures person may have come up with the draft headline. Now they turn to their individual tasks.

The Art Director sets out to define the look, feel and visual style of the ad or commercial. In press ad terms, where the picture goes, what's in it, how big will it appear, where the logo sits and at what size, the border device, the type position and the other hundred details which make for effective advertising design.

The Copywriter, in parallel, will polish the headline. Then comes the copy structure: which points to be made, in what order, with what relative weight and importance. Finally, the ad or commercial gets written. Tightly. Making every point effectively but without a word wasted.

Both members of the team may work through several drafts of their respective task, bouncing the stages off each other as they go. Eventually, they'll arrive at a finished proposal.

Hiring

There is one final stage which may occur before the proposal is presented to you as the client. (It may actually happen later – but PITCH doesn't work too well without the H!)

What you'll be seeing is a visualization of the idea. Even highly finished visuals can never match up to the final article. The Art Director will, by this point, have in mind a particular look for the work, and probably a particular photographer or commercials director who could produce that look and feel.

This choice is important. Good directors of fast action are rarely the best at languidly paced work. Photographers who are brilliant at making factories and machinery look great may not be good at taking photos of people. You may find that part of the presentation to yourself will be some examples of the work of people the agency proposes to use to produce the work.

Execution and standards

When you have approved the proposals the agency goes into overdrive, executing the work – turning the idea into real advertising – and ensuring that the quality is maintained to standard throughout. These issues are dealt with in more detail in Chapter 15.

THE OTHER 'CREATIVES'

I have portrayed this stage of advertising development as a two-person job so far, but this may be far from the truth. There will have been liaison between media and creative as the suitability of media and space sizes or length of time spots have been refined. This input and coordination is, of course, essential for a meaningful proposition. (I've yet to be presented with a TV commercial by creative matched to a *press* schedule from the media department, but, as a client, I have had creative recommending colour double-page spreads while media were telling me I should be using whole-page black and white to get the frequency and coverage. I sacked the agency!)

The main input, however, will come from the account planner or the account handler where he or she fills this role. A good account person will be an intrinsic part of the creative process. If their input is helpful, constructive and of genuine benefit, it will be welcomed by the great majority of creative teams. But the planner is there as guardian of the proposition, and this can lead to the occasional full and frank exchange of views! If the team drift off the brief, a good account planner will gently nudge them right back on target. It would be naive to suggest that this guarantees that every piece of work will be spot-on to the brief when you see it. But nine times out of ten it should be, otherwise you may have a problem with the planner.

Even if media and account planning are happy with the work, it still has one last hurdle to jump before it comes in front of you: the Creative Director. He or she is guardian of the agency's product. A strong director will reject work which does not come up to the agency's standards – no matter how logically it can be shown to meet the brief.

So, the proposals have had an often painful birth and traumatic infancy. Then they have to face the initiation ceremony: the client presentation. We'll deal with that shortly.

BE CREATIVE

1 Go back to the propositions you developed from earlier chapters. Can you make them more motivating? Redraft each in three different forms and leave them overnight. Which works best after the overnight test?
2 Ask a friend or member of the family to give you a headline and brief product description from a press ad – without your seeing the ad. Develop your own using the process described. Now go to the original. How do they compare? Did you at any stage strike the idea which the agency used?

3 Choose two ads which you think look particularly good. Try to analyse why you felt that.
4 Now choose two which you think are well written. What makes them well written?

Further reading

Bernstein, D., *Creative Advertising*, Longman.
Longman, K. (1971), *Advertising*, Harcourt Brace Jovanovich, New York.
Hopkins C. (1987), *My Life in Advertising and Scientific Advertising*, Crown Publishers, New York.
White R. (1988), *Advertising: What is it and how to do it*, McGraw-Hill.

12 Reaching the audience

Defining media objectives – A look at media channels – Selecting specific media – Creativity in media planning – Assessing your own use of media

We now know why we are advertising, what we want to say and to whom we want to deliver the message. It's time for the media experts to get to work. Their function: to take the message to the audience in the most cost-effective way which will meet your advertising objectives.

In working towards the media plan there will be (or there should be!) a good deal of interaction between media and creative departments. One element of the media planner's task will be to select media which are complementary to the creative solution. After all, a great idea for a TV commercial may not work too well on a poster!

There are two fundamental stages in the media operation, the planning and the buying. However, the total development process is much more complex (Figure 12.1). It involves a combination of rational and intuitive processes to produce as close to the optimum as possible.

At its very best, media planning can be as creative as any discipline within an agency – or, indeed, in marketing as a whole.

START WITH OBJECTIVES

Like anything else, media planning can only be done well if it is done, and measured, against specific target achievements. The media objectives are the next level down in the chain which runs from corporate objectives through marketing objectives, communications objectives and advertising objectives.

In effect, the media objectives are the translation of the advertising objectives into terms which allow the media expert to plan and buy. So, for example, if the advertising objective is to raise awareness from, say, 30% to 40%, media's job would be to look at how that awareness had been built in the past, and develop a plan to meet the objective. If previous advertising had reached, say, 60% of the audience to achieve 30% awareness, the media objective is likely to be to cover at least 80% of the audience.

However, 'coverage' of the audience is only one aspect of building awareness. It's not enough to see or receive a message in order to remember it. A combination of conventional wisdom and research

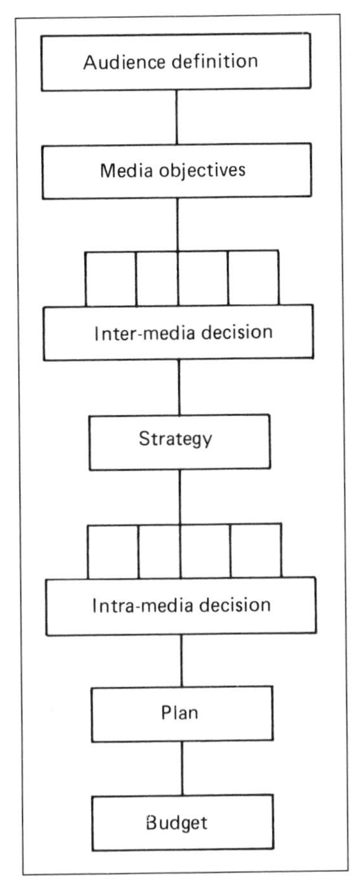

Figure 12.1 The media planning process

suggests that the average individual needs to be exposed to an advertising message at least three times before it sinks in. And that's just to get it in there – what does it take to make it stay put?

You and I may recognize a flowing white stripe on a red background instantly. It says Coke. But it only says Coke because hundreds of millions of dollars have been invested over decades to ensure its instant recognizability.

Defining the media objective – in quantified and measurable terms – is not an exact science. It is, as said earlier, a balance of the rational and the intuitive – but with intuition based on experience. The objective must contain the two elements of coverage and frequency of exposure. It is testimony to the difficulty of setting media objectives that few books on advertising even tackle the issue. Yet applying rational analysis to past performance can provide a basis for establishing meaningful objectives. On a simplistic level, if our objective is to increase responses from 200 per month to 300 per month then the media objective might be to increase 'weight' by 50% – where 'weight' is percentage coverage multiplied by frequency of appearance.

Don't shirk the exercise. With no objective you're lost. With an imprecise objective, at least you have an anchor for your future learning.

THE PLANNER'S OVERVIEW

At the start of the planning process, the planner has several aspects of the task in mind: meeting the objectives; matching the media to the target audience; ensuring that the media can deliver the creative solution; and choosing an environment which is right for the message, the product and you, the advertiser.

He or she will be aided by a great deal of in-depth knowledge of the characteristics of the main media. It's worth gaining at least a basic level of understanding of these characteristics.

Television

From the creative viewpoint, TV is attractive. It offers colour, movement, sound, vision and mood. It is a highly persuasive medium which allows immense latitude for the team's creative talents. Television delivers the advertising message to an audience which is in a relaxed and secure state of mind, in a receptive, domestic environment. Its position as the most powerful of advertising media is rarely disputed.

The media planner gets genuine mass coverage – almost 100% of UK households own at least one set. Yet using the immense amount of research available on viewing habits, the planner can use TV to reach your specific, defined target audience. Indeed, by intelligent use of the available information it is possible to construct a schedule which will deliver the target percentage coverage of that audience at the target frequency. As an advertiser, you'll find this coverage/frequency quoted as television ratings (TVRs). One rating point is equivalent to 1% cover of the audience. Thus, for example, a schedule giving 500 TVRs at 75% cover means that all members of the defined audience would have the opportunity to see your commercial an average of five times (500 ÷ 100% of audience). At 75% cover, the average opportunities to see (OTS) would be 500 ÷ 75, or 6.67 OTS. In today's market, the media planner has an increasing number of options in building the schedule, including national and regional commercial stations plus various satellite and cable channels.

There's an attraction for the advertiser, too, in being able to regionalize the medium. The coverage limitations in ITV contractors' contracts means that TV can be used just as effectively on a regional basis as nationally. Indeed, the use of regional television creates an impression for the viewer that the brand being advertised is a national brand. This has distinct advantages for the regional operator, who is in competition with much larger, national competitors. Television is also a fairly prestigious medium and does lend some of that prestige to the brand or product being advertised.

Selective buying of advertising spots within specific TV programmes can give a reasonable degree of control over the environment in which your commercial appears. You could, to use a simple example, advertise sports goods only during the breaks in sports programmes.

But TV advertising is not without its limitations – the first of which is budget! The costs start with production of the commercial itself. However, the popular press stories of commercials costing £1 million do not represent the norm. While it's not difficult to run up a bill of £100 000 on a reasonably complex idea, it is possible to produce a simple commercial (possibly prepared by the TV station itself) for a modest but still five-figure sum.

Buying time on television is normally done in 'spots' of 10, 20, 30, 40, 50 or 60 seconds, although longer spots can be available by negotiation. TV time is expensive. Again, while a regional campaign with 'first-time user' test discounts could cost as little as a few tens of thousands of pounds, national TV is rarely worth considering unless there is a *minimum* of £250 000 available.

But the worst part of TV buying is perhaps the 'pre-empt' system. Basically, TV time is sold at a price dictated by demand. If you book a spot and someone later offers more for that spot – you get gazumped! There are several levels of buying which give ever-increasing security of appearance, right up to the guaranteed spot. Naturally, the price goes up at each stage, and guaranteed appearances come very expensive, at around 75% higher than the 'base' price.

This system makes life hard for the TV buyer who may have to 'book' the same spot several times at ever higher cost before being sure the client's commercial will run. It's tough on the clients, too. They have no way of being certain that the media objectives can be met within their budgets, since no one *knows* what the necessary spots will cost. The role of the TV planner, and his or her experience, is critical in forecasting campaign cost.

One way around the complexity is to buy packages, where the contractors will agree to deliver a given coverage and TVRs within an agreed time period. It's up to the contractors then to run the commercial in spots which will build up to give the contracted frequency and coverage.

Television does also place certain limitations on the creative team. Some are legislative: all scripts and treatments must be approved by the Independent Television Companies Association (ITCA), which supervises adherence to the IBA Code of Practice for TV advertising. Others stem from the nature of the medium. To put it simply, you can't say much – even in 60 seconds. In balancing cost and frequency, most advertisers in fact use 30-second commercials. So the message has to be kept sharp and straightforward. Yet even given such severe time constraints, the best commercials can tell an amazingly detailed story in that short period.

The instantaneous nature of television, which contributes greatly to its impact, also means that repetition is needed to build memorability. Viewers cannot dwell over the message, nor reread to ensure that they understand it. A good guideline would be a minimum of four OTS to establish reasonable awareness, understanding and message retention. Much more would be needed to maintain these effects over time.

Radio

Radio shares some of the characteristics of television as a medium. It can be used to reach a mass market. It offers sound, mood and special effects. And it is sold in roughly the same lengths of time spot.

However, it is also very different. The lack of vision is the most immediately obvious difference. This factor does cause some problems, in selling clothes or food for example. Radio also commands less attention; the listener is rarely focused solely on a radio programme. For the great majority of us, for most of the time, radio is merely background entertainment while we concentrate on cooking, ironing, driving, DIY or some other activity. So in some ways radio advertising needs to work harder to be effective.

It is also worth noting that while radio can be mass-market, it doesn't have to be. The plethora of local commercial stations in the Independent Local Radio Network leaves plenty of choice. Virtually national coverage can be achieved with a network package of popular mainstream stations. But regional campaigns are equally available. Radio audiences, for individual stations, are more diverse than TV audiences. Particular interest groups can be reached through more specialist stations which programme mainly, for example, jazz or sixties music. These more niche stations can offer real targeting advantages to agency and advertiser.

To return for a moment to the nature of radio; its non-visual nature is unique among advertising media. Some creative teams (and clients!) will consider this a major handicap. Conversely, many will agree with the person who once said 'I prefer radio to TV. The pictures are better.'

The lack of visual stimulus can indeed be used to open the listener's imagination and so make radio a much more involving medium than TV, which pumps finished image after finished image at the viewer. Radio stations and their sales agencies will generally have very good data available on their listeners and their listening patterns. As a result, they are good at 'packaging' spots.

To reach an audience of business executives, a 'drive-time' package may prove ideal. Typically, this may consist of, say, 24 spots of 30 seconds, spread over two weeks and guaranteed to be broadcast between 6.30 a.m. and 9.30 a.m. or 4.30 p.m. and 7.00 p.m., precisely the times when that audience is likely to be listening to the car radio. There is a wide variety of such packages available to suit specific audiences.

The 'weight' of package is also important. Like TV, radio is an ephemeral medium. Your commercial has a life of only seconds. Repetition can be crucial to successful message delivery. The frequency of repetition is no exact science. As a guide, I would not consider a campaign which gave fewer than six 'opportunities to hear' and I would want these to occur in a relatively short period to optimize impact and recall.

The final major difference between radio and TV is cost. A radio commercial which does not use famous actors' voices, and only readily available sound effects and music, can cost as little as a few hundred pounds to produce. Airtime is also much cheaper than TV time. Whereas a single showing of a TV commercial can cost tens of thousands of pounds, a regional drive-time package on a single major station like London's Capital Radio can amount to less than £10 000.

National press

If we have a wide choice of radio stations, we are positively spoiled when we move into press. National press is a catch-all title covering newspapers, magazines and comics; dailies, Sundays, weeklies and monthlies. There are many of them and they vary greatly in content, style and hence readership. This is very much to your advantage as an advertiser. The variety is such that it is possible to find appropriate media to cover almost any target audience definition.

All of them have some important characteristics in common. They are used more actively than TV or radio in that the reader makes a specific choice to pick them up and read them. They lack sound and are limited in their ability to convey movement. Most do run full colour these days. They offer more 'space' to deliver a detailed message (although I dispute the common fallacy that TV is unable to deliver in-depth information). They can be particularly useful in leading consumers to the point of purchase by publishing stockist lists and so on. They have a longer life than TV or radio commercials – although you control that life on TV or radio by defining the length of your commercial while the consumer controls it in the press by choosing how long to look at a given page. They also offer a range of space sizes. Yet as advertising environments, they vary a great deal.

National daily newspapers treat news in a 'fast and furious' fashion. They have a life of a day or less. Yet they can be used effectively as part of a long-term advertising strategy, or conversely, for one-off tactical needs. They offer large audiences from several hundred thousands up to many millions. But each has its own audience – the profile of the *Sun's* readership is very different from that of *The Times*. So they do give a certain amount of market segmentation. National newspapers generally offer a high degree of reflected prestige for the advertiser and this is as true of the dailies as of the Sundays.

National Sunday newspapers, apart from the obvious fact that they only appear once a week, share the characteristics of the national dailies. Their key difference lies in the editorial approach. They treat their main stories in much greater depth than a daily can, and they cater more for specific interests within their audiences – as you may have noticed when bringing your *Sunday Times* home in a wheel-barrow these days. The editorial depth is also reflected in the reading depth. Readers spend much more time on their favourite Sunday paper than on a daily. This may give the opportunity to concentrate a limited budget in Sunday papers and create an illusion of constant presence.

Some of these major national papers, both daily and Sunday, can be bought on a regionalized basis, but not all, and only to a limited extent. The *Daily Mirror*, for example, offers a north/south split for England.

Regional newspapers offer some of the characteristics of national press but with a much more local editorial flavour. Naturally, they are excellent for geographic targeting but tend to lose out significantly in audience segmentation. Most also lack the prestige element of the nationals, but there are exceptions such as the *Glasgow Herald* and the

Yorkshire Post, which, in their own areas, are as highly respected as national newspapers.

Free-circulation papers are something of a conundrum. Conventional wisdom says that they are glanced at but not read, since their editorial quality is often highly questionable. Yet some have built strong positions as, for example, the place to look for car or property ads. They need to be assessed carefully for your own specific needs.

General magazines seems a dreadfully general title to use! Indeed, it could be broken down into dozens of categories such as women's magazines, enthusiast and hobby press and so on. They are, of course, usually smaller in size than newspapers and printed on better-quality paper. They have generally a much longer life than newspapers – anything from a few days up to many months or, in the case of something like *National Geographic*, even years. The variety available is such that most audiences can be targeted effectively; from the teenage audience of some of the music magazines, to the car buyer, to the photographic enthusiast. Some can fairly be described as mass-market, having six-figure circulations, others very narrow audiences of a few thousand. One key feature of the magazine market is that you can find the right environment for any product somewhere in the available range of press.

The business press consists of two broad sectors often referred to as horizontal and vertical, respectively. The horizontal press generally aims to reach individuals in certain job roles across a range of industries. They can be as broad as *The Economist* or *Marketing Business*, reaching middle to senior management, or, somewhat narrower, such as *Works Management* or *The Engineer*. The vertical press aims at specific industries or sectors. Here you'll find titles like *Farming News*, *Packaging Today* and my own all-time favourite, *Rubber and Plastics Weekly*!

The UK is particularly well supplied with business press but the research available on readership is, frankly, often not as good as it might be. You may be forced to rely on your own or your agency's experience to make a valid selection in this area.

All areas of the press work to published rate cards which will give prices for various sizes of space – and for various positions. Particularly strong positions such as front and back cover command premium prices – and with good reason. They do help impact and visibility.

However, with very few exceptions like the *Financial Times*, the rates are for negotiation (unlike the United States, where the rates are fixed prices). At times of low demand, ad directors will negotiate, sometimes significantly, off the rate card. Another feature worth noting is last-minute buying. When papers are ready to go to press and the advertising has not all been sold, the publishers will usually take what they can get at the last minute. This can let you buy half-price space, but you do forsake control over a planned schedule.

Cinema

This is a fascinating medium. And it's often badly used. It's the movie which delivers the audience. Major advertisers such as Gordon's Gin follow the film around the country. So they track an audience appropriate to the product. Local advertisers have a tendency to use the local cinema irrespective of what's showing. And there's a lot of difference between a *Ninja Turtles* audience and those who go to see *Fatal Attraction*. Cinema is good at delivering youngish audiences but of little help for the 'grey power' movement.

I'm often surprised that creative teams don't push harder to get cinema onto the media schedule – it's a wonderful creative opportunity. After all, look what a good movie director can achieve!

Cinema is highly flexible in buying terms. You can buy packages of 'screens', or screens showing, say, only 'U' and 'PG' films, or a 'follow the film' package, or even guaranteed audience delivery.

Coverage takes time to build on cinema and campaigns need to be fairly long. The ideal probably occurs somewhere around six months, with 10–12 weeks being a working minimum.

Outdoor media

We'll ignore free media – like the sides of your vehicles and the signage on your premises – on the basis that you should be using them already! But that still leaves us with taxi sides, bus sides and rears, ad-shell posters at bus stops, moving signs at Piccadilly Circus, 16- and 48-sheet poster sites, hot air balloons and other opportunities.

Standard poster sites range from four-sheet at 60 inches × 40 inches right up to huge 96-sheet sites at 10 feet high by 40 feet (sorry, the UK is still going metric – inch by inch!). They are, like cinema, a highly flexible medium which can be bought literally site by site or in a variety of packages. These packages can be purchased locally, regionally or nationally and are often classified as light-, medium- or heavy-weight campaigns.

Posters lack audience selectivity, although this can be overcome by tactical buying – for example, car park sites for products aimed at motorists or railway termini for commuters. However, they are probably at their most effective, as are all outdoor media, for mass-market products.

These basic aspects of the medium are shared by the other outdoor options. In addition to those already mentioned, the planner will consider Tube cards, parking meters, sports ground banners or even the sides of those airships which used to float over London before the company went bust yet again!

These then are the main and most frequently used media under consideration as the planner starts to consider how to meet the objectives set.

THE INTER-MEDIA DECISION

The great majority of good media plans hinge on one main medium, often with others used for support. The choice of this medium will be dependent on a number of factors including the objective, the audience and the needs of the creative solution. And, of course, the choice of main medium may change over time as a campaign moves from phase to phase.

To help in determining the key choice the planner will combine the client's experience with that of the agency and add a good measure of rational analysis of research available through sources such as the National Readership Survey and Target Group Index.

The following few examples of planning all featured on the winners' list in the Media Week Advertising Awards. They serve to illustrate well-thought-out outcomes of the inter-media stage of planning.

WCRS for BMW

Television was chosen to prime the prospective audience and establish the values of the BMW marque. Colour press advertising supported the TV in building brand values but went much further in delivering more practical information on the range.

O&M for Guinness

The Draught Guinness creative team conceived a series of witty topical advertising ideas. The media objective was to use them in a way such that good coverage and OTS would be achieved without any specific ad being seen more than once or twice a year by any individual.

National press was a natural choice. It allowed many executions at relatively low production cost, and there were enough publications available to rotate the ads between segments of the audience.

BBH for Häagen-Dazs

The target audience for this luxurious ice-cream had been hard to define. It came down to something along the lines of 'people who believe quality is worth paying for – and that they themselves are worth a treat'. The now-famous creative work demanded a 'personal' medium. TV does not qualify; it's a social or family event. Press is much more personal in that it is generally read alone. However, newspapers were not seen as right because of their 'quick-read' nature. BBH wanted the ads, like the product, to be savoured.

The result? A campaign in up-market colour magazines and the colour supplements of quality Sunday papers.

Defining the support

Generally, one medium will stand out. The next task in strategy development is to decide whether it can fully meet the objectives.

At the launch of a new, inexpensive consumer product (those classic, fast-moving consumer goods), television may be necessary both to persuade the trade to stock it and to build awareness rapidly. But you may need trade magazines to help sell the TV campaign to your distributors; advertising your forthcoming advertising! Your marketing plan may lead to adding regional press to pull consumers to the point of sale. Perhaps you'll add precinct posters which scream 'Available right here, right now.' Each medium will have been selected to perform a specific function, the whole structure built to meet the total objectives.

Now the planner can move to the next stage.

THE INTRA-MEDIA DECISION

Let's assume that we've decided on our lead medium – where to next? Into research data is where.

All the well-established media have extensive research on who reads, sees, watches or listens to them. The media owner can usually provide detailed information on the audience by age, sex, social position, region and more. Provided you have been able to define your audience in such terms, it is relatively easy to pull together information from, say, various newspapers for comparison purposes. Such an analysis gives two important pieces of information; first, how many individuals in our target market are covered by each newspaper and, second, how cost-effective each is in reaching that particular audience. The latter point is usually expressed as the cost of reaching each thousand people who fall within our target market. Hence candidate media for consideration are ranked by cost per thousand (CPT), the best candidate being the one with the lowest CPT.

This ranking can be done either on circulation figures for each (for example, the audited figure for the average number of a particular newspaper sold each day) or on more nebulous figures such as 'readership'. It is certainly true that some media are bought by one person but read by several. The value of this 'pass-on' readership is a subject of regular debate. It would take half the book to argue the pros and cons: I suggest you take your agency's advice.

The intra-media judgement is similar for TV. But rather than a choice of many channels, it is often one between different programme spots.

In beginning to build the final media list, we need to look in more depth at issues such as overlap readership. Many people, to use our newspaper example, read more than one paper on a regular basis. If we take no account of this we simply add up all the coverages given by the chosen papers – and may grossly overstate the coverage likely to be achieved. Major agencies will have access to a method of analysing overlap readership by computer, thus eliminating the potential distortion in the figures.

Building the schedule

The plan is beginning to take shape and the planner will move towards summarizing the overall proposal in a media schedule. This is the final document which will be presented to you, the client, for approval.

Putting the schedule together is a detailed task. It necessitates taking into account seasonality of your market and issues such as regional weighting. It must also deal with positioning in various media.

We looked briefly at positioning in our overview of key media options. If posters are chosen, should they be spread generally or only in certain towns? If newspapers, should we be on the City pages, the sports pages or is 'run of paper' (i.e. anywhere!) just as good? There's no magic answer to this one; previous results and experience of the particular medium are the guides.

CREATIVITY IN MEDIA PLANNING

I said earlier in this chapter that media can be as creative as any department in an agency. The evidence exists to prove the point.

The Ogilvy & Mather/Guinness campaign mentioned a couple of pages earlier is a good example of creative placement of a tactical campaign. The famous 'Eau' campaign by Perrier once featured an advertisement entitled 'Heaule'. A media planner and creative team got together and came up with the idea of having a 'hole' in the previous page which partly revealed the ad. How the planner managed to persuade publishers on that one remains a mystery. But creative!

The Economist's red and white poster campaign is a wonderful example of using an unusual choice of medium to reach a business audience and combining it with brilliant creative work to produce results. The Häagen-Dazs choice of magazines, rather than the more conventional TV for ice-cream advertising, proved to be inspired.

THE LAST STAGE

You've agreed the schedule in principle. Now the agency moves out of its intellectual high ground. And into the bazaar.

The media team's last task is to buy your space or time at the lowest possible cost. Naturally, the ad manager of the station or publisher has been given the job of selling that very same commodity at the highest possible price.

The law of supply and demand works extremely efficiently in media. In a healthy market the sellers will stick to published rates like superglue. In a soft market the media buyer will drag the price to the floor. And the situation can change from hour to hour in media like TV and daily press.

ARE YOU USING THE RIGHT MEDIA?

1 Did you agree objectives for your last campaign?
2 Looking back at the media you used, do you feel they were right? Why?
3 What changes would you make next time round?
4 Consider all the options which might reach your target market. Are there any which you should test?
5 Watch the main news stories over the next week. See if you can spot one with relevance to your sector. Could you identify a tactical advertising opportunity?

Further reading

Davis, M. (1992), *The Effective Use of Advertising Media*, Hutchinson.

13 Assessing the proposals

The form of presentation – The media proposal – Judging creative work – Exercising and developing your judgement

The ability to judge advertising varies greatly from client to client and from one person to another person within client companies. This is not surprising among, for example, heavy engineering companies where advertising is relatively unimportant in the grand scale of things and commands a very small portion of total expenditure. Such companies would rarely buy the best talent to fill such a (to them) relatively unimportant role. More surprisingly, the same problem can be found even in major fmcg companies where young product managers can command significant budgets yet have little experience and even less formal training in judging advertising.

I suspect that those with an eagle eye for great advertising are born that way but I also believe that a little training and a lot of exposure can create a better than average judge. What follows in this chapter doesn't purport to turn you into a good judge but it will help you along the road and, with luck, encourage you to work at developing the 'eye'.

THE PRESENTATION

The presentation of the proposals can range from an informal meeting, right up to the formal pitch with full audio-visual support, dry ice and all. For small tactical campaigns or tweaks to existing work, the less formal, the better. For major campaigns, you should insist on a full presentation with appropriate supporting documentation.

For your part, you owe it to the agency to allow them to present the work to its best advantage. Ideally, that would be at the agency – where the display and audio-visual facilities will almost certainly be in place. If this is impractical then do as much as you can to help by organizing video, overhead projection and so on as required. (One cry from the heart: if press advertising is to be shown on boards, do arrange some form of shelving or several flipchart stands so that they can be propped up for viewing!)

Opinion varies greatly on who should present the proposals. Some prefer only the Account Handler on the grounds that it's easier to question the proposals if the main authors are not present. Others prefer the full team to be present so they can 'see the whites of their eyes'. Decide what works best for you.

Don't question the proposals until the end. If something is unclear, by all means ask for clarification but, otherwise, let the presenter show you the logic and continuity of thinking all the way to its conclusion. But do make notes of queries as they arise.

The order of presentation of the elements of the proposal is a constant problem. Logic suggests that it should answer the key questions in the order they would naturally arise:

Have they understood my brief?
What's the advertising proposition?
Have they turned it into a powerful idea?
How will they take it to my market cost-effectively?

The problem is simply this: we and you are going to get most excited about the creative work – but it does not naturally come last. The result is that the media proposals are an anti-climax, which does nothing for the creative work, the media or the presentation.

Agencies, therefore, will generally hold the creative work to the end in order to build dramatic tension. That's probably a fair compromise. The presentation will be more interesting for all concerned and that's a good trade-off for the slight illogicality.

How long should the presentation be? The short answer is long enough to cover the ground, short enough to be interesting. It is rare for even a major presentation to need more than 90 minutes, and 60 minutes is a better target in most cases. If you've allowed more than an hour, do both sides a favour and plan a five-minute break in the middle. Apart from the benefit to personal plumbing systems, research shows you'll remember more of the presentation as a result. (I lied about the creative work being presented last. They'll still leave the budget to the end – at least I do! After all, the euphoria of good creative may make the pill easier to swallow.)

THE REPLAY OF THE BRIEF

All new business pitches will (and all major campaign presentations should) begin with the agency feeding back the brief to the client. It is important that you are confident that the brief has been fully understood and the agency should be prepared to demonstrate that understanding clearly. This part of the presentation is where the brief will be fleshed out with any research that has been undertaken. The key objective must be to watch the logic flow.

Do the results really lead to the conclusions drawn? Are the assumptions being made valid? Do they correspond to known fact? Close attention to this section is critical – or you may find out too late that the advertising castle has been built on sand. Keep a weather eye out for the adman's greatest skill – post-rationalization. Are they working forwards logically towards the creative and media proposals; or did they work imaginatively back from them?

The culmination of this first part will be the proposition and the support for it. Does the proposition genuinely reflect the motivation of the market and your product's or company's ability to deliver? Is that view fully supported by any research which has been presented? Is it the 'most motivating and differentiating' thing you can say? Assuming that you're happy with the proposition, ensure that the proposed support is the best you can offer.

In replaying the brief, the agency will have reviewed and, possibly with research, have refined the target audience definition. Now you'll want to know how they're going to reach them.

THE MEDIA PROPOSAL

Remember, you are looking for five key elements in the media proposal:

It must be addressed to *your* target market.
It must be developed from defined objectives.
It should have a clear strategy.
It should achieve its targets on coverage and frequency.
It should do so cost-effectively.

If the proposal presented delivers against all five then you're on your way to success. But how will you know if it does?

Target market definition

This should, of course, be straightforward – after all, you've already defined the market in your brief. The problem is that you may have defined it in marketing but not necessarily in media terms.

Your brief may have identified 'single home-owners with a liking for music', for example. That's not a description you'll find in newspaper circulation breakdowns. So some translation is essential before the media planner can get to work. As mentioned in Chapter 4, the planner will use whatever research is available (such as TGI and NRS) in order to produce a description which is usable in media selection. A series of cross-analyses might redefine your target to something along the lines of 'home-owners in one-person households; generally aged 24–44 years; predominately male but with a rising population of females; living mainly in London and the South-east; liking music, theatre and eating out'. This combination of demographic and lifestyle elements gives the media specialist something to work with. (This sort of translation can take place at a number of stages: you may have provided it; the account planner may put it together; or it may be left to the media planner. Whichever route is chosen, it must be done.) The approach, as mentioned in Chapter 10, is fundamentally the same for business audiences although the result will contain different sorts of information.

The important aspect of the audience definition, to the media planner, is that it must be capable of comparison with the information available about the candidate media. What you must do is understand and be comfortable with the translation process. The end result must be as close as possible to the original definition. The danger of loose definition is particularly high in business markets. The sort of flawed logic which can arise goes something like: we have a target of key political and business figures, they are mainly male and A social classification; therefore our target is AB business executives.

It is true that 'AB business executives' will capture the great majority of your targets. The flaw is that it will also include around three to four million business executives whom you don't want to reach. The potential wastage inherent in a plan based on this loose translation is very high indeed. Watch the process – and make sure that what you started with is close to what you end up with.

Are the objectives clear?

If you haven't specified media objectives, has the agency set its own parameters? In sophisticated consumer markets it's relatively easy to establish the size and make-up of your target market. So it should be fairly easy, using logical development of the overall advertising objectives, to end up with a reasonable set of media objectives.

The task may be somewhat tougher in specialist markets where there are few available data on audience size. Without solid knowledge of audience size, it is, of course, a nonsense to set coverage objectives. They can never be measured. However, if the client's advertising history is known, objectives could be set in comparison with previous years rather than in the absolute. For example, we might set out to achieve 20% more coverage at the same OTS for the same budget in real terms.

Once again, watch the logical flow and ensure that the objectives set are realistic yet likely to achieve your advertising goals. At a ridiculous level, if you are chasing a 40% market share, 35% coverage is unlikely to be of great assistance.

A last word on media objectives. Ask how achievement will be measured. If the system is not thought through and agreed in advance, there will never be agreement afterwards on whether media did its job.

Does the strategy stand up?

Is the agency proposing that you go head-to-head with your competitors, in more or less the same media? Or is the strategy to pick off the audience from a different direction? The first is likely to make sense where you can match competitor spend. A more lateral approach might make a small budget go further.

The proposal may be based on a wide selection of media, or use a very short media list to create an affordable, 'bigger' presence in each – 'concentrate to dominate'. If your task is to sell millions of BT shares in a short time, the former would be ideal. In most cases the latter approach is more effective. The target audience spread should be the guide to the breadth of media required.

Hitting coverage and frequency targets

These two factors are comparatively easy to assess in most single-medium campaigns. It's possible, for example, to produce a computer run against a national press campaign, a run which will measure overlap or duplicated readership. The analysis will give a reasonably accurate picture of net coverage and opportunities to see. The calculation, as we have seen earlier, is more difficult for TV and relies a great deal on the in-depth experience of the planner who needs to predict audiences for particular TV programmes. But the good ones get it about right.

Multi-media campaigns create more problems. Press, radio, and posters all measure their audiences differently – and with little reference to the others. So the inter-media judgement requires informed comparison of the different data, and multi-media campaigns are extremely difficult to judge with any high degree of accuracy. Again, solid experience becomes a remarkably valuable commodity.

While there are few absolutes in measurement of coverage and frequency, a good planner *can* get pretty close – certainly close enough for a fair degree of confidence that the campaign will work. Make sure they've persuaded you to share that confidence.

Is it cost-effective?

Welcome to the crunch! Any fool could achieve virtually total coverage of a given market, with high frequency of exposure – if there's an unlimited budget available. The real skill is in optimizing frequency and coverage at a budget which represents value for money.

One common route by which agencies measure this is the use of 'impacts'. The number of impacts in a campaign is simply the number of times the message is put in front of the target audience. A sample calculation is shown Figure 13.1. While accepting the inexactitudes of measuring coverage and frequency, cost per 1000 impacts does at least provide a simple method of comparing value between different campaign shapes or media selections.

Audience size × % coverage × frequency = number of impacts

Figure 13.1 Calculating impacts

What you need to look for is – did the agency consider all the sensible options? Why was TV chosen for the main medium? Why no packs of cheap product-enquiry cards for enquiry generation? Which options were combined and how did effectiveness compare? And, normally, you'll be comparing the proposals with previous years' figures.

The other significant factor which affects cost-effectiveness is the agency's negotiating ability. In an on-going agency relationship you'll have knowledge of that. If it's a new agency pitch, ask for a demonstration of buying performance on their other accounts.

So far, so good. But there's one important question you'll have to come back to: is the media right to make the most of the creative solution? And vice versa?

CREATIVITY – WHAT WORKS?

Have a look at Figure 13.2. It seems a paradox to talk about 'rules' in an industry based on creativity, originality and innovation. George Bernard Shaw would certainly have found it at least curious: 'The golden rule is that there are no golden rules.'

Figure 13.2 Characteristics of effective advertising

Yet an examination of great campaigns over the decades shows they consistently reflect the five points. Not through any slavish or conscious adherence but, rather, because good creatives automatically build their thinking around them. And they break them occasionally. But they'll only very rarely break more than one in any given ad or campaign. Perhaps a case of rules being for the guidance of wise men and the obedience of fools!

Getting attention It's simple. If advertising doesn't get noticed, it doesn't get seen or read. If it doesn't get seen or read, it can't help you to sell. And the only thing you'll have achieved is to contribute to the well-being of the media owner.

Successful advertising is highly visible and probably 'different'. That difference from the norm is frequently the key to impact and visibility.

The ad shown in Figure 13.3 was one of a series which appeared in the specialist chemicals press. Such magazines are full of pictures of molecules and beakers. The ad achieved astonishing recall levels precisely because it was different (and, of course, had a proposition of interest to its audience). Which leads us to our second point.

Keep it relevant Visibility is easy to achieve. Anything from a naked body to an elephant playing the piano can stop the reader or viewer. But what message will they take away from the advertising?

The problem is that only the image will be remembered. Unless it is relevant to the message. And that relevance must be credible. The naked figure may work in an advertisement for showers, the elephant for some form of memory course.

The Harcros ad is highly relevant to chemicals buyers. It offers big company strength with local, personal service. As is the computer ad in Figure 13.4, again one in a campaign of three – this time in the

REASSURANCE. FOR THOSE WHO FEAR WORKING WITH MONSTERS.

You've spent years building a relationship with your friendly local chemical company.

It understands how you work.

You understand how it works.

You're happy.

Suddenly, everything seems to change.

The name 'Harcros Chemical Group' either replaces or appears alongside some of the best regarded names in the business.

In Britain, the change affects British Chrome and Chemicals, Deanshanger Oxides, Lankro and Durham Chemicals.

In America, companies you knew as American Chrome and Chemicals, Thompson-Hayward, Long Island Chemical, New England Chemical, Wayne Chemical, Northland Chemical, and Harrisons and Crosfield (Pacific) one day, all have Harcros Chemical Group on their nameplates the next.

Tinstab changes in France.

Harrisons and Crosfield in Canada.

Haagen Chemie and Limox follow suit in the Netherlands.

Even in Australia – where the name has been Harcros Chemicals for years – a new logo appears beside it.

Has a new corporate monster been born?

Will a distant head office dictate changes far from suitable for local operations?

The answer is, a monstrous 'No.'

And the power behind the denial comes directly from the force that made the companies what they are today.

You see, long before the names changed, the companies already formed a group.

Its name used to be Harrisons and Crosfield.

It is now Harcros Chemical Group.

And, though you'll see more of the name, the companies won't hear more from head office.

The new identity will in no way affect individual companies' freedom to respond to your needs.

The difference is, should one Harcros Chemicals face a problem, there are now fifteen others to share it.

And it's a reassuring fact that a problem shared, is a problem gone.

HARCROS
CHEMICAL GROUP

Only our resources are monstrous.

Figure 13.3 (Reproduced with kind permission of Harcros Chemical Group)

AND FOR HIS NEXT TRICK, HE'LL BUY A PC WITHOUT PROPER SUPPORT

He doesn't care that Hewlett-Packard offer the industry's best support service.

He doesn't want next-day engineer call-out, with 90% of problems solved on-site, within minutes.

He doesn't need a free HELPLINE service, for software problems.

He's not impressed that Hewlett-Packard quality means a cost of ownership that's half that of the industry leader.

And he's unmoved by our free one-year, on-site warranty.

But then, he enjoys living dangerously.

You may not.

Vectra range of IBM-compatible PCs. For your dealer, see page 11

HEWLETT PACKARD

A more intelligent approach to computing

Figure 13.4

national press. The visual is an intriguing but highly relevant extreme illustration of the risks of poor service.

Brand clearly Remember those Leonard Rossiter and Joan Collins ads for vermouth? Are you sure who was advertising? Good advertising establishes clearly who is doing the advertising. You're investing money for your benefit – not your competitor's. But this doesn't mean using a huge logo or letting the name dominate the ad or commercial.

Advertising can brand by being distinctive. Levi jeans commercials are uniquely theirs. Häagen Dazs' latest campaign for its ice-cream (Figure 13.5) is instantly recognizable. Conversely, the brand or its logo can become the ad. Silk Cut and *The Economist* have both used poster campaigns where this is the case.

Stick with it Strong advertising ideas have very long legs. They can run and run. If you doubt it, think about PG Tips, those flour graders, Captain Birds Eye and the rest.

In sophisticated markets, long-term brand values are much more important than individual ads, campaigns or propositions. They deliver consistent positioning. They build familiarity and preference.

The problem is, clients usually get fed up with their advertising long before the market does! You're surrounded by your own advertising, seeing it day in, day out; so it's understandable. The new enthusiastic product manager comes in, wanting to make a mark. One easy way is to change the advertising. It's also understandable. It's also seriously wrong. Frequent changes in your advertising strategy leave your audience bewildered – and buying from someone else. Long-term consistency beats one-off brilliance. Every time.

Offer benefits It's been said a million times. But it is an incontrovertible truth. So here's the million and first time. People buy benefits, not features.

Advertising is not compulsory reading, listening or viewing – unless you make it so. All you have to do is answer one question for your audience: 'What's in this for me?' The benefit has to be right up-front. Usually it's in the headline of a press ad. It's even possible to deliver a complex benefit message like 'an insight on what's going on in the world' with no words. My all-time favourite poster did just that (see Figure 13.19, page 152).

The nature of the benefit will vary with the product. It can be rational and tangible and based on hard fact; 5% more productivity. Or emotional and intangible like Levi jeans, perfumes or many other consumer products.

"Before eating, always let Häagen-Dazs
TEMPER
or soften for ten minutes. Only when allowed to
TEMPER
can the full flavour be appreciated."
Häagen-Dazs
Dedicated to Pleasure.

Figure 13.5

Those are the golden rules. Be wise. Be guided by them.

In Chapter 11 we covered some of the proven techniques which can help advertising work; testimonials, demonstration, slice of life and so on. We could add 'problem/solution', where we deliberately set up the problem which the product addresses and prove it can solve it. Or 'flagging the sufferer', where the target audience is flagged in the headline; 'Over 30 and no pension?' All these have a potential contribution to make. Here are a few more useful tips:

- The average reader looks at, or at least is exposed to, a magazine ad for about 2.5 seconds. So the advertisement must communicate quickly. If the benefit has to be decoded, you're lost.
- Research into memory shows that images are recalled more easily if they have one or more of the properties of exaggeration, humour, absurdity, sensual appeal, great simplicity or movement.
- News sells products. If the product or service is new, say so. This is particularly true in many business markets where specialist press is a key source of up-to-date information.
- Let the copy run as far as it needs to. The short versus long copy argument is perennial. Readership falls off rapidly in the first 50 words but drops little between 50 and 500 words. Keep it tight, keep it succinct, cut out every *superfluous* word. But take the space to deliver the promise fully and effectively. If the proposition is right, the target market will read it.
- Use short sentences: rarely more than a dozen words. Avoid complex structure with multiple sub-clauses. Use short paragraphs of two to three sentences, and simple words: 'use' rather than 'utilize'.
- Make sure the copy addresses the reader or viewer as an individual in his or her language. 'We' and 'you' is generally much more appropriate, and powerful, than a more impersonal form. 'You'll' is much friendlier and more readable than 'you will'.
- Pictures which hint at a story work much better than more 'static' shots. If the reader says 'What's going on here?', you've got him or her hooked.
- Puns rarely make good headlines. Don't be clever for the sake of it. If it delivers the benefit effectively, fine. If not, scrap it.
- Don't clutter the advertising. Simple and bold with a single focal point is the key to capturing and holding attention.

That lot should keep you going for a while!

One lesson that comes through is that advertising needs to be different to succeed. By definition, 'different' advertising is untried, untested. It takes a brave client to approve it. How brave are you feeling?

ASSESSING THE CREATIVE PROPOSALS

Immediately before the presentation, re-read the brief thoroughly. Above all, have the proposition clearly in mind – it must be the anchor for your judgement.

A major presentation of creative work should, ideally, cover the following points:

The advertising environment
Competitive advertising
The creative strategy or platform
The proposed advertisements

As a client, I often found agencies ignored the first two. Yet if they have confidence in their work they should be delighted to show it against your competitors' work. There is one danger, however. You will be seeing visualizations of your own ads, and these can never match the polished production values of finished work.

This brings us to the crux of looking at creative work at this stage:

> You must learn to assess *ideas* before you begin to worry about advertisements.

If an idea is strong there will be dozens of ways of implementing it. That's precisely why agencies are well advised to present the creative strategy before showing the ads. Frankly, that's not always possible - many ideas don't spark into life until they're shown 'in action', so to speak.

One case in point is the famous Heineken campaign – 'Reaches the parts other beers cannot reach'. Trade gossip has it that few people within the agency (let alone the client) understood the line. Yet now we've all seen the campaign in several executions it's an idea which is strong, relevant and *effectively* different.

How do I judge?

You can *prepare* to judge. You must read the brief and have the proposition fresh in mind, as we've just said. But you can do more. You can be prepared to *be* your target market.

Spend some time reviewing all you know about who they are, what they're like, their concerns and attitudes. The perfect judge of advertising would be the consummate actor. They'd be 'in role' to react to the proposals. Never forget that, ultimately, your or your agency's opinions are of no consequence. The only reaction which contributes to your bottom line is that of the market.

The crunch has come. The commercials or the ads have been unveiled. What now?!

The first thing to say is that if you've had no automatic reaction there's probably something seriously wrong with the creative work. Either that or you're way out of touch with your market. (We won't pursue the latter possibility!)

If you gasp, feel a tightening in the gut or get annoyed – something's happening. It still doesn't mean that the work is right but it suggests that it has a chance. Register that reaction, either mentally or by making a note. It's the only *first* reaction you'll have. And you may try to talk yourself out of it later. Remember it – it's probably the most important part of your judgement.

Having recorded the emotional reaction, begin to explore the rational reaction. What is the campaign saying; what message would the reader, listener or viewer take out? Compare those with the proposition. If they coincide, you're well on the way.

Glance round at your competitors' ads on the other wall or wherever they're displayed. Would this campaign stand out among their work? Does it have the impact to fight and win the battle for attention? Is it clearly *your* ad?

Is the idea campaignable? If the agency has shown several executions and thought about a few more, then the idea probably has the legs it needs.

Finally, in your role-play as target market – does it clearly, without decoding, offer you a benefit? Yes?

Tell the agency you'll run with the idea. You've just checked against the 'golden rules' and the campaign does motivate and does differentiate. Have the courage of your convictions and be prepared to fight the internal battles from the 'safety-first' mob who'll want some rather more invisible advertising.

Now the time is right to scrutinize the specifics and dissect the individual elements. Is the opening shot quite right? Should the branding be a little stronger? Can the headline be tweaked a little further?

There's a danger of over-analysing at this point, too. Your market won't analyse your ads. They won't be overly literal in their interpretation. Do make sure the work is factually accurate, meets all legal and corporate guidelines and gives the right image of the company. Beyond that, respect the professionalism of your creative team and, at the very least, give their views careful consideration before insisting on any detailed changes.

What if you don't like it?

Rejecting creative proposals is almost an art form in itself. The key skill involved is the ability to reject the work and not the workers.

Having read this far, you'll be aware that good advertising doesn't happen by accident. It's the result of a great deal of work by both you and the agency. There's one more thing which it is critical to appreciate: good creatives are like any other artistic individuals. They strive to make their next piece of work their best ever. And part of their souls goes into that work.

Handing the agency a response like 'It doesn't do anything for me' not only fails to make you the greatest judge of advertising but it creates a demotivated team. Worse, it gives the team no guidance in where to go next.

In the extreme case of the work leaving you cold, push briefly through the process of rational analysis. Then explain that while it works for you on an intellectual level (assuming it does), it fails to get to you emotionally. Try to illustrate what you mean by reference to other advertising, either that of your competitors or simply a couple of campaigns which you really like on an emotional level, irrespective of the product involved.

If the idea is a stunner but the wrong message is coming out, the discussion is easy. Tell them it's a brilliant idea but off-strategy. (Then have a private session with your account handler and find out why it happened.) If the problems are in the detail of execution, they should be easily resolved.

Your objectives are two-fold: to say 'no' without demotivating the team and to give them a steer on how they can solve the problem.

Learn to judge better

You cannot learn to judge advertising solely from a book. You need guidance in what to look for and while books can help, they're an imperfect substitute for looking at lots of advertising, including TV and radio, and discussing it with people who are good judges.

If you use an agency, invite their team to meet for a drink after work; on condition that each brings a favourite ad, not in your sector and not done by their agency. Each has to 'present' and assess the ad. The choice and the discussion which follows can be an excellent learning experience. In training staff within our own agency we often go one better by asking each to bring a bad ad as well as a good one. The discussion often serves to prove that one person's meat is another's poison!

In an attempt to provide you with some help, I've chosen some campaigns which I believe to be good, effective advertising. They're not all for famous brands and I've used press and poster examples to show you don't need megabucks to do great ads.

Corporate advertising is an area of growing importance as companies recognize that the company is, in many cases, the 'brand'. There is lots of it around – but not all of it good.

The UCB ad (Figure 13.6) is one of a long campaign of ads all positioning the company as a specialist mortgage lender, committed to financial intermediaries. For me it works (although it's better in the original colour) because it has a definitive style unique to UCB and, unlike most corporate advertising, it offers a benefit. The branding is strong and the art direction tight and clean.

Most research among audiences for financial advertising suggests that there's a great deal of confusion between brands. But there is good work being done. The Bradford & Bingley, for example, has been built from nothing into a respected name. The ad shown (Figure 13.7) is one which appeals to me a great deal (maybe it was being a student during the 1960s which does it!). B&B is the only top-ten building society which is not tied to one supplier of investment products. The proposition: we can give independent advice. It's well translated in a way which reaches out to a particular target audience. It's consistent with much of their other work and the branding is clear – not only through the logo but through the whole look, feel and tone of voice. The original ran with green headline underlined in red. I didn't find that particularly attractive but it certainly had real impact in the national press.

The fmcg market produces some great advertising, amongst which is the campaign represented by Figure 13.8. The brand name breaks every rule in the book; brilliantly. Indeed the brand name is the whole proposition, for which the manufacturer received lots of hassle. The butter lobby demanded the removal of the 'butter' – unsuccessfully – and from their complaint a great campaign was born.

The ad uses the cover-up of the word to create a teaser element. The headline supports the visual well. The pack and hand were in colour. The whole campaign was unmissable. Only one moan: the copy pushes its luck a bit on this particular example. It got a bit wordy with the word 'word'.

Next, a low-budget campaign. Look at Figure 13.9. The headline says it all. A simple linguistic twist captures the proposition nicely.

Recruitment advertising is an area which is often given little attention. Yet every ad is making a statement about the company and should be viewed as an opportunity to state the values in which the company believes and to promote its image.

Are you using
a specialised
mortgage lender
with more
staying power?
U could B
If you need greater commitment from a mortgage provider, you'll appreciate UCB.
Want a full product range to choose from? UCB continues to offer a complete range of innovative products for both residential and commercial mortgages.
Want to be sure your reputation is safe?
Not only do we refuse to cross-sell clients.
We stay healthy by matching a £4 billion loan book with prudent lending. A policy which has contributed to 20 years of successful growth.
And we're backed by Compagnie Bancaire, Europe's top specialised financial services group. Their AA credit rating means ready access to competitive funds for you to sell.
Want superior support? UCB is the only specialised lender with a 17-branch network staffed by loan professionals who'll actually visit you.
To find out more call UCB.
No-one has more stamina.
UCB Group plc, UCB House,
Wallington, Surrey SM6 0DY.
Telephone: (0628) 778732.
U COULD B
WITH
UCB
UCB Group provides residential mortgages, commercial mortgages and an invoice discounting service.
UCB Group plc. Registered office: UCB House, Railway Approach, Wallington, Surrey SM6 0DY
Registered in England No. 964802.

Figure 13.6

IF YOU BELIEVE IN A FREE SOCIETY, WHY NOT JOIN ONE?

To some extent all building societies are free. Certainly all are free to give you advice.

But talk to them about recommending a particular financial product and then you'll start to hear a different story.

Then you'll find that whilst all are free, some are more so than others.

That's because most are tied to a single supplier for their investment products. So the only ones they can sell you are the only ones they have.

Not so Bradford & Bingley.

We are the only top ten building society that is free to give independent advice. We answer to no-one.

As a result, we are able to select products from any insurance or investment company you care to mention.

It isn't hard to see how this has many benefits. For instance, as an independent Financial Intermediary, we are the only top ten society that can offer you a tax exempt savings plan through our high street branches for your children, grandchildren or even godchildren.

It is a way for you to invest money on their behalf which pays a lump sum after a minimum of ten years without any of it going to the taxman.

However, children aren't the only ones who can benefit from our independent status. It has, for example, enabled us to offer the MarketMaster Growth Bond. This is an equity based investment which, on its fifth anniversary, guarantees at least the return of your original capital, irrespective of the vagaries of the Stock Market.

Then there's pensions. Here we won't be selling you one of our policies because we don't have any to sell.

What we do have is access to over 120 of everyone else's. As well as a free advisory service to help you find the one best suited to your needs.

Of course, whether or not you come to talk to us is entirely up to you.

But if you'd like more information, call us on **0800 900 979**. Next time you find yourself with a few moments free.

The MarketMaster Growth Bond is supplied by Scottish Provident Institution, a member of LAUTRO. The levels and bases of taxation may change. The reliefs from taxation are those that currently apply and the value of such reliefs depends on individual circumstances. The value of shares and units can fall as well as rise and the return may be less than the amount invested. Bradford & Bingley Building Society is Regulated in the Conduct of Investment Business by SIB.

Figure 13.7

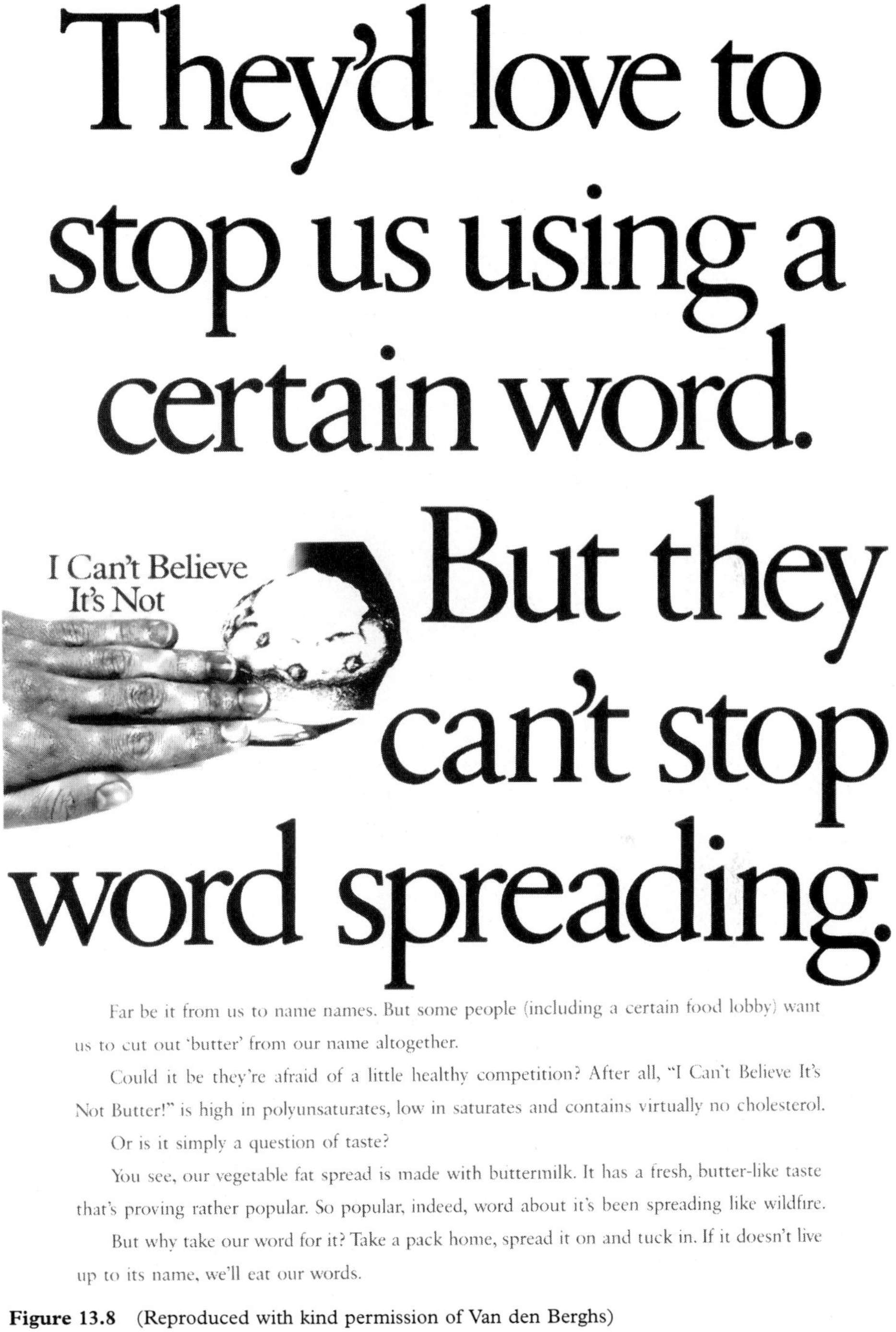

They'd love to stop us using a certain word.

I Can't Believe It's Not

But they can't stop word spreading.

Far be it from us to name names. But some people (including a certain food lobby) want us to cut out 'butter' from our name altogether.

Could it be they're afraid of a little healthy competition? After all, "I Can't Believe It's Not Butter!" is high in polyunsaturates, low in saturates and contains virtually no cholesterol.

Or is it simply a question of taste?

You see, our vegetable fat spread is made with buttermilk. It has a fresh, butter-like taste that's proving rather popular. So popular, indeed, word about it's been spreading like wildfire.

But why take our word for it? Take a pack home, spread it on and tuck in. If it doesn't live up to its name, we'll eat our words.

Figure 13.8 (Reproduced with kind permission of Van den Berghs)

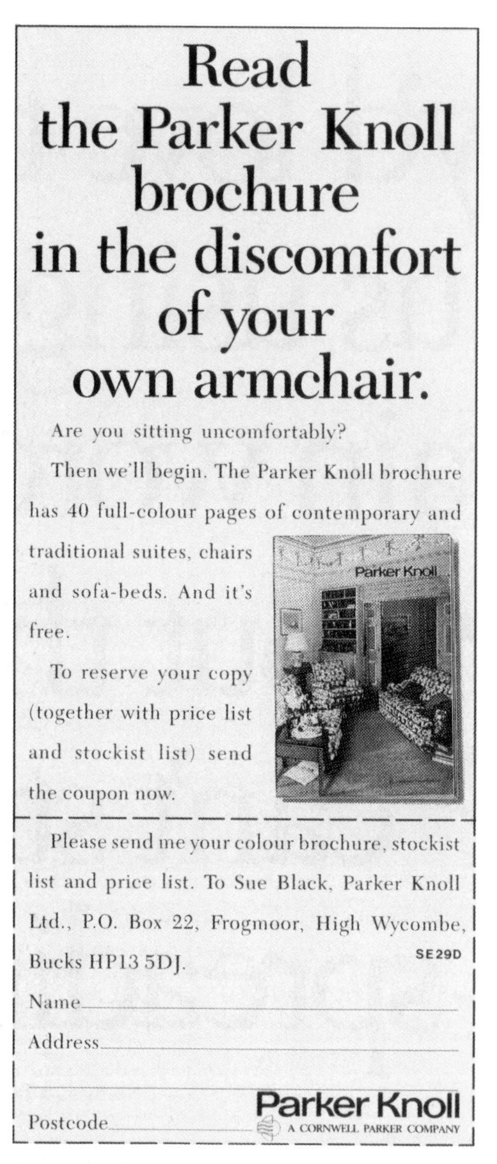

Figure 13.9

Zurich Insurance (Figure 13.10) does it well. The headline says something positive about the company's attitudes and professionalism. Parcelforce (Figure 13.11) is in the same category. It's also extremely well written; the job sounds worth having.

Issues advertising is a particular challenge; how to deal sensitively with subjects of immense emotional complexity. I've chosen two examples which work well. The first (Figure 13.12) was issued by the

Knowing our customer is the first step. Being better known ourselves is the next.

As one of the largest insurance companies in Europe, Zurich has a reputation for quality and service. In the UK, our next objective is to significantly improve our market position through the development of new products and innovative marketing strategies.

But first we need good market intelligence – to understand our customers, our competitors and our own strengths. Equally, people must get to know us. Achieving that ambition means we can now offer two exciting career opportunities within the Marketing Department of our Commercial Lines Division.

Research Assistant

c. £19,000

Reporting to the Marketing Manager, you'll undertake research and present reports on competitor products, trade sectors and customer needs. You'll also be coordinating the activities of external research agencies as well as generating your own projects. As a source of market information, you'll be heavily involved with new product development.

More than anything, we're looking for a self-starter with fresh ideas. Insurance experience is not as important as a minimum of three years within market research. As well as a degree, you'll need good database skills and the personal credibility to convert your ideas.

Marketing Assistant

c. £17,000

Working with Underwriting, Claims and Legal colleagues, you'll help prepare marketing and promotional programmes for new products and activities. In addition, you'll coordinate the activities of design agencies, to ensure projects are completed to time, to cost and to the high quality standards we demand. Of graduate calibre, you'll need previous financial services experience, together with a high level of self-motivation. Familiarity with PC systems and their potential application is also essential.

For both positions, we can offer excellent career prospects, plus benefits including relocation assistance where appropriate, mortgage assistance, non-contributory pension scheme with life assurance, permanent health insurance (subject to a qualifying period) and generous insurance discounts. Zurich Insurance operates a non-smoking policy.

Please send your CV to Caroline Caddick, Manpower Services Department, Zurich Insurance Company, Zurich House, Stanhope Road, Portsmouth, Hampshire PO1 1DU. Alternatively, telephone (0705) 853028 (24 hour answerphone) for an application form.

Zurich Insurance is committed to equality of opportunity. All applicants will be judged solely on their merits.

ZURICH
INSURANCE

Figure 13.10 (Reproduced with kind permission of Zurich Insurance Company)

Sales Professionals

How far could you go with the parcel market leader?

As a Sales Executive with Parcelforce, how far you progress – and how fast – is down to how well you perform.

Based at one of six Sales Offices around the UK, you'll promote our full range of distribution services.

It's a demanding role, both physically and intellectually. You must be confident, highly motivated and commercially aware, with at least 2 years' successful sales experience – ideally in distribution.

Whilst managing our existing accounts is important, the emphasis for you will be on building new client relationships to achieve our ambitious growth targets.

As market leader, we've become accustomed to thinking big.

And thinking ahead. To help you develop your skills in selling a tailored service, we offer a highly regarded training programme and a clearly defined career path into management.

Plus a starting salary of up to £17K (depending on experience), a company car, performance bonuses, 22 days' holiday and pension plan.

So if you're looking not just for high rewards, but for personal challenge and job satisfaction, Parcelforce has the power to deliver.

Please write, with a full CV to Stacy Slater at Parcelforce Headquarters, Solaris Court, Davy Avenue, Knowlhill, Milton Keynes MK5 8PP.

Royal Mail Parcelforce is an equal opportunities employer.

UK wide

Figure 13.11

Embassy of Kuwait in London to remind the public that Saddam Hussein still held hostages after the Gulf War. It balances the joy of the liberation of Kuwait with the cloud cast on that joy by the hostage position. It would have been easy to go too far and picture a screaming child or a jail cell. But enough is known of Saddam's behaviour for it to be unnecessary. The result is a balanced but powerful piece of communication.

The London Lighthouse ad (Figure 13.13) stopped me right in my tracks. No threats, no sob story – which are what we've come to expect in association with AIDS. The headline is riveting, the art direction excellent. The copy has room to breathe, the illustrations maintain visual interest without fighting with the headline. And the coupon hanging out on its own on the right says clearly 'I expect you to do something'. A nice example of telling a story to create effective advertising.

Figure 13.14 is another, but a story about a product. Headline full of intrigue, leading into a genuinely interesting – and true – story. The copy reads like a well-written novel. It has pace and it flows. A fine example of the testimonial approach used to convert a straightforward proposition into a creative solution with bite. I'll remember Gore-tex – but must they insist on using the brand name in capital letters throughout the text?

Business advertising is often, mistakenly, seen as offering fewer creative opportunities than, for example, fmcg products. Figure 13.15 makes a nonsense of this attitude. Redland were fighting a hard battle to command a premium price for their premium products – in this case, a range of roof tiles. The brief was simple: demonstrate the benefits arising from our excellent quality.

The ad does so with impact and style. It was one of a campaign of ads all of which drove the quality message home with headlines full of impact and with tight art direction. Who said roof tiles were boring?

Let's round-off this section with a look at some good poster work. I've chosen two campaigns which have all the attributes of good poster work; they are eye-catching, pithy and put their respective messages across with admirable brevity. And both must have been very good value in production costs, since they rely almost exclusively on the power of words.

The Polytechnic of Central London (now University of Westminster) work (Figure 13.16–13.18) was done by some of my colleagues. The tone of voice and humour is on target for a bright, young audience. Isn't it the kind of college you would like to have gone to?

Sadly, over 2,000 Kuwaitis are still waiting for liberation.

On 26 February 1991, Kuwait was liberated from the cruel hand of Saddam Hussein.

But for many families, the celebrations were tinged with sadness. Their loved ones remained in the clutches of the Iraqi regime. With little prospect of release.

Over 2,000 Kuwaitis are still held in appalling conditions in Iraq's jails. Anyone who saw the evidence of torture and victimisation that Saddam's men left in Kuwait will fear for their safety.

As Kuwait shares your joy at the release of John McCarthy and Jackie Mann, we ask you to remember the fate of the Kuwaiti hostages.

Please add your voice to those demanding that the dictator Saddam Hussein meet his obligations to the United Nations by freeing these victims.

We have much to thank you for

The people of Kuwait have much to celebrate, and many people to thank. Not least in the United Kingdom.

Our countries have enjoyed a long and fruitful relationship. And in our hour of need, you did not let us down.

Your country supported us, and your forces fought with courage and professionalism by our side.

For this, our country owes you a debt which can never be repaid, and will never be forgotten.

The legacy of Saddam

Even amidst the joy of liberation, we knew that a massive task awaited us.

Burning oil wells threatened a major ecological disaster. Our infrastructure was in ruins. Even our hospitals had been ransacked and the equipment and medicines carried off to Baghdad.

Today, we are meeting the challenge of reconstruction with vigour. Our water, electricity and communications are back in operation. Almost 500 oil wells have been successfully capped, and work continues to save the environment.

Many British companies have been awarded contracts to assist in this task. We actively encourage more to submit tenders, for a huge amount of work still remains.

The rule of law prevails

Inevitably, in the aftermath of the invasion, feelings were running high. Tragically, this anger spilled over into lawlessness.

The Government has acted swiftly and positively. In a major public statement, the Crown Prince has emphasised that no Kuwaiti stands above the law, and that any crime would be punished to the law's full extent.

Thankfully, the situation is now much calmer, and the rule of law prevails. We are able, at last, to concentrate our energies on rebuilding our country.

" Thank you " says too little

That Kuwait has a future at all, is thanks to the alliance in which the United Kingdom played such a major role.

Words are inadequate to express our thanks. You have a permanent place in the hearts of all Kuwaitis.

Even in the hearts of those who are not yet free.

"When your soldiers died on Kuwaiti soil, they symbolised bonds of friendship which even the Butcher of Baghdad could not break.

We admire them for their bravery, we honour them for their commitment and we respect them for their belief in freedom."

Emir of Kuwait

Issued by the Embassy of the State of Kuwait, London.

Figure 13.12

HOW I SURVIVED AIDS.

At 9.37am, on Monday the 8th of June (which also happened to be my birthday), my doctor told me I had AIDS. The first person I went to was my brother. I told him I was thinking of killing myself. "Why bother?", he said, "You already have."

That was six years ago.

You see, the problem at that time was that no-one – not the doctors, nor their hospitals, not the media nor their public – really knew enough about HIV infection or AIDS. Or even if there was a difference. The only thing they were certain of was that if you caught it, in no time at all, you were dead.

One year later, I wasn't dead.

It was around this time, that I first came into contact with the London Lighthouse. I remember the phone call vividly.

"I think I'm dying", I blurted down the receiver. "Don't worry", was the reply, "That's what I said when I first phoned."

Suddenly, I was back in reality. I wasn't the only person in the world with the virus.

A day later I was one of a dozen 'me's' perched on beanbags, drinking coffee and exorcising demons. I was amongst new friends (well let's face it, most of the old ones scarpered in the time it takes to say Acquired Immune Deficiency Syndrome). The difference with these people was that they were prepared to listen – really listen. With open hearts.

AIDS never hurt me maliciously. People did.

London Lighthouse restored my self-respect. I never thought I was much of an artist, but with a little encouragement from one of the painting therapists, I uncovered a hidden talent. Simple pastimes, like a night at the theatre or a game of monopoly (as long as I'm the 'Top Hat'), are pleasures I'd forgotten how to savour.

My renaissance is complete.

Yes, sometimes I get ill, but the challenge of AIDS has brought out the real person in me. More honest. More positive. More assertive. The Lighthouse worked miracles for me. Now I work for the Lighthouse. I've got a new career out in the community. Helping men and women affected by HIV and AIDS to face up to it like I did; not as a victim dying but as a person living. As for the future? Well, I've already paid for next year's holiday. I'm going to Cornwall to celebrate my birthday.

The London Lighthouse is never short of love and compassion. Money is another matter. Show your compassion. Make a donation.

NAME

ADDRESS

POSTCODE

I enclose my cheque/PO made payable to FT 30/11

London Lighthouse for £

☐ Please debit my credit card Visa/MasterCard

Account number

Expiry date

Signature

☐ I would like to know more about the work of London Lighthouse. Please send me an information pack.

Please return to: London Lighthouse, 111/117 Lancaster Road, London W11 1QT. Tel: 071-792 1200. Thank you for listening.

London Lighthouse

A centre for people facing the challenge of AIDS

London Lighthouse is registered under the Data Protection Act 1984. Reg. Charity Number 295171.

Figure 13.13 (Client: W. L. Gore & Associates, Agency: Barrington Johnson Lorains & Partners)

A spirited testimonial for Gore-Tex® fabric. From a man who came back from the dead.

"I am alive! I am alive!" yelled the ghostlike figure rising to its feet.

Moments later, Keizo Funatsu of Osaka, Japan was safely back in the arms of his tearful colleagues.

Just 16 miles from the finish, the 1990 International Trans-Antarctica Expedition had nearly ended in disaster.

At 4.30pm the previous afternoon (13½ hours earlier), Keizo had walked out in a blinding snowstorm to check on his dogs.

Losing his way between ski markers, he was disorientated in the raging whiteout.

A skilled survivor, Keizo knew instinctively that there was only one way to stay alive. He must bury himself.

Scraping a shallow trench with pliers, the only tool he had, he curled up in it like a sled dog allowing the swirling snow to cover him and act as a insulating blanket.

KEIZO FUNATSU'S ORIGINAL JACKET MADE BY THE NORTH FACE

At 6pm, they knew he was gone. Clenching a rope tied to a sled to help them find their way, the men circled slowly, shouting his name into the blizzard "Keizo! - Keizo! - Keizo!"

Hampered by darkness, storm and a temperature of -29°C, the team with understandable reluctance, postponed its search at 10.30pm.

Seven and a half hours would pass before Keizo, without hurt or frostbite, could rejoin the land of the living.

His own words tell it best. "Finally, I heard the voice outside the ditch and I knew they were close to me...I was very happy to see my friends...everybody had watering eyes, crying and wet. I cried, yes I cried too."

A happy ending. But the hole which he had frantically dug to survive could so easily have been his frozen tomb.

He owes his life to his team-mates. To the fact that he kept his head and waited.

And to the fact that he, like the others, was protected head to toe from aching cold in GORE-TEX® fabric.

In temperatures of 54° below and winds of 90mph.

'All well and good,' you may say. 'But what has a lost Antarctic explorer got to do with me?'

Simple. The same miraculous fabric will protect you outdoors in Britain.

Waterproof and windproof, yet breathable at the same time, it keeps you dry from the elements and dry when you perspire.

Thanks to billions of pores per square inch that prevent water getting through while allowing your body's moisture to escape.

Faced with 6 million ski strides, GORE-TEX fabric wasn't only the first choice in Antarctica, it was the only choice.

It's available in the best leisure and sportswear by such famous and respected names as Berghaus, Mulberry, Musto, The North Face, John Partridge, Phoenix, Pringle, Pro Quip, Sprayway, Sunderland and Timberland. Durable garments which, in most cases, can also easily be washed. (A miracle in itself.)

And the guarantee is as remarkable as the fabric. All GORE-TEX fabric garments are 'Guaranteed To Keep You Dry' for 3 years. (In the UK or Antarctica.)

So look for the 'Guaranteed To Keep You Dry' diamond when you shop. It's your promise that the complete garment - and not just the fabric - is 100% waterproof.

Ring free on 0800 838527 and we will send you a colour brochure featuring a wide range of clothing made with waterproof, windproof and breathable GORE-TEX fabric.

But inevitably, the final word must surely go to Keizo Funatsu, living proof that it works like we say.

Who simply said with gusto "GORE-TEX fabric saved my life."

GORE-TEX® fabrics

Guaranteed to keep you dry.

GORE-TEX IS A REGISTERED TRADE MARK AND 'GUARANTEED TO KEEP YOU DRY' A TRADE MARK OF W.L. GORE & ASSOCIATES INC.

Figure 13.14

Extremely violent fans have made these terraces safer.

The storms of 1990, though far from the fiercest Britain has seen, went through an astonishing number of the nation's roofs.

Over £1 billion-worth of damage was caused, to more than 3 million roofs.

Not a single properly fixed Redland roof, however, was damaged by the force of wind alone.

Every time nature tests us, the unsurpassed value of Redland's research and development programme is proved.

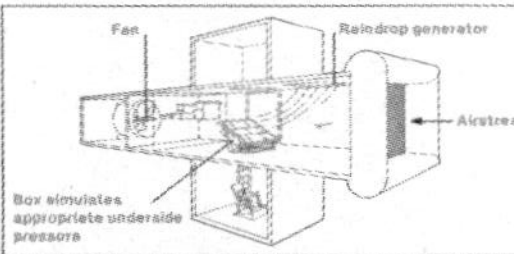

Only Redland has tested products in its own wind tunnels for 25 years.

We have two wind tunnels, our competitors, none.

Every roof tile Redland designs is battered by wind and driven rain until, quite simply, it cannot be bettered.

Compared to our testers, nature is kind.

We even built our own wind- and rain-monitoring station, so we'd always know just how bad the weather can be.

Redland likes to know its enemy.

More than 6 million readings, taken over 7 years, have each helped Redland establish a reputation for practical technical expertise and product excellence that's second to none.

The fact is, Redland sets standards.

Redland's unique double guarantee has become a triple guarantee.

You get guaranteed roof tile durability.

Guaranteed weathertightness.

Now the integrity of the fixing is guaranteed as well.

Use Redland's new Roof Specification Service and we not only provide a detailed fixing specification absolutely free – we guarantee the roof's permanent security against primary weather damage as well.

Phone the Redland Roof Tiles Technical Hotline on 0737 233733, and we'll send you a free model specification, including the terms of our guarantee.

No-one puts more into roofs than Redland.

Which is why we've got so many fans.

Redland Roof Tiles Limited, Redland House, Reigate, Surrey RH2 0SJ.

Figure 13.15

Figure 13.16 Poster for business courses

Speak freely in Russia,
China or the Middle East.

Polytechnic of Central London

Or Japan, Germany or in any one of the 26 languages we teach, full or part-time,
from beginner to degree and beyond, right in the Heart of London. To learn more, phone 071-911 5000.

PCL
THE POLYTECHNIC
OF CENTRAL LONDON

Figure 13.17 Poster for language courses

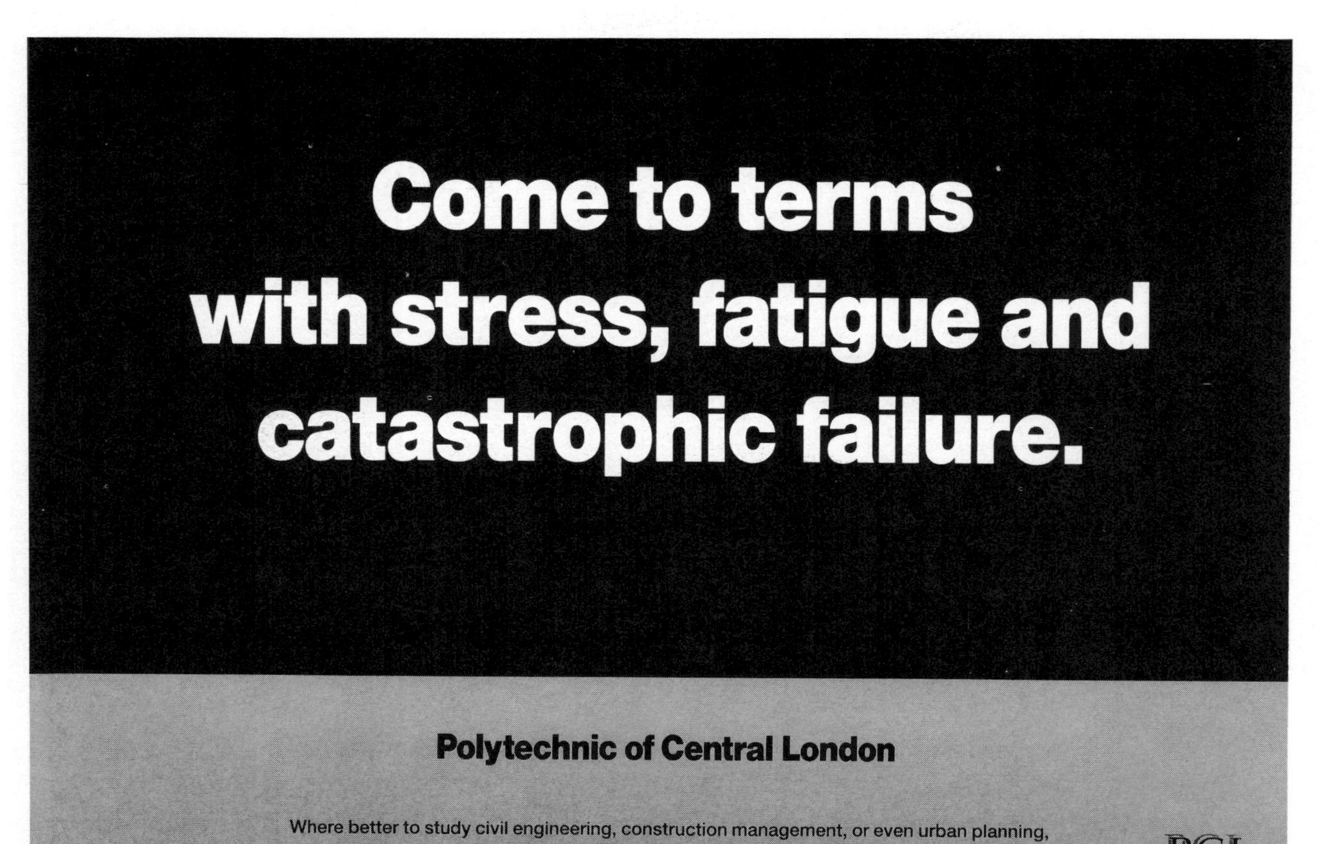

Figure 13.18 Poster for civil engineering courses

The Economist poster campaign is a delight in each of its many executions. I have chosen to illustrate two (see Figures 13.19 and 13.20).

The first (Figure 13.19) is the ultimate in economy of words – it uses none! The original is white lettering out of red, as is *The Economist*'s logo. The early stages of the campaign had built awareness to the point where the client could be that bit braver. The keyhole poster says everything the client could want.

The second illustration is a brilliant combination of media and creative skills – I'd suspect that the creative came first. For those not familiar with the London 'cabbie', it's essential to know that each spends months going around central London on a moped, learning streets and routes. Only after a tough examination do they become cabbies. The learning process is colloquially known as 'the knowledge'. So here's a message which could only work on one particular outdoor medium, taxi sides, in only one city. But how it works!

DO YOU TRUST YOUR JUDGEMENT?

1 I selected the above advertisements mostly from a normal week's reading, and from the posters I saw that week. Try the exercise for yourself. Clip out ads which catch your eye and assess them against the 'Golden Rules':
   - They stopped you, so they must have impact but is it relevant to the product proposition?
   - Is the branding clear? Is it part of a long-term campaign? If you recognized the advertiser or brand even before you saw a logo, then someone's doing a good job. Remember that branding comes not only through the mention of a name or the positioning of a logo but also through the whole look, feel, tone of voice and positioning
   - Finally, and most importantly, does the ad offer anything? Try to imagine the target market for the message and assess whether those people would find a benefit, and find it easily and immediately, in the ad.
2 Go back to your own advertising and look at what you've run over the last year or two. How do you feel about those ads now? Do they score well against the 'rules'? Put them on a wall with your competitors' advertising. Do your ads stand out through the clutter, do they leap off the wall in comparison? Are you developing an individual look and feel which is becoming an asset to your brand?
3 If not, start writing some new briefs. Now!

Figure 13.19

Figure 13.20

Further reading

Designer's and Art Directors Association, *D & AD Awards*, Internos Books, London.

Levenson, Bob, *A History of the Advertising that changed the History of Advertising*, Willard Books, New York.

14 Research into advertising

Why we use research – Types of research – Advertising research – Using an agency – A research exercise

The focus of this chapter will be the specific application of research in developing effective advertising and, to some extent, in measuring its results. However, we must inevitably look at research in the wider context, particularly at the stages which have relevance to preparing a better brief.

It constantly strikes me as curious that even fairly substantial advertisers, spending six-figure advertising budgets, often fight shy of investing in good research. Fact, as they say, is stranger than fiction! Perhaps we can win a few converts.

WHY RESEARCH?

Quite simply, for the same reason as you require any other piece of business information: to reduce the risk of your decisions. Decades of research have proven the effectiveness of advertising – but failed to identify precisely how it works. There's no formula for success so, by definition, it's a risk activity. Is there any other area of your business in which you would consider spending a substantial sum of money without assessing the risk attached to that investment?

The combination of the right proposition, differentiating and motivational, delivered with the right creative solution, can improve advertising effectiveness several fold. But let's be conservative and say, for example, that research might give a 10% improvement in your advertising. Your budget is, let's say, £100 000.

Spending £10 000 on research would be a good investment. Of course, you only 'break even' on the financial 'cost' – but you'll build a stronger brand as a result. Spend a bit less, you may get a financial as well as a brand benefit (with the proviso that to spend too little for meaningful results is simply money wasted).

THE FIRST QUESTION

Before you embark on any research, however, there is one critical question to ask yourself – what will I do with the results?

To digress slightly for a moment, the computer age has enabled companies to produce mountains of financial data, quickly and relatively easily. We face, as a result, a tendency to produce management information which tells us everything, down to the number of bars of soap used last month. And it will be analysed in dozens of different ways. How many managers can genuinely make effective use of such an amount of data? It's often a case of 'We can do it, so we will'.

The same trend is found in companies with in-house research departments. Management can be guilty of measuring such departments as much by the quantity as by the results of their research. And much good work never finds a useful application. Hence my question – what will I do with the results?

One good discipline is to make your decisions before you do the research! Curious though it sounds, it does concentrate the mind. The technique is to project the possible results, (let's say three options) then to decide what action you would take if each one were to happen. When the results are received, the decision is already made.

Objective setting

Developing these scenarios will lead you from a general idea of what you want to know towards specific research objectives. Research is cheaper, more efficient and a great deal more effective when it is carried out to meet specific objectives. We'll deal with typical objectives as we look at the various stages or applications of research later in this chapter.

TYPES OF RESEARCH

Research can take many forms. And while few advertisers would want to become experts in the more esoteric areas such as sample design, a basic understanding of types of research is essential – if only to understand proposals from external agencies.

Qualitative and quantitative

The words are fairly self-explanatory. *Qualitative* research is intended to give information on the more emotional, less quantifiable aspects of marketing. Its results are not statistically 'robust', to use the industry jargon; they cannot be relied upon in a mathematical sense. However, they can be of immense value in indicating, for example, the likely impact of a particular advertising execution on its target audience. Qualitative research involves a relatively low number of interviews, often done in considerable depth.

In contrast, *quantitative research*, as its name indicates, is intended to provide measurable information and is often used as a 'prediction' of future results. Its use in direct mail will serve to illustrate its application.

Assuming that we have defined our target market and identified a mailing list which accurately reflects it, we wish to test our creative execution for its ability to generate response. If it's a small list, we may well simply mail and measure results. If it's several million names, however, we'd almost certainly want to test it on a lower cost basis than a full mailing.

A genuinely random sample is drawn from the list. The size of that sample will depend on how confident you want to be that the test result will be repeated in a full mailing. And here I have to get slightly technical!

Contrary to common belief, the sample size has nothing whatsoever to do with the size of the 'population' – unless that population is very small. Rather, the size is determined by how many examples are needed to eliminate the risk of bias in the results. There are three parameters to consider: the level of 'confidence'; the acceptable 'variance' and the estimated response rate. Don't lose sleep over how these are calculated. The size required for an adequate sample can be identified from tables in relevant books.

To return to our example, which will make the above gobbledegook a little clearer.

If we mail 4500 people in our test mailing, assuming a 3% response rate, we can be 95% confident that mailing to the whole list of millions would give the same result plus or minus ½%. So we can be sure that if we mailed that list twenty times we'd get the original result plus or minus ½% (the variance) on nineteen of those mailings. To be 99% confident, our test mailing needs to be 10 500. (Don't make the mistake of asking a statistician why – unless you have a couple of days to spare.)

Thus we see a predictive application of quantitative research. (This is a very simplified example. The construction of a genuinely random sample requires specialist expertise.)

Desk and field

The definitions are fairly simple: desk research is what you can get from published sources, field research is getting out and talking to the market.

The value of desk research is greatly underestimated. Yet an immense amount of valuable information is readily and relatively cheaply available for most markets. At a basic level, you'll find statistics giving a broad overview of market size and trends, available from sources such as governmental departments and trade associations. This level of information may be enough to establish market share, relative competitive position and basic trends. The Society of Motor Manufacturers and Traders can, for example, give chapter and verse on car registrations by make, model, year – even by postcode, and all for a modest fee. For more details, plus analysis, reports from organizations such as Mintel and the *Financial Times* provide extensive information for a few hundred pounds.

Information services such as the Chartered Institute of Marketing's 'Infomark' give access to a wide variety of databases containing useful information on most markets, again for only a modest search fee. 'Clippings' services from organizations like Media Monitor and Tearsheets can offer you a file of, say, the last 12 months' advertising in your sector. This particular service really only covers mainstream media but represents good value for a price in the low hundreds of pounds. And don't forget your local library. It's free!

Field research is a catch-all heading for a variety of activities, including postal surveys, telephone interviews and face-to-face interviews. There is a low-cost method of using such research in the form of 'omnibus' surveys. These can be found in most consumer sectors and some areas of business-to-business marketing. The omnibus is usually based on a rolling sample and is done on a very regular (sometimes monthly) basis. Its cost is shared by a number of companies interested in a specific market or target audience. You simply 'buy' one or more questions on a particular month's survey.

Beyond this level we move into the area of specially commissioned research – and the cost rises. The techniques used will vary, depending on the audience, the objectives, the timescale, the budget and whether qualitative or quantitative results are required.

A few brief words on the characteristics of the most commonly used methodologies:

Omnibus research: Useful where simple questions can help. But only suitable for either yes/no answers or tick boxes allowing the respondent to choose from a few optional answers. Such surveys can be useful for 'tracking' research. The same questions can be repeated over time and any shift in the answers identified. Limited use but fairly cheap.

Postal surveys: These are pre-printed questionnaires sent to a sample taken from the target audience for filling in and returning. They can carry a reasonable amount of information – but too long, and response falls off. They are fairly cost-effective but are time consuming and rely entirely on the recipient's goodwill in filling them in. Response rates are difficult to predict (I'd always take a research agency's view on this) and so it's difficult to be sure that you'll have enough responses for a viable sample. If a typical response rate is 10% in a given sector, you'll need to post ten times as many as the final sample you need. That can kill its cost-effectiveness and make other techniques more attractive. Postal surveys are generally used for quantitative work.

Telephone research: Just what it says. Recruiting the sample can be difficult – all those people not at home when you call! The telephone is widely used in both qualitative and quantitative research. And you can elicit a surprising amount of information once you get someone on the phone. You know exactly where you stand at any given time in reaching your target sample size. Telephone research is fairly expensive.

Doorstep surveys: These are the clipboards at the door or in the shopping precinct. Cost-effective and quick. But rough and ready in terms of identifying specialist audiences of any sort and hence generally only used for consumer products sold to a wide audience. Relatively low cost.

Focus groups: This technique involves getting a small sample, usually no more than a dozen or so from the target market, into a room for a discussion. A particularly useful technique for advertising testing. A typical group would cost around £2500 to run.

Depth interviews: These can produce excellent qualitative information extracted by a skilled interviewer during a one-to-one session lasting anywhere from 20 minutes to 2 hours. They require highly qualified and experienced personnel and hence are expensive. For a programme of, say 100 interviews, the cost is likely to be over £200 per interview.

APPLY IT TO ADVERTISING

Research which contributes to effective advertising solutions begins long before the brief to the agency. Figure 14.1 shows the areas where it can have a role to play. Media and evaluation research have been touched on in the relevant chapters and will not be covered here.

Audience identification

Marketing theory states that we should identify a need, then satisfy it profitably. Where this is the case, or where a product is already established, the audience will be known. However, where a technical development gives rise to a new product idea, or an idea for a new service is generated, we may have a product looking for a market. In

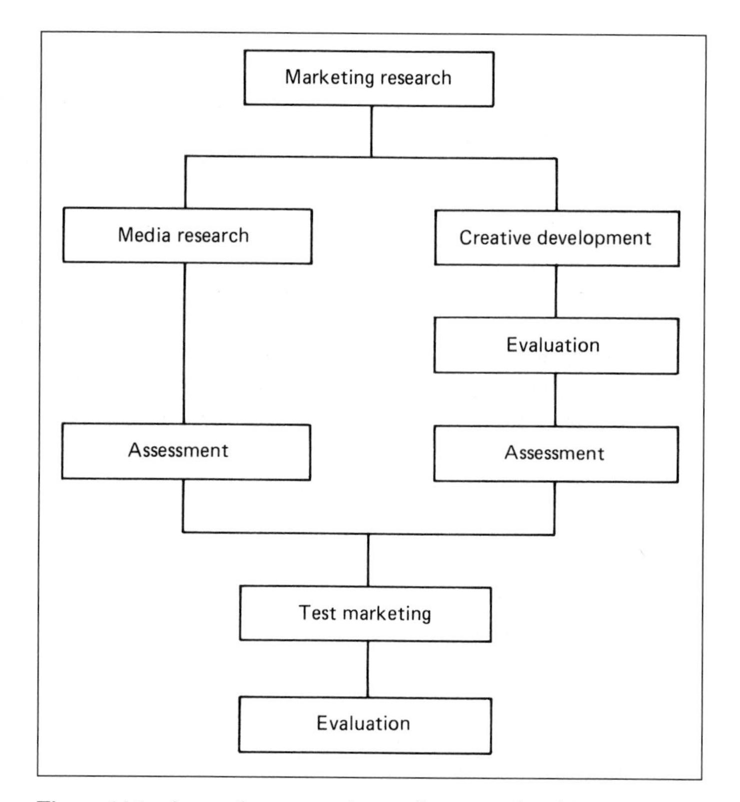

Figure 14.1 Areas where research contributes to advertising

such a case we can make an intuitive guess as to the potential market, then test our hypothesis for validity using research. Typically, this might involve a series of focus groups, testing interest among several potential audiences and gradually narrowing down to the most likely.

Of course, it's not enough to know there's an opportunity for profit – we need to know if there's profit in the opportunity. So the next stage is quantitative research to identify the potential market size.

Both aspects of this information are important. Advertising budget will be wasted unless the audience can be accurately targeted, and media objectives can only be set with any reality if we know the audience size.

The research objectives might read as follows:

1 To describe the most likely target market for product X, in terms of geographic location, age, sex, demographic and lifestyle profiles.
2 To quantify the audience identified in (1) and establish the propensity to purchase product X.

Inside their minds

Earlier, we established firmly the need to understand that audience – to appreciate what your sector, brand or products mean to them. Research is almost essential in achieving a meaningful level of understanding. Again, a combination of qualitative and quantitative techniques is likely to be needed. Depth interviews or focus groups, as appropriate to audience and product, will establish the areas or aspects of the sector or product which are of importance to the market. Broader survey work can then help to check the ranking of these aspects. We learn what counts.

Qualitative techniques are essential to get 'inside' the brand and tell us what makes it really appeal. These are the beyond-the-rational elements of the brand. Through this process we can identify where our competitive edge lies, and we have the basis of another key element of the brief: the proposition.

The research objectives might be:

1 To establish the audience's view of the key benefits sought from products in sector Y.
2 To measure how well product X delivers those benefits.
3 To identify the key emotional values implicit in the brand.

Advertising development

You agree the final proposition with the agency. Off the team go and get to work.

The creative team will face dilemmas at various stages of development. Most are not arrogant enough to believe they know it all – and would find it extremely valuable to let the market help resolve some of those dilemmas, producing more effective creative solutions as a result. The wise client will allow the agency a budget for relevant research to solve such problems.

The team may wish to test alternative headlines, copy approaches or whole creative concepts. Normally, this will be at an early stage in the creative process, using rough visuals shown within focus groups as the research mechanism. You may wish to go the same route if you've been presented with creative proposals about which you are unsure. Indeed, the agency may recommend it.

Normally, testing will be of one of three forms: testing alternative approaches; testing new ideas against your existing advertising; or testing against competitors' ads. The first has no real problems but the others throw up a particular issue.

Your market is not made up of advertising experts. Nor do you want them to judge the 'advertising'. Rather, you or the agency are looking for the audience's reaction to a particular execution of a message. To make effective comparisons, and thus achieve that objective, everything they see in the research must be to the same standards. This may mean producing roughs of last year's, or of competitors' advertising so they are of the same standard as the new ideas. If not, the participants will be heavily influenced by the finished ads and no valuable information on the new ideas will be gained.

A word of warning. This type of research is best used to eliminate bad advertising. It can also eliminate brilliant advertising. The outcome can therefore be that the bland, middle-of-the-road solution wins. This is most definitely not the objective. To protect against this danger, it is critical that the researcher used to run the focus groups is a specialist in creative research. And, ideally, the recordings of the group session should be analysed by a second expert to eliminate researcher bias.

Using test campaigns

The ultimate test of advertising is in the marketplace. It is possible to use the test marketing approach outlined in the direct mail example given a few pages ago.

Using one or a few ITV regions, or regional parts of national press circulation, you could put your campaign to the test in the real world. Confidence levels can never be quite as high as in direct mail because we can never have a truly representative sample – the geographic nature of the test prevents it. However, regional tests can be done and research can be used to assess the effect in the test areas.

Assessing results

This introduces the last area where research can help. This has been dealt with more fully elsewhere, so to close this chapter it is enough to say that the role of research is to learn the lessons from today's campaign to help produce tomorrow's.

WHY USE AN AGENCY?

Many larger companies run in-house research departments. Yet even they will use external researchers for fieldwork. To some extent, this is for practical reasons; few companies, even the largest, could keep a full team of interviewers on staff and fully employed. Agencies are a convenient and more cost-effective source for that expertise.

However, the more important reason concerns the quality of the ultimate results. There is some justification for the argument that bad research is worse than no research – it lulls you into a false belief that you have reduced risk when you may simply have hidden it under a cloak of illusory knowledge.

A good agency brings several areas of specialist expertise to the table, including:

- Understanding of research methodologies and what's likely to get you the best information
- Advice on sample design
- Questionnaire or discussion guide design
- Recruitment of interviewees
- Results analysis.

Each of these stages is important to the final outcome.

For me, however, the two key things the agency provides are anonymity and objectivity. If the respondent knows who is doing the research (before we want them to) the results will be biased, and your own people doing the interviewing will virtually guarantee bias.

STILL NO BUDGET?

If you're not yet convinced, at the very least, do the free research from your desk. And accept the fact that you'll never get optimum benefit from your advertising!

ARE YOU A KNOW-ALL?

1. Take one product or sector of your business and identify the gaps in your knowledge. What would you like to know which you don't at present?
2. Now ask yourself why you want to know those things. What might the answers be?
3. Develop three scenarios of possible answers and identify what action you would take if each were to happen.
4. Examine one of your current advertisements. Could knowing more have helped to improve it? Repeat steps 1–3 but specifically with advertising in mind.

Further reading

Chisnall, P. M. (1986), *Marketing Research*, McGraw-Hill.

Wooster, R. and Downham, J. (eds) (1986), *Consumer Market Research Handbook*, Van Nostrand Reinhold.

15 Approvals, production and control

Agency systems – The approval process – The production process and timescales

Advertising is an expensive business. Even if your budget is relatively small, it will feel a lot to you. But there are many clients who allow it to be more expensive than it need be. To keep it as cost-effective as possible requires effort from both client and agency – and systems which allow both efficient processing of the work and tight cost control.

AGENCY SYSTEMS

Systems do vary between agencies and some are better than others. The good ones, however, even though they vary, share a common objective: no surprises.

A good system should ensure that work is completed to deadline, to quality and within budget. It should, as far as practicable, eliminate last-minute panics and unexpected costs. In the agency's own interests, it should help to allocate and control workflow for optimum use of agency resources – and, of course, allow the agency to measure the profitability of its work for any particular client.

As an example of what I believe to be a good system, I'll describe some elements of one that I use on a daily basis.

The key elements

The process starts and ends with the principal account handler. It is his or her responsibility to deliver what the client requires, within budget.

The anchor for control is the system whereby every piece of work, no matter how small, will have a job number allocated to it. The job cost record for that number will then hold all costs related to that specific task, whether it's the production of an expensive TV commercial or simply a courier charge for delivering urgent artwork. The benefit to the client is that every invoice should be easily identifiable back to the specific task – with no 'dumping' of small charges onto other jobs.

The job cost record will track costs in two areas: first, the charge-out cost of any time spent on the job by 'chargeable' individuals - account management, creative, media and production as appropriate; second, any external costs incurred on the client's behalf. Ultimately, these will come together in the invoice to the client, which is finally checked and sent by the account handler. (Note that media space and time is normally booked and invoiced separately.)

Estimates and cost controls

Figure 15.1 shows the points at which estimates are produced and the control of estimated costs up to the point of invoicing the client. The process starts at the point where the creative team has produced rough

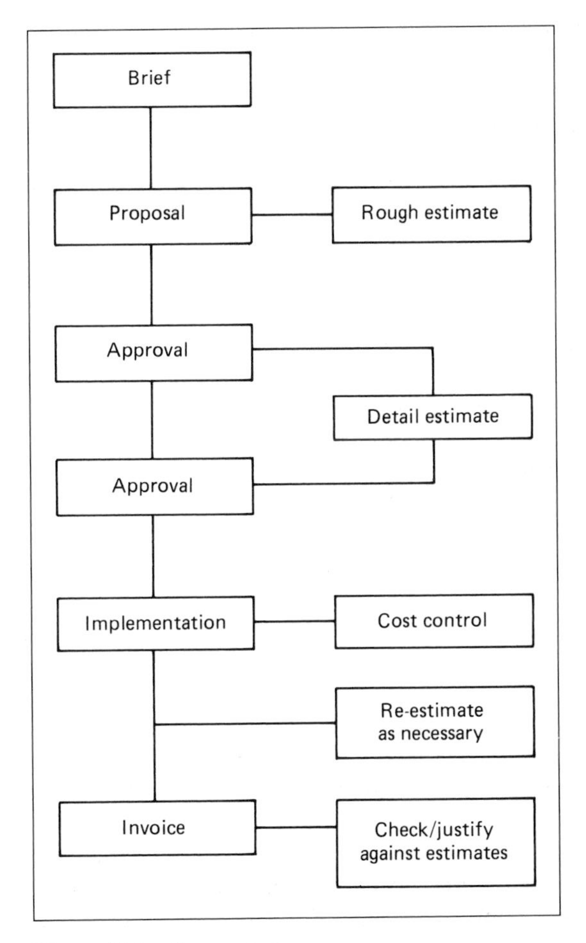

Figure 15.1 Cost control

ideas. If they are to be presented to you at this point, then a very rough estimate will normally be given. This is generally based on experience rather than discussions with relevant suppliers. It will simply provide a 'ballpark' figure.

When the basic ideas have been approved for further work, the development process continues. The next time you see the work it should be a reasonably finished design with full draft copy – and a detailed estimate, based on discussions with suppliers. (However, even this is an estimate *not* a quotation. Some costs cannot be forecast with a high degree of accuracy. These will be identified later in the chapter as we look at production processes.)

Approval at this stage kicks the production team into serious action. They'll take competitive estimates for external costs as well as processing the internal side of the work. When the external work is finally placed, the estimate from the suppliers used will go onto the job cost record. If any change to the specification of the work while it's in progress looks likely to cause a significant cost increase, then an updated estimate will be sent to the client as soon as possible.

Internal time usage will be monitored by both the account handler and the production manager as the job goes through its stages. As external invoices come in, each will be checked against its relevant estimate and contested if there is any unjustified cost increase. The final invoice is checked against the client estimate by the account handler.

There are many other elements to the total system. Underlying all of them is a philosophy that no one can incur costs for your account without the specific authority of the account handler.

YOUR APPROVAL PROCESS

It follows that the account handler needs to be certain of your instructions authorizing action (and, hence, expenditure) by the agency. From your side, you also need a clear approval process with a clear identification of *who* can authorize the next stage of action at each point. If this does not exist, you're asking for misunderstandings and unnecessary expense – and opening gaps for things to fall through.

The money stealers

We have to go right back to the brief to see where things can start going wrong. Getting the proposition wrong is more common than one might hope. The agency puts creative proposals on the table focused, let's say, on the productivity benefits of a piece of equipment.

The client responds by saying that 'reliability' isn't featured strongly enough. In discussion it transpires that the proposition should indeed have been built around reliability, but the client didn't register it until a different proposal had been presented.

The inexperienced client may see this as no big deal – and start tinkering with the ad to bring the reliability of the product out a bit more. That's a waste of time – the brief needs to be changed. If it isn't, mediocre advertising will result; if it is, hours of creative time have been wasted – at the client's cost. The solution is to agree the proposition *before* the creative process starts.

The second area where money is wasted refers back to the approval process. The keen young brand manager wants to make a name. So work is approved and the agency authorized to take it to a fully developed stage. Then the boss sees it and rejects it. The later this occurs, the more that rejection will cost. And the cost has arisen because no clear lines of authority existed within the client's organization. If the system had stipulated that the brand manager could issue the brief and approve up to copy and visual or storyboard stage, but that the work must then be checked with the next level up the management tree, a great deal of time, effort, money and motivation might have been saved.

Then there's mankind's greatest desire. I've had Figure 15.2 on my wall for many years. Regrettably, I don't know its origin or I would gladly attribute it. I give copies to all my clients!

If your approval process involves a dozen people, they'll all feel the need to tinker: it's human nature. But, although it's natural, it's destructive and expensive. Keep the chain of approval short and you'll keep the advertising tighter, more powerful and less expensive to

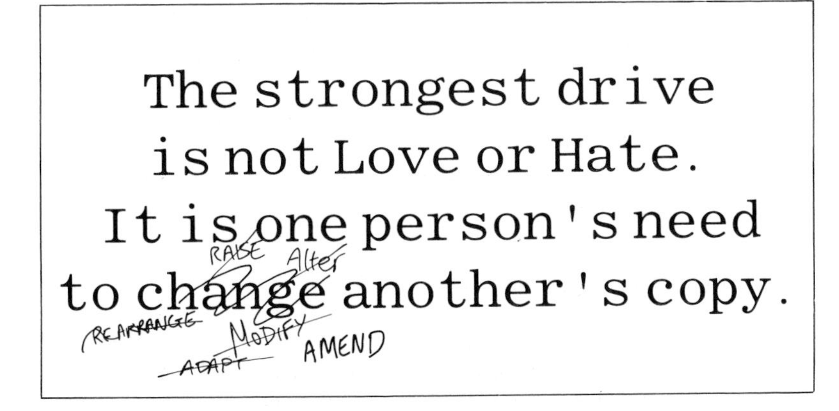

Figure 15.2

produce. Again, the later in the process this tinkering occurs, the more expensive it becomes. Deciding to change a visual or photograph at proof stage is an extremely pricey hobby and definitely not one which is to be encouraged.

Time is the other great thief. There are few occasions in life where the 'eternal triangle' does not apply:

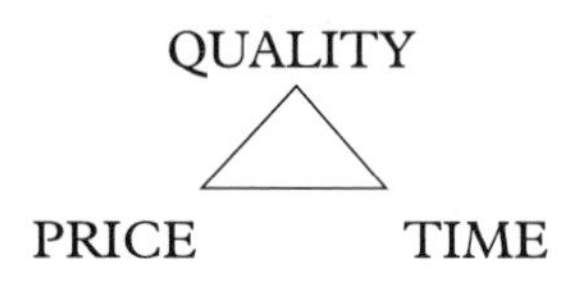

The rule says simply 'you can't have all three'. For any practical purposes, we cannot expect to get top quality at a competitive price and have it delivered yesterday! And time is the ultimate arbiter of the truth of the statement.

The processes involved in producing good advertising need time to get the best quality from them. You cannot make a creative team produce a great campaign more quickly by paying them more. Ideas don't respond to money. No more can you get printers to turn proofs around in half an hour by doubling the payment – they simply cannot set up a proofing press that quickly.

So there are physical limitations. Overnight work costs overtime rates for the workers involved and results in rush charges. Giving priority to your work may mean pushing someone else back in the queue. So your work needs to offer more profit to justify the move. Increased costs.

The sections on production processes give outline timings which allow work to be produced to a high standard at competitive rates. Unless the situation really demands a shorter deadline, stick with those guidelines.

Which raises the subject of planning. If the communications plan has been well put together and is being effectively managed, then adequate time will have been built in so that briefs are given early enough to allow sufficient time for the work to be done cost-effectively.

In my experience, both as client and within an agency, the majority of cost overruns are self-inflicted. By client, not agency!

THE PRODUCTION PROCESS

This section will outline the stages of production involved in a press ad, a radio commercial and a TV commercial. Some stages are similar for all three but will be covered as appropriate under each heading for the purpose of completeness.

The information given is not intended to be an exhaustive description of every stage but rather to offer sufficient knowledge to gain a good overview of the key stages and the implications, in time and cost, of decision making at each. These stages are the 'ES' of the PITCHES process.

Production for press

'Press' is a somewhat catch-all term for media ranging from daily newspapers to annual directories. The different lifespans of various types of press has an influence on both the creative and the production aspects of advertising.

Daily newspapers, by their nature, are put together overnight. It follows that you could change your advertising on a daily basis if you so chose, and you could produce a tactical ad, responding to a news item, in a matter of hours. Reproduction materials (i.e. what the newspaper needs in order to print your ad) are normally only required a couple of days in advance – and, in exceptional circumstances, can even be delivered right up to press time.

A monthly magazine, in contrast, normally works to an editorial plan established months in advance. Typically, a specific issue of a colour magazine will be 'closed' up to six weeks before issue date. Creatively, topical advertising is more limited – although knowledge of the forthcoming editorial content does mean that ads can be topical to the magazine itself. The production team needs to supply 'repro' materials before that six-week closing date, or by 'copy date' as it is more commonly known.

An extreme example of the timing issue is found in *Yellow Pages*. Regional issues of *Yellow Pages* are generally updated on an 18-month cycle. So advertising must not be time-sensitive and copy dates are a long way in advance of issue date.

For the purpose of outlining the production process let's assume that we are running a full-colour advertisement in a monthly magazine. The key stages of production are shown in Figure 15.3.

Earlier, we established that some areas of cost are difficult to estimate accurately in advance. The first of these occurs between your brief and the agency's creative proposals.

It is virtually impossible to predict how long it will take a creative team to generate the right, effective advertising solution. After all, how long does it take to have a good idea? Some come in minutes or hours, some in days or even weeks.

If you pay your agency only through media commission – because your media budget is large – this problem is the agency's, not yours. If, however, like most advertisers, you pay for creative time by the hour, this can cause problems. Ask your agency to put a rough figure

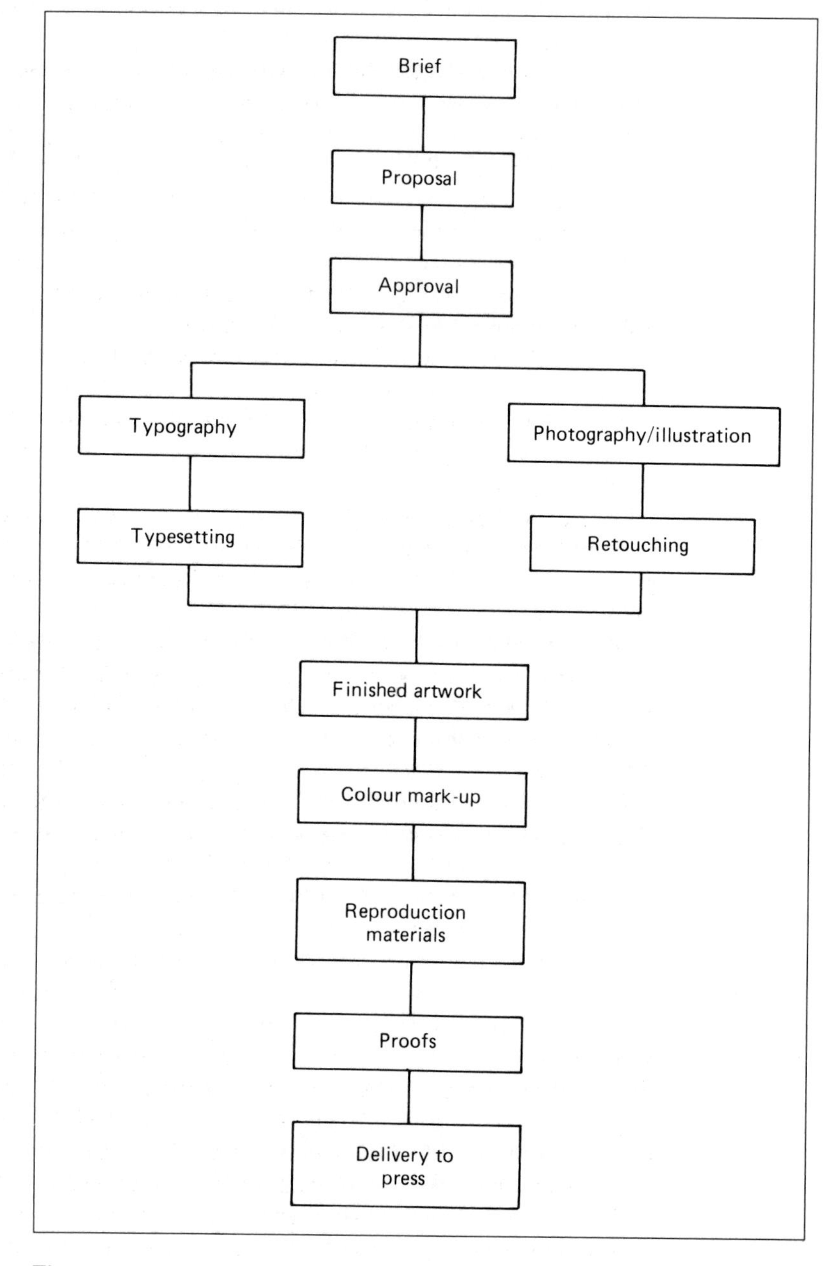

Figure 15.3 Production for press

on this stage and to control to it. But be flexible: don't compromise on the quality of the basic idea. It is the foundation of the success of your advertising.

As soon as you have given final approval of copy and visual, the detail work starts. Inside the agency the *typographer* is set to work. His or her job is to make the final text look as good as it can on paper. This includes ensuring either that your approved typefaces are used or appropriate ones selected. Then the task is to fit the words in the space available - which means measuring every word, every space between words, every space between individual letters and the spaces between the lines, and then balancing that lot so the text is easy on the eye and encourages the prospect to read it.

Mercifully, desktop publishing now takes most of the drudgery out of the typographer's job. But it will never be a substitute for a good 'eye'. The typographer is one of the great unsung heroes of the agency world. Good typography has a major impact on an ad, yet it is all too rarely recognized.

Having designed the type, the typographer will commission the final *typesetting*. Figures 15.4 and 15.5 show two forms of setting – galley and 'set to fit'; the former is becoming rare. The implications of these will become clear later when we discuss artwork.

External work such as *photography* or *illustration* will be commissioned, in parallel with or before the typographical work. Specific artists will have been chosen to suit the subject matter and the mood or feel which the creative work is seeking to establish. The Art Director, together with the production manager, will brief the work.

It is difficult to generalize about the time this stage will take. A simple product shot of a small fmcg product might be a few hours' photography, with results in a couple of days. A major location shoot may take weeks of planning to identify location, assemble props, cast models, prepare wardrobe and take the shots.

This is a second area where costs can escalate. If your new product isn't ready on the scheduled date, photographer and models will still be paid. On an outdoor shoot, the weather cannot be guaranteed. And some things are just more difficult to shoot than were first thought. All or any of these can extend photography time and push up costs.

So ensure that the planning is properly done and that you do your part as promised. Then either pray that the weather will be right or, on a major shoot, insure yourself against the wrong weather.

There's another area of photography which can cause raised eyebrows – *retouching*. If you have just paid a top photographer several thousand pounds a day to take a picture, why on earth should it need to be retouched afterwards? The reality is that the camera has limitations even in the hands of the best photographer. And creative

Method of acoustic appraisal
The basic requirements of an acoustic appraisal are shown in Diagram 1.2.
The site survey or inspection will enable important site-specific information to be obtained, such as whether there are any local noise and/or vibration sources which may affect any new development, e.g. transportation routes or industry, or whether there are any nearby noise-sensitive areas for example housing.
In setting design criteria for a development, reference will need to be made to such documentation as British Standards, to establish acceptable intrusive noise or vibration levels in a development, or possibly planning conditions, which ensure that a development will not affect a nearby noise-sensitive area. In some cases, research studies may need to be referred to in addition to, or in the absence of, relevant standards.
A prediction exercise would, in the majority of cases, be based on measured data taking account of site-specific details. Although it would be possible to undertake prediction without measured site data in situations where there is sufficiently reliable published information, e.g. noise due to road traffic, a site inspection would provide site-specific factors which would assist in the exercise. Prediction of vibration on a site is extremely complicated and measurement must always be the preferred method.
The differences between the predicted noise or vibration climate and the design criteria will identify the scale of any potential problem. An assessment will need to determine whether any additional control measures are necessary and practicable. Obviously, small differences may not warrant huge expenditure and agreement must be sought with all interested parties to determine the best course of action. Where control methods are required, the appraisal should identify the best methods.

Site analysis

Site inspection
The site survey is probably the most important part of an acoustic appraisal, whether it is only a site inspection or a full measurement survey, since it will determine the location of noise-sensitive areas and noise sources and other local factors needed to make an accurate assessment, e.g. local shielding. If a full survey is being undertaken, the initial site inspection or pilot survey will identify the preferred measurement locations.
The items that need to be considered in undertaking an inspection are identified in Diagram 1.3. Diagram 1.3 also gives a checklist of the likely aims of an inspection. This includes reference to local topography, particularly embankments or cuttings, which would provide significant acoustic shielding but the details of which would not easily be determined from maps or plans. In determining transportation routes, data such as type and gradient of road or type of railway track proximity to airports – civil or military – need to be obtained.
Measurement locations need to be selected to be representative of the local noise or vibration climate and take account of site practicalities. This would include whether noise measurements need to be made at heights greater than 1.5 m to obtain appropriate data. Short-period indicative measurements taken during a site inspection are helpful and can establish the preferred monitoring locations.

Figure 15.4 Galley setting

8 **Environmental acoustics**

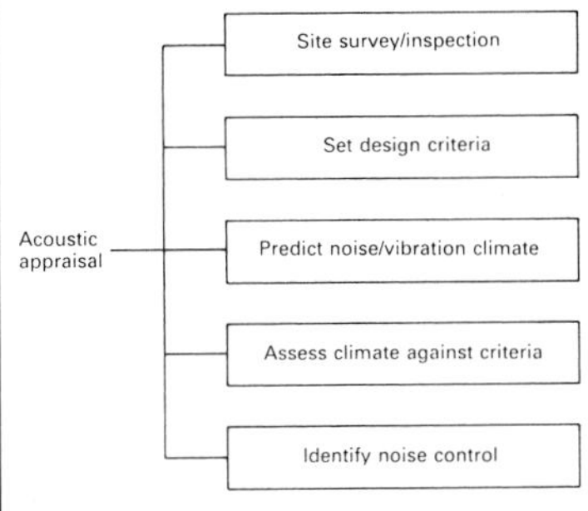

Daigram 1.2 *Acoustic appraisal: requirements*

Method of acoustic appraisal
The basic requirements of an acoustic appraisal are shown in Diagram 1.2.

The site survey or inspection will enable important site-specific information to be obtained, such as whether there are any local noise and/or vibration sources which may affect any new development, e.g. transportation routes or industry, or whether there are any nearby noise-sensitive areas for example housing.

In setting design criteria for a development, reference will need to be made to such documentation as British Standards, to establish acceptable intrusive noise or vibration levels in a development, or possibly planning conditions, which ensure that a development will not affect a nearby noise-sensitive area. In some cases, research studies may need to be referred to in addition to, or in the absence of, relevant standards.

A prediction exercise would, in the majority of cases, be based on measured data taking account of site-specific details. Although it would be possible to undertake prediction without measured site data in situations where there is sufficiently reliable published information, e.g. noise due to road traffic, a site inspection would provide site-specific factors which would assist in the exercise. Prediction of vibration on a site is extremely complicated and measurement must always be the preferred method.

The differences between the predicted noise or vibration climate and the design criteria will identify the scale of any potential problem. An assessment will need to determine whether any additional control measures are necessary and practicable. Obviously, small differences may not warrant huge expenditure and agreement must be sought with all interested parties to determine the best course of action. Where control methods are required, the appraisal should identify the best methods.

Site analysis

Site inspection
The site survey is probably the most important part of an acoustic appraisal, whether it is only a site inspection or a full measurement survey, since it will determine the location of noise-sensitive areas and noise sources and other local factors needed to make an accurate assessment, e.g. local shielding. If a full survey is being undertaken, the initial site inspection or pilot survey will identify the preferred measurement locations.

The items that need to be considered in undertaking an inspection are identified in Diagram 1.3. Diagram 1.3 also gives a checklist of the likely aims of an inspection. This includes reference to local topography, particularly embankments or cuttings, which would provide significant acoustic shielding but the details of which would not easily be determined from maps or plans. In determining transportation routes, data such as type and gradient of road or type of railway track proximity to airports – civil or military – need to be obtained.

Measurement locations need to be selected to be representative of the local noise or vibration climate and take account of site practicalities. This would include whether noise measurements need to be made at heights greater than 1.5 m to obtain appropriate data. Short-period indicative measurements taken during a site inspection are helpful and can establish the preferred monitoring locations.

Site inspection to determine

Development location
Location of nearest dwellings or other buildings and periods of operation
Noise-producing activities near the site
Vibration sources
Local topography
Transportation routes
Measurement locations
Indicative noise levels by short measurement

Obtain base data including up-to-date plans identifying site location

Contact local authority to discuss local factors i.e. noise-sensitive areas
Major noise/vibration sources in area
Complaints received

Organize site access and check that abnormal activities such as site investigations will not be taking place

Diagram 1.3 *Site inspection*

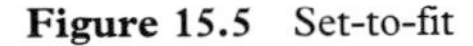

Figure 15.5 Set-to-fit

teams often create images which cannot be fully delivered by the camera. At one extreme this may require the combining of several photographs to produce the final image: a process known as photocomposition. At the other end, it can be as simple as painting out all background so the image appears as a 'cut-out' on the page. Figure 15.6 shows a photograph no camera could have taken. The options were genetic engineering to grow the horns this big, or retouching!

Retouching, whether manual or by computer, is also difficult to estimate accurately in advance. The extent required will only really be known when the photographs are done. On a complex photocomposition, with perhaps seven or eight elements, trial and error may be the only route to precisely the right result.

Again, ask the agency for a rough estimate. But ensure that you understand what they are proposing to do to achieve the final result and ask for a 'worst possible' figure so that you know the downside cost.

Another fact which is often not realized is that many of today's photographic subjects are actually models. They are frequently easier to control than the real thing, and what might have been an expensive location shoot can turn into a studio project. Good models usually turn out looking more realistic than the real thing! But don't get too excited about saving money. You'll need it to pay the model maker.

Illustration is much more controllable. But do allow time for changes. Remember, the illustrator is interpreting in his or her own style what is in the art director's mind. It may not be absolutely right first time.

It is tempting to use illustration rather than photography, simply because cost is easier to control. Resist the temptation! There are times when illustration is ideal to execute an advertising idea, but more often photography is the better medium – it has a reality which illustration can never achieve. (Note that, since the 1988 Copyright Act, another cost element has to be allowed for. Basically photographers, illustrators and other creative suppliers now need to be paid for the *usage* of their work, so it is necessary to negotiate this element up-front.)

At last we have all of the elements, the words and the pictures. The next stage is to prepare the *finished artwork* (sometimes known as 'mechanical artwork' or simply 'the mechanical'). This will be done by the studio, either in-house or commissioned externally by the agency.

Artwork is something of a patchwork quilt. It is prepared by sticking the various elements of the ad to a backing board, in exactly the right size and position. It sounds simple. But it isn't!

Figure 15.6 Retouching for impact

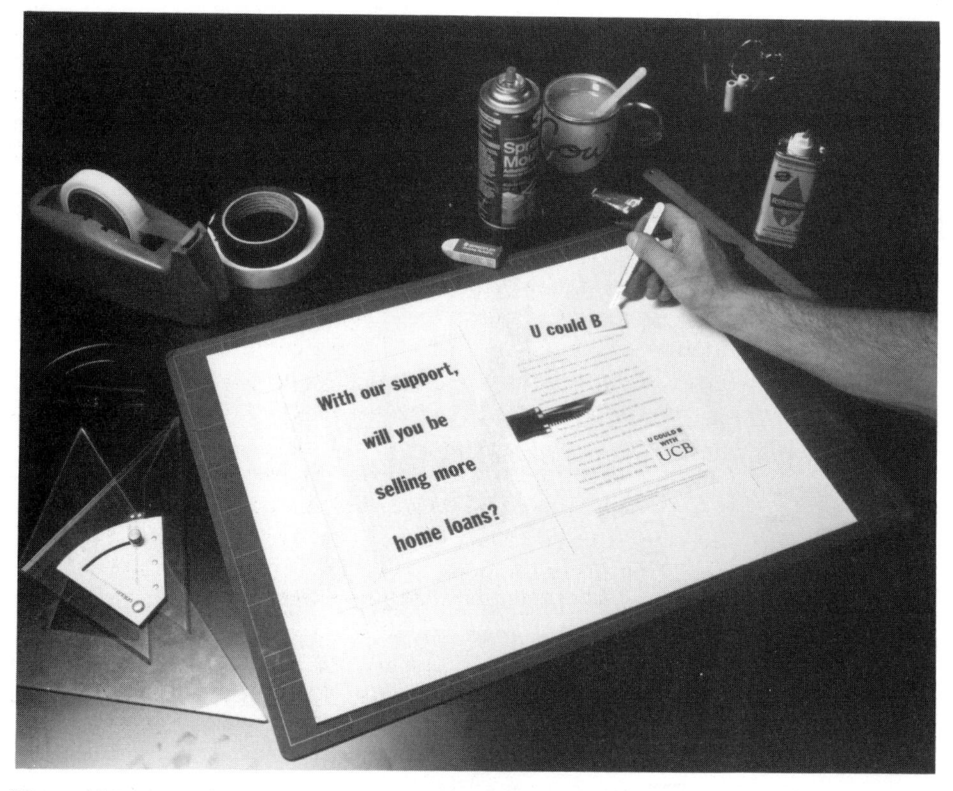

Figure 15.7

Studio work is a craft skill. It requires great attention to detail and a steady hand. Simple artworks can be virtually taken straight from the typesetting system and stuck down. But most require considerable building up to the final ad. Figure 15.7 shows a board in a semi-completed stage with the final element being mounted.

Finished artwork is always black type on a white background. Reversing white type out of a black background or adding colour are done at a later stage. I make this basic point to avoid any possible risk of a repetition of an experience of several years ago, when a client returned four artwork boards with 'This should be in colour' written across each. Goodbye to over a thousand pounds' worth of artwork!

Hence, the *colour mark-up*. The artwork will have an overlay sheet over it, on which the Art Director will mark colour instructions using standard colour references – in UK, using 'PMS' numbers.

The finished artwork will then be submitted for your approval. Don't give it a cursory glance, then sign it off. This is your last chance to change anything at a remotely sensible cost. However, nor is it the time to start rewriting the ad! Go through the artwork carefully, check every comma and full stop. Ensure that the address and telephone number are correct. Check that the transparencies (large slides of the photographs), the photographs or illustrations are exactly as they should appear. Recognize that, in signing off the artwork, you are authorizing the agency to go to press with the work exactly as presented – on your responsibility.

If you're consistently presented with artwork which has errors in it, someone is getting sloppy. Tell your agency that the quality is unacceptable – and ensure that it doesn't continue.

It is worth mentioning that you may be given several different artworks for the same ad. This will be a function of the media chosen. Even so-called 'A4'-sized magazines vary quite a bit in the size of a finished advertisement. In such cases, you have a choice of whether to produce artwork to the smallest size and allow it to 'float' in the other magazines, or to produce more than one artwork. Any sensible agency will take a balanced view on this issue. Allowing an extra millimetre or two of white space (or 'float') around an ad is usually acceptable, but 5 or 6 millimetres may make the ad look somewhat ridiculous.

The problem can be worse with ads which 'bleed', i.e. those that go right out to the edges of the paper. Take agency advice on the optimum treatment of artwork so you get the impact you seek, at a reasonable cost.

The artworks and illustrative materials will then go to a 'repro house' for *reproduction materials* to be produced. Specific requirements will vary by medium. For a black and white (or 'mono') ad in national press, artwork or a PMT (photomechanical transfer) of the artwork may be all that is required. For colour ads, such as in our example, a full set of colour films will be needed. These are produced by specialist repro houses. The process is the same for poster work – and indeed for any printing process including, for example, brochure work.

When the repro is complete the ads will be run off on a proofing press – giving you your first look at the finished article (although you may have seen 'proofs' from the computer work earlier). *Any* change made at this stage will be very expensive. Not only will the artwork require changing but printing films will have to be remade. The *only* purpose of scrutinizing proofs is to check that the ad is printing properly with the right clarity and colour balance, and that the repro house has followed the Art Director's instructions accurately. Finally, the films are supplied to the publisher.

Just as the quality of the underlying idea is critical to the effectiveness of your advertising, so is production quality. The investment you make in producing your advertising will have a major impact on the image of your product and company. Skimp on quality and the ad looks cheap. And cheap ads come from cheap companies – in the mind of the reader.

Part of your investment is time. Make sure you provide enough to get the job done, both right and cost-effectively (remember the triangle!).

While it's difficult to generalize on things like the time needed for photography, the following would be a reasonable timescale for an ad of average complexity (times in *working* days):

Brief to copy and visual	15
First approval	5
Detailed estimate	5
Approval to produce	2
To artwork and photography	15
Approval of artwork, etc.	5
Repro and proofing	10
	57

That's almost 12 working weeks before copy date. Of course, it's somewhat idealistic, but then you should be aiming for an ideal result. This kind of timetable allows for discussion, revisions and corrections. It allows for everything to be done at 'normal' cost with no rush charges. It ensures that your agency will love you!

Production for radio

Figure 15.8 summarizes what needs to be done to turn out the radio commercial. The first three stages will, of course, be common to producing any advertising. But then enters a new dimension – statutory control of broadcast advertising.

Press advertising is subject only to the voluntary 'British Code of Advertising Practice' aimed at ensuring that it is 'legal, decent, honest and truthful'. The only control is exercised after the event, through the Advertising Standards Authority. Such control is normally only instigated by formal complaints from members of the public to the ASA about a particular advertisement. Broadcast advertising is, however, directly monitored and controlled by the Independent Broadcasting Authority. IBA clearance is essential before any commercial can be transmitted. The first stage of this approval must be completed prior to producing the commercial for two reasons: you'll avoid annoying the IBA, and you'll avoid wasting money if, for any reason, the script is rejected.

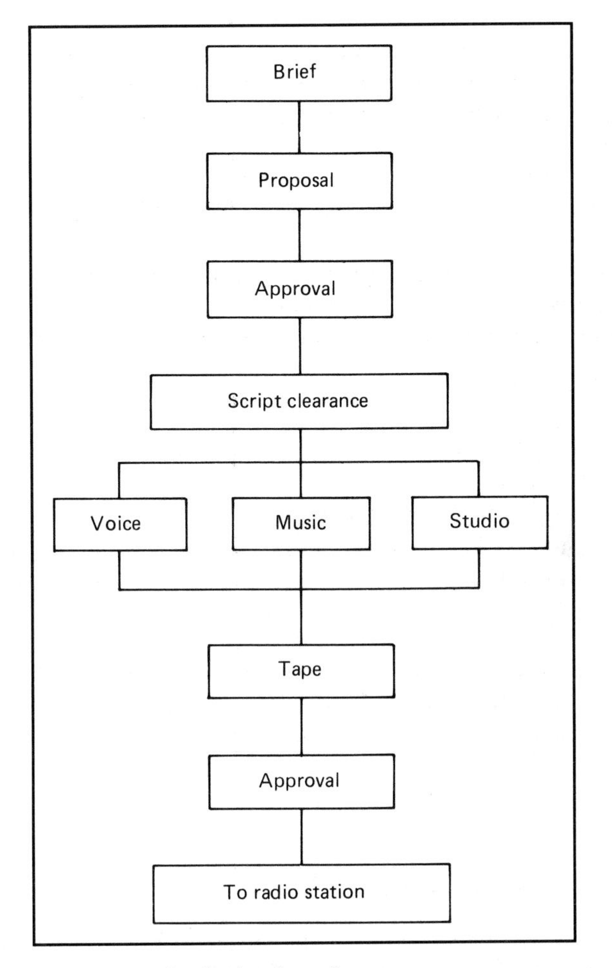

Figure 15.8 Production for radio

Assuming that the script is cleared, it's time to recruit a 'voice' and book the recording studio. It may well be that the idea was submitted for your approval with a voice already identified – particularly if a 'personality' is an integral part of the idea. The studio will be briefed carefully by the creative and production team to ensure that the right sound effects and background music are available. If existing music is to be used, that use will also need to be agreed – with not one but two sets of people. The first, the Music Copyright Protection Company, represents the composer, the second, the Performing Rights Association, represents the performer.

Even classical music, which is long since out of copyright, involves using a specific recording of that piece. And thus will cost money (including repeat fees *every* time the commercial is broadcast – so remember to budget for them).

The alternatives are twofold: either use 'off-the-shelf' music of which all studios carry a stock, or commission a new piece for the commercial.

Note that, although the music is organized at this point, the availability of a particular piece of music for use in advertising should have been checked in principle by the agency prior to presenting their proposals to you.

Actual recording of the commercial is not a particularly time-consuming exercise if the voiceover artist is familiar with how radio commercials work. The outcome of the recording session is a master tape which must again be cleared by the IBA and, naturally, by you the client. Finally, copy tapes are circulated to the radio stations to be used.

Radio can be very quick to produce. As a medium it can be used tactically to respond to events as they happen. However, the timetable below gives a more general view of how long you should allow for a 'normal' radio campaign (times in *working* days):

Brief to script	15
Approval by you	5
IBA script approval	5
Detailed estimate	5
Recording	2
IBA final/your approval	5
Duplication and despatch	2
	39

As with the press timetable, this is idealistic. Some stages can run in parallel to save time. However, allowing this time assures the right quality at the optimum cost.

As an aside, it's worth noting that the script initially approved often goes through minor changes during production – which is one reason the IBA approves at two points. The changes can arise for a number of reasons, slight time over-runs, a 'voice' being more comfortable with one word than another, for example. These should never change the idea or wording in any fundamental manner.

Production for television

Production of a TV commercial can range from telling the station what you want, to the kind of complex project which would not disgrace a blockbuster movie. At the former end of the scale a few hundred pounds may buy you a still picture on-screen plus a voiceover; at the latter end, a major shoot with complex visual effects might set you back half-a-million pounds or more. And, either way, you only end up with a 30-second commercial.

All TV stations offer a service for producing simple commercials, usually for local advertisers, at low cost. Anything more complex will involve an agency and a separate production company. But in both cases, although the complexity varies enormously, the basic stages are the same (Figure 15.9).

You will see the agency proposals either as a storyboard of hand-drawn pictures illustrating the action or as an 'animatic' which is essentially the storyboard put onto video in a manner which gives more movement and feeling of action. You will be asked to approve this with a written script (which may be presented on paper or as a rough recording).

Now, it's back to the IBA, in the guise of the Independent Television Companies Association. The commercial must be approved at this point.

As with radio scripts, a TV script will rarely be rejected outright - unless it breaches the basic Code of Practice. More likely, the ITCA would ask for proof of claims made or give guidance on desirable amendments. The clearance process normally takes only a few days but if particularly complex (for example, scientific) claims are made, proof and clearance can take several weeks.

The approved script and treatment moves into production. The agency's producer now carries the can for getting the concept successfully onto film. His or her first task is to select a production company to do the job.

This is a particularly important choice. The transition from concept to finished work is more difficult in TV than in any other area of advertising. The choice may be made because they have a director who seems ideal for the style, mood, feel and content of the commercial.

It may well be that more than one company are strong candidates for the job. The producer may brief two or three and ask for a presentation on how they would execute the brief and at what cost.

Through whichever route, a production company will be selected and signed up. During this process you will be presented with a cost estimate. The production company will use the standard AFVPA (Advertising Film and Video Producers Association) forms. The agency will add costs not covered, including performers' fees and repeat fees, voiceovers, music costs, artworks and insurance. You'll see a total estimate for your approval prior to a contract being signed with the production company.

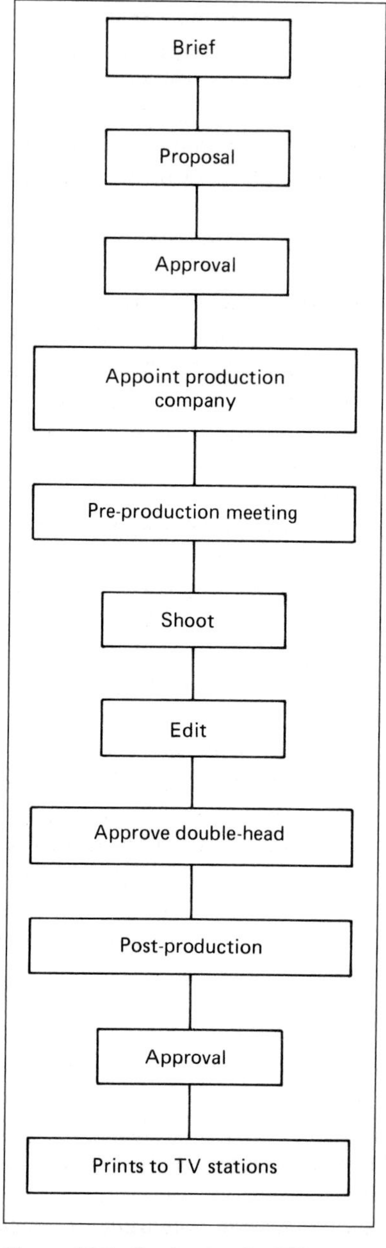

Figure 15.9 Production for TV

One or more pre-production meetings will be held, attended by agency, production company and client. Every detail of the commercial will be worked out and planned; from set design and props through casting, music, wardrobe, special effects and titles, to how every shot will be achieved.

Now it's time to shoot the movie! If you go on-set, you'll find it like Oxford Street on a busy Saturday. I won't bore you by listing all the attendees. Suffice it to say that, if you attend a shoot, you'll see why TV production is so expensive.

The shot footage goes into an editing suite to produce the rough cut. This will again require your approval. At this point visual and sound will be on separate reels, hence the expression 'double-head'. They will be synchronized so that you can see the effect so far. (On a commercial which is heavily reliant on purely visual elements or which might cause the ITCA concern, it is worth running it across to them for guidance at this point. Changes at a later stage can be astronomically expensive and sometimes impossible.)

The commercial now moves into post-production, where visual and sound are married, titles added and special effects work or changes between scenes are completed. The finished commercial is now ready for approval by you and the ITCA, then to be sent to the television stations.

Timescales are extremely difficult to generalize; a simple commercial done by the station can take a couple of weeks from start to finish. A big project can take many months. Either way, the timetable must be agreed in detail at a pre-production meeting.

TV production is not for the faint-hearted. It is expensive and time-consuming and a great deal of expertise is needed to find a safe path through its minefields. If you are likely to be using TV in your own advertising, read further on the subject so that you can talk to the specialists on equal terms, not because you're in danger of being taken advantage of, but because you need enough knowledge to know all the implications of the many decisions involved at the various stages.

DO YOU KNOW ENOUGH?

1 Do you understand your agency's systems? Do you receive enough forewarning of costs?
2 How many people are involved in your own approvals process? If it's more than three, review the necessity for each to be involved. If anyone does not have a definitive role and responsibility for advertising, cut them out of the process.

3 Review your advertising planning; look at the last four or five jobs you gave the agency. Did you allow enough time? Why not? Identify how you can improve your planning to create the time to do the job well.

Further reading

Information Transfer (1986), *The Print Book*, National Extension College, Cambridge.

16 Your action plan

If you're like any other busy executive, you'll have fitted reading this book into a busy schedule. You'll have read it cover to cover, without stopping to do the reviews or exercises at the end of each chapter. So much for my best intentions!

However, now we are reaching the end, you do have a serious choice facing you. You can either put the book down, regard it as good, bad or indifferent, and forget it, or you can identify the elements which could help you create better advertising, and implement them. If the former, thanks for buying the book – the royalties will come in handy. If the latter, you'll need to develop an action plan, so read on.

SHORT-TERM IMPROVEMENTS

Focus on your next advertisement or campaign. And bear in mind how you handled the last one. Go back to Chapter 10 and prepare a detailed written brief. If time and funds permit, commission any necessary research to tighten and sharpen the brief. Think through how you'll present it, and bring it to life for the agency. Above all, work on the proposition. Ensure that it is meaningful; gather competitive advertising and check that your proposition is better, stronger and different. While the agency is working on the brief, take the opportunity to work through Chapter 13 and prepare yourself to assess the proposals which will be presented. Look for immediate improvement in both the creative and the media work. If you can achieve that, you'll get immediate benefits.

MEDIUM-TERM ACTION

Review the integration of your communications. Check that you have identified all your key audiences and the messages for each – see Chapters 4–6.

Re-examine all your communications activities, from PR to point-of-sale material and set a programme for developing consistency of message and, progressively, consistency of look, tone of voice, style and feel. In simplistic terms, do the press article, advertising, brochure and video all deliver the same message; do they all 'feel' like the same company?

At the same time, plan to develop an 'eye' for good advertising. Use the tips in Chapter 13. Read Ogilvy and Bernstein in their respective books on advertising. Get into the habit of appraising advertising - from the market's perspective – as you read the paper or watch TV.

Set up appraisal sessions with your agency; play the 'good ad/bad ad' game. Set up role reversals; make the agency brief you and your colleagues on a 'neutral' product, do some ads then ask the agency to assess the results.

LONG-TERM ACTION

Ultimately, this is what this book is about. Plan to re-read it, perhaps a chapter per month, and respond to the questions and issues raised by each chapter. Take the opportunity to reassess every aspect of your advertising, from broad planning right down to the smallest tactical activity. In a small company you may be able to do so within a year. In a large one the process may take much longer. The one thing you can be sure of is, the longer you put off the start date, the longer it will be before you are getting all of the potential benefits.

CARE ABOUT ADVERTISING

One last word. I have given recognition in several places in this book to the fact that advertising is often a relatively small part of your job. However, no matter how small a part it is, you need to care about getting it right if you really want it to be effective.

So go on, have fun. Seriously!

Index